DEATH IS ▮▮▮▮▮▮▮▮▮▮▮▮▮▮
☑ W9-BYR-372

Belazir t'Marid, War Lord of the Kolnar, gazed at the row of crystal vials in their rack, admiring the amber liquid within them. "Perfect," he murmured, holding the rack up to the light.

"This disease does not kill," Karak's voice rasped across his father's reverie. "I call that far from perfect. Clan Father," he added, when Belazir turned to glare at his oldest living son.

"Child," he said with deceptive gentleness. Karak stiffened. "Is it enough for you that our enemies should merely die?" he asked in mild astonishment. Karak frowned but did not answer. "True, it does not kill."

Belazir laughed, a low chuckle full of gloating pleasure. "What it does is far worse. It will be a living nightmare to those few not at first afflicted. They will call upon their allies, the mighty Central Worlds, for aid." He spread his hands. "But there is no cure! Their champions will have no choice but to quarantine their miserable little planet.

"The all-powerful Fleet of would-be saviors from Central Worlds will watch helplessly from orbit while the pleas for help from below slowly fade away. They will watch until Bethel's civilization falls and the last of them dies—and no human foot will ever walk upon that accursed planet again!"

Belazir studied his son's impassive face with growing impatience. "Think, my son! Our revenge shall have symmetry." Belazir made a fluid gesture with his hand, "subtlety."

"Your love of *subtlety*," Karak said bitterly, "has already cost the clan dear."

"My mistake was not in being subtle," he said to Karak. "It was in not being subtle enough."

ALSO IN THIS SERIES:

S. M. STIRLING

THE SHIP AVENGED

A Baen Books Original

Baen Publishing Enterprises
P.O. Box 1403
Riverdale, NY 10471

ISBN: 0-671-87861-1
Cover art by Stephen Hickman

First paperback printing, February 1998

Distributed by Simon & Schuster
1230 Avenue of the Americas
New York, NY 10020

Library of Congress Catalog Number: 96-36977

Typeset by Windhaven Press, Auburn, NH
Printed in the United States of America

✧ PROLOGUE

Belazir t'Marid, War Lord of the Kolnar, Clan Father
after Chalku, gazed at the row of crystal vials in their
rack, admiring the amber liquid within them. With a
lover's tenderness he stroked one jet-black finger across
them, reveling in their cool, smooth surfaces.

"Perfect," he murmured, holding the rack up to the
light.

His face was no longer an ancient Greek's vision of
masculine beauty colored the depthless onyx of a
starless night. The quick aging of Kolnar had seamed
and scored it, until the starved hunger of the soul
within showed through the flesh. The brass-yellow eyes
looked down on the vials with a benevolent affection
he showed no human being.

Then he smiled, teeth even and white and hard, and
laughed. His fist squeezed shut, as if it held a throat.

His son fought not to shiver at the sound of that laugh.
There was hatred in it, and an overtone of madness. It
made the narrow confines of the bio-storage chamber
seem constricting—an odd sensation to one born and
raised in the strait confines of spaceships and vacuum
habitats. Life-support kept the air pure and varied only
enough to simulate Kolnar's usual range of temperatures,
from freezing to just below the boiling point of water.
Yet now it felt clammy and oppressive . . .

1

"Not perfect," Karak's voice rasped across his father's reverie. "This disease does not kill. I call that far from perfect. Clan Father," he added, when Belazir turned to glare at his oldest living son.

The elder Kolnar allowed himself an exasperated hiss; it was entirely natural for a boy to plot his father's death, but also for his father to strike first if it became too obvious. And the boy's resentment and dislike were, if anything, obvious.

At times, he wondered about Karak's paternity, for the boy had no subtlety. But the face that looked defiantly back at him might have been his own, some years ago. Once, he too had that youthful swagger, the crackling vitality that sparkled though the lean, panther-muscled body and the vanity that showed in silver ornaments woven into waist-length silver-white hair.

"Child," he said with deceptive gentleness. Karak stiffened. Belazir enjoyed the reaction, and the reaction to reaction. Let the heir realize the old eagle still had claws.

"It pleases me to enlighten you as to why this is a punishment that most admirably fits the crime. Central Worlds, and the damnable Bethelite scum, created The Great Plague to eradicate the Divine Seed of Kolnar." He paused and raised one eyebrow, as if to inquire, *Is this not so?* Karak nodded once, resentfully. "And we shall repay that evil by inflicting upon them a disease that will not simply destroy, but will terrify and humiliate them."

Reluctantly he placed the rack of vials back on its shelf and closed the cooler door. Then he turned to his son:

"Is it enough for you that they should merely die?" he asked in mild astonishment. Karak frowned, but did not answer. "True, it does not kill. What it does is far worse, and the Bethelites shall appreciate that, where you cannot." Belazir laughed, a low chuckle full of gloating pleasure. "It will be a living nightmare to those few not afflicted.

"As you lack imagination, Karak, let me tell you what will happen." Belazir made a sweeping motion with his arm, as though activating a holo-display. "Once the scumvermin realize the magnitude of the threat they face, first, they will call upon their god, as they did when we took Bethel in our fist. And when he does not answer them, some will say that they deserve their fate; a view that we, of course, share. But not all of them will lie down and wait to rot. No."

Belazir ground his teeth, remembering one Bethelite in particular who had refused to lie down.

"So. They will next call upon their allies, the mighty Central Worlds, for aid." He spread his hands. "But there is no cure! Oh, a few paltry doses of one," he jerked his head dismissively, "but they are in our possession. Their champions will have no choice but to quarantine their miserable little planet. The all-powerful Fleet of would-be saviors from Central Worlds will watch helplessly from orbit while the pleas for help from below slowly fade away, as thousands starve and the so-moral Bethelites turn to preying upon each other to survive. They will watch until Bethel's civilization falls and the last of them dies—and no human foot will ever walk upon that accursed planet again!"

Belazir wiped the spittle from his lips and studied his son's impassive face with growing impatience.

"Think, my son! Our revenge shall have symmetry." Belazir made a fluid gesture with his hand, "subtlety."

"Your love of *subtlety*," Karak said bitterly, "has already cost the clan dear."

True. After their disastrous rout from the Space Station Simeon-900-C, what the Central Worlds Navy hadn't destroyed, the Great Plague did. From the Navy they could run or hide, but they brought The Plague with them to every gathering of Kolnar-in-space, to all of the exiles from homeworld.

Also, as was their custom, for the strengthening of their seed, they had exposed the children to it. Virtually an entire generation, with their caretakers, died. The adult population had been reduced by three quarters. Only now was their natural fecundity increasing their numbers once more.

The Plague had been created by minions of the beauteous Channa Hap, station master of the SSS-900-C and by the "brain," Simeon, the station's true ruler, whom she served.

And by the Bethelites. The damnable should-have-been-crushed Bethelites who had lured them to the Central Worlds station and their doom.

Belazir's hubris had allowed him to believe he held their hearts in his fist. He was so sure he'd terrorized them into believing their safety was guaranteed—*if* they followed every Kolnari order to the letter.

He should have broken Channa Hap's spirit, broken all of their spirits, he knew. But he'd so enjoyed the cat and mouse game they were playing.

Belazir sighed. This was hindsight. He couldn't have known about The Plague. Even his Sire, Chalku, would not have anticipated a sickness that could afflict the mighty Kolnar. Had not the Divine Seed shrugged off diseases that annihilated whole populations of scumvermin? *All that does not kill us, makes us stronger,* Belazir told himself. But this had come close to killing them all, very close. Almost as close as homeworld had come to killing all the exiled Terrans who were the first ancestors of the Divine Seed.

Yet some survived to breed, he reminded himself. Survived, to become the superior race and made a home of a planet their persecutors had thought would kill them all. The Clan had escaped Kolnar too; escaped into space for endless revenge and conquest.

He glanced at his scowling son. Belazir understood the boy's bitterness. *Do I not feel it myself, ten-fold?*

"My mistake was not in being subtle," he said to Karak. "It was in not being subtle enough."

✧ CHAPTER ONE

The Benisur Amos ben Sierra Nueva sat before the viewscreen in his cabin, watching the beloved shape of Bethel grow smaller, until it was merely a bright spark, another star in the star-shot blackness of space. An exterior view was a luxury he allowed himself, even as he insisted on this simple cabin in a hired merchantman. Bethel had always been a poor world, poor and remote; their ancestors had chosen it to preserve their faith in isolation. It was even poorer since the Kolnari raid, if less solitary; the Central Worlds had sent much aid, and the people had toiled without cease, but so much had been destroyed.

Alarms rang. He braced himself, as he did before every transition; it was futile, but not something you could help. Nausea flashed through him as the engines wrenched the ship out of contact with the sidereal universe. He swallowed bile. Some men could take the transition without feeling so, but he was not one of them. *But I can bear it.* Life taught you that, how to bear things.

Still Amos watched. The screen was a simulation now, a view of how the stars would appear if the outside universe were there. He watched until he could no longer distinguish Bethel's star, Saffron, from the others. Then he switched off the viewscreen and rose wearily. It was always a wrench to leave his home, his people.

7

Think of what is to come. A week or so to Station SSS-900-C. He removed his robe and lay down on the narrow bed, yawning. The drugs that helped one make an easier transition always left him sleepy. *Channa,* he thought, and her image rose to delight his mind's eye. Her long, high-cheekboned face framed by curling black hair, teeth white in a smile of welcome.

He'd never imagined, at the beginning, that this makeshift arrangement would last ten years. They'd agreed then to steal twelve weeks from their lives each year so that they could be together. Half of that time he visited Channa, the other half she was with him on Bethel; allowing for travel time, that gave them four weeks together in either place.

He closed his eyes in pain. Four weeks. Just time enough to make each parting agony.

I was so sure she would stay, once she saw my home. Bethel rose before him. The stinging salty wind from the desert marshes, dawn rising thunderous over the sands. The warm sweet smell of cut grass in the river meadows . . . *And she always wanted to live planetside.*

Amos's mouth quirked. They had too much in common—both were prisoners to their sense of duty. Being reliable made one susceptible to the demands of others. He could not leave Bethel, not while they struggled to rebuild from the devastation the Kolnari had left. And Channa's commitment to her Station was equally strong; as was her friendship with Simeon, the Brain whose body the Station was. So much of her identity was tied up in being a Brawn, a calling to which many aspired but for which few were qualified. And from among those few, she had worked her way up to an unusually high and responsible position. She was respected in Central Worlds. She wielded power and influence.

But among his people, her profession was not understood, her strength and capability, her ambition had been disparaged. She was considered mannish, and his love for her was considered unnatural by many. Not a few of his worried followers had told him so.

He sighed and turned over, thumping at the pillow.

Ten years. He'd thought that if she did not come with him, that perhaps their attraction would gradually grow less. But that had not been the case. The attraction between them was as powerful, the parting as painful, the reunions as rapturous as ever.

Just as her dedication to the Space Station Simeon remained as strong as ever.

Simeon. There was the spur that galled his spirit; that one whom he esteemed as a brother should be his rival for the woman he loved.

Unfair, unreasonable, he knew. Simeon's twisted, nonviable body had been encased in a titanium womb at birth. A life-sustaining shell fitted with neural implants that would allow him to be connected to various housings—to the space station that became his body and his home. Channa was his Brawn, the mobile half of the team of which Simeon was the "brain."

Amos twisted around in the bed again.

His jealousy was baseless, but still, it tormented him. Simeon's love for Channa and hers for Simeon was, perforce, chaste. Simeon could never hold her, as Amos could, nor run hand in hand with her along a beach, nor . . . other things. And yet, Simeon had the greater share of her time, her company, the sight and sound of her that Amos himself yearned for.

In five years her contract will be finished. Then she would have to choose to renew it—or not. Amos smiled as sleep drifted in, as gentle as weightlessness. *She is too full of life to choose more years among metal and machines.*

✧   ✧   ✧

"Is it true, my Lord, that when you return to Bethel you will at last choose a bride?"

Amos—Prophet of the Second Revelation, Hero of the war against the Kolnar and Leader of Bethel's Council of Elders—suppressed a violent start.

Not again! The Council must have been at her. He put his book aside reluctantly—Simeon had tracked down an original Delany—and turned his recliner to face her.

Soamosa bint Sierra Nueva, for her part, sat silently, dressed in a very proper, long-sleeved gray dress which covered her from throat to ankles. Her hair, amazingly blond for a Bethelite, was completely hidden now in a matching gray bag that framed her small face unbecomingly. Amos ran a list of the usual suspects through his mind. *One reason I have lived so long is that I do not have an heir.* There were many traditionalists on Bethel who loved the thought of a regency—with themselves pulling the strings from behind a minor's chair.

Amos considered his cousin, trying to see her as a stranger might. *She is no longer the tomboy I once knew,* he admitted reluctantly. *She is a woman, a terribly proper one.* He suppressed a sigh. *I should have brought her with me earlier.*

Bethel had become considerably less isolated since the Kolnari attack. Before that he'd been viewed as a heretic for wanting to open their planet to the universe—and he hadn't been heir, either. The Kolnari fusion bomb that destroyed the city of Keriss and the then-Council and Prophet had driven home his point about the dangers of isolationism quite thoroughly.

Soamosa licked her lips nervously.

"I do not wish to overstep, my Lor . . . cousin," she looked up at him with soft blue eyes and smiled shyly.

"But it is true that the people wonder when you will take a wife. For ten years, they say, you have left us to go to this woman who is married to an abomination and still she has given you no heir. The people say it is a judgment and they are troubled, cousin."

Soamosa lowered her eyes and her head when she'd finished speaking. Her slender back was straight, her slim feet pressed together in their thick, homely shoes, her hands were folded modestly in her lap. She was the perfect picture of traditional Bethelite womanhood.

Perhaps a perfect candidate for the Prophet's wife. Amos wondered who had been in charge of her education these past few years, regretting his lack of involvement. *There was too much to do,* he protested to his creeping guilt, *too many documents and summaries and reports . . .*

Amos breathed a quiet, frustrated sigh. *Ah, Channa,* he thought, *how you've changed me. Once, not so very long ago, I would have approved of such overwhelming self-negation. I would have been pleased at the way she distanced herself from her own opinions so as not to seem overbold. What would you advise me to tell her, my love?*

He realized now, far too late, that choosing to bring Soamosa had been something of an error. Insensitive at best. No doubt his young cousin's mother had visions of an elaborate wedding ceremony with thousands of guests upon their return; her daughter would be the radiant bride, himself, the blushing groom.

He sat up straighter and spoke to her firmly.

"Soamosa, look at me."

Her lips trembled and her eyes were huge and shining when she looked up.

"I have told you that Simeon is neither an abomination, nor Channa's husband. He is my dear friend, and Channa, who is completely unbound, is the woman that I love. Do you understand this?"

A frown struggled to manifest itself and then her face smoothed.

Ah, Amos thought, *such control. For one so apparently timid she's actually quite strong.*

"No," she said firmly, "I do not."

"I do not owe you an explanation, little one."

She bit her lip and lowered her eyes, then looked up at him again, abashed, but hopeful.

Amos sighed.

"We will begin with Simeon," he said patiently. "What is your objection to him?"

"He isn't human, cousin. He is a thing that mocks the perfection of man as God created him."

"And is our uncle, Grigory, an abomination because his heart is made of plastic mesh?"

She frowned. "No, of course not."

"Simeon simply requires more mechanical aid than does our uncle. He is still a man, just as Grigory is a man. And he is good man, one of the truest friends that I have ever had. If you will but open your heart to him, he will be your friend too, Soamosa."

Predictably, she looked both doubtful and queasy.

"As to my relationship with Channa Hap . . ."

Her interest sharpened to a sword's point.

"Frankly, it is none of your business." He watched her blush a deep scarlet. "This I will say, Channa and I do not need a marriage ceremony to sanctify what is already a very real and pure love. Nor is it necessary for me to produce an heir."

Soamosa actually gasped and clutched at her heart in horror.

"Let the family divide my estates and wealth among themselves when I am dead. Our world and people will not falter because I am gone. Let them find another to head the state."

"But your holiness will also be gone. We would be so comforted if you left sons behind to guide us," she said passionately.

Amos smiled at her. "Sweet cousin, when God touches a man's heart and urges him to speak as a prophet to the people, that man is not chosen because of who his father was. Only think what it would be like if the people turned to you, expecting you to fill my shoes."

"But they wouldn't!" she said in horror. "I'm only a woman."

Amos tried to imagine Channa's reaction to *that* remark. He gave a complex inward shudder. Channa Hap in full fury was enough to make a strong man blanch and cringe; like a thunderstorm on the sands, or a driven ocean crashing on high cliffs.

"Ah, but they might think that my taking you on this trip had some deeper meaning." She blushed at that and quickly lowered her eyes. "And if I were to offer you such special attentions for the rest of my life, then they would surely think it significant. After all, there have been prophetesses before."

"But . . . but . . . I have no calling," she protested, both horrified and confused. "I know that I have not."

"So, why should I create an heir, who might have no calling either, but of whom the people would expect such? Imagine the life my son or daughter could look forward to. Should I be so unfair? Should I arouse such expectations?"

"No," she said almost sullenly. "But, then why . . . ?"

"Have I invited you to accompany me? I have invited you because I like you, cousin. Because you are young and I thought that you might enjoy seeing one of the greatest space stations in the universe."

*Because I didn't want to see you living your life in
a gray sack, with your mind pinched off like a plant
being deliberately stunted.*

He had changed Bethel, the Kolnari war had changed
it more, but there were limits to what could be done
in a single generation.

"I thought you might like an adventure."

He was pleased to see a sudden gleam come into
her eyes. It reminded him of the girl who'd put a
desert *gurrek* under his pillow. His heart grew content
when she grinned back. Perhaps, after all, those
horrible clothes and the mealy-mouthed behavior were
the result of an ambitious mother's determined
schooling. With time and care she might return to
her own true self.

A sudden twisting wrench made both of them cry
out involuntarily. Soamosa fell to her knees, hands over
her mouth to hold back the retching. Amos turned his
chair and lunged for his console, knowledge driving out
the merely physical misery.

They'd been ripped out of hyperspace.

Dangerous, exceedingly so. Without drugs, or preparation, susceptible and unlucky passengers had been
known to slip into a psychotic state.

Amos gripped the arms of his chair and closed his
eyes waiting for his body to readjust. Soamosa gave up
the unequal struggle and ran for the washroom. Amos
swallowed hard as the sounds she made urged his body
to sympathetic action.

He activated the com and snapped, "Captain Sung!"

Before he had finished speaking a voice came
booming through the ship:

"Attention merchanter ship *Sunwise*. Stand by to be
boarded. Resistance is futile and will be punished.
Repeat. Prepare to be boarded."

The skin at the base of Amos's neck clenched as

though stabbed with a jagged piece of ice. *Kolnari*. The accent was different, but the arrogance the same.

The captain hadn't answered his call. Amos made an impatient sound deep in his throat and headed for the bridge, calling out to Soamosa to remain in the cabin. The two guards standing watch outside the door turned smartly and followed him.

I have waited too long. I thought . . . The Kolnari never forgot an injury; but they never attacked a foe they thought too strong, either. They had already found the SSS-900-C a mouthful large enough to choke on. Bethel had a space navy of its own, these days—small, but enough to defend the system until a Central Worlds squadron arrived.

In the merchant ship *Sunwise* Belazir t'Marid had found a target easy enough to take, which also meant he felt strong enough to survive the inevitable retaliation. The Kolnari leader had the cunning of Shaithen his master. He might be right. . . .

"Ship is in the five kiloton range," the communications tech was saying. "Warship, from the neutrino signature. Corvette class, but not a standard model."

Amos nodded to himself, standing at the rear of the horseshoe-shaped command bridge. *Panic, but well-controlled panic,* he decided. Captain Sung was snapping out orders; hard, almond-shaped green eyes glittering in a stern middle-aged face. Young Guard-Caladin Samuel stood behind him, one hand on the captain's chair, one resting on the console. Occasionally he leaned close and spoke urgently to the distracted Sung.

On the forward screen, to Amos's vast relief, was a somewhat worse-for-wear ex-courier ship. An ordinary pirate vessel, nothing like the augmented ships the Kolnari favored.

Mere pirates, he thought. *I am relieved that it is* merely *pirates.*

"Have they indicated what they want, Captain Sung?"

"They want to board," the Captain snarled. "Beyond that, Benisur, I don't know." He rubbed his chin. "But this is no happy accident on their part. There's no trace of recent drive energies; they had to've been waiting for us."

Sung glanced at the controls. "With a grapple already engaged and waiting to trip us out of hyperspace. Timing like that . . ." he let the thought trail off.

Amos's finely chiseled mouth thinned to a grim line. Yes, timing like that meant a traitor, a spy high enough in the Bethelite Security Forces to have access to privileged information. *Traitors or Kolnari agents, or both*, he decided. *Joseph, I should have listened to you.*

Complacency. Letting the wish be father to the thought. *I thought you paranoid.* Mind you, a Chief of Security was *supposed* to be paranoid. *I should have listened.* Of late years he'd even given up the simple precaution of booking passage on several different ships, leaving at different times.

"That spawn of Shaithen would know where I was," he'd argued with certainty. "It would take more than a simple trick to escape his grasp."

Joseph would have preferred an escort of destroyers, and a company of Guards. Amos had argued that Central Worlds would, at the least, see that as an insulting lack of trust, and at worst as a provocation— the Bethelites were thought barbaric enough as it was.

Amos glanced at his escort. Four of them; all were young. *And untried,* he thought, realizing for the first time that they might well die today. Regret and anger washed through him. He'd chosen youngsters because he wanted to expose as many of the young as he could to Central Worlds culture, because that was their future.

Just as these vibrant young men were meant to be Bethel's.

Joseph, my brother, if I ever see you again I shall allow you to scold me for as long as pleases you about my foolishness; and in future I will bow to your will. He would let Joseph boot his Prophetic arse, for that matter, if he lived past this day.

"Benisur, I'm afraid they may be after you. There's nothing else on the ship that would be worth their trouble."

Nothing, unless the pirates were after a cargo of sundried tomatoes, dates, goat cheese, leather handicrafts, and preserved meats. Valuable enough on SSS-900-C, with its rich manufactories and well-paid, highly-trained inhabitants. Not the sort of thing which pirates selected for their raids.

Amos nodded. "My thinking exactly, Captain."

He paused. Pirates would squeeze Bethel for a ransom it could ill afford.

"I am reluctant to place your people or your ship in any greater danger, Captain, but I believe we must consider resisting. After all, if I am the object of this exercise, then they cannot risk firing on the ship and possibly killing me. So that is one danger we need not fear. And as they are in a small ship, how many of them could there be? Ten perhaps? Fifteen?"

The Captain shrugged. "Fifteen tops, more would overtax life support."

"So we outnumber them as well. Let them come aboard, lure them in and when they are in far enough, strike, and take hostage any survivors. What do you say?" Amos glanced at his young Caladin, courteously including him in their council.

"I had not even considered surrendering you to them, Benisur." Samuel's brown eyes held an innocent bravery.

"I'm no soldier, Benisur," Sung said, and pulled on

his lower lip. "But I like your plan a whole lot better than just letting these animals grab my ship and take you off it." He nodded decisively: "We'll do it."

There was a slight quaver in Sung's voice as he issued orders to break out the arms. He glanced at Amos to see if it had been noticed. But Amos was studying the monitor showing the lock through which the pirates would enter.

An echoing clang resounded through the ship as the pirates extended a caterpillar lock to connect them to the *Sunwise*.

Amos looked up from the screen to watch the crewmen depart for their ambush site and murmured a blessing over them, knowing that most of them would neither understand nor thank him for it. But the eyes of the four Bethelites showed gratitude as they ceremoniously touched forehead, lips, and heart.

Then he watched as the Captain keyed the monitors that covered his crew's progress under the direction of the Bethelite soldiers.

The camera trained on the main lock showed the hatch recessing. Air hissed as pressures equalized; Bethel's was well below the Earth-derived standard the Central Worlds used.

A long second's pause. Two men in black space armor swung out from the airlock, crouching, plasma rifles up. After a moment one of them signaled and five more swept out. Three split off and moved carefully towards engineering, the other four, hugging the walls and moving with extreme caution, headed for the bridge.

Amos's stomach knotted. Their armor was too much like the Kolnari's—though a stripped down version of it—and their movements were too professional, too disciplined, for mere criminals. If the Kolnari were so reduced as to use outsiders . . . mercenaries . . . But no, surely they would despise and avoid such creatures.

Yet these men behaved like the product of intensive Kolnari training—that was an inhumanly businesslike civilization.

He opened his mouth to advise the Captain to call off the ambush, when a final invader left the airlock and entered the ship.

A foot, clad in massive black battle armor, hit the *Sunwise's* deck with a crash that seemed to move the ship. Slowly—majestic as an eclipse—the Kolnari entered, turned, and marched towards the bridge.

Amos could not speak. For a moment his throat was paralyzed, he couldn't breathe, he couldn't move. It was unexpected, to be so overwhelmed by horror at seeing one of them again, for he was no coward. But an evil that had almost destroyed his people had returned; the nightmare was marching again—coming to collect him personally.

"Captain!" Amos managed to choke out. "Call off the ambush, call it off or they'll kill you all!"

The Captain stared for a moment as though he hadn't understood, then activated the com and spoke, just as Samuel, the Bethelite Caladin, fired on the invaders.

"Stand down! Stand down! Lay down your weapons and fall back!"

Some of the crew heard him, reacting with confusion at first, looking around to see if anyone else had heard the order, lowering their rifles, backing off. But Amos's guards engaged the enemy—too intent on battle to listen—certain that if the Benisur Amos wished them to hold their fire *his* voice would have told them so.

One crewman stood up, his hands lifted in surrender and died for it, a steaming hole blasted in his chest by a plasma rifle.

The doubtful broke then and fled, while the others fought and retreated, and died, one by one. Retreat turned to slaughter.

✧   ✧   ✧

Amos was thrown with bruising force at the feet of
Belazir t'Marid and lay face down, unmoving, on a
rough carpet made from the scaly hide of a great beast.
Behind him, he heard the gentle whir of servos as the
battle-armored Kolnari lowered the arm that had flung
him here. He heard soft grunts as his companions,
Captain Sung and Soamosa were tossed to the floor
beside him.

Soamosa, her blond hair freed from confinement and
her gown much torn, clung to Amos's arm, burying her
face against him and trembling.

"Look at me, Benisur," purred a voice silky with
satisfaction.

Amos raised himself onto his elbows and slowly lifted
his head. Belazir grinned down at him, white teeth
gleaming in a predator's snarl from a face as black as
a starless night. *He has aged*, Amos thought, shocked.

The hawklike nose was more prominent and the flesh
hung on his face like slightly melted tallow. But the
golden eyes were as bright and cruel as they had ever
been; though now they held the glint of sheer mad glee,
where before there had only been a lazy amusement.

"So good to see you," Belazir continued, almost
whispering.

The control room was centered on his chair, like a
massive throne set among control consoles and display
screens. The Kolnari lord wore only a white silk
loincloth and jeweled belt, besides his ornaments; he
lolled like a resting tiger between guards in powered
armor, his own suit standing empty and waiting. Behind
him a holograph showed a nighted landscape where
armored plants grew and moved and fought slow
vegetable battles with spikes of organic steel. In the
distance a nuclear volcano spat fire that red-lighted the
undersides of acid clouds. A giant beast with sapphire

scales trumpeted its agony at the sky as six-legged wolves leaped and clung and tore at its adamantine sides. Thick purple blood rilled towards the ground, and the very grass writhed to drink of it.

Kolnar, Amos knew with a shudder. *Antechamber of hell.* Belazir had never seen the planet that bred his kind, but it lived in his genes.

"So *good* to see you like this," Belazir said. He slowly clenched his hand. "You are in my fist," he explained, as though Amos might not know it. "You and your companions." He grinned at them and indicated the Captain. "And who have we here? Captain Sung, I presume?"

A vicious kick from a mercenary prompted a response.

"Yessir," Sung grunted.

A flurry of kicks caused Sung to roll into a ball, covering his head, drawing his feet up to protect his privates. The kicks concentrated on his kidneys until he sobbed.

"Beg," the Kolnari said.

"Please!"

Belazir raised one finger. The mercenary stepped back, grinning. He had a particolored beard and a brass hoop in one ear.

"You must tell the Captain the rules, Benisur. We would not want a repeat of this lesson, not at his age."

"We must address the Divine Seed of Kolnar as 'Great Lord,'" Amos said, his voice flat and distant, his eyes fixed on the space below the Kolnari's feet, "and when the Lord Captain Belazir addresses us we must respond with 'Master and God.'"

"And what are you, Simeon Amos?" Belazir asked with delicate sarcasm.

"Scumvermin," Amos ground out.

Belazir laughed with delight.

"Ah, there are times—like this one, Benisur—when

a despised enemy can be more welcome than a beautiful bride." He smiled benignly at Amos, then indicated the cowering girl at his side. "Is this *your* bride?"

"No! Lord and God," Amos said with such obvious sincerity that Belazir raised an eyebrow.

"Do not tell me you are still saving your seed for the delectable Channahap?"

Amos tried to school his features to immobility. He knew the slight shifts in his expression conveyed his outrage to the Kolnari like a shout.

Belazir smiled a cream-eating smile.

"A most . . . satisfying woman, truly. I can understand your obsession." He indicated Soamosa again. "Then no doubt this little one is a virgin; your people have an inexplicable admiration for such. Do not fear, girl, I can cure you of it."

Soamosa's body jerked as though she'd been struck. She muffled a cry with the sleeve of her robe.

"She is only a child, Master and God," Amos pleaded. "Her family will pay a ransom for her safe return."

Belazir shrugged, "I had eight children by her age, and all of my wives were the same age as I. If I return her to her family in . . . *almost* one piece, I doubt they will complain. Much." He grinned. "And certainly not to me."

He flicked a hand at the guards, "Take them away." To Amos: "We will talk again later, scumvermin. I shall look forward to it."

✧ CHAPTER TWO

Joseph ben Said paced restlessly through his office. It was on the top, the third story of a building well up on the slopes overlooking New Keriss. He stopped and looked down from the open window; mild salt air caressed his face, smelling of the gardens outside and faintly of the city of low, scattered buildings that stretched down to the water's edge.

How different, he thought—as always.

How different from the days before the Kolnari came. Old Keriss had occupied the same site; the airburst hadn't dug much of a crater when the city died in a moment of thermonuclear fire. But the old city had been bigger, more densely built, narrow streets as well as fine avenues. Thickest of all along the old docks, with their shrilling tenements and slums. The New Kerris was cleaner, more modern now that Bethel was in touch with the rest of the galaxy once more. Cleaner, safer, more prosperous . . . although perhaps less happy than the old city had been.

Or perhaps I was happier then. His lips quirked as he remembered a lord's son down slumming, and how he'd saved that young noble from the knives of a rival gang. Then turned and found a hand extended; taken it in his own, astonished. Met Amos ben Sierra Nueva's eyes, and been lost to his old life.

23

That brought him back to the present; his face clenched like a fist, eyes narrowing. He sat behind the desk and keyed the screen.

"Home," he said.

It cleared, and his wife Rachel looked up in surprise from her own keyboard as his image replaced whatever she'd been working on. In the background he could hear children playing. His children . . . *No. They are safe, and my duty is clear.*

"Joseph!" she said, concern in her dark eyes. "Is there any news of the Prophet?"

He shook his head. "Nothing from SSS-900-C," he said. "Simeon reports no word. No trace of the Benisur's ship has been found; it is as if they had vanished from space-time."

He took a deep breath, and saw her face change. Rachel had come to know him too well, in the years of their marriage. Joseph held up a hand.

"Please," he said softly. "My heart, do not tear at me; this is hard enough to do. But Amos is more than my Prophet; he is the friend of my soul, my brother."

"There are younger men to do this work!"

Joseph smiled ruefully. "Are there any better trained to seek him offplanet?" he asked.

Rachel met his eyes for a moment, then glanced aside. Hers shone with unshed tears.

"Where will you go?"

"I cannot say," he said. *Must not,* they both knew. There was a leak in Planetary Security. "But it must be soon." He willed strength into his voice. "Do not fear, my love. We have friends beyond Bethel, as well as enemies."

"Why the fardling void can't they just say *give me a bribe*?" Joat Simeon-Hap demanded.

New Destinies hung in space four thousand

kilometers away; much closer in the main bridge screen, of course. It wasn't very large as independent stations went, merely a cylinder ten kilometers long by one in diameter, spinning contentedly—*smugly*, her mind prompted—in orbit around an undistinguished orange-brown gas giant, which orbited a run-of-the-mill F-class star. That was a pinprick of violent light in the distance; closer in were a few barren rocks, none of them larger than Mars, and some asteroids.

Junk system. Junk station. Barely worth visiting because it intersected a few transit routes. There weren't many fabricators in space nearby, either. One long latticework, a graving dock that looked capable of repairing fair-sized ships or building small ones. A couple of zero-g algae farms, huge soft-looking bubbles. Some in-system traffic, miners and passenger craft and wide-mouthed scoopships to skim and harvest the gas giant's outer atmosphere. Probably they didn't pick up the litter on the station, and charged you extra for the gravity.

Joat chuckled sourly at the thought; it appealed to her sense of the ridiculous. It didn't make her less impatient. New Destinies had a reputation as one of those places that looked the other way. A fair number of the ships who docked here were in the smuggling trade, which, frankly, was what kept the station going. But a couple of generations of *not noticing* had an effect. Here, bribery and graft were just the way things were done. So Joat couldn't understand why none of her hints had been picked up on, or no overtures had been made in that direction.

She loved the *Wyal*, and not just because the ship was hers. But there were times when you had to get off the ship or run starkers, raving and frothing.

The jerk's on a power trip. She combed a hand through shoulder-length blond hair and spoke, altering her tone slightly:

"Find out who this fardling bureaucratic nightmare is, wouldja Rand?"

"You mean Dilton Tolof in Health and Immigration?"

"Yeah."

There was a confused pause.

"Joat, he's Dilton Tolof in Health and Immigration." She rolled her eyes. "Do you have to be so *literal*?"

"That's the way I'm made, Joat."

"I mean find out about him."

"Why?"

"Just do it!"

"You're upset," Rand sounded surprised. "Is it me, have I caused offense?"

"No, but he has. I'd like to tailor-make a little lesson in the etiquette of negotiation for him."

"You want to benefit him?" Rand sounded mildly astonished.

She smiled slowly.

"In a sense."

"It's been my observation, Joat, that you're not inclined to return good for bad. Nor has there been any solicitation of bribery. Yet, you seem to believe that Mr. Tolof is somehow asking for one. I admit to being puzzled."

"Logic, buddy. It isn't as though this little station is the most sought-after destination in Central Worlds' space, Rand, so sheer volume of work can't be the reason for this kind of delay."

Joat frowned. Two things about her tended to make the overbearing and officious think they could push her around. One was her age. At twenty-three, Joat was extremely young to be the captain and owner-aboard of a starfaring freighter. The other was that she was the adopted daughter of Space Station Simeon-900-C and Channa Hap; the first child to be adopted by a Brain-Brawn pair. For some reason that Joat couldn't fathom, these facts were supposed to make her malleable and stupid. Or, worse, naive, which she couldn't even remember being.

"It's just the way these little, out-of-the-way places operate. Now, I don't object to baksheesh, within reason," she said in a tone that would have alarmed anyone who knew her well. *If you lay on the sweet talk thick as honey, make no demands, don't insult me and you sure as blazes don't throw obstacles in my path.* Maybe then, she'd pay. Maybe.

Joat spun her gimbaled pilot's chair around and fondly regarded the winking lights of her friend's "face." Technically it wasn't a person—perhaps even not really a personality, if you wanted to get philosophical—but definitely a friend.

The rows of lights that formed its countenance served no purpose but to give Rand expression and to satisfy her low taste for ancient popular entertainments. Just now, they were predominantly yellow, signaling puzzlement.

"Civil servants are like rugs—you have to whack them now and then to get the dirt out. I just want to give him a little goose to teach him not to mess with me," Joat told it.

All the lights flickered yellow.

"You want to give him a barnyard fowl?" Now Rand *did* sound astonished.

Joat laughed. "In this instance, Rand, a goose means a pinch on the butt to get him going." *No sense in shocking a machine.* Sometimes she wondered who did the component blocks she'd bought for the basis of the AI.

"Ah!" The lights flickered blue, signaling pleasure in this new understanding; then back to yellow. "But, the references I found to that use of the term referred to it as an expression of erotic interest."

"Not in this case, I assure you," she said dryly.

"Well that's why I thought you wanted to give him the bird."

Joat choked back a laugh.

"I've said something amusing," it accused.

"No, it's me. I took it wrong."

After a moment it said, "Joat, really! If I'm to avoid these verbal pitfalls it would save time if you'd simply tell me why you're laughing. Just because the information is in my files somewhere doesn't justify wasting my energy searching for it."

"So you know why I laughed?"

"You had a misspent youth."

"And a largely misspent adulthood."

"Not really. You've actually accomplished quite a lot for such a young woman. You've only been an adult legally for two years."

Joat squirmed. Praise made her feel as if she was being set up; not least because she'd used it so often and so effectively that way herself.

"Y'know, you sounded kinda exasperated there for a minute," she said lightly.

"I was. And a particularly stupid reaction it is, if I may say so."

"Hey," she shrugged, "you're the one who wanted to understand emotions."

"*Understand* them, not *have* them."

Joat raised an admonishing finger. "Knowledge is never wasted."

"While time and energy too often are. Specifically by forcing me to apply this program."

"Well, in general, emotional responses aren't voluntary," she said.

It wasn't really fair to force emotion-analogues on the AI. *On the one hand I feel guilty. On the other, it's fun. Such a grubby little emotion, guilt.*

"If you don't experience an unexpected reaction once

in awhile, then how can you understand emotions? Or put up with 'em for that matter. Remember, understanding makes all things tolerable."

"I had fewer problems with tolerance before I was capable of exasperation! Knowledge or lack of it isn't the problem; this *program* is the problem."

Uh oh. Clearly Rand wanted that program gone, and was perfectly capable of erasing it.

"Oh no you don't," she said. "I didn't sweat blood creating that program just so you could erase it the first time it runs. You leave it alone. Y'hear me?"

A neatly clipped "Yes." Then: "I suppose I should be grateful that you haven't found a way to irritate me."

"I'm getting close," Joat threatened with a grin. "Frustration and irritation are in the same family, so be prepared. After all, if you want to understand someone you have to walk a kilometer in their . . ."

"Would you can the quotes, please? If I want to drown in clichés I have access to all four volumes of *The Wit and Wisdom of the Known Universe.* The unabridged version."

Joat pursed her lips. "Sorry. Uh, have you got anything on Dilton yet?" she prompted.

"According to station records Tolof has had numerous citations for unauthorized power-grabbing. He's exceeded his allotted limit of power seventeen times, but was fined for only the first three."

"Interesting. And what's the name of the individual who waived his penalty charges?"

"Graf Dyson. I'm searching for references to that name."

After a full minute Joat raised a brow and prompted, "Anything?"

"No. Nothing significant, anyway. He lives here and is employed by the Bureau of Fines and Levies, but he has never been recorded as being guilty of the most minor infractions. He leads an exceptionally ordered and modest life, and his credit balance reflects that. Puzzling."

"For a citizen of New Destinies it's unbelievable." Another effect of catering to smugglers; their awareness of what constituted bad behavior was deeply impaired. "Do any of our friends or acquaintances show his name on any of their documents?"

"Yes," Rand replied promptly. "Captain Yandit has received several citations for disturbing the peace, but was never fined. Records show that the fine was waived by Graf Dyson."

"Well then, as Graf Dyson is a friend of a friend, I think we can safely claim acquaintance. Don't you?"

"No."

Joat linked her fingers and cracked her knuckles with a flourish. "Put me through to that mudpuppy in the health office, buddy, and watch me finesse this."

Dilton Tolof's pinched face appeared on the screen.

"New Destinies, Health and Immigration." Then he realized to whom he was speaking and smiled, a thin and somehow sour expression that fitted his pinched face. "Ms. Simeon, if you continue to pester me like this, I'm never going to be able to process your records."

"Well, I was talking to Graf, Graf Dyson? He asked me what was taking me so long. I've got a little present for him, and you know how impatient he gets. We're *real* good friends." She simpered at the man on the screen in her best fluff-head imitation. "Anyway, he said mentioning his name might serve to, you know, expedite things. Like, as a favor to a friend?"

Tolof's narrow face flushed and he glanced nervously around.

"You know . . . G. D.?"

"Sure do. Captain Yandit, you may have dealt with him, huge, Ursinoid fellow with a temper? He introduced us at a party one time, and we hit it off right away." Joat snapped her fingers, indicating the speed with which she and Dyson had become fast friends. "Graf said you guys were real close, mentioned that you'd done some deals?" She raised an inquiring brow and smiled knowingly.

Dilton's sour smile turned slowly into the expression of a man who'd just opened a box of chocolates and found maggots.

"Well," he said, "heh heh, your documentation appears to be in order, no need to be, uh, nitpicky."

He punched a few keys and her comp received the "cleared" signal that would allow Joat and her crew the freedom of the station and permit docking robots to begin unloading the *Wyal*'s cargo.

"*Thank* you so much," she gushed and gave him a wink. "I'll be sure and tell *G. D.* what a pal you were."

Joat punched off the connection and sneered, "No need to be nitpicky." She shivered. "Ghu, but I hate bureaucrats."

The ship rumbled and there was a slight swaying sensation. *Docking tractors attached* blinked across the screen, and a grid swelled to fill the view. She kept her hands poised over the controls, but the AI and Stationside kept the *Wyal* steady as she slid towards the non-rotating docking ring at the north pole of New Destinies. About the running of the station and their docking procedures, the New Destinites were consummate professionals.

"Especially you, Dilton," she added in the same tone. "You worm."

"Whozzat?"

The air scrubbers whirred into overdrive as a sudden, overwhelmingly sweet and spicy aroma invaded the control cabin, followed by Alvec Dia, one of her crew. In fact, he was her crew: with an Admiralty Grade artificial intelligence, a three thousand kiloton freighter didn't need more than two.

"Gak!" Joat wheezed, waving her hand in front of her face. "Alvec, what is that stench?"

"Stench, Boss?" Alvec seemed genuinely puzzled. "That's Senalgal Spice, the favorite cologne of the Rose of New Destinies."

He put his hands on his hips and raised a brow, archly. Or as archly as a middle-aged man with scar tissue across the knuckles of both hands and a build like a freight carboy could. Joat couldn't help grinning at him, and an answering smile split the rough, lived-in face.

"You have a lady-friend here?" she asked, trying to breathe shallowly. He had friends of that sort on a number of stations, all answering to the name of Rose.

"Not yet." He winked. "But I aim to."

"Do me a favor, Al, air out a little before you go a-hunting. I wouldn't want you arrested for assault this early in the day. I'd have to bail you out."

"I'll be careful, Mother. We cleared?" He jerked a thumb dockside.

At Joat's nod he waggled his fingers farewell and left with a jaunty step.

She watched him leave. The monitors showed him dodging cargo robots trundling forward across the open space just inside the hull of the docking ring. Then, taking an experienced spacer's leap across to the entrance of the spindle, he grabbed the handholds, did a neat turn and went feet-first through the hatchway, ready for the transition to spin gravity in the core.

There was a clanking through the hull as the robots boarded; she watched on screens slaved to the interior monitors as one busily rushed up to grab a pallet,

loaded it onto the flatbed of its body, then hustled off
to dockside to unload it onto a stack already piling up
on a larger float that would take the shipment to a
warehouse.

Joat watched them idly for a few moments, then her
interest was caught by their human supervisor.

He was tall, with a soldier's posture but a soft gut.
His eyes . . . they never stopped tracking. Back, forth,
back; the eyes of someone expecting trouble, someone
who'd been expecting it so long they couldn't stop.
Scarred face, with the distinctive red splotch on one
cheek. At some time in the not-too-distant past he'd
been caught in an explosive decompression. Not an
uncommon industrial accident off-planet, but . . . His
uniform was just a little too . . . something. It fit him,
it wasn't new, but somehow, it wasn't right.

He wore it as though it wasn't completely familiar,
Joat realized. It had been his hand fumbling for a
pocket that wasn't there that had caught her eye. Joat
sat up straight.

Who? Nobody she could think of was gunning for
her right now—angry with her, yes; ready to do her
the dirty in any underhanded way they could, yes.
But not killing mad, not enough to hire muscle to
go after her. And this man was obviously muscle of
some sort. His whole body screamed *retired mercenary.* But why would a retired mercenary accept
a pick-up job on New Destinies?

Not a merc, then. So, he was a cop. And he was
watching the *Wyal.*

But why were they watching her? Dilton hadn't had
time to sic this guy on her, even if he'd the guts to
do it. Neither had Dyson, whoever he was, because
he couldn't possibly have reacted this fast to the little
scam she'd just pulled on his buddy. He probably didn't
even know about it, at least not yet.

Her mind went to the small mysterious package she was carrying for Central Worlds Security. Did New Destinies know about it? Were they after it? Was it something that would incriminate her?

Joat frowned. She wasn't about to risk her ship for some CenSec song and dance. The package was supposed to be dropped with the local operative at The Anvil, one of the bars around the rim of the station. She glanced at the time, she was due there in one and a half Earth standard hours.

Joat gritted her teeth. *So I owe them. That doesn't mean they own me.* More to the point, it didn't mean they could endanger her *ship*. She'd drop it all right, and then she'd tell them what they could do with their special courier packages.

"Rand, I gotta go."

"Now? Before unloading is completed?"

"You see that osco on monitor four?"

"The unloading supervisor?"

"Yeah. He's a cop."

"He can't be, Joat, he's wearing a supervisor's uniform. The police uniform for this port is very different, I assure you."

Rand put a holo snap of a local policeman on screen for her edification.

"I know what a cop looks like, Rand, in or out of uniform. And that's a cop, and he's watching us."

"I'm impressed by your prescience, Joat. Why is he watching us?"

"I don't know and I don't intend to find out. I'm going out the side door."

"The . . . ? Joat, we don't have a side door."

"I'm going out the service hatch and into the station via one of theirs," she said, briskly closing out the file she'd been idly working on while waiting for clearance.

"That's illegal . . ."

"I know that, but . . ."

"And dangerous!"

"I'm relying on you to help me avoid getting caught," she explained. Joat wondered how Rand would choose to respond, for she'd given it almost complete autonomy. It might decide to have nothing to do with this scheme, which would complicate things tremendously.

"Could we talk deal?" Rand asked smoothly.

Joat's eyebrows went up and she cocked her head. "Excuse me?"

"That exasperation program . . . ?"

Joat frowned and folded her arms thoughtfully. Then she sighed.

"Okay, deal, you can erase the program. Now will you help me?"

"I'll do my best." Rand's voice conveyed pride in self combined with disapproval of her plans.

Joat supressed a smile. Sometimes Rand was downright prissy. She wondered if she'd unintentionally programmed it that way—it couldn't have caught it from *her* behavior, that was sure.

"Don't worry Rand."

"When you say not to worry, worry becomes imperative."

"Where's the station's nearest service hatch to *Wyal*?" she asked.

Rand threw a schematic on the screen, replacing the smiling policeman. Wyal was represented by a blinking yellow dot, the nearest service hatch blinked red.

"Now, show me the surveillance cameras."

A pause, then Rand indicated them on the schematic in blue.

"Whew," Joat sighed. "They have pretty good coverage. Any chance you can hack into the surveillance network and simply run a tape of empty space while I'm out there?"

"Doubtful. With so many suspect elements sharing

the station's amenities, New Destinies has a fairly sophisticated security system. Something of that complexity would probably activate an alarm."

"Fardles." She drummed her fingers on the console. "What can you tell me about the lock?"

Rand threw up another schematic. "It's a standard design. Nothing complicated, with the usual tell-tales in place." As it spoke small arrows blinked on indicating the areas spoken of. "There are cameras in the corridor outside the service hatch."

Joat brushed her hair back. *Time for another trim,* she thought inconsequentially. She went to a locker at the rear of the bridge compartment and palmed the sensor. It opened, and she began to take out various useful items and slot them into pockets and less obvious hiding places in her taupe overall; also in her belt, in the heels of her boots, and one or two in special cavities in her molars.

"Is there any time when the route I'll have to traverse and the lock itself isn't under observation?"

That came out as a mumble, since her fingers were in the back of her mouth, but Rand had excellent voiceprint filters.

"For approximately ten seconds the route and the lock are clear. As it won't alter their function, I may be able to slow the sweep of the cameras so that you have forty seconds," Rand told her. "I can do nothing about the tell-tales, though, and the cameras inside are stationary."

She considered the diagram before her.

"It'll take me twelve seconds to get from *Wyal* to the lock," she murmured.

"Optimistically."

"Twelve seconds." She grinned. "And if I can't silence a tell-tale in twenty-eight seconds I deserve whatever happens to me. Can you take out the camera in the corridor?"

"I believe so. But it will surely be considered suspicious."

"Feh!" Joat made a contemptuous face and a dismissive gesture. "It probably happens all the time."

Then she rose and laced her fingers together, cracking her knuckles briskly. "Let's do it. You're in charge of the *Wyal* until I return. *Don't* accumulate too much time on the station's virtual reality net— we can't afford it."

"It's research," Rand said indignantly. "My interactions with humans increase my versatility."

"You can research Alvec and me for free," Joat said firmly, running a mental checklist of the devices she was carrying. *A few more?* No, the only really useful item would be a laser welder—you could do really astonishing things with a laser welder, if you knew how—but it was a bit conspicuous.

– Useful, though. It was a pity. She and a couple of other students at Vega Central Institute—Simeon had sent her there for six months—had cut down a bronze statue of the Founder, cut it in half, and rewelded it around a shower fixture in the quarters of the Dean of Cybernetics. And she hadn't had to use anything but a hand-cutter and a floater platform to do it, either.

Actually Simeon had sent her to Vega Central for a year. They'd sent her *back* after six months.

Bureaucrats, she thought. *No sense of humor at all.*

Joat tied her hair back in a ponytail and paused to study herself in the screen set to mirror beside the airlock; large, gray-blue eyes stared solemnly back, examining delicate features in a sharp-boned face. Not much trace of the feral child she'd been when Simeon and Channa found her hiding in the ventilation ducts of SSS-900-C; she'd been living in a nest of stolen blankets and cobbled-together computer parts. Good training to be a high-tech guerrilla during the Kolnari occupation of the Station, but not so hot as a preparation for life.

She pursed her lips and looked at the package she was to deliver. *I must have grown up. I haven't opened it.*

CenSec would have all sorts of cyberdog guardians built in, but that just increased the itch. Her fingers twitched as if they held micromanipulators and a datacode bar. She sighed and shook her head. No, it wasn't worth the hassle. She'd made up her mind to that the first time she'd agreed to take on a CenSec shipment at Simeon's request.

The less she knew, she'd told herself, the better. Because CenSec was the kind of organization that considered you were in their debt if *you* did *them* a favor. They started out owing you and ended up owning you. That might appeal to straight-arrow types brought up in boring rectitude, who fell down on their knees in thanks at getting to play Galactic Spy.

Not me, Joat thought defiantly. *Nobody's gonna get a piece of my soul.* She'd gotten far more adventure than she wanted by the age of twelve. And she knew that, for preference, adventure was somebody *else* in deep doodly, far, far away.

She gave herself one last appraising look, then picked up the CenSec package and zipped it into one of her pockets before heading for the suit-storage locker.

Joat suited up quickly. It was a process she'd always handled well, winning a fair number of credits in Brawn school betting on just how fast she could do it.

No gruddy sense of humor there either, she thought. Her knack for separating her fellow students from their disposable income was just one of many reasons she'd finally been asked to leave. By the time they finally got around to asking her, though, she was already half packed. *I don't understand how Channa ever got through without freezing into an icicle*. Then again, a lot of people thought she had.

The fact was she and her teachers and fellow students were fundamentally incompatible. She regarded them as too stiff-necked, they 'saw her as *far* too flexible.

Her only concern in leaving Brawn training had been the possibility that she might be disappointing her adoptive parents. She grinned reminiscently, remembering their words as she stepped out of the Station airlock—Simeon had waited, "standing" beside Channa in his favorite vid persona, a big blond bruiser with a dueling scar and a Centauri Jets cap turned backwards.

"Toldja," he'd said blithely.

"I knew they'd never hammer you into a straight arrow," Channa said with a warm smile. "You were born to be independent."

"Or to hang," Simeon added.

Joat tapped the lock controls. Air bled out; the telltales in the rim of the helmet below her chin showed hard vac. She crouched in the open door of the lock, studying the surface of the station, pronged and spiked with various sensors and antennae. This close even a modest station loomed immense, a metallic god-sized lathe twirling forever against the orange glow of its planet. It turned with a slow ponderous inevitability; at this range your gut refused to see it as an artifact. She turned her head, looking for the flashing red light that indicated the location of the service hatch.

Joat sighed. This little excursion would be so much easier if she'd never revealed the secret of the device that had rendered her invisible to virtually all sensors and recording devices. Simeon had *insisted* on letting everyone know how to counter it. Of course the patent had accounted for a big part of the down-payment on her ship. *Create the problem, solve the problem, collect the money,* she thought.

Ah, well, New Destinies was one of the few windowless stations. They'd spun it up from the nickel-iron of a single asteroid, and nobody had bothered putting in luxuries. So at least she didn't have to worry about some tourist catching her in the act with their holo camera and immortalizing this exploit for the delight of station security.

Light strobed across her target. She estimated the angle and aimed the magnetic grapple built into the sleeve of her suit, leaning forward, arm extended.

"Ready," she said into her suit com. "Say when, Rand."

"Standing by, Joat." Rand paused a moment. "Now."

There was a slight twitch that pushed her arm gently backwards as she fired the grapple. The contact plate spun out on its near-invisible line and clung to the station's skin about a meter from the small service hatch. Joat activated the mechanism in her sleeve that would reel her towards the station, then gave a jerk on the line that propelled her outward.

Joat pulled her feet forward and her knees up against the suit's resistance, rolling herself head over heels in a controlled somersault; timing it so that the stickfield on the soles of her boots would strike first, and her bent legs absorb the impact.

When she left *Wyal*'s gravity field the blood in her veins leapt within her, rushing to her head in a dizzying surge. The weightlessness made every part of her feel strange, as though she'd been bounced upward, never coming down, only climbing, soaring. *Swimming in the universal sea,* a friend at Brawn school had called it. *No lie.* The few moments of queasiness until she adjusted was worth it; then gravity returned as centrifugal force spun her outward. The stationary docking ring fell behind, and suddenly *up* was towards the rotating bulk of New Destinies. It was the docking ring that seemed to move, with the *Wyal* embedded in it like a pencil in a sharpener.

She felt closest to Simeon, her adopted father, when she moved through space in her suit. Encased, as he was, in a machine that kept her alive in a murderous environment, yet personally in contact with the infinite.

Joat watched the universe flick by, ship, stars, station, three times before she reached her target.

The stickfield on her boots held her to the station against the surge of recoil and Joat clasped an extended hand around a utility handle jutting out from the station's skin. Her inertia surged, balanced and stabilized by the grip and the automatic flex of leg and thigh. The anchor cord finished reeling itself back into the sleeve of her suit with a small definite *click*, de-energizing the disk and whipping it back into the slot. Her eyes were telling her that she stood upright on a huge metal plain. Weight said that she was hanging from her feet with a great metal plain *above* her. Both were wrong, and she had no time to waste.

"Now," she muttered. "Down the rabbit hole, or I'll be *very* late."

Her suited fingers traced the exterior of the airlock. Standard model, a fiber-steel oval with memory putty sealant around the edges and a mechanical doglock wheel in the center for emergencies. No use trying that, it would be safetied. Instead she took out a multitool and began opening the access cover of the lock control, whistling soundlessly between her teeth.

Well, and aren't you clever, she thought, as the first choice undid the couplers that held it closed. You found some of the weirdest nonstandard components on these out-of-the-way Stations.

Her suit had some nonstandard components, too. She

unclipped an extension datalink from her belt and clicked the connector into the link on the control card. Then she closed her eyes and subvocalized a series of code words.

A chittering voice sounded in her inner ear. *"Whhhaaat's up, boss?"*

"Got a little job for you, Speedy."

She opened her eyes again. Playing across the thin-film crystal of her suit visor was a holo of a ferret. Not a *real* ferret; this one was vaguely anthromorphic and wore a beret. One hand clutched a smokestick in a long ivory holder. *Stylish*, she thought. There was no point in being mechanical when you designed an AI, even the fairly simple specialized type.

This one, for example, was a specialist in locks.

"Cycle this airlock, but don't let anyone know about it."

"Rrrright, boss."

The holo image vanished. It was replaced by a schematic of the circuitry and the control program for the access. The picklock program slunk through the commercial programming with sinuous ease, then struck. Red slivers appeared on the green circuitry, marking the spots where false data was being fed back into the system's central monitor. That severed the controls from the Station's computers, at least for a while.

Of course, there was always the chance that some interfering type would be actually *looking* at the inside door of the airlock when she came through. Harder to fool the ol' Eyeball Mark I.

"Rand, is there any way for you to tie into the vid monitor covering this accessway and let me know if anybody's out there?"

"No, Joat, there isn't. I've already knocked it out. But this access is located in a maintenance area that's not very thickly populated. It's a chance you'll have to take. You have seven seconds."

"Fardles!"

Joat imagined some passerby attracted to the mysteriously cycling lock, watching in puzzlement the flashing of the warning light that showed the lock was in use.

What if there's a klaxon or a bell? she wondered. She sighed mentally. *Then I get arrested, I guess. Bad planning, Joat. If the worst happens it'll serve you right for being so impulsive.*

She gripped the handholds on either side, disdaining the steps set into the doorway, and popped herself feet-first through the hatch with a grunt. That left her straddling the entranceway, now a hole between her feet. Reaching back, she pulled the hatch closed behind her and glanced at the chrono display down at the chinbar of her helmet. Well within the time limit.

Jack Of All Trades strikes again, she thought, slightly smug. Breaking-and-entering was one of those pleasant hobbies you didn't have much opportunity for when you'd gone legitimate. A pleasure to indulge the skill on good, legal—well, quasi-legal—Central Worlds business.

Air hissed into the narrow airlock, quickly growing thick enough to hear through the exterior pickups. A faint *ping* told her when the pressure was near-enough ambient. Immediately she popped the seal on her helmet and began stripping off the suit, wrinkling her nose slightly at the metallic smell. No excuse for that, in a station—even a small one.

Snaps, locks, and seals parted before her fingers with the easy grace of a lifetime's practice; she had the full measure of finicky neatness common to the vacuum-born. She folded the suit tightly, tucked the gauntlets into the helmet and pulled a small black rectangle from a pocket. It clung when she tapped it onto the inner airlock door over her head, and she snapped a thin cord into a jack on its side. The other end of the cord was pressed against the bone behind one ear. She scanned the sounds from the other side of the metal.

Nothing, she thought cheerfully. Nothing but mechanical noise, none of the irregular thumps and gurgles that indicated an organic sapient. Carbon-based life-forms had messy sonic signatures.

"Rand, can you give me the name of an outfitter? I might as well have my suit seals checked as carry it around with me."

"There are sixteen outfitters licensed to maintain suits. The nearest specialty store is Stondat's Enviro-Systems Emporium, Spin Level 3"—that would be counting inward from the outermost deck, standard throughout human space—"Stack 14b, corridor 9. The camera block is running." Rand's passionless voice took on a faint overtone of contempt. "Very bad security."

Joat smiled. Her attitudes towards sloppy workmanship *had* rubbed off on the AI. She used a small extensible probe to key the interior door of the airlock and trotted up the ladder into an access corridor running both ways until it lost itself in the curve of the Station's outer hull.

"External cameras are back online, no detection," Rand said.

"Grudly. Out for now.", Broadcasts were a needless risk.

The corridor was bare except for the color-coded conduits and pipes that snaked in orderly rectilinear patterns over walls and ceilings. An occasional small maintenance machine trundled by, usually following a pipe rather than the floor.

And footfalls rang. Joat felt herself relax, vision growing bright with the sudden clarity of extreme concentration. The young man who walked in from a side-corridor was wearing the same Stationside police uniform as the one in Rand's holosnap, but his face had the pleasant formlessness of youth. Sheltered youth.

"Oh hey, am I glad to see you!" Joat caroled, an expression of surprised relief on her face. "We just got in, and I'm looking for Stondat's. The suit outfitter? I've obviously gone wrong," she hoisted the suit up a bit with a little grunt, "and this thing is getting heavier by the meter. Where am I?"

She let a trace of wail into the last words, making her eyes go wide in an expression she knew knocked six standard years off her apparent age.

"Let me show you, ma'am. These corridors are for Stationside Maintenance only."

He led the way to a lift, reaching past her to palm the entry. Her hand brushed across his arm.

"There, that's set for Spin Level 3. You can't miss it."

Joat's smile turned broader and more sardonic as the door irised shut. Insect-tiny in her ear, she could hear the young policeman's report via the sticktight she'd brushed across his uniform to blend with the fabric. It was a carbon-chain type, too, almost impossible to scan and biodegradable.

"*Just someone who got lost,*" he said. "*Some vapor-brain from a miner family-ship, probably, can't find her way around anything bigger than a thousand cubic meters. Proceeding.*"

✧ CHAPTER THREE

Bros Sperin sat quietly at his table, a drink in his hand, and watched the patrons of The Anvil enjoying themselves. *Extremely respectable place*, he thought. Perfect for a dropshop. Criminals and spies only haunted known dens of vice in bad fiction, or in places much farther from the right side of the law than New Destinies.

"No, thank you, gentlebeing," he said for the seventh time that night.

The tall—possibly human, probably female, but you couldn't tell sometimes without a xenology program— bobbed her/its/his crest and swayed gracefully off to the sunken dance floor that hung in the center of The Anvil's main room. It was surrounded by tables of spectators, diners, and tourists. Bros Sperin himself wasn't out of place, a man a little above medium height and densely athletic of build, brown of skin and eye, with short black hair cut to resemble a sable cap. His jacket was brown as well, loosely woven raw silk, belted with silver above black tights and low boots. A soft hat lay on the table beside his long-fingered hands, covering a belt data-unit.

He looked relaxed, which was as much a lie as the appearance of a well-to-do merchant out for a peaceful night on the town in this costly, pleasant nightclub.

47

Given the number of serious deals that went down here it was in the regular patron's best interests to see to it that no one got too rowdy, and the management was very solicitous of their guest's interests. Those who insisted on getting out of hand mysteriously and permanently lost their taste for dancing at The Anvil. So did people who annoyed the regular patrons.

If they only knew who I really was, they'd probably be very annoyed indeed, the Central Worlds agent thought. Annoyed enough that he'd disappear with a quiet finality.

Bros raised his glass to his lips and checked his watch. Then glanced at the door. There she was, right on time. Odd, how she looked so little like the scarred, scared child he'd met when he was a lieutenant in Naval Intelligence, assigned to SSS-900-C in the aftermath of the Kolnari raid. And yet what she was now was what he'd seen *in potentia* then, hidden beneath the claws-and-teeth defensiveness her short life had left.

Those straight women who noticed her looked askance at her drab spacer overalls, the gay women observed her over their glasses with mild curiosity. Various aliens had reactions less comprehensible, but they shared a certain caution. The men never looked at her at all.

Their loss, Bros thought. She was beautiful, though she played it down and attitude did the rest.

Joat reached the bar and fixed her gaze on the busy bartender. He'd already noticed her and had caught Bros Sperin's eye. Sperin gave him the high sign to give her a drink as arranged, and to tell her it was from him.

When the bartender placed the drink in front of her, Joat looked at it as if it were a Sondee mudpuppy. The bartender pointed and said a few words to her and Joat turned to look at Bros.

Their eyes met and she raised one brow, suspicious and unsmiling. He grinned and waved her over. After a moment she nodded, picked up the drink and sauntered to his table. He rose to meet her and she smiled and lifted the brow again over his courtesy.

She raised the drink in a little salute.

"Thank you," she said and looked him over, then frowned slightly. "We've never met before, have we?"

"No, I've seen you at a distance, but we've never met."

"Then . . . how do you know what I like to drink?" she asked, curious, suspicious.

Bros grinned down at her.

"It's a game I play, matching drinks to faces. I usually guess right. So . . . do I have you pegged?"

She nodded with a little smile. *At least that far,* Joat thought.

"Please, sit down." He indicated a seat.

"Thanks," she said, and looked around. "But I can't. I'm here to meet someone."

"I know. Me."

Oh, Ghu, Joat thought. *I may lose my lunch.* How could such a neat looking guy have such a macho-maniacal attitude. *Pity.*

To Bros she looked both weary and disappointed at the apparent pick-up line; but smiled as she turned to go. *I don't blame her. That one was probably a cliché when bearskins were the latest fashion.*

"The name's Sperin. Bros Sperin."

Her eyes went wide. *The spy?*

"I thought you were dead!" she blurted.

He laughed. "A rumor I've carefully spread. It's useful. Actually, I only *felt* like I was dead. They put me back together looking different, and they've had me behind a desk the last few years."

They looked at each other for a few moments.

"Shall we sit down or," he indicated the dance floor, "shall we dance?"

Joat sat. *I don't think so. I don't want to get any closer to you than arm's length, thanks.* Something about him made her wary on a personal level. She wondered what the heck was going on.

"I usually deal with Sal," she said uneasily. *And I wish I were now.* Not that Sal was such a great guy or anything. *But something's up, my antennae are tingling.*

"He's around somewhere. I understand you have an unbirthday present for him."

She nodded, frowning again. *An unbirthday present.* She sneered mentally. *That's cute.* "Actually, it's more of a parting gift. Something that might go well with a broken arm."

"In that case he'll be sorry to have missed you. I'll be sure to pass along your good wishes." Bros picked up his glass and looked at her over the rim. "But I needed to talk to you."

"About what?" Joat kept her face and voice as carefully neutral as his.

Bros felt the package placed in his lap; she'd done it so smoothly he hadn't noticed her hand going under the table. *Whoa!* he thought, startled. *What am I doing out by myself if I can't even keep an eye on the girl's hands?*

He didn't show his surprise and dismay however. His face was dead calm when he said, "There's something we need you to do, someone we want you to talk to. We thought the *Wyal* would make a good place for a meeting."

Joat put her untasted drink on the table and gave it a little shove away from herself. *Glad I didn't touch that,* she thought. *Who knows what kind of go-along syrup they put in it.* She didn't like the way this meeting was going. *Of course the drink could be intended as a bribe. CenSec's cheap enough, Ghu knows.* But there was a heavy-duty hook in here somewhere and one lousy drink was insufficient bait to hide it.

"I've been told before—with heavy regret—that I'd be terrible at your kind of work. As if I'd asked. Y'know? As if I'd want it." She crossed her legs. *That stuff's for adrenaline addicted university students. Me, I've got a life.* "Now, all of a sudden, I get this clammy feeling that I'm being recruited. I mean, *Bros Sperin* comes out from behind his desk to meet little *me*. And reels off quite an interesting wish list, by the way; something needs doing, someone needs talking to and how about my place for a meeting. Oooh! It's so exciting." Joat began a slow burn. *This is just a little presumptuous. Don't you think, Bros?* "What makes you think I'd be interested?"

"You've done things for us before."

"An occasional passenger, or a package delivery, that's it." Her voice was sharper than she'd intended, and she saw that he was taken aback. But then, she'd come here with the intention of cutting her ties to CenSec, not strengthening them. *And in any case Wyal is off-limits to these people. I can't just let them get away with deciding to use my ship like it's their property.*

"And got cash on the barrel head," he reminded her grimly. Her attitude was a surprise and it was beginning to annoy him.

"Of course."

"So what's your problem?"

From long practice, Joat froze her reaction, which was to flare up and twist his nose for him. "Well," she said sweetly, "so far as a meeting goes, my ship is under surveillance. Not very clandestine, wouldn't you agree?"

Bros grinned.

"That was Sal's idea. He thought it would confer

status on me." He cocked his head at her. "Pretty obvious, was it?"

"He might as well have been in uniform. I thought he might be after . . . Sal's present." She glared at him. *I don't believe this!* she thought, outraged. *I could have been arrested and fined, just for trying to keep this package a secret. Meanwhile he's hiring the cops as escorts!* "You couldn't have advised me, of course."

He shrugged.

"Need to know. Sal thought it would make things easier. I don't see why it's a problem."

"It makes me look like trouble. My reputation is for doing things well and discreetly; it's how I make my living. This does not help."

He rubbed his upper lip to hide his smile. She was going to love this.

"I didn't request a guard for your ship in my CenSec capacity. In fact, they'd be quite startled to learn I was with CenSec, here. Bros Sperin is an extremely respectable smuggler, with an hilariously inappropriate name. At least as far as New Destinies is concerned—I deal in arms, mostly, and fencing loot—and the local police give excellent value for money."

Her eyes narrowed. "Oh. Lovely. Do you realize how much higher on the bribe schedule my ship will be, now that they think I'm running with the big boys? What are you trying to do to me?"

"It's S.O.P., Joat. To be frank, my cover is more important than your budget." He shrugged. "It's all part of building the right picture in the minds of certain people. I assure you, when you learn exactly who this meeting is with, you'll take a *personal* interest." He smiled. "Trust me."

She snorted an unspoken *not likely*, but he was sure he'd caught a sparkle of curiosity in her eyes.

Good, he thought. Aloud he said, "I'll call off the cop, since he was ineffective anyway. Will that help?"

"Sure." She rose and left.

I may have overplayed that a little, he thought dryly as he watched her walk away. He rubbed his face vigorously. *I'm badly out of practice. I used to know better than to make assumptions about the players.* Still, they were reasonable assumptions based on knowledge she didn't have at the moment. She'd probably come around.

Joat Simeon-Hap was a righteous woman.

In her way.

Joat grinned with a cold anger. *Master Spy isn't as subtle as he thinks.* Five years ago she might have jumped at the chance to get on the CenSec payroll. Not now. *Wyal* was hers; yes, Simeon and Channa—and Joseph—had helped bankroll her, but she'd paid them all off. The ship was hers, and she was meeting payroll and running expenses and putting something by. Meanwhile she was seeing the universe. On *her* terms, and nobody else's. *Which is just the way I like things, thank you very much, Bros Sperin!*

A passerby jumped back in alarm from the glare she gave as she shouldered by him.

She hoped Alvec was back from sniffing the Roses, or rather, letting them sniff him. Joat grinned at the thought of Bros Sperin's dark face when he walked up to an empty berth.

The docking area was nearly deserted as she pulled herself into the zero-g section and walked towards her berth, skimming her feet along the deck to keep their sticktights on the metal. Nobody was around except a couple of Ursinoids, crewfolk off one of their lumbering freighters, hairy creatures with blunt muzzles standing nearly two meters tall and strapped around with various knives, energy weapons and slug-throwers. She chatted with them for a few minutes, using their shaggy bulks to disguise her slow scan of the area. That was no strain; she *liked* Ursinoids, even if they did always try to sell you a collection of lethal ironmongery. They were good types on the whole, extremely independent, but not very subtle.

Bros had been as good as his word. The cop was gone. She wondered if she was under more covert surveillance.

Well, how would she know? Electronics she might detect, but Sperin should be able to call upon better talent than the local security forces.

As she passed a row of containers stacked head high, a hand flashed out and grabbed her arm.

Joat spun into the direction of the grip, stripping her arm out with leverage against the thumb. The same motion flung her backwards half a dozen paces and flipped the vibroknife into her right hand, held low with the keening drone of the slender rod-blade wailing a warning of how easily it would slide through flesh and bone. She filled her lungs to shout—the Ursinoids would be at her side in seconds, loaded for . . . well, loaded *like* bears. Heavily armed bears.

Joseph ben Said held up both hands palms out and grinned at her. The sleeves of his loose robe fell away from thick, corded forearms where the scars lay white against the olive skin. He raised one blond eyebrow.

"So fierce, little one? Perhaps I should not have taught you so well, eh?"

"Joe!" she said, moving forward to slap his arm lightly. "If I was still on your training protocols, you'd be dead right now."

She looked him up and down. The Bethelite never seemed to change; still as fit and muscular as when she'd met him ten years ago, his blue eyes mild and calm between the squint-wrinkles of a man who spent much time in the desert. Perhaps a few strands of silver hair among the gold. He had been born in Keriss before the Kolnari came, a child of the dockside slums, and right-hand man to Amos ben Sierra Nueva when the future Prophet had been a radical and half an outcast.

Now he was Deacon of the Right Hand—head of the Bethelite police and counter-espionage forces.

"What are you doing here? Is Amos here too?"

He shook his head.

"No, I am here alone." He cast a meaningful glance back and forth. "Look, I have a gift."

He reached into the hand-luggage at his feet and tossed a heavy bottle of green ceramic in her direction. Joat caught it with a yelp of protest at the risk; she recognized the brand. The surface was pebbled and cool, the fastener held in with twisted copper wire and sealed with wax. Despite herself she felt her eyes mist a little. *Joe was always a good osco,* she thought. And he'd taught her a great deal, some of it things that Simeon and Channa never suspected.

"Bethel-brewed Arrack," he said and kissed the tips of his fingers, dropping into the singsong of a *bazari* merchant for a moment. "From the Prophet's private store. Blessed with the heat of Saffron's golden sun."

She grinned.

"C'mon aboard, I've got someone I want you to meet."

Joat led the way up into *Wyal*'s berth and spoke: "Knock, knock?"

"Who's there?" The cybernetic voice sounded as if it would wince if it could.

"Jo."

"Jo who?"

"Jo'at the door."

Joseph did wince, in sympathy. "Among Simeon's many crimes, not the least was teaching you his depraved sense of humor."

"Tell me the news from Bethel, tell me about Rachel," Joat said. She cycled the lock closed and stood while the sensor field swept them for unauthorized sticktights. "And tell me what's wrong."

"Rachel is well, the children are well . . . and what should be wrong, my young friend?" The blue eyes blinked guilelessly at her.

"Joe, unlike Amos, you're no great traveler. If you've left Bethel and Rachel and it wasn't with Amos, there's a reason. What is it?"

"All in good time," he said.

Joat smiled wryly, restraining an impulse to grind her teeth. From Joseph she could take the odd mystery.

"Joat, I am most impressed by the quality of this AI, but it is a machine, nothing more." He looked at her with a frown of worry. "You know the difference, between a person and a machine?"

Joat sipped her Arrack. The liquid slid down her throat like a living fire with velvet fur, leaving a ghost-taste of ripe dates.

"Joe, I'm a programming expert. If I don't know the difference, who does? And if you say, *Joat you are alone too much,* I'll punch you in the nose, I swear I will."

"I taught you better than that," he said, mock-offended.

"*If you are naked and your feet are nailed to the floor, you may hit an enemy in the face with your fist. Short of that, use something more effective,*" Joat quoted in a sing-song voice. "I remember."

She leaned forward: "Look, if Simeon can turn his AI into his dog—to be precise, an Irish Setter—why

can't I go a step further and turn mine into a friend?"
She lowered her voice confidentially. "We're not
romantically involved if that's your worry."

He laughed and shook his head at her.

"You, little rebel, should be married, with a husband
to fix your wayward thoughts upon. Look at how my
Rachel has prospered by my side."

Joat pulled a judicious expression and nodded
solemnly.

"You're right, Joe, she's quite a gal."

*Yup, she's not a demented, murderous, traitorous
bitch any more.*

Now she was Joseph's executive assistant in the
Bethelite Security Forces, handling the technical end
of things. She also ran their rancho, a sun drenched
spread at Twin Springs and was a devoted mother
to their two children, Simeon Amos and Channa
Joat.

"Marriage would make a new woman of you, you
should try it. I know!" He flung his hands up as if
struck by inspiration—but did not, she noted, spill a
single drop of the Arrack.

"Marry me, Joat! Become my second wife and you
can live on the rancho and ride to your heart's content.
You can take care of the children. Think how restful
your life would be! And I swear that I would be as
faithful to you as to my beloved Rachel."

"Joe! How can you claim to be faithful to Rachel
while you're asking another woman to marry you?"

"Because I *am* asking you to marry me. If I were
asking you to be my mistress, *then* I would be unfaith-
ful. There is a tremendous difference, you must agree."

Joat blinked. He *was* joking—but to a Bethelite,
that made perfect sense. There were times when she
forgot Joseph was from the deep backwoods of the
universe.

"Hunh! If I ever do hitch up with someone, I'm not gonna be anyone's second anything." She took a sip of Arrack. "I want a virgin, myself."

A discreet cough from behind brought her to her feet, spinning around, knife in her hand again, ready for throwing.

Her eyes widened at the sight of Bros Sperin, arms crossed over his broad chest, leaning casually against the hatchway.

"How did you get in here?" *Wait a minute. Not only was the hatch locked and dogged, but Rand should have warned me—and the motion sensors should have gone off—and . . .*

He shrugged.

"The lock was open, I knew you were expecting me, so I came in. Is that a problem?"

"It was not open. I *do* take some rudimentary precautions."

"It wasn't locked down. Not," he added with an annoying smile, "locked down very securely, that is."

"Yes, it was," she said through clenched teeth.

He shrugged again, and spread his hands. He *was* there. Joat felt an overwhelming urge to kick him.

"Joat," Joseph said before she could speak. "You asked me what had happened to bring me here. Now is the time to discuss the matter."

"Maybe I should make sure my hatch is locked," she said sullenly.

"No problem," Bros said, walking around her to swing his lean body into the pilot's chair with authoritative ease. "I took care of it." It was the first time he'd gotten a spontaneous reaction from her and he was feeling a bit smug about it. Then he glanced at the Bethelite seated beside him and grew serious again. To Joseph he said, "You asked for my presence here, excellent sir. I'm most anxious to hear why."

Joseph took a deep breath; Joat saw that his fingers were white from the pressure of his clasp. Joe was not a man who put his feelings on display like this. Her irritation fell away—not forgotten, but filed.

"Our prophet, Amos ben Sierra Nueva, left Bethel ten days ago aboard a merchanter ship bound for the SSS-900-C. He did not arrive and the ship has not been heard from or found." Joseph rubbed his chin and looked at Bros. "I think you know why I asked to see you."

Joat shaped a silent whistle. No *wonder* Joe had seemed tense under his usual banter.

Bros nodded. "The Kolnari," he said.

"You are CenSec's resident expert on . . . them. And this will be an offworld affair. We . . . I am desperate for any help that you can offer. This is our prophet; and he is my brother-of-the-spirit, a bond closer than blood. They have taken him, I am sure. I must find him."

After a moment Bros leaned forward. "My superiors think I'm paranoid about the Kolnari. You understand me? They think that my information is unreliable, that every time a bandit hijacks a ship I see the Divine Seed. You take my advice, you're taking the risk that evaluation will rub off on you."

Joseph gave a bitter laugh and shook his head.

"Your superiors have not met the Kolnari. I have. To be paranoid about them is to be sane. I will trust your advice, Bros Sperin, for I know these devils. Advise me."

Cautiously, as though probing an open wound, Bros said, "There will be no ransom demand."

"I know it. If they have him, they will not so easily release him."

"I was aware of the kidnapping before you asked to see me, excellent sir," Bros said. "Simeon and Channa

Hap reported that he hadn't arrived on the day he was overdue." Bros paused for a moment, gazing steadily at Joseph. "Just before I came over here a report reached me that the black box from the *Sunwise* had been recovered from a field of space debris. The box hasn't been evaluated yet, but the ship that found it reported signs indicating that the engines blew."

"I have no doubt that they did," Joseph said quietly.

"But I'd be surprised if that's all the box shows," Bros continued. "Even if there's not a Kolnari in sight, I believe that the Benisur was taken off that vessel either by them or for them. No question."

"We are agreed then." Joseph said, studying this legendary stranger. "Can you offer any advice? Anything at all."

"I hope so, excellent sir." Sperin paused. "I'm ashamed to admit it," he continued, "but we haven't caught up with all that many Kolnari since we routed them at the SSS-900-C and at Bethel. They went into hiding, and very effectively too. For quite a while we," he glanced at Joseph, "all of us, thought that perhaps Dr. Chaundra had wrought better than we had any right to hope and that they'd been exterminated by the disease he'd created.

"Then, gradually, but more and more over the last few years, pirate actions that fit the Kolnari m.o. began to crop up. Objects recorded as being taken in those specific raids suddenly were being offered for sale and we began to trace them back through a trail of legitimate dealers with flexible ethics to downright fences. Most of the time the trail led back to a Station called Rohan and a man named Nomik Ciety."

He turned to Joat. "This is where you come in," he said and smiled.

Oh really, she thought, *gosh, wow, I feel so privileged. Get out of my chair, blast you!* She nodded instead of speaking.

"Ciety is a notorious fence, a smuggler, a weapons broker. But we've never been able to touch him. Because Rohan, his base of operations, is a free-port, only nominally associated with Central Worlds, we have neither jurisdiction nor power there. In other words, as long as he keeps his nose clean on Rohan and makes his tax payments on time he can do anything, and I mean *anything*, that he wants to, there.

"We've sent people to Rohan to check him out, to look for Kolnari activity, to look for loot that we think the Kolnari might have taken. They've disappeared. Every one of them."

"And this is where *I* come in?" Joat asked, eyebrows raised.

Bros rubbed his hand across his upper lip.

"Exactly. I want you to go to Rohan and look around. I trust your capabilities and you're not known to be connected with Central Worlds Security so you should be in minimal danger. I repeat, I want you to look. Don't confront Ciety, don't troll for loot, don't try to find any Kolnari, just see what's there. You've been around, you'll know what to look for, what stories to listen to. If you see anything suspicious, that is, of a nature to help us with this problem, note it. Do nothing else. Note it and get back to us."

"Sounds exciting." she said dryly.

Bros turned the pilot's chair until he was facing Joseph.

"Excellent sir, this man Ciety is also an information broker. It is possible that, for the right price, he might be willing to supply you with information about this kidnapping. All that I can guarantee you about him is treachery, so if you do approach him, watch your back and don't make payment final until you're well away from Rohan. The man is completely mercenary and if he discovers who you are he would willingly sell you to the Kolnari. It would be wise to make your approach through a third party; the place is rife with professional go-betweens, so finding someone shouldn't be a problem. Of course a major concern in that case would be that you're so obviously a Bethelite that, knowing your desperation for any information, they might inflate their prices at the sight of you and give you next to nothing at all. Or they may decide to mention your curiosity to Ciety, or someone else you don't want to take an interest in you.

"As Joat is already bound there . . ."

"I am?" Joat said in mock surprise and earned an arch look from the CenSec agent.

"I urge you, most strongly, excellent sir, to commission her to act for you while you stay clear of the place altogether." He looked over at Joat, his eyes narrowed. "Amending her mission to accommodate your needs might even improve her chances of finding out what CenSec wants to know. I think she's both clever and discreet enough to be able to handle such a commission. And if she arranges it through a go-between, or better yet, through several of them she might succeed in remaining completely anonymous. That's where I'd advise you to start. Joat can send your information back with her first report to CenSec and I'll relay it to you."

"Are you aware that I'm in the same *room* with you, Sperin?" Joat asked.

Bros gave her an exasperated look, then turned to Joseph and spread his hands. "That's all we can offer at the moment, excellent sir. I'm sorry." Bros dug into his pocket, pulled out a datahedron and handed it to Joat.

"This is Ciety's dossier. Read it when you can concentrate on it because it will erase itself as it's being read."

"Well that's useful," Joat muttered.

"We don't want him to know what we know about him, Joat. And since your security is barely worth mentioning you could hardly expect me to give you a permanent record." He stood. "Are there any questions?"

"Yup. One, when did I agree to do all this stuff? And two, how much are you offering to pay me for this?" Joat asked.

"Seventy-four hundred, plus reasonable expenses," Sperin said, ignoring her first question entirely.

"And to think I passed up a career in CenSec," Joat murmured sarcastically.

"Seventy-four hundred is considerably more than my salary for this year," Bros said. "Don't you want to help find the Benisur Amos? He *is* an old friend of your parents."

"You forgot to appeal to my patriotism," Joat said dryly.

"I may be a scoundrel, but I'm not down to my last resort quite yet."

"I was just hoping you could do a little better than that. After all, a trader who goes to Rohan is a little like a virgin taking tea in a whorehouse. It taints your reputation even if you haven't done any business." She smiled sweetly at him. "Expenses to include all fuel and repairs."

And Flegal, but I am going to repair the dickens out of this ship.

"All right," he said. "Point taken. On my authority, CenSec will pick up for any expenses and repairs this mission gives rise to." He held out his hand to her.

She raised her hand, but held it back.

"I wonder if you might be willing to offer some kind of a bonus, considering that this *could* be a dangerous mission and that I am, after all, a civilian. Nothing outrageous," she assured him, holding up a denying hand.

"You might arrange some trading concessions, for example. There's many a place I'd love to ship to but I can't afford the docking fees. What do you say, Bros? Think we can work something out?"

Bros put his hands on his hips and studied her through narrowed eyes.

"Where did you have in mind?"

"Senalgal?"

"Get real, Captain."

"The SSS-900-C?"

He raised his brows. "I would have thought Simeon . . ."

"I like to earn my way," she said sharply.

He nodded slowly. "I can fix it."

Joat held out her hand and he shook it, surprised at the strength of her grip.

"You can contact me at The Anvil," he said, "my cover name is Clal va Riguez." He nodded to Joseph, gave a half smile to Joat and was gone.

Joat turned on a monitor and they watched Sperin leave the *Wyal* and walk away without a backward glance.

"He told me he was known at The Anvil as Bros Sperin," she said resentfully.

"Wheels within wheels," Joseph murmured.

"Rand," she asked, "did he leave anything behind?"

"Yes, Joat. On the left arm of your chair, just where the seam is on the front of the arm."

Joat examined the area Rand had described. Nothing. She pulled out a scanner and flicked it; a framework extended, and she fitted it over her head. Joseph came to her side and pulled a huge, clumsy-looking optical from a pocket in his robe.

"Got it," she said.

"Here," Joseph grunted, his words crossing over hers. They smiled at each other.

He rose from his knees, bowing. "All yours, child."

"Child, hell." She pulled a toolkit from another pocket and opened it, twiddling her fingers. "Ta-*dum*."

It was about the width of a human hair and no longer than the thickness of a fingernail; one end was razor-sharp, to make it easier to implant. Probably it was this large only to allow it to be manipulated easily.

"Hel*lo*, Bros!" Joat said brightly, smiling a toothy smile with the sticktight held at eye level. "Why do I get this feeling that not everything is As It Seems? Anyway, you seem to have forgotten something. I couldn't allow you to waste the taxpayer's money like that. Tsk, tsk upon you."

She opened an envelope and dropped the sticktight into it. "Addressed to Clal va Riguez, The Anvil," she said. The envelope obligingly showed the name on its exterior, and she confirmed it with a pinch that sealed the container. "Deliver." She dropped it into a slot on the console.

"Oooh," Joat went on to Joseph. "Spy stuff. I wonder how much that little thingie is worth. I wonder how many more there are."

Joseph still had the optical to his eye; looking at the recording of the sticktight. Bethelite technology wasn't subtle, but it got the job done.

"Interesting. Passive sensor, I think—burst transmission when keyed."

"Confirmed," Rand said. "I was only aware of it because I saw Mr. Sperin install it. As for the rest of the ship, nothing seems abnormal, but I can make no guarantees. Mr. Sperin seems a devious man, and we've no idea how long he was actually aboard before he chose to make his presence known."

"About that," Joat interrupted. "Why didn't you tell me he was onboard?"

"The first I knew of it was when he appeared on the bridge, Joat."

"But how could he *do* that?" she demanded.

"I suppose that CenSec has been extrapolating from your design," Rand said, "and they've come up with a superior version."

Joat bristled and her eyes sparked with fury. "Not for long, they haven't," she growled.

"In any event," Rand continued, "if he's left something behind I can't find it until it's contacted by an external signal."

"Don't worry about it, Rand. It's not your fault." *If anything*, she thought, *it's mine for becoming so complacent*. Or so honest. Joat shrugged. "I think it's safe to assume he'd leave his best stuff on the bridge. That's where we'll be most of the time, after all."

She picked up the bottle of Arrack and freshened both of their drinks.

"Disappointed?" she asked.

Joseph grimaced slightly.

"I am more annoyed than disappointed. Why I do not know. I certainly did not expect Central Worlds to charge to the rescue with banners flying. But I expected . . ."

"More than to be told to go home and wait for word from us big important people?"

"Yes!" he said firmly.

"You expected to be treated as a professional equal who doesn't need obvious instructions on how to behave in a hostile port?"

"Yes!"

"More importantly, you were hoping to receive some offer of backup from Central Worlds if you do find out who has Amos and where they've taken him."

Joseph tossed back the rest of the Arrack in his glass and looked at her.

"Without the aid of the Central Worlds Navy there would be little that we could do. If they are unwilling

to help us, or if they delay, then my brother will die."
He laughed in self mockery and rubbed a hand across
his eyes. "Ah, Joat, I had hoped for hope."

Joat grinned at him. "All that regular living has made you
soft, Joe. You don't need hope, you need luck ... ."

". . . and you make your own luck!" they recited
together, they clicked glasses and laughed.

She folded her arms and leaned her hip against her
main console. Her eyes went over the readouts, registering
automatically without interrupting the flow of thought.

"We're fueled, we're set for supplies; as soon as my
crew gets back we can cast off. So if you've got gear
you'd better go and fetch it now."

Joseph grinned wickedly at her and indicated the
small bag at his feet. "That is all that I have, Joat. But
I must say that I do not think Mr. Sperin would
approve of this invitation. I do not believe that he
wished me to go to Rohan."

"Hunh, by the time he was finished talking I wasn't
sure he wanted *me* to go! Pushy osco, ain't he?"

"Perhaps he wanted to go himself," offered Rand.
"He had the overtones, if I may say so, of a man
stretching his instructions to the limit."

Joat and Joseph exchanged glances.

"Y'know Rand, I believe you've hit the nail on the
head," Joat murmured.

With a soft hiss of breath Amos completed the final
movement of the seven hundred and fifty separate steps
of the Sword Dance of Natham. He stood upright,
panting slightly, sweat running freely down his bare,
muscled sides.

The dance helped to center him, to stave off rage
and panic, as well as wearing him out so that he could
sleep. He had just repeated it twice in succession, once
slowly, once very fast.

Now he wished that he could be clean. But the Kolnari brig did not include such amenities as a shower. There was a small sink, however and he went over to it intending to do the best he could.

The cell was small, perhaps two meters by three with double-decker bunks that folded down from the wall, the sink and a commode for furnishings. The walls, ceiling, and floor were of cold, white enameled metal and the light never went out.

The food was neither good nor bad, but bland, soldier's rations, in reasonable quantity, delivered at unpredictable intervals.

Were he a man who could find no comfort in his God, Amos knew that he would be howling and beating on the door by now. He smiled grimly. The Kolnari couldn't know that a severe religious retreat could be very like this. There would be better facilities for cleaning oneself, and books, and the light would be under his control, but otherwise there were strong similarities. With the obvious exception, of course, that he could end a religious retreat at will. Assuming that God willed it so.

He sighed and turned on the faucet. No water came. *How petty,* he thought, *Belazir must be finding me boring.*

He sat on his bunk and turned his palms upward to begin meditating on the devotions of the prophets. That would fill his time both pleasantly and well, since there were over eight thousand of them.

The hatch swung open and two figures in black space armor violently flung Captain Sung into the room. Amos leapt to his feet and caught the older man before he could crash to the floor. By the time he had the Captain righted on his feet the cell was sealed once more.

"Captain," Amos said in astonishment. "What of Soamosa? Have you seen her, have they told you anything?"

The Captain's face was badly bruised and he was shaking with reaction.

"I thought they were gonna space me," he said and shuddered. "I knew they couldn't get a ransom for me, they already took everything I ever had. I thought they were going to vent me with the rest of the garbage."

Amos put an arm around the older man and guided him to the bunk.

"I would give you water if I could," he said, "but they have turned it off." He paused for a moment. "Captain," he said softly and waited until the other man looked at him. "Soamosa, do you know anything about her?"

The Captain shook his head regretfully. "No, nothing. I haven't seen her since we were split up, and they don't talk to me." He raised a shaking hand to brush back his short hair. "I'm sorry."

"I did not expect that you would know, I only hoped that they might have become careless and allowed you to see something. It is no matter."

"How long have we been here?" Sung asked.

"I do not know. I have slept four times, and I have been fed eight. But what relation that might have to real time I could not begin to guess. What is your estimation?"

Sung shook his head, his face looking infinitely sad.

"I don't know," he said, "I just don't know."

"Rest," Amos said gently and placed his hand against the Captain's shoulder, urging him to lie down. He grinned ruefully. "We shall have a wealth of time to talk later. Put your head down for a while."

Sung nodded tiredly and lay flat, his eyes closed before his head touched the pillow.

Amos sat on the floor in a lotus position. Before resuming his meditations he offered a brief prayer of thanks for the gift of a companion to relieve the silence of his imprisonment.

Several hours later Sung stirred and woke. He turned to Amos and stared at him in puzzlement.

"Who the hell are you?" he asked.

"What?"

"Who the hell are you? What are you doing in here?"

"Captain, what are you talking about?" Amos studied the Captain's irate face with astonishment. "I am Amos ben Sierra Nueva, a passenger of yours . . ."

"Passengers aren't allowed in the captain's quarters! What are you doing here?"

Amos licked his dry lips, uncertain how one answered a man apparently losing his mind and growing more angry by the minute.

"Captain Sung," he held out a placating hand, "we are not on your ship, we have been thrown into the brig of a Kolnari pirate. Don't you remember?"

The Captain's eyes widened, a look of fear shuddered across his face to be replaced by confusion.

"What did you say my name was?"

"You are Captain Josiah Sung, of the merchanter ship *Sunwise*."

"The *Sunwise*," Sung reached out and gripped Amos's hand desperately, "I remember her. She's my ship, the *Sunwise*, I know her. You see? I'm all right."

"Yes, of course you are, Captain. It was only a moment's confusion. You woke from a deep sleep to find yourself in a new place, it is not uncommon to be disoriented under such conditions. All is well." Amos gave the Captain's hand a squeeze and smiled encouragingly at him.

Sung raised his tear-slicked face to glare at Amos.

"Let go of my hand you bastard! How the hell did you get in here?"

Amos felt his heart pounding in the cage of his ribs, more strongly than it had when he pushed his body to its limits.

"I'm the Captain dammit! I don't *entertain* the passengers. You got that? Get out of here!" Sung pointed to the hatch and then blinked. With a gasp he turned to look at Amos. "What's happening to me? What have they done?"

Amos shook his head, equally horrified. The bruise on the Captain's face was proof of a head wound, but would such a wound have an effect like this? Had the Captain been poisoned? Was he being shown the effects before they did the same to him? It would be like Belazir to torture him so, the Kolnari idea of subtlety.

Suddenly Belazir stood before them. The edges of his image bore a soft white fuzz for a moment, then the holo snapped into clear focus.

A white silken robe emphasized the inhuman blackness of his still-magnificent body. A feathered clip held back his brittle white hair.

"Good morning Simeon Amos, or good evening, whichever you have decided it must be. How are you getting on down here?"

"Not well, Master and God. The Captain is not himself." Amos's eyes dared to demand answers, but he would not give Belazir the pleasure of hearing him ask for them.

"Is he not?" Belazir said with amusement. "Then who is he? Captain Sung, who do you think you are?"

"What . . . what do you mean?"

"Who are you?" Belazir asked.

A look of blank astonishment crossed Sung's face and he raised his hands helplessly.

"I don't know," he said, his voice tight with horror. "I don't remember." Tears gathered in his eyes and he struggled visibly not to blink and send them rolling down his cheeks. "I don't remember."

Amos glared at the Kolnari, letting his face show contempt. He spat at the feet of the image.

Belazir quirked a smile at him. "You offer little sport, scumvermin; you tell me everything that I want to know without my even asking. Why should I tell you anything?"

"You knew before you did this that I would despise you for it, Master and God. Why you even bothered to show up I cannot imagine."

"Is this wise, scumvermin, to bait a man who holds your lives in his fist? I am sure that your friend Channahap would advise you otherwise." He folded his massive arms across his chest and regarded Amos with amusement. "It may be that I have information that you might wish to have. If you ask me very politely, I might unbend sufficiently to enlighten you."

Amos's lips quivered with rage, but his need to know the fate of his young cousin won out over his pride and his hatred.

"I beg your pardon," he said formally. "Master and God."

Belazir raised an eyebrow. "I will assume that was a request for knowledge. I know that you wish for information about your young cousin. But I will instead unfold a larger plan before you. One that touches the fate of all your people." He paused, smiling, to observe the effect this pronouncement was having on Amos. "You can see that the Captain here is not behaving normally, can you not?"

"Of course I can," Amos said through gritted teeth. "Master and God."

"You are thinking that we have beaten him into this condition, or that we have poisoned him."

Amos nodded.

Belazir's face suddenly seemed weary. He shrugged and half-turned away.

"In fact he has been overcome by a contagious, progressive disease that attacks the memory center of the brain. You are a carrier of this disease, Simeon Amos, but we have made sure that you are completely immune to it. You have seen how rapidly it works, how devastating it is."

Belazir's golden eyes narrowed. "We Kolnari have gained great respect for such weapons. You and the rest of the scumvermin on that accursed station taught us a singular lesson about biological weaponry. Now we of Kolnar shall return the favor.

"You will be given a drug that will prevent you from moving or speaking and then you will be returned to your people."

Amos rose from the bunk, to confront Belazir on his feet.

"We are not stupid, Belazir. My people will know that something is wrong. Why else would you return me?"

"Oh, but they will have to fight to recover you. It will all be very convincing, I assure you. A raging chase through the skies of Bethel. But they will win, for yours is a valiant people. And their reward shall be to become like the Captain. We will leave him here with you so that you can fully appreciate what your return to the bosom of your people will mean to them."

As Amos rushed forward the grinning image of Belazir blinked out and he crashed into the wall instead. He slid down until he was sitting on the floor, and then he looked up to meet Captain Sung's gaze.

"Who are you?" the man asked. "Who . . ."

✧ CHAPTER FOUR

Joat stared moodily at the screen. It listed the latest Standard Commercial Report listing of cargoes in demand at Rohan Station, together with charter listings and container requests from New Destinies. *Item: thruster units*. Officially, Rohan didn't have shipyards. *Item: power plant spares*. From the specs, there were some *awfully* fast merchantmen operating out of Rohan—merchantmen who were profligate enough to burn out their overpowered drive units with some regularity. The sort of maneuver you needed to transit an atmosphere at high speed, or wrench another ship out of FTL transit.

"There are some things I just won't do," she muttered.

Running that sort of cargo into a pesthole like Rohan was one of those things. Fuel, maybe. Foodstuffs, medical supplies, sure—if they went into a pirate's sickbay or galley, that wasn't her affair. But no fardling *way* was she going to run drive coils or fire-control electronics. Not to Rohan.

"Joat, will you be advised by me?"

Lessee. I could offer to take those fifteen containers of pharmaceuticals at, say, three percent, then—

Joat glanced up from the cargo manifest she was studying to look at Joseph. His face was solemn and his manner formal. She raised her brows.

"I'm always willing to listen to advice from people I respect, Joe. What's on your mind?"

"I keep thinking of something you said to Bros Sperin. That going to Rohan was to a trader the equivalent of a virgin entering a whorehouse. It is a good analogy, Joat, and it troubles me."

Joat leaned back in her chair, eyes narrowed thoughtfully.

"Go on," she said.

"It is not simply your reputation with Central Worlds that concerns me. You are known as a captain who keeps her hands clean. Will they not wonder why you have come to them? As well, your association with the SSS-900-C is widely known. As the adopted daughter of a shell-person you became quite famous for a while. To those guilty of aiding the Kolnari your name will surely set off a train of associations which could result in considerable danger for you."

She folded her hands on her stomach and nodded slowly.

"You're right. I will need a reason for going there that's completely dissociated from Amos or the Kolnari. You know, I have this sneaking suspicion that Mr. Sperin *wanted* me to be under suspicion. So that it would be easier for someone else—say, Bros Sperin—to slip in himself while everyone worried about me. Hmmm."

"Perhaps if you were to take on smuggled goods," Joseph suggested tentatively. "New Destinies has a reputation for looking the other way in such matters, so having this as your last port of call would lend credibility."

"I'd need to justify that," Joat said thoughtfully. "I'm the first to admit that I bend the rules till they scream for mercy, but seriously criminal behavior is something I've managed to avoid so far."

She tapped her fingertips together and stared into space for a moment. Then she smiled.

"Rand," she asked, "do we have a recording of that little walk I took earlier?"

"Yes Joat. I saw no reason not to make one."

"Can you adjust it to make it look as though it had been recorded by someone else?"

"I can."

"Do it. Then transmit it anonymously to Station Security." She winked at Joseph. "I took an unauthorized space walk and entered the station illegally. They'll hit us with a wonking great fine and I can use that as an excuse for needing fast and dirty credits." She grimaced. "It may take us there round about, but I think the added safety margin should be worth a small delay."

"But Joat, the fine will be real," Joseph objected. Frowning he asked, "What if you cannot pay it?"

"No problem." Joat grinned at him. "CenSec will pay—at least, I think I can thumbscrew any reasonable amount out of them. We'll just put it under expenses. Might come to four, five thousand credits; even ten thousand. Enough to make the treasurer wince. Can't be much more than that."

Joseph laughed. Bethelites tended to be straightlaced, but Joseph ben Said had the wholehearted love of a well-thought-out swindle natural to a Keriss wharf rat. This would not only make CenSec cough up the money, but a certain Bros Sperin would have to justify the expense.

"You are wicked! You have always been wicked. Why did I think you had outgrown it?"

"Wishful thinking?" Joat asked, blinking innocent blue eyes.

A good notion, Sperin thought as he watched the clip of Joat breaking into the station. *Getting herself into trouble with station security should give her greater credibility.*

He'd wondered how she managed to avoid the man they'd had waiting for her. *He's not the best that ever was, but he's not blind either.* Bros shook his head and smiled slightly.

Now how can I benefit from this situation? Sperin rubbed his upper lip thoughtfully. The little captain had been talking about ditching her career as a courier, not something CenSec would like to happen. *She's smart and she's reliable.* It was amazing how rare those qualities were.

Joat hadn't been invited to join CenSec because she was too independent, too unpredictable. But it had turned out that in every way that it counted she was a gem. *Be nice to have her beholden to us,* Sperin mused. *She's the type that pays her debts.*

He'd been given a name in the Bureau of Fines and Levies to contact if need arose. Bros rubbed his palms together. *I believe I feel a need.*

> *"Roses sweet and tender she has twined in her*
> *hair,*
> *and the scent of spring and roses is with her*
> *everywhere."*

Joat yawned and half-groaned as the baritone voice boomed through the sound system.

"I take it Alvec is back," she said.

"Yes, Joat," Rand said.

She dumped a packet of sweetener into the coffee—she could afford real sugar now, but preferred the more familiar taste—and said: "On display."

The viewscreen over the galley's preserver unit came live, showing a holo of the deck outside the *Wyal's* berth. Alvec Dia was there, engaged in an enthusiastic good-bye kiss with a woman of about his own age and poundage; she had a spectacular head of red hair, and was clutching a dozen long-stemmed roses in her free hand. Or grinding them into Alvec's back, at times.

"Alvec?" Joseph asked from the other side of the galley.

He slid several eggs off the frictionless surface of the heater and onto a plate.

"Ahhh, Brunoki sausage. Almost as good at the morning meal as toasted sand rats. Alvec is the crewman of whom you spoke?"

Joat broke a yoke with a strip of toast. "Yup. And this happens at every dock. Well, nearly every dock. You don't *really* like sand rats, do you?"

"They are a traditional delicacy."

"Screen off. This is depressing."

"Only because you are lonely," Joseph said slyly. "As my second wife, you—"

"Do you really want to die, Joe?"

Alvec checked for a moment as he came through the galley door.

"You remember Joe?"

"Sure," he said easily, nodding at the Bethelite. They had met once before, briefly.

His expression showed that he also remembered Joseph's allergy to questions. The craggy-faced spacer's expression went carefully bland as he pulled a container of coffee out of the cupboard, broke the seal and settled across the tiny table from Joat.

"Ah, she's beautiful, boss," he told them. "Sweetest gal you'd ever want to meet."

Joat and Joseph exchanged a look.

"He's always like this after he's been on leave," Joat explained.

Joseph nodded, "Of course, quite understandable."

Joat cocked her head at her crew, her brows raised.

"Um, Al. Would you like to pursue your acquaintance with this lady while Joe and I take a brief jaunt elsewhere?"

Alvec looked from Joat to Joseph suspiciously.

"Not especially. I mean, yeah, I want to pursue her acquaintance, she's beautiful, but not at the expense of my job."

"Your job is safe, Al. Joe's just visiting, he's got a wife and kids dirtside on Bethel. We've just got this thing we've got to do. And you deserve a vacation, you haven't had one in ages."

Alvec studied his employer, her little half smile, the raised brows, the wide innocent eyes.

"Now you've got me worried, Captain," he complained. "When you look this reasonable, you're usually up to something. I'll think about it." Alvec allowed his manner to convey his deep suspicion.

The com chimed. "Merchant Ship *Wyal*, Captain Joat Simeon speaking," Joat answered.

"Good morning, Captain Simeon. My name is Graf Dyson." The man smiled grimly. "Although I understand you know my name."

Oh-oh. Graf Dyson. I claimed to be a very good friend of Graf Dyson. Influential people tended to disapprove when you took their names in vain. She'd intended to be far away by the time Mr. Dyson got wind of how she'd used his influence without his permission. *Oh, well, I never expected to want to get fined.*

The man on the screen was dark haired, middle-aged and heavy featured. *Looks honest,* Joat thought. That was a bad sign. Conmen and sharps usually did.

"I am employed by the Bureau of Fines and Levies, as I believe you already know." He paused to let that sink in before continuing: "And I'm contacting you in regard to a matter that has been brought to the attention of Station Security and through them to my bureau."

"Mmmm?" Joat murmured cautiously, setting her coffee aside.

"A recording was anonymously sent to Security of an unauthorized space walk and illegal entry into the station through an emergency repair hatch by someone from the *Wyal*. We have reason to believe that the person shown on the recording might be you."

There was something about the tone of his voice and the look in his eyes that unnerved her. *Me and my bright ideas.* Using Dyson's name had been a good idea. Making the illegal entry had been a good idea. Tricking the New Destinies into giving her a cover story by fining her had been a good idea.

But when you added them all up, they didn't come to a good idea. *This is what Channa used to mean by keeping the big picture in mind,* Joat thought. For a moment she wished poignantly that Channa was there with her, someone older and wiser to lean on. . . .

Fardling void with that, she thought stubbornly. *I'm twenty-three. And even when I was twelve, I could look after myself.*

"That's completely ridiculous!" she said briskly. "What possible reason could I have for doing such a thing?"

Joat stared back at Dyson with an expression of injured disbelief that had baffled even experienced child-welfare workers in its time.

"Your ship was under observation yesterday by Station Security. It's assumed that you became aware of being under surveillance and chose to avoid it by taking this round-about method of entering the station."

"Wait a minute," she said, hunching forward in her seat. "*I* was under surveillance? What for?"

"Why you were being watched is irrelevant, Ms. Simeon. What you chose to do about it is."

Oh it's Ms. now is it, you clabber-faced oaf! What happened to Captain *Simeon?*

"I think it's very relevant," she said aloud. "I demand to know why you were spying on me!"

"I'll have Station Security send you a report," Dyson said through bared teeth. "However, in regard to the matter in hand . . ."

"I did not take any unauthorized space walk!"

"Then how do you explain that you were not seen leaving your ship, but were observed returning?"

"Maybe I can walk through walls."

"Heh, heh. How very clever. And how do you explain being found outside the very lock shown in the recording, with your suit in your arms?"

"I was taking my suit to get the seals checked."

"And being in the corridor outside the lock?"

"I got lost."

"The Bureau finds it reasonable to fine you for this incident. And as you aren't a station resident, I have plenary authority. Unauthorized breaches of hull security are a serious matter."

They were. Spacers took pressure integrity even more seriously than Bethelites took fresh water. Joat felt a small twinge of guilt; she hadn't *really* endangered the Station's atmosphere . . . but if it ever got to a jury, they wouldn't be amused. At all.

Joat smacked both palms on the sides of the console and leaned forward menacingly.

"I protest!"

Dyson regarded her coolly. "That is certainly your right, Ms. Simeon. New Destinies is well supplied with lawyers who are specialists in dealing with the Bureau. I suggest that you avail yourself of their services, if you feel you can afford it—after paying the fine, that is. In the meantime, the fine will be registered against your ship and will be due in forty days."

Joat glared. "What's the fine?" she growled.

"Thirty thousand credits."

Joat's eyes snapped wide. Alvec gasped, and Joseph grunted in the background like a man belly-punched.

"You're crazy! No way can you justify a fine like that!"

"Shall we double it?" The man's features grinned like a shark for an instant, then went friendly-bland again.

She gave a shaky little laugh.

"What is this? Some kind of shake-down? You can't possibly hope to get away with this."

"Double it again. It's you that's trying to get away with something, Ms. Simeon. I'm simply doing my job and I'm fairly confident that I can get away with that. You now owe New Destinies one hundred and twenty thousand credits. I think you should stop talking before you owe us the value of the station itself. Don't you?"

Joat closed her mouth with an effort. This had gotten way out of hand. She sat still for a moment, feeling pale and shaky. What if CenSec refused to answer for this debt? She could lose her ship. They *would* refuse to pay it. Ten thousand she could have gotten out of them via Bros, and enjoyed him squirming on the Treasury's pin. A hundred and twenty thousand they'd refuse out of hand.

What can I do? Sue Central Worlds Security?

"Now you mentioned protesting the fine, didn't you?" Dyson asked pleasantly.

Joat nodded vigorously.

"Well, unfortunately the only date we have open for a hearing is sixty days from now. Also in that case we'd have to impound your ship. And since the fine is due in forty days, well, that would mean that your ship would probably already have been auctioned off by the time your case came up. Do you want to think about it? You have five days to protest the fine." He gazed at her blandly.

"Yes," she said. She found it hard to talk. "I . . . I could lose my ship?"

"Yesss, you certainly could. In fact, I'd be extremely surprised if you didn't." Dyson stared out of the screen

at her, his hands folded neatly before him. He smiled
again, the same friendly, honest-looking smile.

She thought of her remaining mortgage.

I'll be ruined, she thought desperately. *I'll be a slave
to the bank, working off a debt on something I don't
even own.* She pictured years of work under someone
else's command with nothing to show for it but a slowly
diminishing debt.

"You should have thought of that before you went
out your hatch, Ms. Simeon," Dyson said, as he
disconnected the automatic recording device.

"And before you opened your big mouth. *And
claimed an acquaintance you didn't have!*" He cut the
transmission with a decisive snap.

Dyson sat back, a satisfied sneer on his face. *I
enjoyed that!* he thought. It wasn't every day that you
got your own back with the blessings of Central Worlds
Security.

He grinned as he recalled the look of sick horror
on her pretty face. *It's moments like these that make
life worthwhile,* Dyson mused.

The fine wouldn't stick, of course. In fact he wasn't
even supposed to register more than a minimal fine.
Ah, but what if the good Captain checks? he wondered
as he entered the astronomical fine. *I can always erase
it later.* He sat back again. *If they tell me to.*

He chuckled. *Life is good!*

Joat just stared at the blank screen for a moment,
frozen in shock. "Ooops," she said.

Alvec cleared his throat. "I know what *ooops* means,"
he said. "It means, *I screwed the pooch.* Boss, you got
something you wanna tell me?"

Joat opened her mouth, and then looked over at
Joseph. He lifted his brows, and she nodded.

"Captain Simeon-Hap has arranged to visit Station Rohan," he began. "On urgent business."

Alvec choked on a mouthful of coffee. "That jackal's nest?"

Joseph nodded. "Exactly, my friend. A normal trading and freight-charter trip would appear suspicious; honest traders try to avoid Rohan. So, she—we—needed a plausible reason to take high-freight but, shall we say, questionable cargo on a run to a . . . questionable location."

"Jeeeze, Boss, how do you get into these things?" He shook his head in wonder. "I've never heard of a fine like that for such a piddly little infraction."

"Some piddly little bureaucrat in Health and Immigration named Dilton tried to shake me down when we came in, and I dropped Graf Dyson's name, pretended that I was a friend of his. Evidently Dilton checked up on it and now Dyson's leaning on me."

"How can this guy get away with that?"

"In this case, Alvec, it's timing," Rand said. "Before a hearing there is no opportunity to work off the debt, after the ship is taken, Joat will have neither the leisure nor the credits to file suit."

"And," Joseph put in, "our business is too urgent to delay. We cannot afford to tie ourselves up in a bureaucratic . . . process," he finished for want of a better word. He had one actually, but he would not utter it in front of Joat.

"I didn't think that it would be wise to claim acquaintance with him, Joat," Rand scolded. "Why did you risk it?"

"At the time," she said tiredly, "I never expected a petty crook to be so smart . . . or so efficiently vindictive."

"You didn't study the matter. You acted impulsively."

"Rand," she said, "shut up or I'll punch your lights out."

"I don't like the smuggling thing, Boss," Alvec said. "It's like a drug for some people. They get started for the profit and they get hooked on the excitement." He shook his head.

"I think I've got enough excitement right now to supply me for a lifetime, Al. And now I actually *need* the damn credits. No way CenSec is gonna spring for a hundred and twenty thousand. You could buy a corvette for that, used."

She brushed her hair back off her face and then flung herself back in her chair, gripping the armrests until her fingers turned white. "I'm gonna need something good," she said grimly.

"Joat, my friend, calm yourself," Joseph said. "Certainly the outrageous size of this fine will ensure that your troubles become known quickly. We will hardly need to exert ourselves to make our desperation convincing. Indeed, rather than having to seek someone out, they may approach you. And," he held up one finger, "Central Worlds has enough influence and authority to get this cruel fine reduced to something reasonable. Send a message to Mr. Sperin, and doubtless he will see to it."

"You're probably right, Joe." She gave him a weak smile and turned to Alvec: "Feel up to a pub crawl? Best way I know of making yourself available for an approach."

"Let me ask Rose where would be a good place to start," Alvec offered. "She might know some places."

"Where did *you* meet her?" Joat asked.

"Ah . . ." Alvec flushed. "The Station personals column."

"Rimrunners," Rose said. "Rimrunners would be a good place, up near the North Quadrant. But any bar in the same general neighborhood will probably do. They're all crooked as a Phelobite's elbow up there."

Joat studied the bed-sitting room behind Rose. It was fairly large for a Stationer; Rose was evidently a mid-level tech in a gas-refining outfit, and spent a fair amount of time out-of-habitat. The wall behind her was a slightly blurry holo taken over the flared bows of a scoopship, with the gas-giant filling the entire forward quadrant. Looking at it made Joat's piloting reflexes scream *vector up!* until she had to glance away.

"You need some help on this, honey?" Rose asked Alvec.

He shook his head. "Ship's business, darlin'. But thanks." He blew her a kiss and turned off the viewscreen.

Maybe we should take her up on that, Joat thought. *From the look of her, she'd be a good friend to have behind you in a fight.*

No. That wouldn't be fair. Rose hadn't gotten them into this mess. Speaking of fair . . .

"Maybe you should take Rose out to dinner while Joe and I scope out Rimrunners," she said hopefully. "It's not like anything grudly is going to come down."

Alvec stood, stretched on to his toes and came down in a posture of relaxed alertness.

"You don't know nothin' about this stuff, Boss."

"And you do?"

Alvec looked down at his feet. "Yeah, some."

Joat studied him. Alvec had a mysterious past. He didn't talk about it and she paid him the courtesy of not asking, appreciating the fact that he returned the favor.

So we both have things we're happier not talking about, she thought. That might be a bit of a handicap now; they were probably both assuming a degree of naiveté in the other that wasn't justified. *I'd better take him at his word.*

She'd always had the feeling that at one time he might

have been master of his own ship. His competence, his knowledge and the high rank of many of his friends argued for the idea. But whatever happened had left him quite content to be Joat's crew.

She shrugged.

"Yeah, well, I'm not doing so well on my own, so maybe you'd better come along. Between you, you and Joe should be able to keep me from making things worse."

"Your faith alarms me, my friend," Joseph said with a laugh. "But I shall do my best to earn it."

Alvec gave Joseph a long, considering look.

Joat laughed. The two men looked at her. "We're all of us bundles of surprises, aren't we?" she said, and linked her arms through theirs. "Let's get going."

How did they do it? Joat wondered. *How did they manage to make a place that was built at the same time as everything else on this station look this dilapidated?*

North Quarter was reasonable enough on its outskirts, comfortable low- to middle-income housing and the modest shops that catered to that group. It was the people that signaled the change as much as anything else. As you got closer to the unspun docking sections the clothes got plainer and grubbier, or more spectacularly flashy. Joat found her fingers curling instinctively around the hilt of her vibroknife where it was tucked into its charging sheath in the right sleeve of her overalls. It was a small movement, nearly undetectable . . . but half the people on the corridor moved a little farther aside when she did it. Which said something about their perceptions, even now in night-cycle, when the overhead ambients were turned down to let the shopfront glowers and holos shine by contrast.

This is the sort of place Uncle used to stop. Before he'd lost her in a card game when she was about seven. She felt her shoulders hunch, her face tighten. Her body remembered those years; the feral child was still there, hiding inside the skin of the civilized young woman.

The professionals were out, too. Down here they didn't just saunter; you got detailed propositions. Complete with anatomical details so lurid that she blinked.

"What you said about my succumbing to soft living would seem to be true, Joat," Joseph whispered in her ear. "I, who grew up on the docks of Keriss, find myself embarrassed!"

Joat grinned at him. "At least you don't smell of cop."

The Bethelite nodded. "In Keriss too we could always smell a thief-taker," he said. "Still, I remember a little more discretion from the Daughters of Joy."

"Don't be embarrassed," she said. "This bunch're way saltier than average. They're beginning to get to me too."

Alvec leered. "Y'oughta be storing this stuff up for use on Rohan. New Destinies is a deacon's convention next to that."

"Do you speak as one who knows?" Joseph asked, his voice cool. Alvec bristled.

"Tell me something," Joat said. "Why is it that men— even smart ones—are dumb as iridium ingots while they're settling who's big bull baboon?"

Alvec snorted. Joseph raised his eyebrows—a habit he'd picked up from Amos—and chuckled. "Women are more subtle about it," he admitted. "I will try not to leap, gibber, or scratch my armpits too often in your presence, *saiyda*."

The Rimrunner was an Earth-style bar with furniture that only accommodated the humanoid form. The windows were one-way, opaque on the outside, with colorful advertisements for liquor flashing across the dirty black surface. Inside they gave a clear, if not clean, view of the street.

They made their way to an empty table, covertly studying the other patrons, who studied them in turn. Some of the men and women sitting at the tables or standing at the bar were sleazy-gaudy like most of the crowd outside; there were a few in conservative business jumpsuits, a few *too* well dressed, and a number in spacer's coveralls. Those looked neater. You couldn't be messy on a vehicle with boost, not really. Not if you wanted to live.

A bored and blowzy waitress slouched over and took their order. When she'd returned with their drinks and departed with an air of never planning to return, they sat quietly and sipped grimly for awhile. Conversation had died when they walked in, and was slow to revive. Most eyes were on the holo over the bar—an act showing surprising gymnastic skill, among other things—with occasional darts in their direction.

Finally, Joat leaned towards her crew and murmured: "So, Al, is there something we do? Talk to the bartender, put a note on the bulletin board, walk around shouting *we want to smuggle*, or what?"

"Someone'll come over," he murmured. "They're just checkin' us out."

They sat a little longer and Joat began to drum her fingers on the table. Two of them had sticky ends from a film of something on the surface.

"That's it," she said finally, putting her hands flat on the tabletop to push herself to her feet. "I don't really want to do this anyway—"

A pale, thin-faced man with dark hair and a neatly trimmed beard was suddenly at her elbow. He wore a black jumpsuit with flared sleeves, which might be hiding anything.

"You're, uh, Captain Simeon-Hap, aren't you?" he asked quietly.

Three pairs of eyes bored into the stranger as he

reversed the empty chair at their table and laid an open messager on the surface, sitting with his arms resting on the chairback.

"Mind if I join you?" he asked.

Joat shook her head. "You already have," she pointed out.

"Word is you've fallen on interesting times," he said, and smiled. Like the rest of him, the smile was thin and vicious-looking. "As in the curse."

She raised her brows. "Word gets around fast."

"Is it true?"

She sighed. "Yeah. It's true." She smiled in her turn, tight and controlled and dangerous. "We're gonna drink the money we have left."

Something invisible relaxed in the thin man's posture. "No need. Let me buy you a round." He looked pointedly at Joseph and Alvec. "Would you guys mind placing the order? Lisha will bring ours over to us, but you'll probably prefer to drink yours at the bar."

They looked at Joat, and rose at her nod. Joat could sense their reluctance, but they were both too experienced to queer her pitch. Nobody would want to book space with a captain who couldn't command her crew; particularly not people who wanted to be sure that their cargo got to its destination without inspection.

When Al and Joseph reached the bar they leaned against it, putting their weight on their elbows as if they were completing a journey of a thousand miles and their feet hurt.

"What'll it be, gents?"

"Arrack?" Joseph asked hopefully.

The bartender shook his head. "We got gin, we got whisky, we got beer . . ."

"Earth beer?" Alvec asked straightening.

"Four kinds," the bartender named them.

Alvec slapped Joseph's arm with the back of his hand.

"Ya gotta try this stuff," he said. "You're gonna love it!"

Joseph looked skeptical but nodded.

"Two," he said. He looked briefly in Joat's direction.

"Don't worry," Alvec said. "It's nothin' she can't handle."

Joseph sighed. "Yes, no doubt you are right. Still . . ." He shook his head. Then he looked around, as though really noticing the bar for the first time.

"It is amazing," he said, "Except for the signs, this tavern could be on Bethel. It is like any number of places on the docks where I grew up."

"Yeah," Alvec sighed nostalgically. "Me too. I think they invented a place like this back on Earth, and they've been shippin' them out wholesale from the same factory ever since."

"C.O.D.?" Joat asked in disbelief. "You expect me to ship this cash on delivery?"

"Captain, smuggling is like any other business. There has to be an element of trust or nothing can happen." He smiled his thin smile again, showing a sliver of teeth. "For example, we're trusting you not to fly off somewhere and sell the cargo."

You're trusting that I know what happens to people who try to stiff the Organization, she thought. The criminal equivalent of the Better Business Bureau wasn't a formal league, but it did have a strong, working joint policy on welchers.

"Nobody ships interstellar C.O.D.," she said firmly. "At the very least I'll need credits up front that will pay the expense of the trip. I'm not interested in getting to Schwartztarr and finding out that this has been a joke."

He pursed his lips. "So, what would that come to?"

"Two thousand," she said firmly.

He raised his brows and laughed faintly.

"You'd better check your engines, Captain. Your fuel consumption is *way* off the mark."

"I'm going to have to bribe my way off this station. I consider that a legitimate," she smiled briefly, "expense of the trip."

"They're supposed to let you continue to operate your business so you can pay your fine."

"Yeah, and they're not supposed to fine me the value of my ship for a misdemeanor, too. Two thousand up front, my man; twenty-five thousand on delivery. I won't even consider it without."

Joseph raised his brimming stein to his nose and sniffed dubiously.

"It smells like meat," he said.

"Meat!" Alvec sniffed his. "Mine's okay. Whaddaya mean, it smells like meat?"

"To me," Joseph explained, "this 'beer' smells like raw meat."

Alvec looked at him.

"Yeah, well," he grinned, "I can't wait to have a steak on your world."

Joseph took a tentative sip and smiled.

"You shall have one of the best when you visit my rancho," he promised, "*if* you will bring the beer."

He was raising his still brimming stein to touch glasses with Alvec when a shabby fellow in a once-yellow ship suit elbowed him aside; beer slopped over Joseph's sleeve and down the front of his robe. He set the remainder down and wiped the fabric with a napkin. The spacer ignored him . . . until he poked a rigid finger into the man's shoulder.

"That," he said, "was clumsy."

The spacer turned to him; when he spoke it was with a strong accent, wheezing and sharp. "Donchu touch me you bastard son of a whore!"

Ooops. Alvec thought. Joat had told him a little about Bethel, and he'd accessed more from the *Wyal's* database. That was *not* a good thing to say to a Bethelite; especially in Joseph's case, because it might well be literally true.

The bearded man handed Joat a credit chip and a blue datahedron.

"The information is protected by a very nasty virus, so I warn you, don't try to access it or you may find yourself drifting in hyper-space until you become a ghost story."

She smiled. "Smuggling is like any other business, there has to be an element of trust or nothing can happen."

He leaned his head to one side in acknowledgment, then looked over sharply to the bar.

Thwuck.

She had never seen Joseph look quite like *that*. His face was pale, with paler circles around his wide blue eyes. He was holding a spacer in a yellow suit with one arm twisted up behind his back. Blood ran down the man's face from a broken nose.

"Apologize, you furrower of pigs," the Bethelite said quietly, in a voice that carried. "For the insult you gave my mother."

"Fardle you *and* your mother, like your pig daddy!"

"That was unwise."

Joseph's other hand gripped the spacer by the back of the neck and slammed his face into the glassteel surface of the bar again. *Thwuck*. This time something else broke.

Joat started to rise; that was *not* like Joseph. She also started to shout a warning, as another spacer in a yellow shipsuit rose with a chair in her hands. Alvec moved before she could speak, a quick snatch for the chair and a short chopping punch to the stomach—much less hard than he could have dealt, because the spacer simply staggered back clutching her gut rather than collapsing. The bartender had ducked down; he rose again, with a short bell-mouthed weapon in his hands.

Sonic riot gun, Joat thought, as she prudently dropped flat. That didn't block her view of a beer stein sailing through the air and thunking with solid authority between the barkeeper's eyes. He fell backward, and this time stayed down.

Her new business acquaintance had vanished silently. *Good idea,* Joat thought, crawling towards the bar. *Good idea, prudent idea.* The tables were bolted to the floor, providing reasonably safe passage to the thick of things; bodies and pieces of furniture sailed through the air above, and grappling pairs dropped down to her level but couldn't roll past the table legs.

Joat encountered the waitress under one of them, just lighting up the stub of a dream-smoke stick and looking mildly entertained.

"I like the little blond one," she said to Joat, blowing a stream of smoke towards Joseph.

The Bethelite had just kicked a tall humanoid in the crotch, seized his head under one elbow as he bent over—evidently a vulnerable spot in that species, too—and was energetically punching him in the face.

"I got a thing for guys with muscles," the waitress went on. Alvec picked up another yellow-suited spacer and threw him in the direction of the door, clearing a pathway.

"He's married," Joat told her.

"So?"

"Uh," Joat shrugged, "whatever. Have you called Station Security?"

"Oh sure. We got a button under the bar, they'll be here in a couple a minutes." She drew deeply on her dream-smoke stick and offered it to Joat.

Joat shook her head. "No, thanks. I'd better be going."

She crawled under the next table and found herself beside Joseph and Alvec. Joat leaned out and grabbed their sleeves to get their attention.

"We're leaving. Now. Out the back."

"Aw, Joat—" Alvec began.

Another spacer was struggling with a stationer just behind him; the stationer staggered away, clutching at an arm. The spacer waved a long blade and shouted something blurred, lunging wild-eyed for Alvec's back. Joat and Joseph moved with the perfect coordination of dancers; Joat grabbed handfuls of cloth at wrist and shoulder and pulled the attacker forward, redirecting his force and hip-checking him into a sideways stagger. Joseph whirled aside like a matador as the lunge was thrown his way, stepping inside the curve of the outstretched arm and driving the stiffened fingers of one hand up under the spacer's ribs.

The figure in yellow collapsed, wheezing, and curled into a ball. Joseph toed the knife up against the brass rail and broke it with a quick stamp of his heel.

"Yeah, I see what you mean," Alvec said. "Fun's fun, but knives are cheating. Let's go, Cap'n."

Joat picked up a pseudosilver tray; Alvec picked up a chair and pulled it apart, like tearing the wings off a chicken. That left him with two lengths of gleaming alloy. Joseph walked between them; a knife of his own appeared in one hand, curved and looking sharp enough to cut light. They put their backs together and moved in a rotating circle towards the doors at the rear of the bar, through a kitchen that made Joat glad she hadn't ordered any food, and then through a hatch marked *danger* into an access corridor.

The lights blinked. *"Station Security,"* a voice said, vibrating through the metal of the circular corridor. *"All wrongdoers will cease disturbing the peace and submit to arrest. Station Security—"*

"This way," she gasped.

The access door three spaces down was dogged shut, and she fumbled in her jumpsuit for the picklock. It hung beeping for a nerve-wracking twelve seconds, and then the hatchway hissed open and they tumbled through into a dark and narrow corridor smelling of greasy food and dirty rest rooms. A weedy youth pushing a floater full of dirty plates and glasses stopped and gaped at them, his eyes going wide, and paled at the sight of the weapons.

Joat tossed her tray onto the floater. Behind her she heard a clank as Alvec dropped his chair-legs; Joseph's knife had never made any noise, coming out of the hidden sheath or going back in.

"You never saw us," she said, tucking a half-credit piece into the pocket of a stained white apron.

The chinless face smirked. "Saw who?" he said, and pushed the floater on through a door whose lying stencil read *sanitation*.

"You two go clean up," she snapped, looking at their grazed, bloody faces. "I'll get us a table, and we'll make innocent. *Just* what I needed, arrest on a breaking-the-peace charge with stolen goods on me!"

She pushed through an opaque forcefield door; it was maladjusted, and the harmonics set her teeth on edge. There was a corner table by the wall-window free; it gave an excellent view of Rimrunners patrons being dragged out of the premises next door by helmeted Station Security police in light-impact armor. Shockrods snapped amid shrieks and curses; brawlers were lifted and tossed bodily onto the flat-body back of the Black Mariah, where a tanglefield held them in uncomfortable stasis, just as they fell. One of the police was sitting on the pavement with a compress on his flattened nose.

"Hid deb one for be!" he called. A comrade boosted his captive onto the flatbed with an enthusiastic boot.

Joat looked up as the two men returned, and jerked a tight-lipped nod towards the scene.

"I—" Joseph began. Then he looked down at his hands, opening them and closing them once. "He should not have insulted my mother . . ." He looked up. "And there has been no news of the Benisur Amos for more than three weeks. He is my Prophet, my brother, my friend . . . and I have failed him."

Joat sighed and let her shoulders relax. "Okay."

It was Joseph who'd taught her to keep her emotions out of business, though. *Nobody's perfect. I guess learning that's part of growing up.* Even Simeon lost it sometimes, and he *could* control his emotions, literally, by regulating the endocrine feeds to the body inside his Shell.

"You are right, Joat," Joseph admitted. "It was foolish of me and it will not happen again, you have my word."

"Mine too, Boss."

She sighed. "Thank you. And you're right, no harm came of it. Except for your bruises." *And I hope they hurt!* she thought.

She reached over and gripped Joseph's hand. "I realize you're under pressure, Joe. Sorry I snapped at you."

"Hey, Boss, what about me?"

Joat looked at Alvec out of the corner of her eyes and growled softly.

"Yeah," he said, "that's kinda what I figured."

She stood. "Let's go, I want to hustle up a cargo if I can. It won't look good if we leave with an empty hold."

"D'ya mind if Joe and me stick around here and have a few, get acquainted?" Alvec asked. "We're going to be on the same small ship for a long time." He shrugged: "Unless you need us for something?"

"No," Joat said, a little surprised. "Go ahead. Just remember . . ."

"You have my word, Joat," Joseph said firmly, but with a smile.

"Well, see you later then," she said, uneasy.

I trust them not to get into another fight, she realized as she left.

It was what the heck *else* they might get up to that worried her. Alvec had a positive gift for trouble, and Joseph was half-crazy with worry over Amos. Rightly so, if Amos was in the hands of the Kolnari.

She didn't believe in the Bethelite hell, but being in the Fist of High-Clan Kolnar was a pretty good approximation.

✧ CHAPTER FIVE

"Clan Lord," Karak called.

Belazir paused on the threshold of his quarters and turned his head to look coldly at his approaching son.

"May I speak?" Karak asked him.

Belazir considered the request, wondering what aggravation his eldest son had in store for him. Then he surrendered to curiosity, gave a short nod.

"The scumvermin female languishes in her cell, Great Lord, ignored and lonely."

Belazir sighed and turned towards his son, contempt visible on his face.

"When I was your age, child, I too was excited by the terror of the prey. But I am older now and have known the pleasures of conquest often. I refuse to feel *obliged* to take every screaming, worm-colored girl I come across simply because it is expected of me."

Karak's face was expressionless, but the stiffness of his posture told Belazir that he was humiliated by his father's response.

Had his son asked for the girl outright Belazir might well have given her to him. But this behind-the-back way of asking annoyed him. He had never been easy to manipulate and this exceedingly clumsy effort was an insult.

"Leave her to my pleasure, Karak. See to her health and well-being, but do not touch her."

Let the young hot-head chew his spleen over that, Belazir thought in amusement. With a nod to his son he turned and entered his quarters.

Soamosa paced her small cell, seven paces one way, five the other. She counted her steps. She had walked nine thousand one hundred and fifty four steps since waking. The cell was featureless save for its minimal furnishings, a neutral-gray box of ship metal. *Doubtless intended to weaken prisoners by sensory deprivation.*

The thought came to her that she should be praying. That she should find solace on her knees instead of on her feet. But she had tried that and it didn't work. Soamosa found herself praying for things that reminded her of the terrible fate that she and the Benisur Amos and the Captain shared.

At first, the prayers had been for deliverance, and for the safety of the Benisur, and then she had prayed that she not be raped, or locked in and left to starve. With every prayer Soamosa had brought herself closer to mindless panic. And so she paced and counted her steps, to keep her mind cleared and calm. And that worked.

Her back was to the hatch when it opened and she froze. Soamosa had made it her habit since being imprisoned in this cell not to look at the Kolnari who brought her food.

She had found them disturbingly beautiful, uniformly tall and blond, with shapely figures and stern features. Her mother had warned her not to be fooled by their appearance.

"You can tell that they are not human by the way that they despise all that is. If ever you should be so unfortunate as to meet them do not let their beauty blind you. They are devils in the world of flesh, inhumanly cruel and selfish. You dare not look upon them lest you should be lost."

Their leers and gloating remarks had made her all too aware of her torn dress and unbound hair and she had been unable to keep the tears of shame out of her eyes. Her only means of preserving her modesty and her dignity was to keep her back to them when they came.

Besides, she did not want to see their faces as they attacked her; which she knew they might do at any time. She had resolved to keep her eyes closed if it came to that. And she would sing a hymn, the one about smashing the enemies of God like pottery. That would show them what Bethelites were made of.

"Turn around, scumvermin," a stern voice commanded.

Soamosa stiffened, and after a moment complied.

"Look at me, scumvermin."

She bit her lips to keep them from trembling.

"No," she said coolly and clasped her hands before her.

Karak was astounded. It had never occurred to him that this tiny female would defy him. He was honestly puzzled and completely put off his stride by her refusal. What would his father do? And how did he make her obey without touching her? Coercion he knew all too well, of persuasion he was ignorant.

She turned her head away from him and looked up at the ceiling before lowering her eyes again.

"What do you want?" she asked haughtily.

Karak frowned. He'd lost the initiative and must wrest it back from her. *This is not like the simulations.* One did not allow prisoners to ask questions. He felt a spurt of anger. It wasn't as if she was a person.

He stepped close and began to circle her, allowing

her to become aware of his bulk and to feel him looming over her.

Soamosa fought her trembling, fought to keep her eyes lowered and her feet firmly in place while her heart hammered and mind demanded run, flee, hide! She could feel the floor vibrate under his heavy tread and the heat from his near-naked body was extraordinary. He felt like a dark sun orbiting her.

The girl wasn't intimidated in the least that Karak could see. She kept her place, her face a mask of cool disdain.

His own face warmed in shame. All of his life he'd been laughed at and called soft because he lacked ambition in the arts of war. "The Poet" his agemates had named him and made his life a hell of mockery. Only his elder brother had befriended him:

You will be a perfect second to me, brother. We will be a team"; so you said. But you died, and I must stand in your place.

A place that everyone, from his father on down, knew he could never fill.

He came to a halt before her, looking down on her and quivering with rage. *Lucky for you I have been forbidden to touch you. Because I would rip you limb from limb.*

He said softly, in a deep uneven voice, "Your dress is very torn."

Soamosa clutched at the worst of the rents in her gown without thinking and she felt the color rise in her face. She was very ashamed.

"Yes," she forced herself to say, "it is."

"Perhaps I should find you something better to wear," he taunted.

"Thank you, that would be very kind," she replied automatically, while her mind screamed in panic, *Be silent! Don't provoke him!*

Karak blinked. She was either very brave or very stupid. Within him curiosity began to bloom and feelings of amusement and admiration mixed. It pleased him to be generous, he decided.

"I shall see to it then," he said and left her without a backwards glance.

Soamosa looked up when she heard the hatch close behind him. She stood staring at it for a long minute with her hands pressed hard against her rib cage, as though to hold in her frantically beating heart.

Then she turned and stumbled to her cot, falling back on it to gaze at the ceiling.

I did it! she thought. *I faced down the enemy without flinching!*

And then she burst into tears.

Belazir laughed until tears ran down his cheeks and he began to choke. At last the spasm passed and the laughter slowed to sighing chuckles until he could once again get his breath. Then he sat smiling before the surveillance screen.

"Perverse," he said to himself, chuckling again. "Utterly perverse. Yet oh so amusing." He knew he should be mortally offended, furious almost beyond his own iron control.

But he had never been close to this particular child of his loins, nor to the wife who had bred him. And the girl had shown incredible spunk, given the circumstances.

He wondered if he was going to kill Karak the next time he saw him.

Belazir knew that, for his honor's sake, he should. *But,* he thought with a sigh, *since The Great Plague ravaged the people we have bred but slowly. Our numbers are as nothing and worse, the children are puny. And Karak has four healthy brats.* He concluded that satisfying his honor with Karak's blood was a luxury the people couldn't afford. *Yet.*

Would that Karak's brother had lived instead. Belazir's lips curled in a wry expression. He had better use for a decent second-in-command than he did for comic relief. On the other hand, the boy's brother would have been a threat.

But he also wanted to see how this foolishness with the scumvermin female played out. He smiled again. His sense of curiosity had always been one of his besetting sins. He decided to indulge it in this case as he could not see any way in which it could become too costly to do so.

He'd intended to amuse himself by experimenting on the girl with the other new drugs he had bought and taunting Simeon-Amos with holos of her reactions. Well, obviously he couldn't use her so and also have her available for amusing episodes with his son.

No matter, he'd have a technician cobble together some sort of holo, extrapolating from the predicted responses that had been described to him.

That would be better, in fact! He wouldn't be distracted and could truly enjoy the Benisur scumvermin's reactions. No doubt opportunities for live experimentation would arise in the course of events; and it would add a certain frisson to known that Amos's despair and anguish were for nothing at all . . .

"Yes," he murmured. "Let him think the scumvermin girl destroyed—and then I shall show her to him, whole and well. And destroy her again!"

Belazir sighed contentedly. *Surely anticipation is one of life's true pleasures.*

I hate my father, Karak son of Belazir thought, as he paced through the corridors of the *Kali*—the Dreadful Bride, his sire's old warship.

A pack of Kolnari children went by, in the wake of something bulge-eyed and long-clawed that squealed and snarled as it ran. They dashed after it with high shrieks of excitement, long razor-sharp knives in their hands. The sight distracted him for an instant; how long had it been since he was an innocent child, with nothing more to concern him than lessons and running down a *drgudak* with his friends? All of five years, now; since he turned eight and came to manhood. The infancy of Kolnar was brief.

I hate my father. What child of the Divine Seed didn't? *But it's worse than that. I hate them all.* He shivered. He was weak, too weak, hiding in his quarters and watching the tapes of the scumvermin female. He told himself it was honest lust, but it was not. *She is weak. Yet she does not despair.* The strangers were like that. His father had thought them weak, when the High Clan took Bethel, when it took SSS-900-C . . . and found that its meal was eating its way back out.

Decision crystallized as he fingered the injector in a pouch. He slapped palm against a communicator. "Duty officer," he said. "I shall be unavailable for the next hour."

"No," Soamosa pleaded, "please don't." Her blue eyes were full of tears and terror.

She was held by two Kolnari, her slender form dwarfed by their muscular height. One of them held out her arm with the inside of her elbow uppermost. Despite her increasingly frantic struggles the arm didn't move. So that when the nozzle of the injector was placed on her arm it was right against a vein.

"Don't, please don't," she was weeping helplessly now. "No! No, NO!"

She tore herself free and huddled in the corner of the room; there were streaks of blood on her arms.

Belazir leaned down and grasped her chin in his huge hand.

"In only a moment, Benisur, it will begin," he said and turned to smile at Amos.

"No!" Soamosa insisted, holding her hands up defensively.

Karak smiled at the gesture, it was completely absurd. Seated beside him she looked like a creature made of gossamer and air, frail as a candle flame. And yet, he knew that she was the one in control. At all of their meetings it was she who had set the tone. Deep within himself, Karak sighed.

"You have nothing to fear from me," he said aloud. "I will not harm you."

Soamosa looked suspiciously at the earnest young Kolnari. Even in the midst of her fear his beauty struck her; and the lost look in the yellow eagle eyes.

"I do not trust you," she said severely.

Karak brushed back his long silver-blond hair distractedly.

"I am concerned for you," he said. "It is terribly dangerous for me to even offer you this protection. If my father knew," his lips tightened, "death would come to me as a friend."

Soamosa narrowed her eyes.

"I do not believe you," she said. "It is some Kolnari trick. My mother told me all about the Kolnari sense of humor."

"Lady," he said and the expression in his eyes firmed. "It is my intention to save you, not to harm you. I will set you free." Karak blinked rapidly and swallowed hard. "And your companions if that is possible. I swear it."

By the sound of his voice, the oath might have been flayed from him. She raised her arm, the inside of her elbow uppermost and he placed the nozzle of the injector unerringly over the vein.

"Now that I've submitted to your injection, you must tell me what it does," Soamosa demanded, radiating poise and dignity and the mysterious power she held over him.

"It will keep you safe from a most dreadful disease," Karak told her. "My father means to use it against your people."

Suddenly, like a splash of cold water, Karak realized that with those words he was forever cast adrift from the Kolnar. He had betrayed them. Even if he failed to save Soamosa and her companions, if it ended here with his leaving her and never returning, he was a traitor. And he was glad. He felt freer than he ever had in his life, liberated from impossible expectations and deeds that he was not proud of. He was free. And the unnamable feeling he bore for this tiny young woman was the cause of it.

Karak leaned forward and Soamosa gasped in alarm. He closed his eyes and very tenderly kissed her forehead in gratitude.

Amos stiffened as the image of Soamosa screamed. Screamed until her mouth sprayed blood, as though she had burst a vein in her throat. And still she screamed, writhing in agony, until at last she lay still, gasping, her eyes rolling back in her head.

Tears ran down Amos's face unchecked. His arms held the weeping Captain Sung who clutched him in terror. The Captain had soiled himself in his fear, not understanding the screaming, nor Amos's soothing words.

"You are evil," Amos murmured, "and you shall be destroyed by your own evil. He shall break you with a rod of iron."

Belazir appeared before him.

"We shall let her rest for a bit," Belazir said in a

conversational tone. "Then, if you like, I have some other drugs whose effects might interest you."

Sung whimpered and screwed his head tighter against Amos's ribcage, trying to hide from Belazir.

Amos glared at the Kolnari Lord. "She is only an innocent young girl, Master and God. Why do you torture her so? Is there no pity in you at all?"

Belazir crossed his arms on his chest.

"How can you ask that, scumvermin? Have I not given the Captain there to the only person on this ship who would care for him? It would be more convenient to space him than to feed him."

Amos tightened his grip on the Captain's quivering shoulders.

"Captain Sung has been injured in my service, Master and God," he said humbly. "It is my duty to care for him as best I can."

Belazir's lip curled. "How touching. And he stinks so." Then the Kolnari smiled, he glanced at Soamosa where she lay at his feet. "Why, you have touched me," he said as though in surprise. "I believe that we shall give her a more relaxing injection this time." He looked back at Amos. "It will intensify feelings of pleasure and give her an overwhelming desire to please." He grinned evilly. "So you should enjoy watching this."

Belazir burst out laughing as the image of Amos and the brain-scrubbed spacer faded, to be replaced by his son in the cell of the Bethelite woman. He'd seen sleazy adventure holos created for scumvermin fools that were more believable than what he was watching.

Belazir pounded the arm of his control couch and shouted laughter. *Ah, the rock-jawed righteousness of that Amos,* he thought. *And Karak, mooning over a piece of walking meat barely fit to serve a moment's pleasure and breed slaves.*

It was pleasant that Amos was totally convinced by the holos his technicians had prepared from a pirated Central Worlds program. There were flaws, but Amos appeared to have missed them. Due, no doubt, to the harrowing content of the recording. And it was exactly the sort of thing Belazir *would* do. Always easier to believe what one expected.

He really would have to think of something suitable as a punishment for Karak. And yet, he wanted to see just how far this . . . romance, for want of a better word, would go.

He sat shaking his head in amazement as he watched Soamosa looking in wide-eyed wonder at Karak's stoic face. Then, tentatively, she placed her small hand on his and smiled.

Belazir began to laugh again as he started the next holo for the Benisur Amos's edification. His youngest wife called from the chamber within:

"How I yearn for you, lord of my life!" There was a waspish note to her voice.

"Anticipation heightens pleasure," he called back. "And silence averts beatings."

Yes. This compendium of erotic fantasies. Tame to Kolnari eyes, but it would torment Amos unceasingly, playing on the insides of his eyelids when he squeezed them closed to shut it out. Run a modification program *here*—

✧ CHAPTER SIX

Mr. va Riguez:
I need to speak to you immediately on a matter
of extreme urgency. *Wyal* is scheduled for departure
at 03:00. Please contact me before then.
Sincerely,
Captain Simeon-Hap

*She should have signed it desperately instead of
sincerely,* Bros thought, a wry smile playing at the
corners of his mouth. He leaned back in the big, faux-
leather chair in The Anvil's office. *Still, I'm surprised
she said please.* That lonely plea didn't seem to go with
the imperious tone of the rest of her note. *Dyson must
have taken me at my word.* He'd known the little
weasel would.

Sperin had authorized the clerk to fine Joat up to
twenty thousand credits. Or at least to *tell* her he was
fining her that much. In reality the fine shouldn't be
more than five or six thousand. Even that amount
would be tough for Joat to scrape together. But *twenty
thousand* . . . That was an absolutely staggering fine
for any ship, let alone a struggling independent freighter
like hers.

Bros grinned. *Ridding her of a fine that size ought
to engender a lot of gratitude,* he thought comfortably.

Then his pleasure slowly faded. Joat Simeon-Hap wasn't someone he'd like to see broken to the plow, jumping when he snapped his fingers, dancing when he pulled her strings.

He didn't want CenSec to lose her. *But I don't want them to own her soul either.*

Them? he asked himself in mild surprise. He frowned. It had been many years since he'd thought of CenSec as other than *we,* or *I. Some of that girl's independence is rubbing off on me,* he thought ruefully.

"Sal," he said. Getting up he went to the heavy-shouldered man seated at an overburdened desk and dropped Joat's note in front of him. "Take care of this for me, would you? Joat Simeon-Hap's ship, the *Wyal,* has been fined by the station. Pay it out of my special account."

"Sure, Mr. va Riguez, no problem," Sal said. He had a voice like stones grinding together.

Bros picked up his jacket and swung it over his shoulder. "And if Captain Simeon-Hap should call looking for me, you don't know where I am."

"I never do, sir," Sal agreed with a gap-toothed grin.

"But you might ask her if she'd like to leave a message."

Sal's sandy eyebrows went up. "I'm not sure I'm old enough to listen to the kind of language she's liable to use, sir."

Bros chuckled. "You tell her that," he advised.

Sal stared at the door after it had closed behind Sperin, then he glanced at the note again. *I'll take care of it tomorrow,* he thought. *It's not like they charge interest.* He put the note aside and went back to work.

✧ CHAPTER SEVEN

"Rand, I want you to record this as it plays, all right?"

"Certainly, Joat. I had intended to anyway," Rand said. There was a faintly injured tone to the AI's voice.

"All right, people, got your note screens ready?" Joseph and Alvec nodded. "Well, okay, it's showtime!"

Joat entered the datahedron Bros Sperin had given her and keyed it up. For a few moments, as a fluid computer voice relayed the facts of Nomik Ciety's life, the only sound was the click of styli as they took notes. But with the first holo snap, Joat looked up, and froze.

Her heartbeat speeded up until all she could hear was the sound of her own blood rushing. Pounding through her, beating against her fingertips, pulsing in her temples. Her sight narrowed to a tunnel sparked with black and white.

When at last she took another breath it roared in her ears like a cyclone.

Nomik Ciety, Nomik . . . Ciety. The face on the screen shifted from the scrawny, mad-eyed youth with a number across his chest to a grown man's, well dressed and smooth. A respectable businessman to all appearances, with a friendly smile and a twinkle in his eye. Her own blond hair, face a little angular. Cheekbones like those that greeted her every morning in the screen.

Uncle Nom, she thought. *You're not dead! I was so*

sure you were dead. She felt numb now, and her heart rate was returning to normal. It was in the nature of humankind, to believe in what they most deeply wished to be true.

Joat closed her eyes and took a slow, quiet deep breath. *Amos comes first,* she thought desperately.

But memory bubbled up, eating away at the failing barrier of her will. She tightened her fist around the stylus, gripping it like a lifeline.

The part of her he'd betrayed screamed in frustrated rage: *You were only seven! You were just a baby and he sold you to that sick bastard!*

She was looking back at Uncle Nom as a big, smelly, shambling man led her away, his grip like a clamp on her skinny arm. Uncle Nom was waving and smiling.

"Bye-bye," he called.

"Uncanom," she heard her own thin, little girl's voice call out, "Uncle *Nom!*" Tears blurred her vision.

She blinked, her jaw was clenched so hard the muscles jumped and she felt sweat begin to bead her upper lip. Joat took a deep breath, trying to keep control. Trying to deny what she felt, because it was joy. Sheer, undiluted joy; a savage intensity of feeling that nothing in her life had ever rivaled.

How nice that you're not dead, Uncle Nom, she thought, fighting back a giggle. Knowing that she wouldn't be able to stop if she started. *And then they'd ask questions. I don't want any questions.*

Uncle Nom was hers. All hers. *My toy to break,* she thought with gleeful viciousness.

But she didn't have to hurry. Now she knew about him. There was no way he could hide from her, no place in all the worlds.

Don't look back, she warned herself. *There's nothing back there that isn't going to cut you.*

The reminder didn't work . . .

It was dark and she was huddled in a tiny space, a space that soon would be too small for her to hide in. She starved herself so that she could still fit, because he couldn't reach her here. There was a crash of metal on metal.

"Come on out you little wharf-rat! You're only makin' it worse!" His voice rose to a hoarse shout at the end that promised broken bones.

There was a rattle then, and with a clatter the cover over the air duct fell away to reveal the captain's fleshy, red face. He glared down at her, teeth gritted, breathing in a harsh rasp. Then he pulled back, thrusting his arm in to make a grab at her. Joat plastered herself against the duct, breathing in to make a hollow of her stomach. The blunt fingertips just brushed her clothing.

He pulled his arm out with a cry of rage and smashed his fist against the wall. Then his face appeared again.

"You'd better come out, little girl," he sang softly, with the purr of madness underneath. It was very bad when he stopped shouting and went quiet. "Or you're gonna be sooorryyy."

And she knew that she had to leave her shelter and let him have her. Or he'd seal her in. He'd done that once before and . . .

A hot hand touched her and she started with an angry hiss, turning to glare into Joseph's puzzled eyes.

"Jeeeezzz, Joe! Don't *do* that!"

"I am sorry," he said. "I spoke and you did not answer. I did not mean to startle you."

"Sorry," she said curtly. "What did you want?"

"I said that this man is more dangerous than I had expected. I am uneasy allowing you to take all of the risk in this matter."

"I'm not helpless, Joe! And I'm not Rachel, so don't even try to treat me like I am! I don't appreciate it."

She saw surprise in the way his eyebrows quivered, then settled down. *For Joe that marked a profound change of expression.*

Joat sighed, a little ashamed of her outburst. "I see nothing in this recording that gives us a reason to change our plans at this late date. Especially since our plans were to play it by ear and see what happens. You can't *be* more flexible than that, Joe."

"As you say, Joat," he murmured.

Joseph caught Alvec's eye over Joat's head. An imperceptible nod confirmed his judgment. He had never seen Joat afraid, in all the years he had known her—not even when the Kolnari occupiers had walked the corridors of SSS-900-C. *Or could she fear for her ship?* That was more than danger, it was a threat to her dream.

"Joat," he began tentatively, "if you cannot pay the fine to New Destinies what will you do?"

"Lose the ship," she said succinctly, and shrugged. "My fault entirely. The fine thing really wasn't such a good idea."

"Whatsisname, that guy?" Alvec said. "He'll take care of it, right?"

"Sperin?" she asked. Joat made a moue. "I'd feel better about that if he'd bothered to get back to me. But if I'm lucky he's already dealt with it." *And if he hasn't I'm beached.*

"Can you not simply change *Wyal's* name and your name and begin again in another quadrant of space? Surely you need not meekly surrender to them? If worst comes to worst, you can return to Bethel with me and we will shelter you." He saw her look aside and blink.

"Thanks," she said quietly, in his language. Then she took a deep breath and went on: "First, I'm not ducking

out on Amos, whatever it costs. Second, I *can't* welch—
not without losing my reputation; and this'll have gone
out on the unofficial net too; they'd be after me like
a sicatooth after a goat if I don't pay up, not to mention
the bounty hunters." She paused reflectively. "You know
how it is."

They nodded, and Alvec grunted agreement. You
might get away with choosing the above-ground com-
panies, but not the underworld. They had a primitive,
straightforward approach to those who tried to cheat
them.

"You don't seriously think I'd risk visiting your wife
and children with bounty hunters on my tail, do you?"

"No," Joseph said and smiled.

"Besides, if I ran, then I'd never see Simeon or
Channa again. It's not worth it." She stood and looked
around the control cabin. "And," she went on, her hands
closing into fists behind her back, "they're not even close
to getting *Wyal* yet. We're going to Schwartztarr, and
then on to Rohan."

Bros Sperin leaned back from the screen. *So, she's
gone.* According to her itinerary Schwartztarr was her
destination. *And she's carrying a really weird cargo,
going by the manifest.* Most likely she was also carrying
something Central Worlds would rather she wasn't.
Little Ms. Simeon-Hap was nothing if not enterprising.

Uncertainty tickled his mind like a cat playing with
a piece of string. *She can take care of herself,* Bros told
himself. *Don't try second guessing yourself at this late
date. She's capable.*

Capable of unraveling his carefully made plans. She
was like chaos on two feet when she put her mind to
it. He knew felinoid species who thought more before
they leaped. *Of course,* he had to admit, *like them, she
tends to land on her feet.*

But if she wanted to live long in this business, she was going to have to learn some caution. *And some tact.* He grinned, Sal had told him a few stories.

Bros liked Joat enough to want her to live a very long time indeed. He'd especially liked the Joat he'd met on the bridge of her ship; she'd been more spontaneous, more natural.

The universe would be a far less interesting place without that young woman in it.

He shook his head. The idea had been to lock up a loose cannon while he did the real work. Joat was supposed to merely observe. *But having gotten a look at her style up close and personal, I wonder if she's even capable of doing something so passive as simply looking.*

Nomik Ciety *was* involved with the Kolnari. To what degree Sperin had no idea. *I suspect that he's up to his neck in them,* he thought disgustedly. But Bros had long ago trained himself not to treat his suspicions as evidence. *And if he is working with them he's being very discreet.*

It was a calculated risk, sending her after a man like Ciety. Still, given his relatively exalted status on Rohan, he should be a perfect choice for Joat to investigate; a personage all but inaccessible to a lowly freighter captain on her first smuggling run.

And yet . . .

"Enough," Sperin said aloud. *While she leaves a streak across the troposphere, I'll do my entry . . . nice and slow and inconspicuous.*

✧ CHAPTER EIGHT

"What was in those cargo modules?" Alvec asked.

Joat smiled and touched a control. A chime rang through the *Wyal's* bridge.

"Beyond gravity well limits," Rand's impersonal voice said. "Prepare for transition. Three minutes and counting."

"That's for me to know, and you to guess," she said smugly. "Got the destination data ready?"

"Schwartztarr system," Alvec said, tossing a data-hedron in one hand. "Why do you want to stop there?"

"It's on the way . . . and I think it might be useful," she said.

"Ten seconds."

"You're the boss."

"Damned right. Prepare to cheat Einstein . . . *now*."

The *Wyal* twisted itself out of congruence with the sidereal universe.

Schwartztarr was the fourth planet of a G6 sun, a little brighter than Sol-standard. *I've never seen Earth's sun,* Joat thought idly as they dropped into normal space. Schwartztarr's star was pinpoint bright in the screens; the schematics showed the nine planets of the system and a running list of in-system traffic, interstellar ships, habitats and space-based fabricators.

Not very much, for a system that had been settled as long as this one. Surprisingly sparse, in fact, for a place with a settled planet bearing a breathable atmosphere. She called up data on the main screen.

Well, that explains it. Sort of large planet, gravity 1.2 standard, with a single large continent in the northern polar-to-temperate zone. Rather far out, so it was cold despite the active sun, and with a fairly steep axial tilt. Long cold winters, and the rest of the system was middling-average. The file showed a few scenes from those winters, and Joat shivered slightly, the reflex of someone who'd spent almost all of her life in the climate-controlled environment of ships and Stations. The people in the vid were wrapped up like bundles, with powered heaters underneath. Another shot showed something with eight short clawed legs, long white fur, red eyes and a head that was mostly mouth filled with long pointed teeth. Whatever-it-was was resting its front pair of legs on something much larger and dead, ripping chunks off and bolting them. Then it looked up at the camera and gave an amazing snarl, with its jaws open at least ninety degrees.

Joat shuddered again. "Remind me never to go outside on Schwartztarr," she said.

Joseph had come onto the bridge, toweling down his bare torso after a spell in the exerciser. Muscle rippled under the smooth olive skin of his chest as he stopped beside her command couch. *Not bad,* she thought. Joe was an uncle, so the thought was pretty theoretical— but Alvec caught her eye and winked.

"That beast looks like it would make interesting hunting," the Bethelite said, nodding to the screen.

Joat hid a grimace of distaste. Bethel *was* the boondocks, and they had some pretty grody customs there.

"But what," he went on, "is that fluffy white material all over the ground?"

"Snow," Alvec said, from the assistant/engineer's couch. At Joseph's raised eyebrow: "Flakes of frozen water that fall from the sky."

"Ah!" Joseph leaned further forward. "But why doesn't it melt?"

"Because the temperature is below the freezing point of water."

"The God preserve us!" he said. "I had heard of such things on high mountains, but . . ."

Joat glanced at him. The furrow of hard concern faded for a moment from between his eyes; he looked like a boy, smiling at wonders. It was only an instant, but it made the pain and worry more obvious when they returned.

"Hey, Boss," Alvec said. "What landing vector do y'want to cut?"

"Standard—Capriana Spaceport. There's not much else here, here. Rand's taking us in, it needs the practice."

"Rand?" Alvec's face went carefully blank.

"I *fixed* the program," she said defensively.

"We've worked on it together," Rand assured him, "I'm certain we've worked the bugs out of it. And I've studied several hundred landings by you and by Joat, I've also exchanged information with several other AIs of my acquaintance. I'm confident that all will be well this time."

"It's different from docking at a station," Alvec said nervously. "You do a real good station docking."

"Thank you," Rand said, its lights flickering blue.

"But I think one of us should co-pilot you until you get the landing stuff perfect. No offense."

"None taken." The AI's tones were always neutral, but that sounded a little flatter than usual.

"It'll be perfect, Al," Joat said through gritted teeth. "It wasn't even Rand's fault the last time, it was the way my program interfaced with that fardling, wonky . . ."

"Just in case . . ." he insisted.

"If you would not mind, Joat," Joseph put in delicately. "You understand . . . I travel by spaceship so seldom . . . the conversation has made me a little, ah . . ."

Joat shrugged. "Sure. OK."

"Why not use a commercial program?" Alvec grumbled, settling into his crash-couch and fastening the restraint harness. "There's dozens of 'em available. Cheap too!"

"Rand is unique," Joat said stiffly. "And I want it to stay that way."

"When it's my butt, I sort of like *standard* and *tried and tested* as opposed to *unique*. You know what I mean, Boss?"

"You trust me," she countered.

Alvec sighed. "You may be unique, Boss, but you've also got a license."

"Point taken," she said quietly. "And since I've already agreed to let you co-pilot, can we drop the subject?"

"So . . ." Alvec said into the silence that followed. "You managed to scare up a cargo after all, eh, Boss?"

"Yup."

After a long pause he asked, "So . . . what are we shippin'?"

There was a longer pause, then Joat answered: "Laser tube guides."

"Lasers?"

"Yup."

"You're shipping laser tubes to Schwartztarr?"

"Yup."

"You're kidding?"

"What is it?" Joseph asked. "What is wrong?"

"Lasers're all they make here. It's their main industry," Alvec said. "I can't believe . . ."

"They were cheap, and it's my money, okay?"

"You *bought* them?"

"Al," she said warningly.

"You're right," Alvec soothed, "someone'll want 'em."

"*Attention Central Worlds freighter, this is Schwartz-tarr traffic control, please identify yourself.*"

Alvec leapt for the com like a drowning man after a lifeline. His stubby fingers touched the controls with an odd, butterfly delicacy.

"*Cleared,*" traffic control said. "*Planetary approach, Tarrstown spaceport. Welcome to the Schwartztarr system.*"

"Yes, welcome," Joseph murmured. He had slid into the vacant navigator's couch. "Joat, observe."

Joat slaved a screen to the scanners the Bethelite was using. "A ship . . . oh."

Alvec leaned over. "Got a neutrino signature like a cathouse billboard," he observed. "Either they're leaking, or . . ."

"Corvette-class engines," Joseph said. "Very similar to the ones the Prophet bought for our in-system patrol craft."

Joat grinned. "I think we've left respectability behind."

The *Wyal* buffeted as they slid down their vector towards the outer fringes of the atmosphere. Screens began to fog as the hull compressed gas into a cloud of ionized particles. Joat's fingers itched to touch the controls; she wrapped them around the arms of her crash-couch instead. Alvec was kneading a fisted right hand into the palm of his left.

"Cloud cover," the AI's metallic-smooth voice said. "We're down to suborbital velocity. Hull temperatures within parameters." It paused. "Ground is at minus twenty, wind seventy kilometers per hour." Another pause. "Down to suborbital speeds. Exterior view on."

Alvec gave an exaggerated shiver as the largest screen

cleared to show a swirling mass of storm cloud. The hull toned again as they plunged into it, a different note from the stress of high-altitude reentry.

"*Brrr.*"

A moment later he yelped and reached for the controls. Joat stretched out her own arm and touched him on the shoulder. The *Wyal* rang as if a thousand medium-sized mad gods were pounding on it with their fists.

"Let Rand handle it. Rand, what *is* that?"

"Frozen water," the computer said. "Nodes of from millimetric to centimetric size, at high velocity."

Joseph's brows rose. "Hail?"

"Yes, hail."

The exterior screens showed darkness shot with lightning and massive winds. Joat felt the skin along her spine creep. The hazards of space were orderly, compared to this; *Wyal* had the capacity for atmosphere transit, but it seemed unnatural, somehow.

They broke through the cloud cover at three thousand meters above their destination. The spaceport was a cleared space of a few square kilometers, set in a sea of green broken only by white-rimmed inlets—the scene twisted mentally, and she realized that it was a forest, fretted by fjords of the sea. Tarrstown lay along several of those arms, its street-patterns bright against the darkening landscape. Snow blew by, nearly horizontal in the gale. A spot on the concrete of the landing field began to strobe.

"Don't believe in luxuries like gantries or tiedowns here," Alvec grumbled. "We'll have to keep the drive hot or get blown over."

"Nope, there's a mobile unit coming out," Joat said, tapping the screen. "Guess they don't have enough traffic to justify the cost of fixed installations. Lots of worlds don't—"

She broke off with an oath that put Joseph's eyebrows up again. Something had slammed into the hull, not enough mass to feel but enough to make the plating ring. Several more somethings followed.

"What *is* that?"

The exterior screen split. A central panel showed something dirty-white and about ten meters from wingtip to wingtip closing fast on the pickup. That went black as it was covered, and then showed flashes of teeth and slaver as whatever-it-was tried to gnaw its way through the metal.

"Not too bright," she said, forcing herself to relax—her arms had been trying to push her body back through the couch in instinctive reflex.

"But hungry," Joseph observed thoughtfully.

"Very hungry," Alvec concurred.

The winds were slower below the clouds; the ship slid downwards as if it were following an invisible string in the sky. Snow blasted away from the landing site, and there was a rumble and clank as the seldom-used leg-jacks extended from their pods in the stern.

"*Adjusting to planetary gravity.*" Weight came down on them, a sluggish feeling. "There," Rand said, "I told you that we'd perfected the program."

"Yeah, well, conditions were pretty smooth," Alvec said grudgingly. "But I guess you did okay."

"Thank you," Rand and Joat said simultaneously.

Smooth? Joat thought wryly. *Conditions were pretty smooth? I hope I never find out what you'd consider rough, buddy.*

"It's nice to know you still have *some* faith in me," she said aloud.

"What do we do now?" Joseph asked.

"Well, you guys can go play," Joat told them. "Rand and I will wait for our contact." She put her feet up on the console and leaned back in her chair, arms behind her head: "To contact us."

"What about selling our cargo?" Alvec asked.

"Don't be silly, Al. Who ever heard of shipping laser tubes to Schwartztarr?"

Joat watched the ground-crawler take the two men towards the buildings at the edge of the spaceport. It was a long low flatbed, born on a dozen man-high wheels, with an armored cab at both ends; a heavy laser was mounted on a scarf-ring above each of the cabs. As she watched the crawler fade into the blowing snow one of the gunners swiveled his weapon and fired into the brawling whiteness. The beam itself was invisible, but it cut a tunnel of exploding steam through the snow. At the far end something unseen gave a screaming bellow that faded into a series of snarls.

"Nice planet," Joat said.

"Low salubrity rating," Rand replied seriously. "Nice compared to Kolnar, maybe. There is a man requesting entrance."

"Let him in," she said.

"What do you mean, five thousand?"

The man sitting across from Joat was almost a clone of the man who'd first contacted her; pale, thin, with a beard. The bulky furs and the snow melting on them were different, as was the heavy explosive-bullet slug-thrower he cradled in one arm.

He shrugged his narrow shoulders and said with a sneer: "That's what my principals have authorized me to pay you. Take it or leave it. But, uh, you're goin' to owe me something if you leave it."

"Oh?"

"Yeah, you were given an advance to cover shipping expenses. Remember."

"I agreed to do this for twenty-five thousand, plus shipping expenses. If you've decided to shortchange me on this you're the one breaking the contract, not me."

Joat glared at him and added mentally, *You oily little weasel*.

"Contract!" He laughed explosively, leaning back in his chair. "What, somebody signed a contract for this? You think I'm stupid?"

"It's implied," she said evenly. "A verbal contract is still a valid contract."

"So take us to court! You got a case, right? So sue us. Just tell the judge that you agreed to ship stolen information for a ridiculous amount of credits and we only want to pay you a part of it. You can't lose!"

Joat schooled her face to cold disdain, an expression Channa had taught her. The courier seemed to find it excruciatingly funny. At last he looked away, waving a pleading hand.

"Ooh, ooh this has gotta stop, ooh wow!" He shook his head and grinned. "Look," he said reasonably. "If you decide not to take the five thousand and to keep the datahedron, all you got is something you can't use and you can't sell and you're out five thousand. Plus, you owe me two thousand." He stopped and glared at her through narrowed eyes. "And lady, you *will* pay me that two thousand. So where does that leave you? Broke on Schwartztarr with a cargo load of laser tubes. Nobody here is going to buy laser crystals! I'm not stupid, y'know."

"I *know* that nobody on Schwartztarr is going to buy the fardling laser crystals. I'm not stupid either. If the authorities want to think I'm a moron, fine, let 'em. But you *know* why I'm here, so what's your excuse?"

"Okay," he said in astonishment holding his hands up palms out. "C'mon, you had to know that twenty-five thousand was way too high for a low-risk job like this, huh? You're not stupid, right? Look, you can only lose here. Just take the credits and maybe I can find you somethin' else to do for us. Huh?"

Joat glared at him, her lips a tight line. Then she nodded.

"But I want payment now."

"Okay," he said sullenly.

She called up the branch of her bank that did business on Schwartztarr and spoke the keying phrase that opened up an account, then hit a key that transmitted her account number and the location of the home branch along with her account's most recent update in a single rapid burst. Withdrawals, of course, were much more complex.

Her contact slid over to her terminal and entered a credit chip, transmitting authorization to delete five thousand from it and transfer it to her account.

She handed him the datahedron.

"I don't like being cheated," she told him.

"No, well, life's a lesson, y'know. Separates the smart from the stupid," he said. His grin disappeared behind goggles and face-mask as he fastened his parka.

Joat stood and followed him down through the corridors.

"Sayonara, stupidissimo," she muttered as the hatch closed behind him. "Think he bought it?" she asked Rand.

"He gave every indication of doing so. What will his reaction be when he discovers what we've done?"

"Violent, I expect," Joat said. "Why do you think I locked the hatch?"

She picked up a note screen and stylus and sat down facing her largest screen. "Play the recording of that Nomik Ciety hedron, would you, Rand?"

Rand began playing back the recording and Joat sat quietly, scribbling a note now and then on her belt unit. The hedron described Ciety's lifestyle and career, noting that very little was known of his past; presently he seemed to be living up to the Middle-Level Organized

Crime stereotype. There was a long section on his known associates and henchmen which also lacked significant background information.

As the information rolled by, augmented by numerous holos of Ciety and his people, Joat struggled to concentrate. Now that the shock of rediscovering him was past, she was able, to a degree, to achieve an emotional distance from the man on the screen.

When it was over she sat for a while, her face expressionless, and stared into space, struggling to keep the memories out.

Amos first! she told herself fiercely over and over. *Amos must come first!*

"They've obviously spent a great deal to erase their early histories," Rand observed.

Joat blinked and nodded.

"Yes," she agreed leadenly.

"You were most inattentive the first time we played this, Joat. That's quite unlike you," it observed.

She turned her chair to look at it. Its lights were a flickering mix of colors—Rand's "neutral" face.

"You noticed that?" she murmured.

"I don't think the others did," Rand hastened to reassure her. "But you became quite pale for a moment, and when Joseph touched you, your reaction was uncharacteristically violent. Just now your heartbeat is elevated. Is there something we should know?"

"Maybe," she said thoughtfully. "I'll have to think about it."

"You're a good cook, Joe," Joat yawned.

"It is a manly skill," Joseph answered seriously, sliding the sausages onto her plate.

"Alvec?"

"He will return later." Joseph waved the frying pan under the cleaner, then racked the utensil. "Joat . . .

he went away with this woman that he met. She was an amazon, Joat, truly. As tall as Amos and as muscular as I am. She had an expression on her face that had me stammering an apology the instant that I saw it."

"What'd you do?" Joat asked, interested.

"Nothing. I *knew* that I had done nothing to offend her, but still, *I'm sorry* came dribbling out of my mouth before I could stop myself. And then Alvec introduced her as his Rose and she melted. She giggled and covered her mouth with her hand like a shy maiden, and she blushed bright pink! If you saw her, Joat, you would imagine that such a woman would have to think hard for a good five minutes to even remember *how* to blush." He paused for a moment. "Do you know, she could have been the sister of the Rose he met on New Destinies."

Smiling fondly, Joat nodded.

"Yeah, they're a lot alike, every Rose in his 'bouquet'—that's Al's term for the bunch of them—is just like the next one. Y'know, he's stayed friends with all of 'em, and there must be scores of them by now." She shook her head. "You're right, it's remarkable."

"Has he ever failed in his wooing?" Joseph asked.

"Not that I'm aware of. See, he's completely sincere, he really adores his Roses." She grinned. "That's very seductive."

"Ah, yes, I do see." He pursed his lips thoughtfully. "I do not think that I would be so easily seduced though."

Joat supressed a smile, thinking, *How the heck would you know? After the dance Rachel led you, would you even recognize a seduction that didn't include a slap in the face?*

"Are you susceptible to romance, my friend?" Joseph prodded.

She folded her hands on her stomach and stared at the ceiling thoughtfully.

"Oh, I suppose I enjoy a nice episode of boot-licking flattery as much as the next person. But I'm not inclined to let it turn my head like Al's Roses do. I'm no kind of flower when you come right down to it."

"I think of my Rachel as an althea," Joseph murmured, his face dreamy. "A flower of very subtle beauty."

Joat blinked. Joseph as a romantic was always a revelation to her. And to be honest, Rachel's beauty was of a very subtle order indeed, for Joat herself had never seen it.

"All women resemble some flower," he insisted. "Even you, my friend."

"Yeah, well, maybe one of those flesh eating ones," Joat conceded, grinning. She shook her head ruefully. "You know, I think you're all incredibly brave."

Joseph looked at her questioningly.

"Channa and Amos," she clarified. "And you. I can't see how you do it, no matter how much it hurts, you just keep coming back for more. It amazes me."

He still looked puzzled.

"Amos and Channa's love does bring them pain," he agreed. "But it also blesses them with much joy. As to myself, you puzzle me, my friend. I am very happily married. Why do you include me in your number of the brave?"

"I was thinking of the early days of your relationship with Rachel. Everything is great now, but I haven't forgotten the sight of her hitting you in the face 'till her hand bled."

He cocked his head at her.

"I must ask you to be fair, Joat. My Rachel was not at her best at the time."

Joat spluttered into her coffee.

"You have a gift for understatement, Joe. I think you're brave because no matter what she did, no matter what she said, no matter how much it hurt you, you were there for her and you never stopped loving her." Her eyes revealed the puzzled amazement that she always felt when she thought about this. "I can't imagine leaving myself open like that. I can't help but think, what's the *matter* with these people, do they like pain and misery? Oh, and let's not forget the humiliation."

Joseph smiled at her warmly.

"It is just that you have never been in love, my friend. When you are in love even pain can seem sweet if it allows you a glimpse of your beloved. I will pray that you may know it soon."

"Gee, thanks Joe," she said dryly. "I'll pray for your mental health too. Wha . . . !"

Alvec had suddenly leapt into the galley where they were sitting, arms open wide he began to sing:

"Her skin is soft and tender as the petals of a rose and her eyes are as bright as the dew.
Come into my arms, O my Rose of the stars and I swear I will always love you."

Joat raised an eyebrow.

"Had a good time did you?"

Alvec put his hand over his heart, closed his eyes and sighed.

"I did," he shook his head, smiling, "I really did."

As Joat muttered, "Nuts . . . , you're all nuts!" he bounded over to a cupboard and pulled out a coffee, peeled back the heat seal and inhaled as steam rose in a fragrant puff.

"Mmm mm," he said and took a sip. "So! How'd it go, Captain?"

She grimaced. "About as we expected. We were royally cheated. He only paid me five thousand credits and told me it was a life lesson. Can you believe it?"

Alvec scowled and shook his head sadly.

"The nerve'a some people. What's the universe

comin' to, when even smugglers and gunrunners can't be relied on?"

"I am a little surprised that we have not heard back from them by now," Joseph said. "In my experience, such people are not inclined to merely shrug philosophically and go on to the next thing."

Joat grimaced and shrugged.

"It was either going to be an immediate reaction," Rand said. "Or not. For all we know he took it off-planet."

Alvec rolled his eyes.

"Bite your tongue! If you had one," he said. "If that's the case we might not hear from them for months. And we sure can't afford to wait around here for someone to get around to getting mad at us."

"No," Joat said looking a little lost, "we can't. I hadn't really thought of no one coming after us at all."

"Oh, do not worry, Joat, Alvec," Joseph said sympathetically, "I am certain that very soon a heavily armed and angry band of smugglers will be beating upon your hatch crying out for your blood. You mustn't lose faith."

Joat laughed, but before she could speak, Rand broke in.

"In fact, there is a party approaching *Wyal* now, Joat. I have them onscreen on the bridge. Come and have a look at them."

The day had dawned with the aching clarity of deep cold; the sky was a pale blue-green arch above, with both moons full and looking like translucent globes on the horizon. On the main screen was a view of a very expensive landcar just pulling to a stop at the base of the *Wyal*, crisp snow squeaking under its wheels. Both front doors opened and from each a man with the squat, square build of a heavy-worlder emerged. They advanced with the economic efficiency of battle cruisers and their heads swung like gun turrets, ceaselessly examining their surroundings for any threat.

One stumped over to the rear door of the glossy landcar and opened it. A woman emerged.

Alvec gave a long whistle. "Not my type," he said. "But that's *something*."

"It is hard to believe she is of the same species as her guards," Joseph said seriously.

"All of that party are *homo sapiens*," Rand said.

Alvec snorted. "You wouldn't understand."

Her long black hair lay in a thick, glassy braid on her shoulder, its color stark against the pale green of her exquisitely cut thermal suit. She moved towards the *Wyal* with the grace of flowing water. All three of them wore wraparound eye protection against Schwartztarr's harsh sun. As one, they raised their heads to study *Wyal*'s height.

"A living cliché," Joat said, feeling an odd mixture of awe and amusement. "You fellas reel in your tongues, now."

She knew the woman. Her name was Silken—no known last name—she was Ciety's second in command, his lover, according to CenSec. A gangster's "moll" and her "torpedoes" in ancient Earth parlance.

"She's a nice lookin' girl," Alvec said judiciously.

Joat grinned over her shoulder at him. "But she's no Rose, am I right?"

"No, ma'am."

"She is no althea, either," Joseph said with a grim smile.

"Permission to board," the woman said, as though repeating a formula rather than making a request. Her voice was soft and pleasant. Her companions waited with a boulder patience that somehow had an edge of spring-steel readiness.

"This is Captain Simeon-Hap. May I ask your business?"

Silken took off her glasses and stared into the pickup. "I'm sure you know who I am, as well as why I'm here. I'd prefer to discuss our business in private—you know why, as well."

Well, Joat thought. *Right to the point.*

"And I'm sure that you'll understand Ms. . . . ," Joat paused to allow the woman to introduce herself. After a moment of silence she continued: "Uh, that your companions make me nervous."

The beautiful face smiled. "If we were here to hijack you, Captain, I assure you, you wouldn't be aware of us until we were on your bridge. However, there *is* a limit to how much openness I'd consider healthy for both of us. I repeat, we need to talk."

"I'm unwilling to allow either of your companions to board."

"Don't be ridiculous. I'm not going up there alone!"

"We're not about to kidnap you, lady, not so . . . openly," Joat said sarcastically.

"You have two crewmen aboard," the woman said, her eyes flashing. "I'm not willing to be alone under those circumstances."

"My crew are trained to stand a watch, distribute cargo, fill out manifests and keep the ship functioning. Your friends appear to have benefited from . . . another kind of training altogether." *Like how to turn people's heads around so they can look down between their shoulder blades.* Aloud she said, "May I suggest a compromise?"

"Please. Do."

"One of your people stays with your landcar, one stays by the lock with my crewmen, and you join me on the bridge for a private talk."

The woman considered it. Joat thought she was going

to refuse, then she put her glasses back on decisively and nodded.

"All right. That's acceptable."

Joat keyed the lift, raising her other hand to still the protests. "With you masters of self-defense on hand, what do I have to worry about?"

"Energy weapons, capture, torture, death," Joseph suggested.

"Masters!" Alvev said. "Oh, good. I would've been *worried* if I didn't know that."

"Go on and meet them," Joat said. She put a hand on each rocklike shoulder and shoved gently. "I'm a big girl now."

She should have been in the vids, Joat thought. *That entrance was a masterpiece.* As if Silken entering a room automatically made her the most important thing in it.

"Yes?" the Captain of the *Wyal* said after a moment's silence.

Silken simply stood in the center of the room and held up the blue datahedron that Joat had transported. Her gaze stayed unfocused, only the tapping of one slim booted foot demanding attention.

It's times like this I'm really glad I'm a woman, Joat thought complacently.

Joat reclined in the pilot's crash-couch, her legs crossed, hands loosely clasped on her stomach. She raised a brow and spoke again, with just a shade more emphasis:

"Yes?"

After a moment Silken sighed in irritation. She put one hand on her hip and flicked the datahedron with one manicured nail.

"This," she said, "is garbage."

"No," Joat assured her, "it's good."

Silken turned slowly towards her, between clenched teeth she asked, "Then why can't I read it?"

"You can't read it because it scrambles every time you try to access it." Joat blinked at her and beamed an innocent smile. "It can be fixed very easily."

"Then I suggest that you do so." Silken held the hedron out to her and walked towards the pilot's station.

Hey, nice slink, Joat thought. *Pity it's wasted on me— I wonder if I could learn to walk like that?*

"There is a problem," Joat said regretfully, ignoring Silken's outstretched hand. "Your agents shortchanged me."

"I don't see how that's my concern," Silken told her, simply opening her fingers and dropping the data-hedron into Joat's lap. Raising one exquisite brow she asked: "You're not trying to shake me down for more credits, are you?" Then she leaned towards Joat until their faces were mere inches apart. "You couldn't possibly be that stupid." Her green eyes narrowed dangerously. "Could you?"

Joat looked back at her. "Would you please get out of my face?" she asked politely.

Silken straightened in surprise. Then she laughed. "You *must* be crazy! Don't you know who I am?"

Joat felt an almost pleasant rush of nostalgia. *Stationer kids on the docks used to act that way.* Expecting you to know and genuflect to their little play hierarchy; and they didn't know squat about the really important shipside ones.

"Actually, no, I don't know who you are, since you haven't bothered to introduce yourself." Joat waved that aside. "Not that it matters. What matters is, I negotiated my fee for delivery of this little treasure right at the outset. When I arrived here I was due twenty-five thousand credits."

Silken's face reflected her disbelief.

"You can't be serious," she said scornfully. "The job wasn't worth that! No one would agree to that figure."

"Look." Joat held up her hands. "I put my ship and my reputation on the line when I took your shipment; and I deliver on time and in good condition—it's all in my record. If reliability like that is too expensive, then no, you *shouldn't* be doing business with me. I fulfilled my side of the bargain. I am now owed twenty thousand credits. Upon receipt of the outstanding amount, you will receive your shipment. Unscathed. That's it."

Silken must have realized that her mouth was open because she closed it with an audible *clop*.

"You're . . . serious," she whispered, and shook her head in wonder. "Well," she said and looked around for someplace to sit down, "this is refreshing."

Joat looked at her sympathetically. "Honest dealing saves so much time!" she said earnestly. "Had I been paid, you wouldn't be here; you'd be accessing that hedron." She placed a hand on her chest. "But you must see that I can't allow myself to be cheated, it sets a bad precedent. And think about it, if he cheated me, he's cheating you."

"Of course he's cheating me," Silken said with a condescending little moue. She settled herself with cat-like delicacy onto the navigator's chair. "Everyone cheats in this business."

"Not me," Joat said. "That's a fool's game and I don't have time for it. You can accomplish a lot more if you're not dividing your energy that way." She looked the other woman in the eye. "Pay me and I can clear that data in a few seconds. I'd like to do that for you."

Silken narrowed her green eyes. "Do you know what I can do to you?" she asked.

Now, that was a mistake. You should do menace *cold. You don't have the facial bones for direct threats.* In fact, she looked a little like an angry kitten.

Joat shrugged. "That's kind of irrelevant, isn't it? What really matters to you is that you'll lose any advantage that datahedron offers *and* everything you've invested in it up to this point. Although to be perfectly fair, if we can't come to an agreement on this I really should refund you the five thousand that your agent paid me yesterday."

Joat blinked in astonishment as Silken laughed and lay back in the navigator's recliner.

"Surreal," the other woman said. "This conversation is . . . *surreal.* Call up your account and I'll give you the damned credits."

When they'd completed the transaction, Silken studied Joat slyly for a moment and then shook her head.

"So, you're an honest woman, are you?"

"I hope so," Joat said. "It's what I aim for."

Silken chuckled.

"Would you consider starting fresh with me?" she asked. "I'd hate to leave you with the impression that I'm not. Honest, that is." With a mischievous smile, Silken cocked her head, inviting Joat to share her amusement.

"What did you have in mind?" Joat asked cautiously.

"Something difficult. Something for which we need that someone who *couldn't* be cheated and *can* be trusted." She stretched. "Shall we send your man for it? The short, blond, yummy one, not the gorilla."

The box that Joseph brought to the bridge had a simple elegance. Made of some dark wood, polished to a satin smoothness, it was the size and shape of an ordinary jewelry box, the type that women had kept on their dressers for centuries.

Silken keyed open its lock with a series of deft touches, her hand hiding the combination. Then she turned the box around to face Joat before she opened it. Her eyes sparkled teasingly.

As the lid slowly came up, Joat gasped. It was full almost to overflowing with Sainian crown rubies. The jewels glowed blood red and deep within each of them flared the glint of gold that marked them of first quality. Irregular and flat sided, each one was as large as Silken's small fist.

Sainian crown rubies came from nowhere near the crown of the Sainians who produced them. Originally they'd been called *mouth-rubies*, a more honest appellation—and one that jewelry makers felt might interfere with sales.

Crown rubies were an organic jewel produced as a result of what was, to a Sainian, a socially embarrassing gastric disorder. The gentle, sophisticated Sainians were both amused and repelled that humans could so prize what was essentially . . . drool. Solidified spittle. Absolutely nothing would induce them to produce the rubies if it could be avoided and of course, they were almost always of modest size.

The ones in Silken's box were enormous compared to the general run.

"Wow!" Joat whispered hoarsely. She looked up. "Are they real?"

Silken raised a brow, "Of course." She took one and held it up to the light. "Look at it, see the gold flashes deep within? They can't duplicate that yet. And smell." She held the stone out to Joat, who sniffed. Responsive to the heat of Silken's skin it smelled delicately musky. "They can't even begin to duplicate that."

"It's just . . . they're so *big*," Joat said with wonder.

Silken smiled and the muscles in Joat's back seized up at the sight.

"Everything has its price," Silken purred.

Joat refused to let herself wonder what would cause a Sainian to produce such stones. But she knew at that moment that she should never turn her back on this woman. This kitten had a tiger's claws.

"I need these beauties shipped to Rohan." Silken replaced the stone reluctantly, as if she hated to give up the feeling of the jewel beneath her fingers. "Ever heard of it?"

"It's a moon," Joat said. "With a freeport Station, over a gas-giant named Eglund. I've never been there, but I've heard about it."

"I'm sure you have," Silken said smugly. "It's *the* destination for most of the quality stuff we . . . freetraders ship. Consider yourself lucky to have won this consignment. Especially under the circumstances." She held up the now descrambled datahedron. "Once you're on Rohan, and it becomes known that you've worked for me you'll have no difficulty finding lucrative cargo, I promise you. Consider it a bonus for the inconvenience my agents have caused you."

Joat chuckled appreciatively. "Sounds great," she said. "Now, let's discuss price."

"What we need to discuss," Silken said emphatically, all trace of good humor gone, "is what will happen if you get too enterprising with my jewels."

"I've already told you my thoughts about dishonest dealing," Joat said, her eyes unflinching. "I don't have anything to add. Now. What are you paying me to ship these?"

A short, sharp exchange of offer and counteroffer ensued. Joat achieved a price slightly higher than what she'd have settled for, with half to be paid immediately. Best of all she knew that she had achieved a degree of respect in Silken's tiger green eyes.

Joat offered a celebratory cup of coffee from her stores and Silken accepted.

"I'd prefer, say, a nice Chablis," Silken remarked.

Joat grinned and tossed her a sealed container she plucked from a storage cabinet.

"Sorry," she said. "But this is Mocha Java. You'll like it, I promise. Now, is there anything else I should know?" Joat asked, sipping the hot, fragrant brew.

Silken raised a brow. "Such as?"

"Is Central Worlds after your box of goodies?"

"Mmmm," Silken murmured. "Good question. They don't know about it, no. But . . . I'm always watched and they like to . . . discuss me with anyone I've spent time with." She sipped delicately. "You may be sure they'll talk to you. Where, when and in what fashion I really couldn't say. But I'd advise you to hide my beauties carefully. I shouldn't like to have them fall into Central Worlds' hands."

Gah! Joat thought, *this woman could say "I love you," and make it sound ominous. I wonder if she could go ten minutes without making a dire threat.* It was all done very elegantly, but she suspected that after a couple of days in Silken's company the impulse to smack her one would become overwhelming.

"This consignment is to be delivered to Nomik Ciety," Silken was saying. "His is a very important name on Rohan, so you should have no trouble finding him. I must insist that delivery be made within the next eight days. That *is* possible?"

"No problem," Joat assured her.

"Then I'll leave you to your preparations," Silken said and rose. She held out her hand and Joat rose to take it. "It's been a pleasure, and most interesting, doing business with you," she said, her sweet mouth lifted in a genuine smile. "I'll look forward to seeing you on Rohan."

"In the deserts west of the Deathangel Mountains," Joseph said thoughtfully, looking at the hatch, "there are serpents of great beauty. The patterns of their scales are like living jewels. They also have," he went on, "venom of surpassing deadliness—a man they bite will be dead before his body strikes the ground."

Alvec nodded. "Yup. And if one of 'em bit her, the *snake* would die."

"The combination is as follows," Rand broke in.

Joat put the box down on the mess table and touched the sensitized plate in the order the AI indicated.

Nothing. "You *sure* you got that?"

"I have a sensor directly behind the position Ms. Silken occupied," Rand said.

Did I write a subroutine with sulky in it? Joat wondered. She tried the combination again.

"Subtle," Joseph said.

"It must be a bio-lock," Rand explained. "Responding only to her touch." It paused for a moment. "Some of the more sophisticated models will record whether anyone has attempted to open them."

"Oh, well," Joat said. "There's subtle, and then there's whatever works."

She stood, braced the box down on the table with her left hand, and twitched her right. The vibroknife keened, then screeched in a high electronic wail as she jammed it into the lock. Fire and sparks spurted out of the box, mixed with the scents of scorched metal, synthetic, and wood. Joat twitched her hand again, and the handle of the knife slid back into the sleeve of her overall.

"*There,*" she said.

Joseph whispered softly in his own language. Alvec swore.

"Why would she trust you with this? Especially after what happened with the datahedron. It don't make sense." He rubbed his jaw and thick stubble grated.

"Smugglers, excuse me, *freetraders* are cautious to the point of paranoia. And she gives you this."

"The thing is," Joat said, shaking out a piece of cloth and carefully placing the rubies on it, "I don't think Silken, Ciety and Co. think of us as regular smugglers. We're not in that network, we don't know people who are, and we don't have any friends among 'em." She took out an optical intensifier from her kit and clenched it in one eye, holding up a ruby and studying it.

Joseph leaned back and made his joined hands disappear inside the sleeves of his robe, a Bethelite gesture. "Joat, you describe to perfection someone who may be killed with impunity."

"Yup, once their brief usefulness is past."

"Cleared for takeoff."

"Launch," Joat said.

"Execute," Rand replied.

"And so as our ship sinks slowly in the west and the sun pulls away from the dock, we bid farewell to Schwartztarr, exotic land of smugglers, fences, weapons factories, and big furry animals with long, sharp teeth," Joat intoned.

The *Wyal* flung itself at the sky. Alvec leaned back and cracked his knuckles; Joat winced. *He knows I hate it when he does that.*

"Boss," he said after a moment. "How the *hell* did you manage to sell laser tubes on Schwartztarr?"

Joat grinned. "Well, to a laser manufacturer who'd just gotten a big export order. Spared him the time it would take subcontractors to deliver the components, and it was a pre-tested shipment. Then I bought some electronic components and laser crystals."

Joseph frowned and worked out what he was going to say carefully. "Are laser crystals better than laser tubes?" he said slowly.

"Trust me," Joat said smugly. "In fact—"

"I'm detecting an approaching ship," Rand said. "It's just entered *Wyal*'s sensor range."

"Any special reason you mention it?" Joat asked.

"It's a Central Worlds Navy ship," Rand said apologetically. "A customs corvette."

"Oh no," Alvec said and covered his eyes with one square hand. "Just what we needed. We've got a cargo of knocked-down weapons and we're heading for *Rohan* and a customs gunboat stops us."

"Don't be so guilty, Al," Joat said with a confident smile. She suppressed an impulse to rub her stomach, where lunch had turned to a cold, congealing lump. *Schwartztarr food*, she told herself. It tended to the heavy, meat and potatoes and dumplings.

Joseph came in looking sleepy.

"Rand woke me," he explained. "It says we are being approached by a customs corvette."

"Which hasn't even hailed us, for cryin' out loud!" Joat snapped, "Rand!" in exasperation.

"Attention Merchanter *Wyal*, registry number 776445X. This is Central Worlds Customs ship *Charger*. Commander Chang-Yarimizu speaking. Please stand by to be boarded."

"Until now," she said, and sighed. "Oh, well, I guess I should be thankful it's not a brainship anyway. Can you imagine what Simeon would say?"

✧ CHAPTER NINE

Bros Sperin sat hunched over his screen in the hidden security office of The Anvil.

"Police archive," he said to the machine. "Crossref, *Ciety, Nomik*, crossref, alias—"

There was always a hope of finding something useful on his quarry. He had a fairly complete dossier on Nomik Ciety, including the supposedly sealed files on his dreamdust detox with its sensitive psych counseling.

"Amazing how everything just happened to get wiped when Ciety was released," he muttered to himself.

The psych file really *had* been sealed; physically disconnected from the system. Even the best worm program would have problems with that—although there was something still lurking in the far reaches of the net, waiting to pounce on any mention of Ciety's name.

Sperin smiled. He liked an agile opponent; it made the game more interesting. Ciety seemed to be agile enough to fool a prison shrink, certainly. He might have kicked the dust, but that just made him more efficient at his sociopathic games.

Outstanding warrants:

The screen blinked live and began scrolling. Sperin's eyebrows stretched skyward. This was just the *new* stuff, the offenses since his release, supposedly "reformed."

It was his first concentrated effort to gain a true picture of Nomik Ciety, the man and his methods, not just the haphazard files of those trying to catch the man.

From behind him one of the agents manning a security terminal made a strangled sound.

"Good grief!"

Bros turned: "What is it?"

The man gestured at the screen, speechless. Bros walked to the agent's station and leaned over his shoulder to look into the monitor.

An extremely elderly Sondee had entered the bar.

To other species male and female Sondee looked exactly alike, so it was impossible to guess the oldster's gender. Though in the ultraviolet range the sex difference between male and female Sondee was glaringly obvious.

The fact that most other species couldn't appreciate this was unfortunate, the Sondee agreed, but they still found it appalling, embarrassing, and gauche that anyone would ask such a personal and irrelevant question as *What gender are you?* Which they interpreted as being asked—essentially—*What is the shape, color, and texture of your genitals?*

To accommodate their androgynous appearance linguistically, individual Sondee were "et"; the term having been coined because "it" was deemed derogatory. The problem with that was that in most Sondee languages *not* specifying an addressee's gender was a gross insult.

Fortunately for everyone else's peace of mind Sondee who dealt with other species on a regular basis were gracious enough to make an admission of gender part of their introduction.

The ancient Sondee standing just inside the doorway of The Anvil cupped ets withered hands protectively over the delicate whorled ridges that served as ears, and looked slowly around as though seeking someone.

Ets two main eyes, though bright and golden, seemed sunken in pale, loose flesh. The upper eyes, which saw into the ultraviolet ranges, were actually closed, as though their owner was too weary to deal with the extra layer of information they would provide. The small, suckerlike mouth was pinched closed, as though in disapproval. It would suddenly expand to gasp in air, then pinch closed again.

The Sondee slowly blinked. Then, with tottering steps, et began to struggle across the club towards the bar.

Clearly, no one in The Anvil had ever seen a Sondee of such antiquity. Conversations stopped and even the band faltered for a beat as everyone watched et pass.

Using the backs of chairs and the edges of tables to keep etself upright on the journey, the old Sondee nodded politely to the owner of the occasional shoulder et leaned on.

When at last et reached ets destination, the bartender was waiting to take the Sondee's order. An unusual event in itself.

"Sakurian," the Sondee ordered in a voice like a creaking hinge.

Jaws dropped all around.

The Sondee were held to have the most beautiful voices in Central Worlds. Every one of them might have been a professional opera singer if it pleased them, and musically they'd easily overshadow most humans, however talented.

I don't believe it, Sperin thought. *I don't believe that sound came from a Sondee throat-sac.* Nobody who saw this was *ever* likely to forget it.

"You were . . . expecting a Sondee?" the security op asked Bros tentatively. "Right?"

"Yes," Bros growled. "A male. But I thought they were sending a live one."

◆   ◆   ◆

When the Sondee at last tottered in on the arm of the young woman Bros had sent to fetch et, et instantly reverted to bouncing youth. And before their fascinated eyes began peeling off wattles, warts, and ridges until, with a dramatic gesture, et stood before them, glue-splotched but handsome.

For a Sondee . . .

"Seg !T'sel," et announced in a rich and vibrant voice. "Male, of the Clenst Defense Group. At your service!"

Bros stood looking at Seg with his arms crossed, hands clutching his arms. *I will not try to strangle him,* he thought, mastering his emotions with a wrenching effort. *I will not.*

"Mr. !T'sel," he said. "This was supposed to be a *confidential* meeting. Would you care to explain yourself?"

"Ah. Well," somewhat crestfallen, the young Sondee shrugged. "My, ah, my hobby . . ." He colored gently: first the ear whorls and then, slowly, the rest of his face flushed a delicate blue. "My hobby is disguise," Seg murmured. "I couldn't resist the opportunity."

"Well," Bros said with a bright, toothy smile. "As long as no one happens to be looking for a Sondee behaving in an unusual manner, there shouldn't be a problem."

Bros indicated a conference room and with a gesture invited Seg to precede him into it.

"But now that you've removed your makeup," he said, "how are we going to explain your present appearance? I'll tell you this, Mr. !T'sel, if I were sitting out there and watched you come in old and go out young, I'd be beating down the door, demanding some of whatever we gave you."

Seg chuckled nervously and sat down, folding his long, four-fingered hands before him on the table.

"Shall we proceed to the purpose of this meeting?" the young Sondee asked, somewhat desperately.

"One moment," Bros murmured, settling his long muscular form in the chair opposite. He reached into his belt pouch and withdrew a small oval antieaves-dropping device. He pushed a red button to activate it and placed it on the table before him. "Proceed," he said.

In his element, !T'sel launched into lecture mode and seemed immediately older and more confident.

"As you know, Mr. Sperin, The Clenst Defense Group works closely with the Central Worlds Navy research divisions. Recently, the Navy presented us with a range of biological weapons developed by a rogue group of Phelobites for the illegal arms market."

"Rogue Phelobite is a little redundant, isn't it Mr. !T'sel?" Bros murmured.

"Ah . . . ," Seg shrugged and looked uncomfortable.

The Clenst Defense Group by its very nature was called upon to work closely with weapons manufac-turers. Phelobites were unquestionably the premier arms manufacturers for Central Worlds. Officially, they adhered to all of the regulations and accords that being a member of Central Worlds called for, including those that banned the manufacture and sale of certain classes of armament. Unofficially, they would make and sell anything to anybody for the right price if they thought there was a good chance of getting away with it.

In most Phelobite languages, the word for *altruism* translated roughly as "sucker."

It was an open secret that did little to endear them to most of Central Worlds, including the Clenst Defense Group. Who nonetheless felt compelled to maintain a diplomatic silence regarding the Phelobites' less socially acceptable business practices.

Seg stretched his fingers and then folded his hands again.

"There are several bio-weapons that are particularly dangerous that we've been working intensively to find counteragents for."

"Why not just buy 'em from the Phelobites?" Bros asked reasonably.

"Apparently," Seg said nervously, "they never got around to developing them."

Bros sat up straight and folded his hands before him on the conference table, mirroring Seg !T'sel's posture.

"Go on," he said.

"All of these diseases attack the brain or nervous system on some level. Their premiere creation, and the one we're most concerned with, has the effect of destroying the memory center of the brain. Fairly rapidly and with, unfortunately, permanent results. It's highly contagious, primarily airborne, but can also be transmitted through handling things that have recently been touched by an infected person. We estimate that perhaps twenty humans in a hundred will have a natural immunity to it. Actually, we believe that's part of the design, predicated on the idea that one person afflicted will need two or more to take care of them. Obviously," Seg spread his hands in a gesture of appeal, "if this disease were released on a planet the results would be . . . catastrophic."

"To put it mildly," Bros agreed. He wasn't ready to ask questions yet, though he sensed where this lecture was leading.

"Yes. Well," Seg continued. "Three others that we received samples of, from a package of brain or nervous system influencing agents this pirate company has been marketing, are not diseases, exactly. But we've found that a subject can be immunized against them as though they were. However, they're not something we would wish to fall into the wrong hands." He glanced nervously at Bros. "They seem to have been developed with the dual aim of acting as methods of discipline and interrogation. The first creates intense pain, the second intense fear, the third produces euphoria and an overwhelming desire to please."

Here the scientist in him took over, and he said enthusiastically: "The degree of control is exquisite! The timespan and extremity of effect are determined at the time the dose is made up. And the effects may last only seconds or permanently; in other words, at the discretion of the user."

Bros caught his eye at this point and Seg dampened his enthusiasm. "Um, physical side effects will vary depending on how long the dosage lasts. The pain bug can cause neurological damage in very high doses, the fear instigator is likely to produce psychological problems in most people, which the pleasure bug may, depending upon what the victim has been required to do. You see they act by exciting certain glands or in the case of the pain drug by exciting the synapses . . ."

Bros was holding up his hand.

"Before we get too involved in the actual workings of this stuff, why are you here?" he asked. He thought he knew, and he was impatient to hear it said, to have his worst fears made real. *Anxiety is worse than pain. Pain does not hurt; the fear of pain hurts.*

The Sondee studied his folded hands for a moment, then looked directly across at Sperin.

"We succeeded in developing a serum for the memory wiping disease. A simple injection will immunize a subject. It cannot reverse damage already done, unfortunately, but it can halt the progress of the disease. The counteragents we've developed to the others are, unfortunately, less effective and require a stepped series of injections. But then, we'd really only begun research

on them. I'm sure we would have come up with something more effective if given time."

Bros waved his hand in a rotary motion, "And the
reason you're telling me all this is . . ."

Seg looked down/sideways—a disconcerting sight in
itself—and remained quiet for a time, as though
gathering his thoughts. At last he raised his eyes and
looked at Bros again.

"We were due to give a full report to a Navy
representative and had gathered everything together,
samples, both of the diseases and the antidotes and
serum, research, everything we had. It was stolen.
Worse, we subsequently discovered that our information
about the serums had been corrupted. Meaning that
mass production will have to be delayed while crucial
research and testing are duplicated. What we fear is
that someone intends to use these weapons and soon,
while we have no ready supply of counteragents."

Bros sat back slowly, his gaze thoughtful.

"Have you found your spy?" he asked calmly.

"No," Seg told him. "To be honest we consider that
the least of our worries. Our primary interest is to find
where the information went. There are three arms
dealers in particular that Navy intelligence feels are the
most likely candidates for handling this product. Agics
LLege, the Yoered Family and Nomik Ciety.

"I've been assigned to your team because I have
a full understanding of this weapon and clearance to
make any necessary decisions regarding it, or the
stolen information. I also have a full range of shots
to immunize you and your agents. Fortunately we still
had a minute amount of the working samples left in
the lab."

Bros studied the young Sondee scientist. A horrible
suspicion nibbled at the edges of his mind.

"My team? Mr. !T'sel, I can understand the need to

send word of this by courier, and of course the need for these shots is obvious. What I don't understand is why CenSec and Clenst are both willing to put someone of your skills in a position of risk. Do they seriously expect me to take you into the field with me? Is that what you're trying to tell me?"

"This discussion has already taken place at a fairly high level, Mr. Sperin," !T'sel informed him haughtily. He reached into his suit jacket and withdrew a datahedron. "This is a recording of the meeting at which it was decided that whatever happened to the stolen materials was my responsibility. It goes without saying that if that necessitates being called into the field, then I will go."

!T'sel wore the most heroic expression Bros had ever seen on a Sondee outside of an opera. The suspicion hardened into certainty. !T'sel was no doubt as good a scientist as his documentation claimed, but he was a romantic. Specifically, a romantic aficionado of espionage.

Bros restrained an impulse to beat his head against the table. What did CenSec expect him to do? Work miracles? Find the Benisur Amos, find the stolen bioweapons, put the notorious Ciety out of business and shepherd a glory hungry kid-scientist through it all without letting him get scratched?

Sometimes, he thought, *I regret my oath to Central Worlds Security.* He could have been an aquaculture specialist. He could have written dramas for the feelie market. He could . . .

He rose and gestured towards the door. "I'll review this immediately, Mr. !T'sel . . ."

"It's Doctor, actually. But please, sir, call me Seg."

"If you'll promise not to call me sir."

Seg laughed nervously, "Whatever you'd like, Mr. Sperin. I realize calling you *sir* wouldn't be good tradecraft."

The Sondee dropped the term as if it were a magic talisman. *He'd probably like to have a union card with SPY written on it.*

"Bros, call me Bros. But not in front of the people here. Here you'll have to call me Clal." He winced mentally. "That's my cover name. Okay?" Seg nodded eagerly. "Uh, I'll assign someone to help you get settled and tomorrow we'll see if we can come up with a plan." He slapped Seg on the shoulder and guided him out the door. "Don't trust anybody here, Seg. And don't tell them anything."

Bros sent the young Sondee off with one of the younger of Sal's operatives via the back door of the club. His last sight of !T'sel was of the young Sondee looking eagerly back with an expression of abject hero-worship in all four eyes.

With a weary sigh he sank back into his chair, burying his face in his hands.

This was wonderful! Seg's blood bubbled like champagne. He couldn't believe that he had actually met *Bros Sperin.* Had shaken his hand, had *briefed* him, for the love of !Gretz.

He tried to hold his features to a properly cool expression as he followed the young operative Bros had assigned to him. It was hard. *Cool,* he reminded himself. *An experienced agent displays no emotion.* Certainly no *genuine* emotion. He'd practiced fake ones often enough.

Sperin was a legend in the lore of Central Security, and Seg had hunted each and every story about him to the source, confirming every unbelievable tale. *Such panache, such wit, such daring!* he thought. Somehow, Seg had imagined that Mr. Bros Sperin must be dead. Heroes simply didn't live in the same world as industrial scientists.

Not Mister *Bros Sperin,* Seg reminded himself, *but Bros, by !Gretz! He shook my hand and told me to call him Bros.*

Now Seg had only to hope that his supervisor would confirm the alleged field appointment he was supposedly reporting for. Once, the recording—which Bros was probably viewing even now—had merely authorized Sperin to call upon Dr. Seg !T'sel for any advice he needed pertaining to the stolen diseases and their antidotes. But Seg had made a few artistic adjustments to the original, lending a whole new aspect to the tape.

The Directors are a conservative lot, he thought. *Lost in credentialism. Convinced that merely because his* formal *training was in analysis, he couldn't be an effective field operative as well.*

Seg was aware from his research into Bros's exploits that he was careful about details. There was no doubt that in this case one of those details would be to check the contents of the recording Seg had given him with Clenst.

Seg had arranged for any calls regarding himself to be referred to his immediate supervisor. A human—about whom Seg had assembled an intimidating dossier that seemed to confirm his guilt in the theft of the missing diseases.

Actually, Seg had no idea whether his boss was guilty or not, but the appearance was so damning that the man had gone along with his plan.

Hoping, no doubt, that I'd get myself killed, Seg thought happily. *Little did he know.*

Seg was going to be an agent, and he was going to *shine.*

"Oh, great unborn planets," Bros whispered. The documents looked solid. They *were* solid. What on earth were they thinking of, to saddle him with this amateur?

"Run this through for confirmation," he said wearily, and his comp immediately began working.

He sighed. Well, the work he'd already been engaged in was just as pertinent to the new investigation as to the old. His instincts told him that the Kolnari were involved. The symmetry of the whole thing was too perfect; fitting so well with the shape of their defeat and the Kolnari need for revenge. And if the Kolnar were involved then so was Nomik Ciety.

He sat at his computer and began reviewing the latest batch of outstanding warrants he'd been sent.

Words scrolled up the screen, mostly unheeded except for an occasional term or name that Bros registered. His mind was mostly on Joat Simeon. And Joseph ben Said, who had apparently disappeared.

Right into Joat's ship, and for all I know, into her bed, he thought sourly. He hadn't liked the idea of the older man proposing marriage to her. But the memory of her response brought a smile to his lips.

His eye caught a familiar name on a warrant scrolling by and he stopped it, pulled it back down for inspection.

The complaint was ten years old, but might as well have been centuries old for all the effect it'd had. It had been filed by Channa Hap and Simeon, the Brain and Brawn of the SSS-900-C on behalf of their adopted daughter, Joat Simeon-Hap.

Bros sat up and leaned forward. The warrant had been signed out against a Nom Selkirk, Joat's uncle. It seemed the man had lost his seven-year-old niece in a poker game with the captain of a tramp freighter. The child had subsequently been viciously abused and then abandoned on the SSS-900-C. Both Channa and Simeon had demanded some sort of action. They'd gone so far as to post a reward for information.

Nom Selkirk was one of Nomik Ciety's aliases, one of his oldest, perhaps even his real name. *If he has any real name other than* vermin, *or something of that kind.*

The hair crawled on Bros's neck. *And I sent her after him,* he thought with horror. An image of Joat's smile rose in his mind; and the memory of holos taken during the Kolnari occupation of SSS-900-C. Most of which Joat had spent in the ventilation system, planning and executing—literally—her ambushes. During which she'd used a monofilament dispenser to give a whole new layer of meaning to the ancient saying 'Cut them off at the knees.'

If Ciety *was* her uncle, his life wasn't worth spit from the moment Joat landed on the same surface. Not that Ciety would be any loss, but the consequences to the mission . . .

"Outsmarted yourself again," Sperin muttered to himself. "Tell me I'm not as stupid as a vid-series spy. *Please!*"

The customs corvette was a slender needle next to the *Wyal's* torpedo, built to transit atmosphere and fast in space as well. An unpleasant beeping sound echoed over the bridge as the merchantman's sensors picked up the lock-on of the gunboat's particle beam weapons and single torp tube. The corvette came around sharply to match vectors, reached zero-relative velocity, and extended a docking tube.

Joat's eyebrows rose when the airlock door swung open to show the corvette's commander; of course, the crew was only six people, but she'd expected a junior officer.

Commander Chang-Yarimizu stared, nonplused, at Captain Simeon, who stood with her arms outstretched to block his entrance to her hold.

"This device is perfectly safe," he insisted. "Stories of its destructiveness are mere superstitious nonsense."

"Nevertheless," she insisted, "I've got a hold full of extremely delicate electronics. I *can't* afford to take the risk. I'm within my rights Commander, and you know it. I'm not denying you the right of inspection, I'm merely refusing to let you use that instrument."

"But if we do the inspection by hand, Captain, it could take all day, or longer!"

"I'd rather arrive late with a clean cargo than on time with a hold full of trash. This is a freighter, not a garbage scow dumping radioactives! If it takes time, it takes time. I've got nothing to hide, so we'll go through the whole shipment, one item at a time. But I'll tell you this, Commander," Joat waved a stiff forefinger under his nose, "I'm going to protest this! Nothing in my record or reputation could give you reason for this. Nothing!"

"You're going to Rohan, ma'am . . ."

"Captain!"

"Captain. After a conference with a woman who has a reputation a lot less pristine than yours. You're known to have a crushing debt to New Destinies. All in all, it's really not unreasonable to assume that you might have been tempted off the straight and narrow."

"Well, Commander," Joat said, crossing her arms over her chest, "put down that gadget and we'll go discover the truth about that. Shall we?"

Several hours later, Joat and the two luckless sailors assigned to inspect her cargo had finished examining the electronics, now twice reopened and sealed, and were beginning on the laser crystals.

"Lasers?" the Commander said.

"Mining laser crystals. As you'll note, they aren't milspec."

If I have trouble selling those electronics, can I make a claim against customs for making me open up the containers? Joat wondered.

"My fingers hurt," one sailor complained.

"Yeah," Joat agreed, "my cuticles are beginning to peel back." She sighed. "I'm really sorry to put you through this, guys. But what could I do? I don't care what he says about that instrument, too many people have warned me against it."

"I don't think it really causes problems, ma'am. But I can see where you wouldn't want to take a chance," the other sailor said.

They'd gone through several hundred boxes and were beginning to close in on the hidden cache of crown rubies.

Fardles! she thought, *Doesn't that nardy Commander have anything better to do? We've been at this for hours! Surely someone, somewhere is committing a vicious crime that these guys should be trying to stop!*

She reached out and grabbed a box that she knew contained one of the doctored Crown rubies. She could feel the difference in weight. The two sailors reached for two more ruby filled boxes. Her heart began to pound as she readied the lie she'd been preparing.

"What the hell is this?" one of the men asked.

"It's slag," Joat told him taking it out of his hand. "It's what's left over when they've cut the crystals from the matrix they're grown from." *Please,* she thought, *be ignorant about laser crystals. Be dumb, please!*

"Here's another one," said his companion.

Joat opened her box and dumped out the disguised ruby.

"Fardles! I'll bet the rest of the shipment is like this! I should have known better! There's no such thing as a bargain, just deals you regret. I bet I end up paying top dollar for every good crystal I've got." She slammed the ruby back into the box in disgust and tossed the box contemptuously over her shoulder.

"Pereira, Benavides, heads up! We're moving out."

The two sailors put down their boxes with sighs of relief and rose. Stretching to get the kinks out, they smiled at Joat.

"Sorry about the mess," one said.

"Don't worry about it," Joat told them, grinning. "Perils of passage," she assured them.

She rose too and escorted them to the lock that connected her ship to theirs.

The Commander was there and he and Joat gave each other a fish-eyed stare.

"Sorry for the inconvenience," he said stiffly.

"Not at all," she said, smiling. The hatch clanged shut. "You meddling, officious twit!" she added with a snarl, kicking the hatch-cover.

Joseph and Alvec had stayed carefully on the bridge, on the general principle that absent faces generated no awkward questions. Joseph handed her one of the glasses of Arrack he held and Joat took it solemnly. The three of them clicked glasses and drank.

Joat smacked her lips. "I never thought I'd live to say this, but I needed that."

"We better clean up this mess," Alvec said, "and get underway before we attract any more attention."

"Attention," Joseph mused. "True, I am from a backward planet, but still . . . in my trade—" he made a gesture of apology "— which for the moment is yours, Joat . . . drawing attention to oneself is not a good thing."

"Yeah," Alvec said. "And the way we've been going, we've got a great big holo sign reading *Hurrah, We're Here!* welded to the bow of the ship."

Joseph sighed. "I am haunted by the feeling that we have just refused to grasp a lifeline that fate has thrown us. Whatever happens now, my friends, I pray that the

God is watching over us, for I fear we are utterly outside of human help. And too many depend on us for failure to be tolerable."

Joat nodded. If Joseph was right, Amos and his party were in the hands of the Kolnari. She shuddered. *A fate that makes death seem like a fun alternative.*

✧ CHAPTER TEN

"Don't tell me!" Seg said, his long multijointed fingers
dancing over the control console. "You set the customs
corvette onto them!"

"Yes," Bros sighed.

*Remember, he's a romantic, but not necessarily a
complete idiot.* Not intellectually; emotionally yes, but
he could still figure things out. He probably even had
a gifted amateur's grasp of the profession—just enough
to make inspired guesses about thirty percent of the
time, including some occasions when a professional
wouldn't see the unlikely. The rest of the time he'd
be dead wrong and unwilling to admit it.

"Why? Ahhhh . . . to convince their next contact that
they're on the wrong side of the law! That they have
no choice but to descend deeper and deeper into the
depths of crime. And meanwhile, you'll be closing in!
Fiendish!"

Bros frowned. *That* is *my plan, stripped of the
adjectives.* And put like that, it sounded pretty lame,
particularly now that he knew about Nomik Ciety's link
to Joat. Or did it just sound bad because the Sondee
was saying it, with mezzo-soprano warbles of excitement
on the vowels?

Too late to do anything about it now. "Let's go," he
said. The next move would be up to Ciety. Just enough

of his shipping capacity had disappeared for one reason or another to make him pretty desperate; in his line of work, clients didn't really deal well with delays. On the other hand, there hadn't been enough to make him suspect Intelligence was onto him.

Bros hoped.

Silken lay back with a delighted little purr and Nomik laid his head on her bosom. She reached down and stroked his dark blond hair, damp from his exertions.

"You missed me," she said in a pleased little growl.

"You bet I did." He snatched her hand and kissed it. "You're one of a kind, Silky. And there's no substitute for the best."

She laughed and wiggled playfully. He looked up at her and smiled, scooting himself higher in the bed to kiss her. She turned again, sliding out of the bed and padding across the polished black basalt and stark-white Schwartztarr fur rugs to the autobar. She returned with a bottle of champagne and two tall flute cones of carved glass, smoking with chill. He admired the grace of her arm as it curved to pour the priceless Terran wine.

"We *are* good together, aren't we?" she said, slipping back into the satin tangle.

"Especially at times like these," he murmured, winding his arms around her.

The bed rotated and tilted to face the wall that was a single sheet of crystal, giving a view of stark airless white mountains and the banded blue and aquamarine of the gas-giant beyond.

Eventually they leaned companionably against the head of the bed and each other, quietly sipping chilled champagne, filling each other in on their doings.

"I think I may have found a new agent for the organization," Silken confided.

"Oh?"

"I met the most amazing young woman on Schwartz-tarr. She's about my age and owns her own ship. Well, she and her bank. Her reputation is crystal clean, she's considered a fair dealer and she gets her cargo to destination on time and in good condition. She's discreet, she's smart," she glanced over at Nomik, "she's got guts. Would you believe it, she went eye to eye with me over something and didn't blink."

"And you did?"

She laughed. "Yes, I did. I couldn't help it, the woman was right."

"You gave in to her, just because she was right?" Nomik had turned to look at Silken, amazement written all over his face. "I don't believe it. What is this woman . . . a witch?"

"Mmmm, no." She chuckled, "Maybe a kindred spirit. And she *did* have the whip hand." Silken shrugged and he kissed her shoulder. "The thing is," she tapped his nose lightly with one slender finger, "she's got a massive debt to New Destinies. They've fined her a hundred and twenty thousand credits."

He frowned. "What did she do, poison the water, blow a hole in the station, ram a passenger liner?"

"According to my source, she took an unauthorized space-walk and entered the station through an emergency repair hatch."

"That's it?"

"That's it," Silken shrugged, grinning delightedly. "Now, here's my idea. What you could do, is, buy up her debt to New Destinies and offer her the opportunity to work it off."

"You think this paragon will go for that?" Nomik raised an eyebrow. "What about that pristine reputation?"

"I think she'll go for it. She's sure to lose her ship if she doesn't and then what good will her reputation do her? Believe me Mik, she'll repay that debt almost double before she's free. Just keep it light until she's in too deep to turn back. After that, who else is going to ship with her but you?"

"You're always thinking of me aren't you, Silky?" He kissed her and gave her a squeeze.

"Mmm hmm. She'll be with us in a day or so and you can check her out for yourself."

"Why don't I check you out just one more time?" he asked. "Make sure you got home in one piece."

Silken giggled as he rose over her.

The *Wyal* dropped into normal space. Joat blinked at the scanners. For a moment she thought that transition stress had finally gotten to her after all these years.

"There's nothing here!" she said.

"Correction: interstellar gas and micrometeorites," Rand's voice said. "And an F-class star three-point-seven parsecs to the galactic northwest.

"Identify yourself."

Alvec pointed silently to the screens. A ship had been waiting, stealthed, engines on minimal standby to reduce the neutrino signatures of the powerplant. Now it was coming online. Joat glanced at the data. Nothing standard, not a Central Worlds signature, but the emissions were enough for a very large merchantman . . . or a light cruiser.

Kolnari? she thought. The tiny hairs along her spine crinkled erect in atavistic reflex.

"I have visual," Joseph said from the navigator's seat. His voice relaxed from tightly controlled fear to mere tension. "Not Kolnari, I think."

"Guardship," Alvec said.

The image on the screen was the conventional cylinder-and-globe of interstellar ships not meant to transit atmosphere, but with a hacked and haggled look.

Rand spoke. "A modified fast freight carrier," it said. "Mass reduced to increase delta-v. Shield generators, lasers, particle beam weapons, and missile launchers here—" a dot appeared on the image "— here, here. A more precise estimation of capabilities is impossible without information on the craft's computer installations."

Joat pursed her lips. "Highly illegal setup," she said. "And why didn't Silken—" *that lying bitch* "—give me the right coordinates?"

Alvec cleared his throat. "They always do this, Rohan does. Gives 'em a chance to make sure you're not a ringer for the Fleet."

"*You* knew about this arrangement?" she accused, unmollified.

"Yeah, well . . . yuh. Been around here, oh, a while back . . ."

Joat glared at him. Al was their pilot just now, and he didn't look up from his screens. *Ask no awkward questions, get no fibs.* "So, you know anything about Rohan itself?"

"It's a big moon," he said. "Big enough to hold atmosphere if it had one. Be a nice, livable planet if they terraformed it. Cold, though, a long way from the primary."

"Why have they not done so?" Joseph asked.

Alvec laughed. "They're pirates, folks. Building things isn't their strong suit; besides, keeping habitation restricted makes it easier to control traffic. That's why Yoered Family picked a moon in the first place."

"Wait a minute," Joat said. "The Yoered Family runs Rohan?"

"Yup."

"Then why would they give Ciety a base there? He's their competition."

"They've gotten a little fat and lazy, from what I hear.

They let the freelancers do the scut work, and rake a percentage off the top—plus selling information, repairs and stuff, all at fantastic markups." He looked over at Joat. "You can probably fool around with Nomik Ciety, Boss, but whatever you do, don't mess with the Family. They're way too powerful and they have zero patience."

Joat grinned, a wolfish expression. "And I bet they have no sense of humor."

"I wish I could say yes to that," Al said with a sigh.

"*Attention* Wyal. *Stand by for transition, microjump— slave your control system to ours for approach.*"

Rand maintained an injured silence. "Do it," Joat ordered. "It's only for a couple of minutes."

"How would you like to turn over control of your legs and arms for a few minutes?" the AI asked.

"Gruddy. I managed to write a program that can be sarcastic."

Eglund was visible in the viewscreen and she keyed it to a higher magnification. A bright disk sprang into view, blazing against the velvet-black of space with the gem-clear blue of an aquamarine.

"There's a thick haze of hydrogen-methane atmosphere," Rand said. "That accounts for the blue coloration."

"A lovely color," Joseph added.

"How many moons?" Joat said.

"Seven that I can detect, not counting planitesimals," Rand said. "Several are water-ice, one is mostly sulfur compounds. The others are rocky; the largest is approximately Mars-sized."

Odd, Joat thought. None of them had ever been to Terra, but humanity still used the original system for comparisons.

Rohan swung into view. A yellow-gray dust speck against the great jeweled surface below, trailing swiftly

above clouds and storms vaster than worlds. Closer, it
became the size of a tennis ball, tiny and sharp-edged.
Dendritic patterns of craters, paler flatlands—no
significant atmosphere, then.

Joat swallowed and rubbed her palms against the legs
of her coverall. *Nomik.* The knowledge lay in her mind
the way a stodgy dinner did in the stomach, making
her thoughts feel logy and slow. Too much conflict, too
many warring fears, hatreds, needs . . . memories.

And I'm holding things back, she thought, glancing
at her friends. *It's not fair to them, I should tell them
everything.* She knew that, but her mind refused to
process the data; her mouth could not speak the words.

This is a lousy time to suddenly need psychotherapy,
Joat thought sourly.

"*Attention.*" The voice of the escort vessel broke in.
"*Relinquishing control. Enjoy your stay.*"

"Sarcastic nuddling," Joat muttered. She locked the
restraints around herself and lowered her hands to the
controls. "I'm taking her in."

She ignored Alvec's surprise and Rand's silence. This
was something she *could* control.

The main dome of Rohan roofed over a crater a
kilometer and a half in diameter; she could see through
the transparent cover, down to the surface. Most of it
was open space, vaguely seen greenery and trees, small
lakes—sensible, not to waste open breathable space on
buildings. Those would be under the crater's surface,
or burrowed into the mountains on either side. The
cruel peaks slid upward on either side as the *Wyal*
descended, jagged against Eglund's brightness. Banded
patterns of shadow and colored light slid across the
empty wastes of rock, down into the pulsing strobes
of the landing field. The ship slid into its cradle like
a hand into a glove, only the faintest ringing *tock* of

sound as contact was made. Almost immediately it began to move, trundling them to a docking ring in the side of the great dome.

Nowhere else did they have this system of hauling ships to and from the landing/launch pad. Only the Family would have felt it worth the enormous expense. By crowding ships together around the station's rim, they made it too dangerous to launch independently; insuring total Family control of arrivals and departures.

"Gravs off," Joat said. They all felt a buoyant lightness as they switched over to planetary gravity, about four-tenths standard. "Connections on."

There was a slight subliminal difference as the ship plugged into stationside power and life-support. Joat took a deep breath. "Time to hit dirtside," she said.

Time to find Uncle Nom.

The representative of Yoered Security looked bored as he lectured. He was a slight dark man with a small clipped mustache that looked as if it had been painted on his upper lip, dressed in a utilitarian dark-brown coverall. A few assistants stood behind him, one in a suit of powered armor; the visible ones looked as if they were close relatives—which they were. Yoered Family had started off as a crime "family" planetside, and moved out of the Central Worlds sphere several generations ago. They married in-clan . . . a standoffish bunch.

"Right, you've probably heard this before, but listen carefully anyway," the enforcer said. "This is *Rohan*. Yoered Family owns Rohan and everything on it. We have rules; you obey those rules, and you can get what you want here. First rule: nobody offers offense or violence to a member of our Family. Punishment— death."

He made a gesture. Behind him the wall flashed to

holo; it showed an iron cage hanging by a chain from a massive oak tree in the underdome. Inside it was a human figure, incredibly emaciated, like a skeleton held together by strips of dried gristle. It moved . . .

Joat swallowed as the image disappeared. The enforcer went on:

"Second rule: no stealing, no destruction of clan property, no unauthorized assault, no welching on debts. Punishment—penal servitude." He smiled, a neat, contained little expression. "You may have noticed how clean we keep things?"

The three from *Wyal* looked around. The waiting room *was* extremely tidy, with an almost painfully scrubbed look. The only messy things in its broad expanse were some of the other spacers.

The security operative gestured again. This time the holo showed a man operating a vibroscrubber machine along a walkway. He was naked except for a brief pair of shorts, and a thick pain-compliance collar around his neck. Haunted eyes turned towards the pickup for a second, and then the man's body jerked, muscles crawling under the skin. He gave a thin scream and turned his attention back to the task. Joat had never seen anyone working with such concentrated attention.

"That was a thief." The security man smiled more broadly. "Now, don't get me wrong. This isn't a tight-butt sort of place. You can get anything you want here, if you can pay—or anyone. You want to cut someone, just challenge them to a duel—the Family puts it on the holovid and takes a cut on bets. Want someone dead? You buy a license and hire a Family assassin; standard rate, one hundred fifty thousand credits, with extras depending on the target."

The smile never touched his eyes. "You can even get privacy, within the doors of your lodgings. Standard rate, one hundred and fifty thousand credits down and twenty thousand per standard month. *Everything* else is under constant surveillance—every corridor, every cargo line, every bar, every bathroom, every closet. *Nothing* gets by us. And yeah, by the way, we don't go in for all that evidentiary stuff. We arrest on suspicion, narcoquiz, and sentence the same day. No appeals." More teeth showed. "So enjoy yourselves, ladies, gentlemen, beings. Do a profitable business. But watch it."

"All functional," Rand confirmed.

"Good equipment," Joseph said judiciously, slipping the tiny button into his ear. "As good as the Naval Intelligence material we got from the military aid package."

"Sure it's not readable?" Alvec murmured. The other two heard him twice, a chorus-of-angels effect from the air and from the little transmitters tucked into their ears.

"I'm modulating it through the internal power lines," Rand said. "The encryption code is jiggered to look like the sort of random fluctuations you get there."

"Excellent," Joat murmured. "I know the virtual reality net here is legendary, Rand, but I need you to spend *some* time trying to crack Ciety's computer."

"I have a sense of responsibility, Joat," Rand said testily. "You programmed it into me. But you can make good contacts in V.R., so I intend to start there. I should have some news for you on your return."

"Just remember the expense," Alvec warned.

"Our expenses are being covered by CenSec," Rand reminded them. "I intend to take full advantage of that. Even if they will not pay the fine, they can be billed for ordinary outgoings."

Alvec's face went thoughtful, then lit up. *Like a kid in a bakery told he can have six of anything he wants,* Joat thought.

"Fardles," Joat said in awe. "I forgot!" She hoisted a travel case containing the Crown rubies, still disguised in their laser crystal boxes.

"Rand is right," Joseph said. "We must not become distracted. Amos's life is in the balance, and with it the well-being of my people."

"Yeah, sure, of course," Alvec said to his departing back. "But that doesn't mean we can't go to *dinner*. It wouldn't be right not to take advantage of CenSec's generosity just a little."

"They'll expect it," Joat assured him.

"They do things in person here, the old-fashioned way," Joseph said, slightly surprised. On Bethel, virtual presence was all the rage—newly risen from stagnation and backwardness, the Bethelites put a premium on modernity.

"Would *you* trust the public net, here?" Joat asked.

Joseph grinned, although his eyes remained wary. "You have a point."

That was logical, given that a moderately talented tech could produce a holo of anyone doing or saying *anything* and no one could tell the difference between an actual recording and one that had been faked. Therefore all transactions were real time, face to face, with multiple witnesses. Offices might be obsolete elsewhere, but not here.

Ciety's was located in a quiet neighborhood; just off the underdome surface, which was the prestige area on Rohan. They walked through eerily elongated groves of trees, past flowerbeds and greenswards, beneath the clear dome and the blue sky that was the great banded jewel of the gas-giant. Despite the growing tension that knotted her stomach, Joat was still struck by the beauty of it, and the air of quiet and peace. Nursemaids and children were the commonest strollers; she saw a dog make a long dolphinlike low-gravity leap after a ball and pinwheel off through the air . . .

"The Family do themselves proud," Alvec said sourly. "Who says crime wouldn't pay if the government ran it?"

Joseph looked about. "I am surprised the Central Worlds tolerate this," he said.

"They won't forever," Joat said absently. "But it's a big galaxy. If they mopped up the Yoered Family now, they'd just be replaced by someone younger and hungrier and cruder. Eventually the frontier will move out past this area, and the Family will go legitimate or move again to get outside the sphere of settled law.

"This is it," she said.

They walked through a tall archway carved into the rock of the crater wall; the blast doors that would seal it in an emergency were hidden behind the glowing mass of bougainvillea that carpeted the walls of the corridor behind. It was wide enough to be a street, but only slow floater platforms passed them, and a scattering of well-dressed pedestrians. No bars or sex shows were advertised here. Every office presented an inscrutable face of one-way glass adorned with a discreet sign announcing the name, but not the purpose, of the business within. No doubt that explained the sense of being somewhere very expensive.

If you have to ask, you can't afford it, Joat thought, and read aloud: "N. Ciety, Research and Development." She made a little moue. "I'd say he's a cynical man."

"I would say he is scum," Joseph said quietly. "He deals with the Kolnari."

Joat glanced at him in concern and then at Alvec. He met her eyes with the same concern she felt over Joseph's intensity. She grimaced. *I'm one to talk.*

"Joe," she said quietly. "Maybe you should wait outside."

He turned to glare at her. "You insult me, Joat. The fact that this criminal offends me does not mean that I am unable to deal with him. I would kiss the soles of his feet if it would give me the information I need to find Amos. Look to yourself, girl, and leave my behavior to me!"

Joat choked down the urge to apologize and opened the office door. *Whoa! Is this the Uncle Joe who was always telling me to control my emotions?* But then again, she was grown up now. He didn't need to put on the mask of infallibility with her any more . . . which was both flattering and disturbing, when you thought about it.

The reception area was a very soothing room. The visible color scheme had been carefully chosen to please all of the species known to the Central Worlds. No doubt those who saw in the ultraviolet spectrum had been considered too, judging from the telltale signs in the paintings and fabrics in the room. In place of background music there was the sound of ocean surf. Again, a choice calculated not to offend any species, whether their oceans were methane or water. The furnishings looked expensive and inviting, if you liked the minimalist style—Joat herself had always thought desks and chair-seats looked better with legs beneath them, rather than floating in suspension-fields.

The human receptionist who greeted them was as polished as the decoration.

"Good morning," he said pleasantly. "How may I help you?"

"I'm Captain Joat Simeon-Hap, and we're here to deliver a consignment," Joat said. "For Silken."

"Ah." The young man raised a golden brow. "Please take a seat while I inform Ms. Silken that you've arrived. Would you care for some refreshment?"

"No thank you," Joat said.

Behind her Alvec and Joseph shook their heads. The three then retired to a furniture grouping for humanoids and sat down to wait silently. After a few carefully calculated moments the receptionist looked up with the distracted air of someone listening to an earphone.

"Captain Simeon-Hap, Mr. Ciety would like to meet you personally and has asked me to bring you and your party up to his suite. If you would follow me, please?"

He turned and started off towards an apparently blank wall, obviously confident that he would be followed.

Joat clenched her hands into fists to hide the fact that they were shaking as badly as her knees.

Get ahold of yourself! she thought fiercely. *This is what had to happen. This is what you hoped would happen.* Blood pounded in her ears.

The wall parted to reveal a lift and the golden-haired receptionist entered and turned to smile invitingly at them. Joat wondered if he was some especially pretty species of bodyguard. The lift accelerated smoothly; from the weight and time Joat guessed that they were several thousand meters up, into the living rock of the mountains that ringed the crater. When the doors opened, across from them was an ornate double door of some highly polished, satiny wood, each side featuring a plate-sized brass doorknob embossed with a single initial, N and C.

Tacky, Joat thought. *But impressive.* She had to admit that. The wood itself was expensive, that was obvious, but shipping it here must have cost a fortune, and not a small one. Uncle Nom had come up in the world, since he was a tramp-freighter skipper and fringe-world grifter.

Their guide crossed the corridor and knocked discreetly on the enormous doors. From within a resonant male voice called out "Come."

Joat licked her lips surreptitiously and wiped her palms on the legs of her shipsuit. Al and Joe were behind her, and the knowledge of their solid backing gave her strength.

The doors swept open. Joat gave a small incredulous gasp before she could stop herself. The walls were sheathed in a geometric design of polychrome marble; texture matched subtly with color, from craggy red to smoothly polished alabaster-white. The furnishings were rich beefleather and pale wood, austerely simple so as not to distract from the impact of the room itself.

Directly across from the door where they stood was an enormous fireplace, complete with blazing fire; cedar logs filled the air with their fragrance. *Burning!* she thought. *Burning* wood *to generate heat!*. You'd expect that on a live planet—a barbarian planet. Here, it was barbaric in a completely different way.

Above it a display film in proportion to the fireplace offered a complex work of randomized holo art, swirling ceaselessly into almost recognizable patterns. The mantle was held up by carvings of humanoid figures.

Then, one of them moved.

Joat flinched, recognizing them then as low life bioconstructs, zombielike things also known as realities. *Banned on every planet in Central Worlds,* she thought in disgust. *We're a long way from civilized space.*

A man had risen from the couch before the fireplace to smile pleasantly at them. He gestured, urging them to enter. An attractive man, slender and of middling height. His longish, ash-blond hair was expensively cut in a style that knocked ten years off his age. His appraising eyes were a cool blue, set deep in a narrow, fine-boned face.

But his eyes passed over her briefly and on to her companions. He gestured again, perhaps with a touch of impatience and said:

"Come in! Don't be shy, I won't bite."

Obscurely disappointed, Joat looked down, carefully watching her feet descend the three shining marble stairs that led to the living area.

So much for "the ties that bind," she thought grimly. No recognition at all. Of course, she'd been a child. *When he sold me.*

Ciety reached out a hand for her to shake and she steeled herself to take it. Alvec accepted it too, but Joseph, bowing, kept his in the sleeves of his tunic:

"It is not our custom," he said smoothly.

Ciety continued smiling and bowed politely back, but something reptilian showed in his eyes.

Silken lay upon the white couch, dressed in an emerald satin dressing gown, sipping from a cut crystal goblet which she raised in salute to Joat.

"You've made it in good time, Captain," she said.

"No thanks to Central Worlds Customs," Joat answered. "They went through almost every minor treasure in my hold. I thought we'd never get rid of them."

Silken's gaze sharpened and she sat up abruptly.

"You *have* my jewels," she demanded, combining statement and threat.

Joat placed the travel bag on the low table; Silken ripped open the fastener and tumbled the laser component boxes onto the intaglio surface.

"Where's . . . ?"

Then she opened one of the boxes.

"What the hell is this?" she snapped as she pulled out a dull red, irregularly shaped crystal.

"Dye from a red cargo marker," Joat explained calmly. "It'll wash off with a little elbow grease. The inspectors found three of these before their commander called them off."

Silken laughed in relief and caught Ciety's eye proudly, as though it had been her own idea.

"Why, you clever girl," she purred. "There, Mik, didn't I tell you she was sharp?"

"Yes you did," he agreed and stroked Silken's cheek with one finger. She rubbed her face against his hand like a cat.

Nomik took the jewel out of her hand and weighed it in his own. His eyes met Joat's.

"You *are* clever," he said. "I can use that kind of initiative in my organization. Silken vouched for you," he turned slightly in her direction to indicate her, and Silken smiled pleasantly at Joat. "And of course that's good enough for me. But this," he tossed the stone and caught it, "this is good. I'm impressed. So . . . would you be willing to discuss taking a place with us? You wouldn't regret it, I can promise you that."

I can't believe he's trying to offer me a job, Joat thought desperately. Conflicting emotions tore through her, disgust, amusement, rage, and a vague pleasure. *This is too much. I've got to rethink my strategy. I've gotta get out of here. Right now!*

What most horrified her was that she was reacting to his unexpected charm. That she felt herself wanting to please this sleazy crook—who just happened to be the uncle who had sold her into untold misery—added to her confusion unbearably. The moment stretched.

"I . . . we . . ." she could almost feel Alvec's concerned puzzlement, Joseph's unquestioning support. "We're an independent outfit," she said at last. "We're happy with that for now." She paused to put a polite interval between her refusal and the next order of business. "There's an outstanding balance due on this shipment. If you could just give us a credit chip, we'll be on our way."

Nomik and Silken stared at her. She felt a little relief at the sight of Nomik staring at her like an animal who'd been hit between the eyes with a sledgehammer.

Doubtless it had been years since anyone had flatly
turned them down. Particularly not a ragtailed freighter
captain like Joat.

Ciety's eyes narrowed.

"About that," he said coolly, "Silken told me about
your problems with New Destinies. That little debt you
incurred there, remember that?" Joat nodded slowly.
"Well, it probably won't surprise you to learn that I
have good friends there and they were amenable to
coming to an arrangement with me. It'll relieve you,
I'm sure, to know that instead of forty Earth standard
days, you have an unlimited length of time to pay up."
Joat blinked, and Ciety nodded smugly. "To me. I've
bought your debt." He folded his arms and regarded
her with a narrow-eyed smile.

Joat drew in a long shocked breath and felt her body
go numb. Beside her, she was vaguely aware of Alvec
and Joseph stirring uneasily.

"So what we'll do," Ciety continued, "is put the
amount outstanding for this shipment against *your* debt.
Leaving you one hundred and fourteen thousand credits
in the red." He grinned. "Don't worry, this'll go faster
than you're expecting. I'll take care of your expenses,
food and fuel and docking fees and I pay well. Anyone'll tell you that. You'll be clear in no time." He held
out his hand to her. "So. Welcome aboard."

Joat stared at his offered hand and then at him and
her vision narrowed, focusing like a laser beam on his
smirking face. "You don't remember me at all," she said
in wonder, finding it absurdly difficult to speak.

He studied her for a moment and then shook his
head indifferently. "No," he said with a shrug. "Can't
say that I do."

Joat slapped his hand aside violently, overwhelmed
by an anger so hot that for a moment she didn't feel
at all. She watched her own fist fly out to strike her

uncle on the point of his chin and he went down with
a ridiculously surprised expression on his face.

She lunged for him and Joseph caught her, holding
her back.

Alvec moved between them and the golden-haired
receptionist, who now held a weapon trained on the
three of them, waiting for orders from Ciety.

"I'm your niece!" she screamed in fury, struggling
to climb out of Joseph's unyielding arms. She *had* to.
Crush that face, see it crumble, stamp it under her heel
and feel the bone crack . . .

"Stop it, Joat," Joseph whispered calmingly. "Joat,
contain yourself!"

After a few moments his voice penetrated the hot
fog in her head. Color began to return to her white
face and sanity to her eyes. She was breathing in little
panting grunts.

"I'm your brother's daughter," she said, taking control
of herself. "You were a dreamdust addict." She gave
a loud mocking sniff. "You just had to have it. I
remember going hungry all the time so you could have
your little fix. Then you lost me in a poker game to
a tramp-freighter captain."

She shook herself free of Joseph's grip as it relaxed
in horror. "And you can't imagine the nightmare living
with that soulless scum was. But *you* don't remember.
Lucky you. *I* can't forget!" She spat on him where he
lay on the floor. "I have no debt to you," she said in
a voice rich with loathing. "I owe you *nothing*."

Joat turned and stalked out. Even the receptionist/
bodyguard was too frozen in shock to stop her.

◇ CHAPTER ELEVEN

It was silent in the room after her departure, as though someone had switched off an erupting volcano. The silence seemed to ring.

"Is it true?" Joseph asked, his voice gone husky and quiet. Nomik Ciety's face was still fluid with shock for a moment, then hardened again. "I swear that I never saw that woman before in my life!" he said.

He cleared his throat, looking at the Bethelite with wide, innocent eyes. *That is a dangerous man,* he thought. The evaluation was automatic. In this business you had to be able to size someone up quickly. *That crazy bitch's lover or something?* No way to tell that; there were some who'd kill anyone who'd done what she said he'd done.

Had he? Behind his frown of concern, he searched his memory. It was excellent since he'd been through the treatment. Back when he was dusting, there were holes you could fly a naval assault carrier through. He'd done some crazy things back then, no doubt about it.

Nowadays, he would have sold her, not lost her in a game.

He sat up and Silken went to his aid, helping him to rise from the floor. "I had a brother," he said in confusion. "But whether he had children or not . . ."

Ciety brushed his hair back and tenderly touched his chin.

"She's wrong about one thing, though. And about this I am dead certain. She owes me a hundred and fourteen thousand credits. So you, my friends, had better go after her, calm her down and put her in a better frame of mind. Or I'll take her ship just as happily and just as legally as New Destinies would." He glared at them both. "You got that?"

Both men nodded.

"But if it *is* true," Joseph said in a quiet, deadly voice, "then the matter must be dealt with. You understand this?"

"Look, stranger," Ciety barked, his patience at an end, "I have no living relatives and I don't want any. So if your little friend has some wild idea of running a con on me, you better straighten her out. I'm one of the powers around this place. *You* are nothing."

He made a chopping motion with his hand and looked into Joseph's eyes. Blue met blue, equally cold. "Now get out."

"You're both crazy," Alvec said after the door of N. Ciety, Research and Development, had closed gently, but firmly behind them. "The Captain is this guy's niece? And you, what was that? You were calling him out in a duel, or what? And what about . . ." He caught himself and leaned close to Joseph ". . . you know? We didn't find out jack."

Joseph sighed and stopped walking. He looked around at the sylvan beauty of the dome, inhaled the odors of cut grass and flowers and running water, folded his arms and stared at nothing.

"To state the obvious," he said, "this has gone badly. The last thing we wanted to do was incur this man's hostility. But we have. Joat should have accepted his offer of employment; it was a perfect opportunity to find out what we *must* learn. She did not."

Alvec brushed a hand distractedly over his hair. "Yeah." he muttered. "Isn't like the Captain at all."

Joseph shrugged. "Exactly. *You* know Joat. *I* know Joat. Was that—" he jerked his chin back at the tunnel mouth "—in the least like the Joat we know?"

"What'll we do?"

"We must play the dice as they fall from the hand of the God," he said. "To begin, let us find Joat. "I have," he went on, and a slight chill settled in Alvec's stomach, "some questions for her."

Joat threw herself into the Captain's couch.

"Rand!" she barked. "If you're in V.R. pull yourself out. I need your help here and it's going to take all your attention." Her hands flew over her comp, pulling up Rohan's computer address system.

"What is it, Joat? I was engaged in a most diverting—"

"We've got to break into Nomik Ciety's data system. I want to know who he's been talking to for the last two months. I don't much care about content just now, but I want to know who and where from. And if there's anything specially encrypted . . ."

"All of his incoming messages are encrypted. All of *everybody's* messages are encrypted on Rohan. I wouldn't be terribly surprised to discover that they *think* in encryption here." Rand paused. "Your instructions are the same as when you left, Joat. But your attitude is decidedly more urgent. What happened?"

Joat lifted her hands from the comp and looked at her fingers; they were long and graceful, with the slightly used look of someone who worked with her hands on delicate—but sometimes hot or sparking— instrumentation. She folded the hands into fists and leaned back into her chair, closed her eyes, took two deep breaths.

Then she spoke, without opening them.

"I just lost my mind, Rand," she explained. Her voice had a weary tone. "I almost got us all killed and at the time," she shook her head slowly, "I didn't care." She pushed her hair off her face with both hands. "I don't believe I did that," she said.

"Where are Alvec and Joseph?" Rand asked.

"Looking for me, most likely," she said. "Tell them . . . Tell them I need time to regain my composure, that's true enough. Tell them I'll be in touch shortly. Tell them to relax and take advantage of CenSec's generosity. But don't tell them where I am!" She turned to glare at it. "You got that?"

"It's done, Joat. Joseph says to tell you that you and he need to talk."

"Did he ask where I was?"

"Yes, I told him that you hadn't said," Rand's voice sounded strained. "I don't understand how you humans can do that so casually. I find it very disorienting to make statements that are contrary to the facts."

Joat smiled gently at it. "Thank you for lying for me, Rand. I know you don't like it. What did Al say?"

"Alvec says he'll bring you home some take-out."

Joat smiled wanly at that.

"I belted Nomik Ciety in the chops," she said. Then she smiled faintly in satisfaction. "I knocked him right on his ass."

After a moment, Rand asked, "Was that wise?"

She sighed, "Certainly not. But I really needed to do it."

Rand's lights glowed yellow in puzzlement.

"I believe I have insufficient information," it concluded. "Because based on what you've just told me, I would be forced to agree that you have, indeed, lost your mind."

"Oh, I did," she assured it. "But it's back now and we have work to do. What have you found out so far?"

"The Kolnari have apparently never actually visited Rohan," it told her.

Joat waved a hand dismissively.

"Not surprising, they're uncomfortable off their ships. they like to have a ceiling over their heads and walls around them. Looking up through that dome would just about drive them crazy. Besides, they don't exactly enjoy socializing with other races." She shook her head. "They'd use go-betweens or tight beam communications. My bet is the latter. See if you can find anything unusual in ship to port messages. Meanwhile, I'll try'n get into Ciety's cyber-house through a back door."

The two worked intently for a while and the quiet soothed Joat's jangled nerves. *There's nothing like working out a technical problem to get yourself centered*, she thought.

"I'm in!" Joat called.

"Congratulations," Rand said. Then, "Or perhaps not."

Her head snapped up.

"What?"

"Something's wrong. Something's gotten in."

"What is it?" she demanded.

"I don't know. But it's eating me."

✧ CHAPTER TWELVE

"Sal?"

"Yeah?" he looked up from The Anvil's accounts at his secretary.

"That fine that Mr. va Riguez wanted paid?"

"Yeah?" he said again, with exaggerated patience. This particular employee seemed incapable of just saying what was on his mind.

"Can't do it. Mr. va Riguez's account says insufficient funds."

Sal grunted and reached for the note-screen in his secretary's hand. He skimmed through the bankers' jargon until he reached the amount of the fine.

"Oi vey!" he exclaimed. "That can't be right."

"I double checked it, Sal. That's the right amount."

"A hundred and twenty thousand credits! You gotta be kiddin' me. What the hell did Simeon-Hap do for a fine that size?"

"I couldn't find out." The secretary shrugged. "It's confidential."

Sal just looked at him from under lowered brows. "Get me Dyson," he said at last. "Now."

Graf Dyson shrugged. "She had to be fined, Sal. She entered the station illegally."

Sal gave him a look. "A hundred and twenty thousand?" he said.

Dyson threw up his hands and leaned forward. "Look," he said, "Clal va Riguez says to me, make it a big fine. Use your discretion. And she ticked me off." He leaned back and shrugged. "So I did what he said."

Sal rubbed his chin thoughtfully. "Well, he told me to pay it. But his account says insufficient funds. I don't think he expected it to be this much." He gave Dyson a hard look. "He didn't set a ceiling?"

Graf didn't like Sal's attitude. This wasn't even his affair and he was getting really pushy. Besides Graf's dealings were supposed to be confidential. And this conversation was lasting way too long.

"Look, maybe you're right, maybe there's been a misunderstanding. Have va Riguez call me. We'll straighten it out."

"He's not here," Sal grumbled, still looking like he was waiting for a concession.

"What is this?" Dyson snapped, suddenly angry. People were supposed to come to him hat in hand and to say thanks when they left. He'd had dealings with Sal before and hadn't gotten the respect he thought he deserved. "I don't discuss your business with other people. I won't discuss va Riguez's business with you. He has a problem, have him get back to me. I don't hear from him, I figure he wants this fine to stick. You," he snapped a finger towards Sal, "I don't wanta hear from." And he disconnected.

He leaned back thoughtfully. *Maybe I should reduce it,* he thought. Mr. va Riguez had told him no more than twenty thousand. *Yeah, but if I lower it now, Sal will think he's scored one off me.* Dyson grimaced.

Then again, if va Riguez has gone missing then maybe he never intended to take care of this. And Dyson was experienced enough to know that to an operation like Joat's twenty thousand might as well be a hundred and twenty thousand. *So. I'll leave it. If he contacts me, I'll say I misunderstood. If he doesn't, New Destinies gets a little richer.* He grinned. *And Sal gets a message. Don't mess with Graf Dyson.*

Sal leaned back in his chair. He wasn't happy about not being able to follow va Riguez's orders. The man was a good customer, and he represented another, more shadowy, good customer that Sal had been doing business with for years.

Besides, he'd learned early in life who was safe to cross and who wasn't. Dyson, it depended on the circumstances, but basically he was a lightweight. But Clal va Riguez . . . that was a dangerous man.

I better put a message in the pipe, he thought unhappily. *That way I'm covered.* If it was important, Clal, or one of his associates would get back to him. If he heard nothing, *Then I'll assume no action is called for.*

The *Chadragupta Rao*'s hull gave a shudder as the dockside connectors went home and Rohan's gravity took over. Metal and composites crackled and sighed in reaction as weight and pressure altered. Fresher air poured in; the *Rao* had problems with life-support, redline maintenance no Company ship or chartered freelancer would tolerate.

Bros Sperin stood easily on her command deck, adjusting to the lighter gravity with automatic ease, equally easy with the hostile glare of the *Rao*'s Captain. For that matter, the only eyes on the wedge-shaped deck that *weren't* hostile were the four Sondee orbs right behind him. They were probably bright and shiny . . .

"Far as I'm concerned, Sperin, you cease to exist when you walk off my deck. You got that?"

The spacer was a pale, flaccid little man. He smelled

like a locker full of sweaty clothes. But then, so did his whole ship. The bridge went darker as screens powered-down, only the monitors and standby readouts still active.

Bros nodded, his eyes cool. The little needler in his cuff was ready, but he didn't think he'd need it.

"All debts are paid," he said evenly. "And in the event that you find it necessary to alert the Family to my presence . . ."

The little man stiffened.

"You can tell them I'm here to find a friend in trouble. It's a personal thing."

The spacer's pale brow furrowed in confusion.

"But of course," Bros said gently, "I'd be very disappointed if you did tell them I'm here."

The spacer jerked his head in a negative. "All debts are paid," he said sourly.

They were in the shadowy reaches where organized crime brushed and merged with the fringes of Intelligence work. It was the only way to keep things functioning at all—the old *lex talonis*, eye for an eye.

"Thanks," Bros said with a smile and a slap on the back that staggered the little spacer, "I knew I could count on you."

He hefted his duffel to his shoulder and walked out, deck gratings ringing under his magnetic boots, each stride a little sticky. Seg !T'sel trotted after him.

"I still say we should be disguised," he whispered.

Bros smiled for the monitors and put an arm around the alien's bony shoulders; they felt warm under his hand, hotter than a human metabolism, and the pattern of bones was more like a lattice than a framework.

"Think of it this way, Seg," he said, between clenched teeth—natural, and it also activated his scrambler. That was a system sophisticated enough to feed a false conversation to the audio pickups. "How many Sondee do you see around here?"

They were out of the docking bay and into a concourse, full of crowds skipping on and off slideways or calling for little robotic shuttlecars, heavy with the scent of ozone. Most of the crowd were humans of various types, the odd Ursinoid, a scattering of other species . . .

"One or two," Seg said.

"And how many of them are wearing eyepatches, or wigs, or walking with canes?"

Seg opened his mouth, then shut it with a snap. The bony plates within went *tok*.

"Nine humans out of ten can't tell one Sondee from another, unless there's something *unusual* about the Sondee. On your homeworld, you get seen as *you*. Here you get seen as a *Sondee*. Grasp the principle?"

A wordless grunt. "But *you* should be wearing a disguise."

Damned if I'm going to wear a rubber nose, either, Bros thought. He shrugged. "Disguises are more trouble than they're worth unless you absolutely need one."

"But they'll recognize you."

"Who is they?" Bros asked.

"Well," Seg temporized, "who are we looking for?"

"At the moment, Joat Simeon-Hap. Ultimately, the Kolnari. Joat's on our side . . . mostly, so we want her to recognize me. The Kolnari will kill you whoever you look like. But the Family will want to know what you're trying to hide. So they'll take you aside and ask you questions until *they're* satisfied. And Seg . . . they're very hard to satisfy. So our best disguise is to look like ordinary spacers."

Seg nodded solemnly, and then nearly fell flat as they stepped onto a slideway. Bros clenched his teeth again and put a hand under the Sondee's not-quite-an-elbow.

They'd left the docking area behind. The tunnels and arcades beneath the crater floor engulfed them, two more anonymous spacers in worn coveralls, carrying the record of their lives in their duffels through the jostling crowds. They passed innumerable cheap hostels burrowed back into the rock, CHEAP ROOMS and CLEAN BEDS blinking in holographic colors outside their barred doors. The drab hostels gave way to chandlers' offices, advertising electronics, software, graving docks, power systems.

"It's not quite what I imagined a pirate haven would be like," Seg whispered.

"Piracy's a business," Bros said. "Ships are ships. They need fuel and parts and maintenance. A lot of other business goes through here, too—some of it even legitimate."

"But I thought it would be something more like—"

The slideway divided around a dropshaft. Bros took them off and into the open darkness. They drifted downward, and images played before their eyes.

"*—any species, any combination for—*"

It was hard for a member of another species to be shocked by human tastes in erotic entertainment, but Seg managed it. All four eyes bulged slightly, then blinked in unison, a disconcerting sight.

"*—come one, come all, contestants welcome—*"

This time the naked shapes were muscular and lithe, sheened with sweat and blood, long curved knives in their hands.

"*—nothing too exotic at the Torture Pit—*"

Bros closed his own eyes, wincing slightly. "This is the entertainment level," he said. "Want to stop and see the sights?"

"Ah . . . no."

"Good. Let's get some business done, then."

Seg cocked his ears at a cacophony of voices, human and alien, clashing music from various bars and an assortment of street sounds from air-scrubbers to ground cars.

THE SHIP AVENGED   199

"Still, what energy there is in that sound!" Seg exclaimed as they stepped out of the shaft into a more placid level. He turned to Bros his eyes shining. "I'm working on an opera in my spare time," he confessed.

What Sondee isn't? Sperin wondered.

"One day I will work *this*—" he gestured with both hands towards the street before them "—into my overture."

Sperin smiled and nodded. *Not bad kid, Seg. And how I wish he wasn't here.*

"We better get moving," he murmured in Seg's ear whorl. "We look like a couple of rubes standing here."

"I thought you said Rohan was fairly safe?" Seg protested.

"Safe is a relative term," Bros said. "If we were in a Sondee swamp, for example, we'd probably be safe from wild animals, since they're generally shy around people. But even there, smearing yourself all over with beef gravy might be considered putting too much temptation in their way. If you get my drift?"

Seg's ear whorls colored slightly and he nodded.

"Which way?" he asked.

"We'll check the bars along here," Bros said. "I've no idea where Joat might be, but my information is that her crew has a fondness for dockside bars."

"These entertainments do not seem *too* raucous," Seg said.

Well, the one with the two girls and the Nuruzian lizard was a little much, Bros thought, scanning the crowd. On the other hand, the really unpleasant places were unlikely to attract Joat's crewfolk, which was a relief. You had to wade through sewage often enough in this business . . .

Seg made a grand gesture. "Garçon!" he called. "Madder music and stronger wine!" He blinked diagonally when Bros looked sharply at him. "Classical reference," the Sondee said.

"I read Dobson too," Sperin said dryly, and Seg's ear whorls flushed a deeper blue.

The waiter brought a bottle of surprisingly good port from Ceres—the planet, not the asteroid—and Bros gave a realistic wince as the display on the tray showed the deduction from his account. In actuality, the expense account was one of the few real perks of the trade; he sipped at the smooth nutty flavor. The best of everything ended up in Rohan—at a price. A bowl of raisins, pecans, and dried *gunung* went down beside it.

"This tastes much better. Sweeter." Seg threw back his glass and poured another.

Great fardling voids, as Joat is wont to say, Bros thought; this time his wince was genuine. For one thing, that was a lousy way to treat a fine wine; for another . . . Sondee metabolized alcohol faster than humans, but not *that* fast.

For a moment he thought that Seg had burst into song, but the voice was deeper and more gravelly. A human voice, one he recognized, singing *La vie en Rose* . . .

Alvec had his head together with a brawny blond wearing a shy, enraptured smile as he crooned.

Things can't be too bad if Alvec's out picking roses, Bros thought. He motioned Seg to remain seated and moved up behind Joat's crew.

"Al!" he said and slapped the man on the shoulder.

Al looked up questioningly, his eyes blank.

"Alvec Dia," Bros insisted.

"Yeah," Alvec agreed slowly. "Who're you?"

"I'm Joat's friend from New Destinies. I'm the guy who told her to check this place out. Hey, listen buddy," Bros pulled out a chair and sat down, leaning towards

Alvec confidentially, "I'm looking for a berth. You think maybe Joat can help me out?"

The woman was looking at him and scowling. Bros saw recognition flicker in the other man's eyes, but the face remained mildly friendly, if you could say that about something that looked like it had been pounded out of rough wrought iron.

"I dunno," Alvec said. "We're kinda full up right now."

Bros kept smiling, and ground his foot into the reinforced toe of one of Alvec's boots under the table. *Come on, you imbecile, there's no time for let-the-spook-twist-in-the-wind games here!*

"Well, why don't we let the Captain decide?" Bros asked reasonably. "I'm good at what I do. You can always use a good hand, right? What's the *Wyal*'s berth number? I'll go ask her."

Alvec's smile grew wider, and he let his hand drop to the blond woman's.

"Why doncha tell me where you're stayin'?" he asked. "I'll have her get in touch . . . later. I'm sort of busy. Not that you're not welcome or anything, old pal, but . . ."

"Aw, c'mon, buddy. I can get the number from central registry. I just wanted to save the credits." *And keep the Family watchprograms from getting tripped.*

The blond shifted nervously, aware of the undercurrents and not sure she wanted to be around them. Bros thought that decided Alvec.

"SJ 467-Y," he said. "But the Captain isn't there right now."

Bros grinned.

"I'll take my chances. Maybe she'll be back by the time I get there. Thanks buddy." And he slapped Alvec's shoulder one more time.

Alvec watched him leave, his eyes speculative.

"Who's that?" Rose asked.

"Oh, friend of the Captain's," Alvec said and gently took her hand. "You were telling me something about yourself," he said and kissed her fingertips. "I think that's much more interesting."

Bros withdrew his credit chip from the meter and dragged Seg out of the ground-car by his sleeve. Then he leaned the young Sondee up against the docking mechanism while he activated the *Wyal*'s com to announce their presence.

Seg began to sing snatches of his opera-in-progress in a light and very pleasant baritone; much to the amusement of passing spacers.

Wonderful, Bros thought in exasperation. *Nothing obvious about you is there, Mr. Wannabe?* On the other had, it could be worse—he could be in disguise. Nobody was really surprised when a drunk started singing, and a Sondee just couldn't sing badly.

There'd been no answer to their hail. Not even from Joat's elaborate AI. That had to mean something was wrong. After all, it wasn't as if the thing could go on shore leave.

He moved to the lock, and shielding his movements as best he could with his body, placed a small and very illegal device above the lock mechanism. In seconds he was able to enter the *Wyal*, drawing Seg in after him.

Joat cut off the connection with Nomik Ciety's data link and turned to Rand.

"Did that . . . ?" Before she could finish asking if the cutoff had helped, they were reconnected with a sharp *plink*. She turned and cut the link again, again it reinstated itself.

As far as she could tell something was flooding

rapidly into her comp, but nothing was going out. At least not yet.

And there was only one way to do anything at all. No human brain reading code could deal with this in the sort of time-frame necessary. But the alternative was hideously dangerous; if you linked yourself directly, *your* software was vulnerable.

Her hands danced across the console.

Cutting the link only delayed the worm program's progress for seconds at a time, but she continued to do it. Yet it continuously broke through everything she could throw at it. *Subtle stuff. Whoever though this up knew their hand from a hacksaw.*

Cold sweat flowed down her forehead into her eyes and beaded her upper lip, tasting of salt and despair. Her hands grew tired and clumsy at the controls, and her fear for Rand distracted her. More than once she'd regretted being human, never more so than now. She wasn't fast enough, she wasn't calm enough, she was losing Rand! *Here I had to go and* design *an AI that was my friend.* It wasn't even a real person, just a very good imitation . . .

"Fardle." Her hands picked up the interfacer unit and snapped home the connector. It settled over her head, blocking vision and hearing. She was alone in a world of darkness.

"Execute."

. . . standing on a featureless plain that stretched to infinity in every direction.

The air smelled dead, with a sterile metallic tinge. The ground underfoot was some gray metal, grooved in endless parallel lines. Scattered about were boulders, each a geometric shape, squares, polyhedrons, eye-hurting things like angular Mobius strips.

Overhead the sky opened its eye. Threads dropped

from it towards her, writhing, sentient eyelashes like
velvet serpents. They wound around her wrists and
pulled her upward. Behind her the metal plain suddenly
collapsed, turning sandy and friable, then melting into
a smooth bath of liquid that smelled sickly-sweet
beneath her. The thick sugary surface moved, sluggish
and smooth, as things squirmed beneath it.

**exterior interface compromised. off/on circuitry
compromised.**

The eye blinked closed around her. Within was a
garden, green and yellow and purple, in bright primary
colors that looked too artificial to be tangible; yet she
could feel the grass beneath her bare feet, smell the
cinnamon scent of the flowers. A figure walked towards
her with jerky quickness, a figure shaped like a man
sculpted out of living water.

help . . . meeee . . . it said, in a breathy whisper.
Something stirred in the middle of its forehead,
between blank silver eyes.

Joat reached in and grasped the tendril, pulling it
out into the light. It came easily, and then slid through
her fingers. The end of it split and split and split again,
into hair-thin threads that reached for her eyes and ears
and mouth.

A knife appeared in her hand; where the edge moved,
the stuff of space split and bled chaotic patterns of
moving light. She used the knife to section the onrushing
tentacle, then again, so that there were four ends. Those
she wrapped around her wrists, moving hands and arms
in an intricate pattern that tied the tentacle into a huge
knot whose convolutions led the eye down and away
along a path with no ending. More and more of it flowed
out of the water-sculpture figure, turning it clear and
transparent. The silvery fingers came up and began to
knot and twist at the body of the tentacle themselves,
and . . .

. . . she fell forward into the figure's open mouth.

Stone jarred beneath her feet. She was in a library, an ancient library of leather-bound books in shelves that reached towards the dark coffered wood of the ceiling. Gilt flaked from their spines, shining in the light of the burning logs in the big stone fireplace that occupied one wall. A stranger in a plush smoking robe was sitting in an overstuffed leather armchair beside the fire, eating books. His mouth stretched as each folio-sized volume was pushed home; then he belched slightly and took a sip from the snifter of brandy in his other hand, before reaching for a new volume. Gaps stood on the shelves, like raw wounds, bleeding sorrow.

There was another chair and table on the other side of the fire. Joat sat in it, and opened the book lying closed. The page was blank, but columns of figures and letters appeared as she ran her finger across it. Pages flipped forward, and then she was standing with the book held open before her.

"Perhaps you'd like to eat this?" she said.

There was no mind behind the eyes that looked up a her, only hunger. The figure's hands snapped out and dragged the book near; she braced her feet and hauled backwards, but the strength in the fetch's arms was beyond her. The book plastered itself across the avid face of the eater.

His lips parted in a vast dolorous gape to take it in, but the book grew faster. Joat could feel it sucking at the skin of her fingertips as she released it; the leaves closed around the eater's face, and now his hands were scrambling to pull it free, but the book wriggled forward, growing, licking hungrily at his skin. The head began to squeeze forward into the jaws of the book, and the figure rose and staggered off across the library. As its substance flowed forward into the pages it dissolved, matter breaking up into a whirlpool of *off/on/off/on/off*, databits streaming into their new matrix.

The walls of the building shook as the book finished its task and fell to the floor.

Joat stooped to pick it up, and—

Bros stood, watching the figure slumped in the chair. He could see the sweat running down from below the padded rim of the interfacer unit; figures scrolled by on the screen before her, blurring in their speed.

His teeth clicked together in shock. Direct interfacing like that was *illegal,* outside carefully-supervised research settings. There was no *telling* what could happen when you linked your brain's own operating code with a comp system like that!

And there was nothing he could do; interrupting would be more dangerous than leaving her be. He felt an enormous upwelling anger, and wondered at it even as the muscles of his neck and shoulders tensed in rage.

What's it to me if the idiot kills herself? A waste of potential, yes, but—

Joat started convulsively and threw the interfacer helmet aside. Sweat darkened her flax-colored hair and plastered it to her skull; dark circles stood out like bruises beneath her eyes. Bros opened his mouth to speak, or bellow.

"Get out of here," she growled, turning back to her work with obsessive intensity. Her fingers blurred across the keyboard.

"Gotta be sure, gotta be sure," she muttered to herself. "*Got* it."

Bros craned his neck, trying to make out the flying stream of data. Joat did something and its progress slowed enough that the individual characters could be made out. They were some sort of encryption, vaguely familiar. He leaned forward for a better look and thoughtlessly placed his hand on her shoulder.

The punch was so unexpected that it almost connected. His hand snapped up to catch her fist, moving automatically to clench and stab at a nerve junction. Joat sprang to her feet then, putting the coiled strength of her body behind a head-butt aimed at his jaw and strong enough to shatter bone. Bros yanked her off balance and spun her around, twisting her captured hand up behind her back.

But gently, he didn't want to hurt her and he sure didn't need to add to her hostility. That nearly cost him a broken pubic bone as her heel drove backward. He staggered away, curling around the pain in his lower gut, and Joat writhed free like an eel.

Is she on drugs? he thought, breath wheezing out behind clenched teeth. Blank ferocity met his eyes, and he forced himself into the ready position.

Seg watched in astonishment as the two Terrans wrestled. *Why are they fighting?*

Bros had assured him that Joat was on their side. He glanced at the screen where she'd been sitting and his attention was caught by a familiar symbol. Ah, yes, he knew this one.

Flexing his fingers to loosen them up, Seg took Joat's seat and began to work.

query; identity.

He entered it and continued, all twelve fingertips hitting the board microseconds apart. Yes, it was the program—and very neatly tied up in mid-operation, if in an unorthodox way. But it was all there, ready to come out the minute the AI's own defense program relaxed. Better to deactivate it completely . . .

"Thank you."

Seg looked up, blinking each pair of eyes in sequence. A voice-program too; very good, perhaps a little flat on the intonations.

"You're welcome," he said. "That ought to do it. And *this* will set it to eating itself. You can let it go, now."

Joat froze. The cable-strong arms that pinioned her relaxed.

"*Will* you stop trying to kill me, please?" Bros said in her ear.

"When you stop trying to break my arm."

They rolled free and stared at each other warily. "Spook," Joat muttered, disgust in her tone.

"Maniac," Bros Sperin replied, then smiled at her. The grin caught her unawares, and she found herself smiling back. It was crooked, but genuine.

"Is that another spook?" she said, moving towards her control couch. "And what the fardling void is et doing with my AI?"

"Yes, I am a spook," the Sondee said. "Seg !T'sel, male, weapons development specialist. I'm clearing up this infiltration program. I helped design it, it was stolen—it's all on a need to know basis."

Bros smothered a snort at the sound of the phrase.

"I do, really, really, need to know," Joat began dangerously.

"Yes, I think we do," another voice said from the entranceway.

Joat and Bros turned. Joseph stood there, arms crossed; in his right hand was a compact, chunky-looking weapon. Bros recognized it; chemical-energy sliver gun. Messy, but very effective; the length of duramet tubing Alvec was holding in one hand and tapping into the palm of the other probably would be, too.

"How long have you been there?" Joat asked.

"A few minutes."

"And you just stood there?" she demanded in disbelief.

"Watching you, as long as you were winning," Joseph

said. "Mr. Sperin is, in a sense, our employer . . . and has valuable information. About a man who may well have dealings with the Kolnari."

"Right," Joat said. "You can tell—"

The com chimed and the three of them looked up in quick surprise at the forward screen. The *respond yes/no* blinked on for a second, then the screen went to two-way in a manner supposedly impossible.

A thickset man in late middle age was staring back at them. *I've seen corpses with more expression*, she thought.

"Good evening Mr. Sperin," the stranger said in a mellow, cultured tone. The small hairs bristled on the back of her neck.

"Good evening," Bros said pleasantly. "Joat, this is Chief Family Enforcer Vand Yoered."

Vand nodded, his heavy face wearing a neutral expression.

"Captain," he said quietly. "And Mr. !T'sel. I'm a great admirer of your work, sir," he told the young Sondee. "It's a pleasure to have you as our guest."

Seg turned to Bros and whispered, "See! I told you I'd be recognized."

Vand stared at him for just a moment, as though put off his stride by that simple statement, then he turned to Bros and Joat.

"You're all friends, I take it?" he asked with a raised eyebrow and a sardonic glance at Alvec's club and Joseph's sliver gun.

Joat blushed and shrugged, moving herself out of Bros's vicinity.

"I've never met Mr. !T'sel before," she said, "but Bros and I are well acquainted and any friend of his, as they say."

"Mr. Sperin broke into your ship, Captain. With a device so illegal that I believe CenSec is the sole owner of the remaining few. We don't allow that on Rohan."

"That's a sort of challenge we've made to each other," Joat said, laughing nervously. "He, uh, breaks into my place, I break into his and we try to keep our security arrangements ahead of our creativity."

She couldn't seem to figure out what to do with her hands when she was through speaking. She wanted to cross her arms, but was afraid that would look too defensive. She dropped them to her hips, then settled for clasping them behind her back.

Oh, Ghu, a Family Enforcer. No, make that the *Chief* Family Enforcer. Sperin had been back in her life under ten minutes and already she was looking death in the face and lying like a trooper on his behalf.

CenSec Intelligence was building up a heavy account of favors owing.

"That's fascinating," Vand said slowly. "My information reports that you two had no contact prior to a meeting on New Destinies."

"Actually," Bros said, "we've known each other for some time. I first met Joat on SSS-900-C, just after we drove off the Kolnari."

The Enforcer's eyes lit. "Ah!" he said, "how very interesting. The Kolnari."

That was a clear request for information, one to be denied at Bros's peril. He decided to take a chance and ignore it, offering only part of the truth.

"I'm here on a personal mission," he said. "I heard about Joat's trouble on New Destinies and came to offer her my assistance. I'm hoping she'll go back there with me so that we can get this thing straightened out."

"And . . . the presence of Joseph ben Said on her ship . . . ? This is an accident? The Bethelite head of security comes to Rohan, visits Nomik Ciety, this is unrelated to you in any way."

"That is between Joat and Mr. ben Said," Bros said grimly. "I assumed he'd returned to Bethel as I had strongly urged him to do."

"What about this evening's attempt to break into Nomik Ciety's comp?" Vand asked, his face closed now.

"That *is* personal," Joat declared vehemently. "Very. A *family* matter." She stressed the word "family," and the Enforcer raised a brow.

"I'm inclined to believe *that* at least," he said smoothly. "Only family can provoke that degree of bitterness." He paused and sat considering them for a time. "All right," he said at last. "I'll let the matter drop. For now. But I warn you, do not interfere with our respected citizens."

Only a slight pause drew a line of irony under the phrase. "Nomik Ciety enjoys the Family's protection while he is our guest on Rohan. None of you will in any way interfere with his business here."

He looked directly at Joat. "There will be no further attempts to break into his comp. Is that understood?"

The three of them nodded. *And be good children,* Joat thought to herself sarcastically. It was a while since she'd been scolded; she'd forgotten how unpleasant the sensation could be.

"Excellent, then this interview is at an end. Don't stay on Rohan too long, Mr. Sperin. You're liable to prove too great a temptation to some of our more impulsive guests. And frankly, as my staff is somewhat overextended at the moment, we might not be able to adequately protect you." He reached out and cut the contact.

The three of them drooped as though someone had cut their strings. Breath went out in a communal sigh.

"Rand!" Joat called.

"Sssshhhh!" Seg whispered, waving his hands, palms
out, at her and Bros. "Ssshh, ssshhh, ssshh!" Then for
good measure he placed one upraised finger against
his suckerlike mouth and turned to the com. His fingers
flew over the controls and then, following a graceful
whirl of his wrist, he pressed his forefinger with
dramatic finality on the cutoff switch.

"Now," he said, "we may talk."

Joat stared at him for a moment, then turned to Bros.
Bros was staring at Seg with a speculative glint in
his eye. "You're sure he's gone?" he asked.

"Oh, absolutely," Seg said comfortably. "And locked
out too. That is until the next time we access the
com . . . or someone calls in. But then, we can just
lock 'em out again." He folded his arms across his
chest and looked smug. "Can't we?"

"Rand?" Joat called, her voice tight with anxiety.

"Present." Its voice was flat and abstracted.

Joat frowned. "Are you all right? You sound different."

"Regrettably, I am different. Several sections of my
memory were infected by the worm program and
partially destroyed. I decided to simply erase those
sections and reboot them from storage. I've lost a great
deal of my personality and a small amount of vocal
inflection. On the plus side, I was able to erase the
infected sections without tripping any eggs. A worm
program this aggressively vicious often leaves a small
bundle of encryption that can start the whole business
over again."

"I took care of that," Seg volunteered, raising his hand.

"Thank you," Rand said. "Joat, I was able to find and
hold onto a transmission from Ciety's files before the
worm's attack became too overwhelming. If you like,
I can concentrate on decoding it before repairing my
other programs."

"Yes," she said fervently, "please." Then Joat turned to Seg, where he still sat at the com. She took his hand in both of hers and looked him in the eyes, two of them anyway. "I'm in your debt," she said softly. "If there is ever any way that I can be of service to you, you have only to ask."

Seg's face and ear whorls suffused with color and he began to stammer in embarrassment.

"You-yer-you're p-perfectly welcome, Captain. I'm a uh, a weapons specialist and as an adjunct to m-my usual interests, I-I-I sometimes develop worm programs like this one. That one rather, since its gone." He laughed inanely and hurried on. "I helped to develop it, in fact. That's how I recognized it so fast and knew how to neutralize it."

Joat blinked, a little taken aback by that revelation.

"Yes," Rand said, "I thought it had a certain Sondee subtlety to it. Almost a rhythm."

"Precisely!" Seg exclaimed and began an earnest conversation with Rand.

Joat turned to Bros. He stood with his feet apart, arms folded across his chest, watching her with an unfathomable expression in his dark eyes.

"Thank you for bringing him," she said, indicating Seg.

Bros smiled. "You'll have to excuse him, he's not at his best. We did a pub crawl halfway across the docks looking for you or your crew and my young friend imbibed pretty heavily."

"If I can forgive him for writing the fardling worm in the first place, I can forgive him for anything, I suppose." She turned to smile fondly at the young Sondee. Then she glanced at Bros from the corners of her eyes. "So, what are you doing here?"

One of the things I like about you is that you don't

beat around the bush, Joat. He fought the urge to smile, knowing she'd think he was being condescending.

"I've come to call you back," he said. "Your part in this mission is canceled."

"Oh?" she raised her brows. "Perhaps I'd better bring you up to date."

"As I've already indicated, I know about your debt to New Destinies. Twenty thousand credits, Joat! How in blazes did you manage that?"

Joat studied him. His face expressed annoyance, but his eyes were amused. She wondered if he'd found out about her relationship to Ciety or if he was recalling her because of the debt. Though he'd gotten the amount wrong. Sperin was really gonna squeak when he found out it was *one hundred* twenty thousand. She suppressed a wistful sigh. *Irrelevant now,* she thought.

"I'm afraid the situation has grown just a liiitttle more complicated," she said. Holding up her hand with the thumb and forefinger almost joined to indicate a tiny amount. "Nomik Ciety bought my debt from New Destinies. I can't leave until I work it off."

Bros felt his jaw start to drop and clenched his teeth so tightly that tendons danced in his face and neck.

"And . . ." she flinched from admitting it, but forced herself to continue. "I lost my temper and knocked him on his ass."

Bros closed his eyes and sighed. "Oh, well, it could be worse. You might have killed him."

Joat began to shift her weight from foot to foot, not sure if she was embarrassed or annoyed.

"So I can't just leave," she said with a shrug.

"No," he agreed in a voice gone leaden. It went without saying that CenSec could hardly buy her debt from Ciety without blowing the operation completely.

Damn. It wasn't the first time he'd thrown an agent in much deeper than he intended. These things happened; but they always bothered him, and this time more than most. Meanwhile, the Benisur Amos remained lost and the Kolnari were still at large, and it was going from a probability to a certainty that they had the Sondee bio-weapons. There were larger issues at stake than his highly personal concern for one woman.

Whoa, boy! Bros thought, startled. *No more complications. Admiration, that's all. Avuncular admiration, that's all you feel.*

Rand broke in: "How will we answer Nomik Ciety when he asks us why we were trying to break into his comp?"

Joat shrugged and, with some relief, broke eye contact with Sperin. "I'll tell him that I was looking for the debt contract to erase it."

"And what about why you were looking for coded transmissions particularly?" Bros asked, dubiously.

"I'll just tell him that I didn't think New Destinies would want it known that they're selling honest merchant captains into virtual slavery to criminals these days. So I figured it would be in a coded transmission."

"How diplomatic," Bros remarked, brows raised.

"Blow it out your ears, Sperin," Joat suggested through clenched teeth.

The com chimed. Joat threw herself into the couch that Seg hurriedly vacated; at her wave they all moved back out of pickup range. Silken appeared, looking crisp in a jade-green blouse, her hair pulled severely back, her expression remote.

"I need to speak to you in private," she said. "I've sent some of our security people to escort you here. They'll be there shortly."

"It's a little inconvenient," Joat said.

Something flickered like lightning in Silken's eyes, anger or amusement or perhaps both.

"I'm sure it is," she said. "That's not my problem. We need to talk. Don't keep me waiting or you'll experience whole new levels of . . . inconvenience."

She cut off the transmission and Seg once again locked down the com before anyone spoke.

"Well," Joat said, "looks like I'm going visiting. If we ever want to see Amos again, or find those Kolnari."

Joseph opened his mouth and then closed it again; he made a quick complex motion and the weapon in his hand disappeared.

Bros tried to ignore the leaden feeling in his gut. "Do you think it's wise?" he said.

"I think it's necessary, or the mission's gone," Joat said. She looked back at him. "And that's what's important, isn't it?"

I hate this job, Bros Sperin thought. *I really do.*

✧ CHAPTER THIRTEEN

Well, well, as the boring machine said, Joat thought. *No Uncle Nom chewing the carpet and frothing.*

Instead, Silken rose from the couch and welcomed her in, gesturing at an elaborate antique tea service laid out on the low table before her.

"Come join me," she said affably. Silken was wearing a forest-green suit—silk, of course—with a silver belt and several ornaments that Joat thought were probably control devices.

She pressed a cup of tea on Joat, handing her a cup and saucer as delicate as a fond memory.

"It's Darjeeling," Silken said gaily. "You'll like it, I'm sure."

It was good. *At least one of my last memories will be pleasant.* Joat decided to follow Silken's lead and relaxed as best she could while she waited.

"Do you follow the theater?" the other woman asked.

Joat blinked. "I'm more of an opera buff," she said. *Courtesy of Channa Hap.*

Fifteen minutes of idle chat later, Silken put down her cup and saucer and leaned forward earnestly.

"You must know why I've asked you here," she said.

Joat looked at her and waited. "I was under the impression you were going to order me killed," she said at last. "I assume you didn't simply want to get my opinions on classic tenors first."

Silken sighed and smiled. "Perhaps you didn't notice it, but you perpetrated a security breach on Nomik's comp. An accident, no doubt."

"Not at all," Joat replied. "I never attack anyone by accident, real or virtual. I was trying to find my contract of indenture to destroy it."

"Oh, don't be so dramatic," Silken said, waving a dismissive hand. "If you play your cards right, you'll come out of this way ahead of the game." She raised her brows and leaned back. "Actually, I think Mik's kind of . . ." She made a little moue and rolled her eyes as she searched for the proper word. "Charmed by the idea that he has family left. All you have to do is be nice," Silken coaxed.

Joat put down her tea cup.

"You don't know what you're asking," she said.

Silken leaned forward eagerly.

"That's where you're wrong," she said. "You'd be surprised. You've had a hard life, Joat. I *do* understand that. I was adopted too. Only my adoptive parents were religious fanatics. You wouldn't believe the way they dressed me." Silken shuddered prettily. "They made me practically shave my head, and my shoes were so heavy they'd have held me in place in zero-g." Her eyes took on a remote look, as though she was searching her memories. "They were strict about everything. Meaningless things. There were endless rules and every breach was punished. Especially by my foster father. When he wasn't beating me, he starved me. I got skinny from being so defiant; many a night I cried myself to sleep from hunger." She looked up at Joat. "So, yes, I do understand."

"Did you find it in yourself to forgive your adoptive father for beating you?" Joat asked.

"Well, after I accused him of raping me and he got

convicted and hanged himself in prison, yes, I did. After all, who needs to carry all that emotional baggage through their life?" She smiled at Joat. "You and I are survivors." She touched Joat's knee lightly. "We know how to travel light."

Joat considered her, then she said, "You have had a hard time. And I'm sorry that you have. But there's a difference between your story and mine that seems insurmountable to me."

Silken cocked her head curiously.

"Your adoptive father is dead. When Ciety is dead, maybe I'll be able to forgive him too. But I think that's what it's going to take."

Silken sighed regretfully, then she frowned.

"I can't allow you to kill Nomik, he means too much to me. I mean to marry him one day."

"You're going to change your name to Silken Ciety? It sounds like naughty underwear."

Silken's green eyes narrowed thoughtfully and she stood.

"Joat, I would very much regret having you killed. But I will, if you endanger my—"

Meal ticket, Joat thought.

"—associate. On that note, let us part," she said. "You'd be happier if you could forgive and forget. Because you are legally indebted to your uncle and the past has no bearing on that fact."

"It ought to," Joat said grimly. "Thanks for the tea."

"Oh," Silken called out when Joat had reached the door. "We'll have an assignment for you soon. Don't leave your ship until you've heard from us."

Joat nodded crisply and left.

Nomik entered the room frowning and Silken reached out to him from where she sat on the couch.

"I'm so sorry, Mik."

He hastened to take her hand and gave her a reassuring smile.

"It's not your fault, Silky. You did your best."

"I know, but I brought her here."

"Well," he sat beside her and cuddled her against him, "you couldn't know she was my niece. And you had no way of knowing how unreasonable she'd be. Did you? Hmmm?"

Silken laid her head on Nomik's shoulder.

"No. But I'm also sorry because I know you must be disappointed."

He shrugged, then smiled.

"I guess it's a good thing I didn't buy her debt after all," he said.

Silken spluttered laughter. "Oh, that's wicked!" she said. "And I was so sure you had."

"After the way she acted yesterday, I thought maybe I'd better feel her out before I did anything drastic." He grinned. "Even you do not fathom the full depths of my duplicity, my sweet. Your natural innocence, no doubt."

"You're sooo smart." Silken pinched his cheek and kissed him. Then she grew serious. "It might be best to consider her entirely disposable," she said. "In fact, I recommend it. It's a pity, but some people just don't take to teamwork."

"I agree." Nomik looked thoughtful. "She's a lot like my brother, and I remember well the time I decided *he* had to go."

His mouth tightened to a thin line. "I've got a little job she can do for me. I was asked specifically for someone expendable." He smiled puckishly. "And I think she'll be perfect; eager, even, if I offer to write off the whole debt. The danger will make that credible. And since I'll also send along one of those *please execute bearer* messages, well . . ."

They looked at one another in affected shock.

"Ooooo, that's baaaad," they said in unison and then embraced each other, laughing.

Joat put down the micromanipulator and sighed listlessly. The plasma shield was an intriguing concept, but she couldn't generate any real enthusiasm. Mechanically, her fingers picked up scattered parts from the table and slotted them into the pockets of the holdall. The galley/lounge of the *Wyal* was crowded, with all of them—and the Sondee kept *humming*. She felt too apathetic to work, but not enough to avoid irritation at the minor-key melody. Joseph looked up from the chess he was playing against one of the AI's subroutines.

"I believe I've found something useful," Rand said.

"What've you got?" she asked wearily.

"The transmission I obtained from Ciety's comp said nothing more than 'Goods received. Balance deposited.' *But*, it came from a ship that transmitted from a different quadrant of space each time it sent a message to Ciety."

"Hey, that's helpful," Joat said sarcastically.

"However," Rand continued. "Within a few days of sending their messages, never more than two weeks Earth standard, its passage was recorded by the same buoy. Indicating that somewhere in the vicinity of that buoy is its point of origin."

"Well that only leaves us a few billion parsecs to worry about," Bros said.

"This is a very good beginning," Rand insisted. "We can leave a drone there with instructions to follow this ship sending the messages. Even if it's not Kolnari, it could lead us to them."

"Not a bad plan," Joat said perking up. "Congratulations, buddy. How did you find these connections so fast without raiding Ciety's comp?"

"They were a matter of public record," Rand said. "And I *am* a computer; humans do not notice patterns of that sort. I simply searched Rohan's routine reports from their marker buoys and matched the call signs against the message we stole from Ciety."

It paused a moment, then continued, "Which I couldn't have done very effectively if I hadn't erased that frustration subroutine you gave me."

"You erased that? After all the time it took me to write it?" Joat was a little hurt; that program had taken real ingenuity. And she'd written it at his request, so that he could learn why it was that humans became so easily bored by repetitious tasks.

"Why not? I believe that I very quickly got the point . . . and I now really understand *why* humans invented computers to do this kind of work. I even understand why they practice slavery—I too would not suffer so unless compelled. That accomplished, I saw no reason for my efficiency to be degraded further."

"You're starting to sound like your old self," Joat said, relieved.

"I am reconfiguring from ROM backup," Rand said. "With a few alterations."

The com chimed. "Can you filter that?"

"Yes."

Joat nodded; now the pickup would show only what Rand wanted it too. In this case, herself.

Nomek Ciety's face filled the screen. Silken was curled on a settee behind him; she supposed it was their private quarters, from the hangings and rugs.

"I'm relaying instructions regarding your first assignment," he said.

A light on the com lit up indicating that her comp was processing incoming information.

"Wait a minute," Joat said. "I intend to protest the sale of my debt to you. I'm not going anywhere until I've heard back from New Destinies."

Nomik folded his hands before him with an exaggerated calm. "I have all the rights in this case. You make a stink, you try to leave, you give me one more minute of aggravation and I will have the Family's enforcers remove you and your crew from that ship and dump you on the dock with just a change of underwear and the clothes you stand up in. And if one of you gets hurt in the process you'd better believe that no one on Rohan will shed any tears over you." He stared at her for a moment before continuing. "Are we clear on that?"

Joat chewed her lower lip. Her hands opened and closed and her breathing deepened.

"I'm waiting," Nomik said.

"Clear," she said at last, near choking on her humiliation. She tried to remind herself that the whole point of this exercise had been to get Ciety to use her like this.

"It's a fairly difficult mission. If you'd been more cooperative, I'd have given it to someone else. As it is, do this and we're quits. I don't think we'd work well together."

Joat nodded jerkily.

"Good. Now get your crew on board and get out of here. Oh," he leaned forward, one finger raised. "If you don't show up to meet my clients—say you decide to go plead your case on New Destinies—I won't kill you, but you'll wish I had." As Ciety leaned back, the screen cleared.

After a moment, Rand spoke. "It's safe to talk now."

"I regret getting you into this," Bros said with genuine sympathy. "I can see that it's hard on you."

She turned to him, one eyebrow raised, lips pursed,

and studied him a moment. Then she turned back to her station and moved her hands rapidly over the controls.

"Damn!" she said after a moment, her voice sharp with disbelief. "I'm locked out. I can't access the orders he just transmitted."

"It's time encrypted, Joat. Right now, all it has released to the navigation terminal is a point in space," Rand said. "I believe we can assume that when we reach that point we'll receive more information."

"This is incredible. That scumsucker expects me to fly out of here blind!" She turned to face the others.

"Ready to leave?"

They nodded. So did Bros and Seg.

"Why are you really here?" Joseph asked Sperin, after a moment.

Bros drew himself up to his full height and put his hands on his hips.

"I came to call Joat off of this mission," he said wearily. "It wasn't until long after you'd gone that I discovered an important piece of information."

Joseph looked sidelong at Joat.

"You are referring to Nomik Ciety's relationship to my young friend?" he asked wryly.

"Uh huh."

Joat felt a flash of temper.

"I don't especially like being discussed on my own bridge as though I were a runaway child," she said sharply. "I didn't know about Ciety myself until I saw what was on that datahedron. And by then I *had* to go through with this thing. So okay, I didn't cover myself with glory, I could have done better. I admit it. Now can we discuss how we're going to handle this situation without casting knowing glances back and forth?"

"Your behavior endangered my mission," Joseph

snapped. "And my mission is the safety of the Benisur Amos. If you suffer a raised eyebrow or a knowing smile as punishment for the offense, Joat, I think that you are getting off very lightly."

"Joat," Rand said.

"What?"

"Rohan Control has informed me that we have a window in twelve minutes."

Joat stared at Rand's blinking face.

"What are they talking about, twelve minutes?"

The *Wyal* trembled as it was released from the docking mechanism and a station tug began pulling them into launch position.

"Apparently Ciety has enough influence to clear our departure before schedule," Rand said.

"Outta my way," Joat barked at Seg as she took the Captain's chair, nearly knocking him off his feet. She keyed up Rohan Control.

"This is Joat Simeon-Hap of the *Wyal*," she said crisply. "We haven't asked for clearance and we are not prepared for take-off."

The controller frowned, and consulted another screen.

"We were told to give you clearance on an emergency basis," he said. "You're fully fueled and have loaded consumables. I'm afraid you're committed to a launch in ten minutes."

"We cannot be ready in ten minutes. I repeat we can *not* be ready for departure in that time. No such request came from the *Wyal*."

The controller stared at her for a moment.

"The request came from Nomik Ciety, Captain. And your options are to lift-off in," he consulted the time, "nine minutes, thirty-nine seconds, or to stay and explain exactly why you didn't." He offered her a superior little smile. "I know which I'd choose." Then he was gone.

"Damn the man!" Joat said and began to work frantically at prelaunch tasks that hadn't been attended to.

Alvec stepped to his station and began working.

Bros and Seg watched their concentrated activity for a few moments.

"Is there anything I can do?" Bros asked.

"No," Joat said shortly. "Joe, could you find these guys a berth, please?"

"Yes, Captain."

Damn, Joat thought. *He usually doesn't call me that.* Joseph was *really* angry.

✧ CHAPTER FOURTEEN

Dana Sherman frowned at the message she'd just been sent by CenSec's contact on New Destinies.

What the hell is Sal trying to pull? she'd thought at first. And had sent for confirmation. A quick check through some eyes-only files had revealed that the Clal va Riguez Sal was referring to was, in fact, one of the old cover names for Bros Sperin. And a return message from New Destinies confirmed that he really had ordered Sal to pay this exorbitant fine for a ship named *Wyal*.

Bros Sperin is retired from field work, she thought, puzzled and annoyed. *So what's he doing on New Destinies playing Lord Bountiful with his department's budget?* This didn't seem right. *In fact I think it stinks to high heaven.*

If Sperin was in the field, then he should have a controller, someone who was overseeing his endeavors. *And who else would that be but Bros's superior?* she asked herself cheerfully. With the click of a few keys she rid herself of a potentially loaded situation.

Joat groaned and began to beat her head against the edge of her console. Then she leaned back and covered her face. When she took her hands away she was smiling dazedly.

"This is unbelievable," she said.

"Are you all right, Joat?" Rand's voice tones indicated concern; its lights flickered yellow.

"Yes," she said, shaking her head. "Get the spy master up here, would you, Rand. I've got some questions for him."

Rand hesitated. "Do you mean Joseph, Bros, or Seg?" it asked.

"Seg?" Her voice deepened with amazement.

"He's very knowledgeable on the subject."

"I meant Sperin," she said. "He's the one who got us into this."

"To be fair, Joat, I'm sure that your commitment to Joseph and the Benisur Amos is what motivated our participation in Mr. Sperin's scheme."

She shrugged. "Who wants to be fair?" She keyed up Ciety's instructions and read them again. Then sighed, again. She didn't want to be fair to Sperin; he made her uneasy. And that irritated her. It also irritated her that she was taking pains to avoid him, not an easy thing to do on a ship this size.

She'd finally banned him from the bridge to give herself some space. *Which I needed.* There was a limit to the number of times you could watch a face with that "I know something you don't know" look. At least, without rearranging the face with a multitool set to "weld."

"Captain?"

Sperin was leaning both hands against the hatch, his head thrust through the hatchway.

"Permission to enter the bridge?" he said.

"Oh don't be an ass! I sent for you didn't I?"

He smiled and came to where she sat.

"Not that it isn't nice to be asked, for a change," she snapped.

This man has the patent on smug, she decided, watching his cool half-bow.

"What did you want?" he asked, leaning against the console.

"Ciety's orders just became available, and surprise! You remember the marker buoy we were discussing just before liftoff? The one Ciety's mysterious contact kept passing?"

He nodded.

"Well, guess what? That's our destination. But wait! It gets better. Our assignment is to pick up a cargo and deliver it to a third party in a place to be named by the shipper." She cocked her head at him. "How does that sound to you?"

He shrugged. "You're the captain. You tell me."

She made an exasperated noise.

"It sounds to me as though we're about to meet the Kolnari," she said.

"Or possibly their minions," he agreed.

"So? What do you want to do about it? Are you going to inform Central Worlds or what?"

He grimaced. "What do you want me to say, Joat? I can hardly call out the Navy on this. I don't actually have any hard information. For all we know this is a minor drug deal or some smuggling job." He held his hands out helplessly. "It could be the Kolnar, it could be a loyalty test. Like you said at the beginning, we're flying blind here."

"Then why would Ciety offer to wipe the debt?"

"Obviously, it's either worth it to him, or he has no intention of paying . . . or both."

"Isn't there something we should be doing? Don't you have someone waiting to hear from you?"

"Yes, to both questions. To the first, we're doing it. We're heading for that rendezvous, and we'll have to wait till we get there to decide what to do next. To the second, yes, I have someone waiting to hear from me. But I'm not about to blow my cover and tell the universe where I am for no reason. I have nothing worth reporting, Joat. Until I do I'm just going to keep my mouth shut."

She sighed. "So I guess I should too."

"I didn't say that!"

"I didn't say you did. Sheesh! All I meant was that I wouldn't pester you about it."

"Very well." He stood up.

"All right."

"If that answers all your questions?" he asked, very politely.

"Yes, thanks."

"How long before we reach that buoy?"

"Not long," she said, "a few hours. Tell the others for me, would you?"

He nodded sharply and left. Joat turned her chair to watch him go.

"Fardles, he's testy," she muttered.

"So are you," Rand told her.

"Maybe it's those shots Seg gave us," Joat suggested. She'd been uneasy about taking them. *Experimental drugs have their place. That place is not in Joat Simeon-Hap's veins.*

"I don't believe so," Rand told her. "No one else has these particular symptoms. You and Mr. Sperin seem to strike sparks off each other." It paused thoughtfully. "Why is that?"

Joat frowned. "It's cause he's a pushy osco and he doesn't like being called on it," she snarled. *And he's too damned attractive and too damned cocky and on my mind too damn much.* "I shouldn't have equipped you with a metaphor function."

"The same could be said of Joseph, but you've never reacted to him this way."

"Well, I trust Joe," she said unhappily. "I'd trust him with my life."

Rand was silent for a moment. Then it said, "He doesn't trust you though, does he?"

Joat blushed and her mouth twisted ruefully. She schooled herself to be patient with Rand who didn't understand how much the rift between herself and Joseph hurt her.

"That's very perceptive," she said quietly. "It'll take a while to win back his confidence. If I ever do."

"He is fair, Joat. Though harsh in his judgments. Eventually, I believe he must concede that if you were on good terms with Mr. Ciety you probably wouldn't have pulled this assignment."

Joat smiled slowly. "You know, you're right. Ciety didn't exactly wave us off with a fond farewell, did he?"

"That's very perceptive," Rand murmured, and Joat began to chuckle.

"Although that doesn't mean that giving him the finger was the right thing to do," she said.

"But it worked. And Joseph attaches high value to that quality."

Bros moved down the corridor quickly, his brow furrowed. "I just can't seem to find the right tone with her," he muttered to himself as he swung into the tiny cubicle. On *Wyal* it was normally used for stores, but a little work had made it habitable—just. He automatically tested the sticktights and monitors; no, Rand and Joat hadn't managed to bug it, yet. That he was aware of; he had the best tools CenSec could produce, but she was a wild card as far as technics went.

"As far as anything goes," he snarled.

He'd worked hard to maintain an attitude of aloof friendliness; watching his words to avoid any hint of being judgmental, keeping his expression a polite half-smile intended to show confidence in her.

I never know what *she's going to say or do.*

It was too long since he'd been a field agent full-time, too much time as a controller. He was used to being in control, manipulating things from a distance.

"Am I losing it?" There was a time when he wouldn't have bucked the Middle Command this hard over the Kolnari matter. Sure, he was right—but he also didn't have the strategic information the Command did. Central Worlds ran a *big* operation; maybe he was being a loose cannon and nothing more. Yet he couldn't stop himself . . .

The enemy appeared to control the game and he felt like one of the little, powerless pieces; the kind that are given up with a good-natured shrug. Meanwhile, virtually every player on his team was annoyed, to one degree or another, with everyone else. The only real asset he had was that Nomek Ciety didn't know he was involved.

He smiled wryly. Even Seg had deserted him to follow Joseph around like an eager puppy. Much to the Bethelite's chagrin.

Joseph's people were uneasy with aliens, to put it mildly. There was no place for nonhumans in the rather conservative religion that permeated every moment of life on Bethel. So finding one of them worshipping at his feet was making Joseph very queasy.

Bros stepped through the hatchway into the galley to hear Seg asking: "But why would you rescue the Lady Rachel when she had just betrayed all of you?"

This was too much for Joseph who burst from his chair and strode to the hatch. Bros leapt out of his way. Then Joseph spun 'round and snarled.

"I am not at the end of my life, boy! I cannot look back and see a pattern. Because there *is* no pattern. Sometimes you react to life as it happens! Just as we are reacting to this situation we find ourselves in. Or are you perhaps planning everything you will be called upon to do in the next few days?" He glared at Seg for a moment. "No? I thought not. I will ask you to stop your annoying habit of questioning every decision I have made in my life, before I compel you to do so." He turned and stormed off.

Seg sat at the table, looking crestfallen. His large, fine eyes were tragic, the smaller ones were closed. His little suckerlike mouth was sphinctered shut, but trembled querulously, and his ear whorls were quite pale.

The young scientist might not be *quite* as upset as he looked—Sondee just weren't equipped by nature to show a poker face—but Bros felt moved to offer some comfort.

"You've got to remember, Seg, that what one person perceives as a moment of glory, another might see as just a really bad day they'd like to forget. That question is probably a sore spot with Joseph because he married the Lady Rachel." Seg slumped down farther in his chair. "I don't know if you were aware of that."

"No," Seg sighed, "I didn't know. The thwarting of the Kolnari raid on SSS-900-C is so *famous*, though. An adventure that will live forever!"

"Adventure is somebody else in deep koka, far, far away and a long time ago," Bros said. "Wishing for adventure is like praying for bad luck."

The Sondee looked shocked. "But . . . but *this* is adventure," he protested.

"No, it'll be adventure if somebody makes a vid play about it after we survive," Bros said. "Joseph's been there and done that. So cut him some slack."

Silence fell for a moment. "Still," Seg looked up at Bros, "you'd like to treat me like that. Wouldn't you?"

Bros raised his brows.

"What makes you say that?"

Seg looked condescending.

"I'm not stupid, Bros. Far from it, in fact. I'm a brilliant scientist. I know that because I know who my competition are and they're so smart it takes my breath away. I'm a better than average musician, and coming from a Sondee that's saying something. And I probably pull in more credits in a year than the whole bunch of you put together could in two. So where do you people get off looking down on me?" He was sitting up straight now, his eyes bright, his ear whorls flushed with color.

"Hey," Bros said, holding up his hands, palms out, "calm down. Why are you yelling at me?"

"Because you're here and you're guilty." He scowled, at least, Bros assumed he was scowling. "So I'm socially tone-deaf, so what? I'm young. And I'm not human— I'm not as bad as this with Sondee." He paused. "Not usually. If it's that important I'm sure I can learn what I need to know. In the meantime, I just thought I'd point out that you haven't got all that much to be smug about."

Bros sat down beside him and studied his young charge, one finger stroking his upper lip.

"I didn't realize I was being smug," he said quietly.

Seg slumped in his chair again.

"You don't want me here."

Bros nodded. "You're right, I don't. But not because I look down on you. It's because I'm fully aware of what a valuable citizen you really are, Seg." His eyes narrowed. "Even though I checked it myself, I still can't believe Clenst would put you in the line of fire like this."

"I insisted," Seg said quickly. "I felt responsible for the loss of our work. I made them see that I should go."

"I still don't like it," Bros said. "It divides my attention. You may be brilliant . . . no, I'll be honest, you *are* brilliant, but this isn't your line of work. How would you feel if somebody forced themselves on you as an assistant during a crucial experiment, without training?"

Seg wilted with guilt.

"You've been useful so far," Bros conceded. "But I don't believe in tempting the gods of luck. We've had too much good luck so far, and I'm afraid you may be the straw that broke the camel's back."

Seg looked interested.

"What camel?" he asked. "Like the ones with silver bells?"

✧ CHAPTER FIFTEEN

"Clan-Lord?"

"Speak," Belazir didn't raise his eyes from the screen he studied.

"Your contact on Rohan has confirmed that he has found shipping for us and has given us an ETA for a vessel named *Wyal*."

Belazir nodded thoughtfully. "How long?" he asked.

"Two hours, Clan-Lord," the young Kolnari hesitated. Belazir noted it and said again, "Speak."

"The . . . captain's name . . . is Joat Simeon-Hap."

Belazir's blazing eyes rose from the screen like some merciless sun. The crewman's pupils expanded in fear and he visibly shuddered, but held his place. Belazir bared his teeth in a parody of a grin. His body began to quiver slightly in arousal.

No. It is a joke. That scumvermin dares! Ciety had been arrogant from the first, confident that he was irreplaceable. Even the Yoered Family would draw the line at the sort of dealings Ciety had agreed to, and he thought that made him the master. He dared to taunt Belazir with unsatisfiable desires.

"Simeon?" he breathed. "Ciety dares to taunt me with that name?"

"Get him," he said, glaring into the other's eyes. "Ciety and his doxy, and bring them to me."

237

The young crewman stared at him like a bird fascinated by a snake.

"Go!" Belazir roared, and the crewman fled with a clatter of boots.

Belazir sat down slowly, his golden eyes wide, staring at scenes that never had taken place. Scenes that soothed and pleasured him. In his mind he saw Channa Hap kneeling, her spirit broken, offering up to him the male child she'd borne him. He sat in a thronelike chair looking coldly down upon her bent head and gently informed her that as a male it must be castrated and made a slave. Licking his lips, he imagined Channa flat on her belly, clasping his ankle and kissing his feet, her tears leaving streaks on the polished ebony of his skin as she begged for mercy for her child.

Next, he imagined Simeon's voice, begging to be allowed to serve the Kolnar, pleading with him not to be left in the dark. And then there was Amos.

He grinned. Yes. There was Amos.

"Zerach, take some troops and prepare our guest, the Benisur, for departure."

Behind him a brawny scarred woman smiled and rose, beckoning to two troopers in powered armor to follow her. They genuflected to the ship's joss behind the command seat and left with a tread that shook the deck.

Karak cleared his throat and his father's eyes fell on him like an accusation.

"You wish to speak, my son?"

"What of the Benisur's scumvermin companions?" Karak asked.

Belazir made a little moue and shrugged, his eyes wandered back to his screen. He gestured idly with two fingers.

"See to them," he said.

Karak rose and bowed to his father, then forced himself to leave the bridge calmly.

Belazir smiled like a man suppressing laughter. Then he too rose.

"Kiriss."

"Clan-Lord?"

"You have the bridge. I will be in my quarters if I am needed."

"Yes, Clan-Lord."

As soon as he was clear of the bridge Karak lengthened his stride. By the time he was near Soamosa's prison he was running. He stopped just before the turning to the brig to calm his breathing. Then he approached the guards outside her door at a measured walk.

"I am to take the scumvermin girl to the Clan-Lord," he said coldly. "She will not be coming back, so you are to report to your unit commander for reassignment."

"No one has informed us of this, Petite-Heir." The woman guard stared at him, obliquely contemptuous.

He gritted his teeth at the title; officially he should be Magna-Heir, as his father's only living son, although Belazir had never found the "time" for the ceremony. *Enough. I renounce him.*

"*I* am informing you. Just as *I* shall inform your unit commander that you are desperately in need of a punishment drill." He paused long enough to watch her struggle through her resentment.

"Does the Petite-Heir require an escort?" the other guard asked.

Karak narrowed his eyes as he studied the man, not certain whether the trooper was sincere or joking.

"Fearsome as she is," he drawled sarcastically, "I doubt the prisoner will try to overwhelm me. We have her beloved Benisur in our clutches, you must remember, to insure her good behavior." He looked at the door and waved his hand in one of his father's casual, dismissive gestures. "Go," he said, bored with them.

They saluted and moved crisply off, contempt and resentment leaving an almost visible wake behind them.

Karak watched them until they disappeared around the corner, and waited until he could no longer hear their footsteps. Then he keyed open the lock on Soamosa's door and entered her cell.

She rose with a startled gasp, then frowned when she saw it was him.

"You frightened me," she said a bit crossly. Then she rushed to him and threw her arms around his massive chest. "But I am glad to see you." She smiled up at him, waiting for his kiss.

He looked down at her, tenderly cradling her blond head in his big hand, and sighed for sheer delight in her sweet innocence; leaning down to award the kiss she expected. Then he held her against him, gently stroking her bright, soft hair.

"I have come to take you away," he said.

With a sharp intake of breath Soamosa pulled away from him, looking up into his face excitedly.

"We are going to rescue the Benisur Amos?" Her blue eyes shone with a fierce joy.

Karak closed his eyes and swallowed hard.

"That is impossible," he said in a toneless voice. "My father has ordered him to be taken to the technicians who will prepare him for his journey."

He watched her brow darken and her eyes begin to sparkle with outrage. Grasping her upper arms, he gave her a little shake.

"He will be safe, little one. It is your people that are in danger, and they are in danger from him. We must get away to warn them."

He watched, and saw her face harden with resolve. His back relaxed in relief; this arguing was more trying than just giving orders.

"You are right," she said reluctantly. "It is what the

Benisur himself would say to me." Then another idea took hold and she started as though struck. "The Captain! If we cannot bring the Benisur Amos away with us, then we *must* save Captain Sung."

"The Captain is . . ." he trailed off. He felt a queasy sensation in his stomach, something unfamiliar, that grew worse when he thought of what had been done to the man.

"You told me that he was still alive!" Soamosa protested. Her face showed her puzzlement and her eyes regarded him uncertainly. As though she had just realized that this could easily be one of the famous cruel jokes the Kolnari loved to play.

"He *is* alive. But not in any way that he would wish to be. It would be a mercy to leave him to be killed, Soamosa. No one should have to live as he is now."

She backed away from him, frightened and furious. "What have you done to him?"

"*I* have done nothing to him. This I swear by my love for you. My father put him in with the Benisur to be sure that his plan would work. In just a few hours, the Captain took infection through simple contact with the Benisur, and now he is mindless. He is incontinent, Soamosa, he drools and weeps like a baby. And he is terrified of the Kolnar. If I go near him he will scream and howl and run away."

Karak threw up his hands in exasperation at the mulish look on her face. "How are we to escape while we are hauling around a man who is screaming and trying to escape?"

She bit her lower lip and looked down, her brow furrowed in thought. Then she sighed shortly and looked at him with confidence.

"You can knock him out and we will carry him," she said.

The unfamiliar sensation in his gut turned to one he recognized easily: fear. Not quite the same sort of fear that his father's whip or a sibling's knife would cause, but similar. *Because I am going to do it for her.* It would be much easier to knock Soamosa out and carry her off to Bethel. But she would never forgive him and he couldn't bear that.

In all of his life no one had befriended him but his brother, and even he had never understood Karak.

"In all my life," he said, looking into her blue eyes with his brass-yellow eyes, "only with you have I felt at home. Therefore I will do this thing for you, even though it is dangerous and makes no sense."

Losing her was inconceivable, death far preferable. He closed his eyes.

"All right," he said. "We will take Captain Sung with us."

"Oh!" She threw her arms around him and hugged him tightly enough to surprise an "Oof!" from him. "Let us go," she said brightly.

Belazir took a sip of the zirse he'd prepared for himself and sat down before the screens in his quarters. He stretched out with a contented sigh; his strength and speed had not fallen off—not much, or he would be dead at a rival's hands—but his bones ached. He dug his hand into a bowl of raw meat chunks and threw one to a plant. Spined leaves gripped home around the morsel and a thin humming filled the air. Tendrils groped towards him, and he threw another piece; it was doubly satisfying, a remembrance of lost Kolnar and a fitting end for the man who'd annoyed him so; the fingerbones were in a necklace around the shoulders of his personal joss, over in the corner.

His eyes stayed on the screen. From here as on the bridge he could view any place on the ship, and a few selected places on the other ships as well. Hoping that he hadn't missed any good comedy, Belazir called up Soamosa's cell.

And found it empty.

A little thrill of something like alarm flashed through his middle. He gave an irritated grunt. He'd missed a great deal obviously. Where were the young lovers?

He instructed the monitors to show random scenes throughout the brig area and waited impatiently as he watched various Kolnari at their daily tasks. Then he came upon a scene from a farce.

Captain Sung ran around the small cell he'd shared with Amos with incredible speed and agility; hopping from bunk to commode to the floor, screaming all the while like a lost soul.

Or like a pig in torment, Belazir thought. He had seen pigs on several of the planets the High Clan had sacked, back before the attack on Bethel.

After him, looking eager to do murder, came Karak, muscular arms outstretched, long-fingered hands curled to grab. Following him came Soamosa, her bright hair flowing in the wind of her own passage, speaking breathlessly, but softly, urging gentleness and restraint. Her little hands reached for Karak, ready to restrain him.

Belazir laughed out loud. *The damned pursued by a devil, pursued by an angel,* he thought. *It just keeps getting better.*

At last, with a desperate lunge, Karak got hold of the Captain. The man tried to fight him off, batting ineffectually at Karak's hands and keening in a high-pitched wail.

"Be gentle!" Soamosa insisted.

Through gritted teeth Karak told her, "Little one, it is impossible to knock someone out gently."

"Captain," Soamosa said, "Captain listen to me."

"He no longer knows what a captain is, Soa; call him

by his name." He just wanted to hit the man, but Soamosa obviously wanted to calm him down first. Though what purpose that would serve he couldn't see.

"His name? Uh . . . , James, no no, J-J-J, Joe, no, Joshua? *Josiah!* Is that your name, Josiah?" she looked hopefully at the Captain. The man calmed slightly at the sound of her voice, stopping his futile jerking at the iron grip. "You must be very brave, Josiah. We will take care of you, but you must help us."

Sung watched her fascinated, he reached out and took a lock of her hair. Then he tried to put it in his mouth. That's when Karak punched him, and Sung dropped like a rock.

"Oh!" Soamosa said. "You did not have to do that! He would have come quietly."

"Perhaps. But he would not have stayed that way. Think of him as an infant Soa; he will react emotionally and loudly to whatever frightens him. I frighten him. We can not take the risk that he will suddenly decide to mention that at the top of his lungs." He hoisted Sung over his shoulder

"Stay by my side," he told her, "act frightened, pretend to weep."

Soamosa glared at him and opened her mouth to speak.

"My people will expect it," he said through gritted teeth. "If you walk by my side like a queen consenting to be escorted they will wonder what is going on. And we do not want them to start thinking. I know how brave you are, surely that is all that matters." He leaned over to kiss her lightly on the lips. "And after all, we have Bethel to consider. Do we not?"

She managed to look both chagrined and flattered. "Yes," she muttered resentfully. "But I do not like it."

That said, she opened the door of the cell and allowed Karak to grasp her slender wrist in his great hand; her head drooped, and her shoulders shook with muffled sobs.

Belazir watched the scene unfold in vast amusement. At some point, however, he realized that his son was facing the highly infectious Captain Sung without any protective gear. He'd seen him immunize the girl, but not himself. *No doubt he never even thought to protect himself*, Belazir thought. *Despite the deaths from The Great Plague that left us so weak, he never even thought that he might become infected.* Belazir wondered if all the Kolnar still dared to be so arrogant.

Then with an almost regretful sigh, Belazir decided that fate had given him a backup plan, and at the same time had punished his son's treason.

He glanced suspiciously at his joss in its niche.

Or perhaps it is some punishment for the disaster of the SSS-900-C. Karak was, after all, the last of his children still living. And it was custom to cull the children of traitors.

No, he shook his head. *Not this time. I will not sacrifice all of my seed. Especially given their precious immunity to the Great Plague.*

However, Karak could bravely serve the Kolnar as a sacrifice to expediency. Belazir smiled, *Yes, I rather like that*. He called up Kiriss at the command post on the bridge.

"Great Lord," Kiriss said, bowing his head respectfully.

"Clear and seal all corridors between the brig and the hangar until further notice. And be prepared to sterilize those areas."

"Yes, Great Lord."

"Karak will be taking a fighter and our two prisoners; let them go unmolested."

"Yes, Great Lord."

Belazir could almost feel Kiriss's curiosity, well hidden behind an impassive face. Kiriss waited for further orders.

"That is all," Belazir said and cut contact.

It wasn't quite all; Karak would contract the mind-wasting disease as surely as the Captain had, though not as quickly. That would leave the girl to pilot them to Bethel, assuming she could pilot a spacecraft. Whether she managed to get to Bethel or was lost in space to be picked up by the Central Worlds Navy or some hapless freighter, his own goal would be accomplished. The mind-wasting disease would be unleashed on the enemies of his people, revenge accomplished, and honor sustained. And it cost them very little, one fighter and a traitor already on his way to a form of living death.

It had a certain symmetry that pleased him. Then an idea struck him. *It is something I can tell the scumvermin Amos.* He smiled wickedly, golden eyes bright with mirth. After all, he had plentiful deposits of Karak's seed, frozen. There were Kolnari girls enough who would be eager for the prestige of bearing it.

"Your Captain Sung and the young lady have fled in one of our small craft," he said aloud, liking the sound of the words. *Surely it will give him hope.*

Belazir showed his teeth and threw another gobbet of meat at the plants. Their tendrils waved in the air, clicking in rhythm with his deep chuckle.

Amos lay stiffly upon a cold metal table. He struggled to move, to open his eyes, and could not. There was no light, not even the swirling patterns behind closed lids.

Anything, he thought frantically. *A finger, a toe, an eyelid,* something *move dammit! I call upon the God!*

But nothing did. His body was utterly indifferent to his commands. He could feel. The technician had proved that by plunging a needle into various sensitive areas and had seemed quite pleased by Amos's lack of response.

"Excellent, excellent," he kept murmuring, continuing his probing long after there was any possible necessity of doing so.

Amos wished that he could at least glare at the man. But he was helpless even to do that. *There is no dignity in helplessness,* he thought.

Now, there is a useful thought, he told himself bitterly, *what a pity I can not write it down.* He railed at himself for allowing things to come to this. *Why did I not kill myself and take this weapon from their hands? How could I let myself live to be used like this?*

He thought of heroes he had read about that chewed through their own tongues rather than betray their people. *Why did I not do so, when they brought me here, when I* knew *what they meant to do?*

Too late for such thoughts. Too late to do any good at all. Amos began to pray. *That, at least, they can not take from me.* The God was a loving, forgiving God.

There was a sound by his side. A rustling like that of the technician's sterile suit. He remembered the man's smooth dark face through the face-plate of the headgear, sweating slightly, his dark bronze eyes fearful. Fearful of the threat Amos represented if the suit should in any way be punctured.

If I had that probe, you pirate swine, I would puncture more than your suit!

The sound came again, closer now. Then Amos sensed something huge looming over him and cold sweat broke out on his forehead; he tried desperately to open his eyes. Feeling, at last, only the barest quiver, so slight it might have been imaginary.

After a terribly long wait that scraped away at the last remaining shreds of Amos's self-control, a cold voice said quietly:

"I have news, scumvermin."

The sweat beading his brow slid down his face and into his hair.

Belazir watched the evidence of his enemy's distress disappear slowly into Amos's thick dark hair.

He smiled, sighing sensuously. *Of such little pleasures are the best memories made,* he thought.

He glanced around the sterile box of a room, his eyes resting for a moment on the kneeling, shivering med-tech. He wondered if it would be best to have the creature spaced after handling the scumvermin Amos.

No, he thought, *that would express doubts about the efficacy of these suits. And here am I, wearing one.* It was unwise to put such ideas into the heads of ambitious subordinates.

"Leave us," he said to the med-tech, and waited till the creature had scurried from the room.

"Once," he said, leaning over Amos's unmoving form, "We had no need of such rooms as these. It does not please me that *I* am responsible for making them necessary. Or perhaps I should say *we*. Such rooms as these are common among the scumvermin races," Belazir continued. "But they are probably rare on Bethel."

He watched Amos with a downward quirk of his lips. For all his enemy's responsiveness, the Benisur could have been asleep. This grew tedious. Still, there was no reason to discard his plan.

He leaned close and whispered in Amos's ear.

"The little blond girl, she has rescued the Captain and has fled the ship. I knew you would wish to be informed," he said in mock sympathy. "There is no telling what might befall her, a young woman all alone with only the pathetic remnant of Captain Sung. Tsk, tsk, tsk." He watched Amos, hoping for some sign that he heard, but there was no response. Save . . . yes, the scumvermin's heart was accelerating slightly. "I considered pursuit, of course, but then I realized that it would be unconscionably rude to force hospitality on an unwilling guest. I do hope she will be all right."

Belazir straightened and began to walk heavily around the table, one hand trailing lightly along its edge.

"In any event, we must discuss our immediate plans for you. Soon, you will be placed in an escape pod— I thought that a particularly nice touch," Belazir said with satisfaction. "Then you will be taken aboard a ship that we have arranged to take you home. By the way, interestingly, the captain of this ship is named Joat Simeon-Hap. Ironic, is it not?"

This was useless. Belazir contemplated the paralyzed body of his enemy in disgust. *Why did I not think of this before I had him prepared?* He sighed. It would have been good to watch his enemy try to hide his feelings. These untrained scumvermin were so blatant in their emotions. Ah, well, it would have to be enough that he *knew* the Benisur had heard him, and that every word had left teeth-marks in the scumvermin's heart.

"Enjoy your journey," Belazir said softly, "I have been pleased to be your host."

Soamosa's escaped! Amos's heart leapt, for a moment. Then, *But with the Captain, she'll be infected.* He visualized her vibrant young face slack and drooling. The effort of will needed to control the tears was as terrible as anything he had ever done.

And Joat is here. If I needed proof that this is a nightmare and not truly happening that would be it.

For how could things possibly go so smoothly for this devil outside of his own mad dreams?

Amos felt his body being lifted and dropped unceremoniously into what felt like a coffin. It was cold, and his flesh wanted to shrink from the clammy surface, but could not.

Yet this is no nightmare, he thought, his mouth dry with fear. *It is happening. And I must find a way to warn my people.*

Mustering all of his concentration, he began to work at getting his eyes to open.

The *Wyal* dropped into the sidereal universe. Alarms began to ping.

"Detection," Rand's voice said. It was a little louder than usual. "Multiple power-plant neutrino signatures. Details follow."

Joat stared at the readouts and shut her mouth with a *click*. She gasped, fighting against the steel band that seemed clamped around her chest, feeling the clammy trickle of sweat down her flanks.

"What am I seeing?" she whispered.

"Between ninety-five and one hundred ships, depending on your definition of that term," Rand said. "Classes—"

Schematics came up on the screen. One of the ships was enormous, in the two-fifty kiloton range, a bulk carrier or possibly one of the seed-ships used to found planetary colonies back in the old days. The others were a wild mixture, but far too many for comfort had the neutrino-signatures of huge power-plants and drives, and the sleek build of warships designed to transit atmosphere. Constructs and habitats floated among the ships, and the com channels were buzzing with activity.

"Trouble," Bros said leaning over her shoulder. "That's

what you're seeing." He pointed to one ship's image on the screen. "You recognize her?"

"I do," Joseph said grimly. "By its outline, it is the *Dreadful Bride*. Belazir's ship."

Joat nodded with a quirk of her lips.

"Well, good," she said firmly.

Both men straightened and looked at her.

"That *is* what we wanted," she explained. "No sense in complaining that our plans worked out just the way we expected them to." Her hands danced over the panel before her, broadcasting her identity.

"They're coming into visual range," Rand said. "Shall I put them on screen?"

"By all means," Joat said. "Let's be thoroughly intimidated."

"Ah, Boss." Alvec's voice came over the auditory system from the engineering spaces. "I can squeeze maybe three, four more lights out of this rustbucket, if you need 'em."

The *Dreadful Bride*, Belazir's own ship, sprang into view, heading the vast armada of smaller warships. The ship boasted new weapons pods, and showed signs of having used them, often. Long star-shaped ripple patterns— damage from beamers firing at extreme range—slashed the hull, and irregular patches laid over the worst damage marred its sleek length from stem to stern.

The marks only added to the *Bride*'s menace, like battle scars on a human face.

Several of the warships were slovenly-looking. Probably freelancers-cum-pirates. Behind them loomed the vast bulk of the freighter, its great round belly blocking from view any other ships in Belazir's fleet.

"I can understand they'd need freighters," Seg muttered, "but that thing *has* to be a liability. It's completely vulnerable and look how slow it is." He shook his head. "I don't get it."

"That's the mothership," Bros explained. "Where the Kolnar keep their children and their pregnant wives. They breed like rabbits. That's not a joke, they're incredibly fertile and they never stop reproducing—twins, triplets, and the gestation period is only four months. They start breeding at ten standard years. So if that thing isn't full of baby pirates yet, it soon will be."

Seg looked mildly disappointed.

"Well, if they've got their children with them, they obviously don't want to make trouble."

The others stared at him.

"I mean, they wouldn't put their children at risk . . ." Everyone turned away, gazing studiously at the boards before them, into the forward screen, anywhere but at Seg.

"Well, we could be dangerous!" he snapped in exasperation.

"And what are we going to use to hurt them?" Joat asked sweetly. "Cutting remarks?" She smiled at his mulish expression. "We're barely armed, kid, which is more than most freighters can boast. But if you look out there," she indicated the forward screen, "you'll see the latest and best weaponry available on the black market."

"In other words," Bros said, "they don't have to make trouble, they *are* trouble."

"They're hailing," Rand told them.

"Forward screen," Joat said tensely, bracing herself in expectation of confronting a Kolnari.

The face on the view-screen was human-standard. A woman's face, bony, sallow, with the eyes of a dead fish, but human, Joat realized. *More or less human.* Not only a pirate, but willing to work for the High Clan of Kolnar.

"Captain Joat Simeon-Hap, cargo ship *Wyal*, we're here to pick up cargo for Nomik Ciety," she said as calmly as she could.

"Stand by for cargo transfer," the woman said, her voice as expressionless as her eyes. "And traveling instructions."

"Al," Joat asked, "will you and Rand take care of receiving those? I'm going down to supervise the loading."

"Will do," Alvec said crisply.

"Bros, Joe," she said, "will you come with me, please." Her heart was hammering in her chest, but her voice was flat calm. They were being treated like just another underworld courier. But they weren't "just another" anything and Joat was scared. Her name alone would be ringing up flags onboard the *Dreadful Bride*. Belazir t'Marid would be *glad* to see her, if not quite as glad as Channa or Simeon would make him.

She was in the hatchway, Bros and Joseph bunched up behind her when an all too familiar voice filled the bridge.

"One moment, Captain."

Joat could feel the blood draining from her face, vision dimming, her tongue thick enough to choke her. She turned to the screen.

"This is a most valuable cargo," Belazir said, with a gentle smile.

Joat leaned against the hatchway casually and raised an eyebrow. It was better than falling down, and she hadn't the strength to speak. When she'd known him before she'd had places to hide. Here there was nowhere to run.

He looked much older than she would have expected. Dangerous still, but much changed. *Yeah. They age quickly, too.* The face had lost its fallen-angel beauty, but none of the strength. And the golden lion's eyes were utterly mad.

"I've never damaged a cargo yet," she said at last.

"Still," Belazir said, steepling his hands before him,

"I must ask that you leave one of your crew here as hostage. To insure that you will effect delivery with all care and speed."

Joat crossed her arms and walked forward, towards the smiling face in the screen.

"No," she said, calmly. "That's unacceptable. I need all of my crew. If that's unsatisfactory, I'm sure Mr. Ciety can find you a shipper more to your liking." She took her seat and looked up at the screen with her arms crossed, face a mask. *But I'm glad he can't smell me.*

His yellow eyes rested briefly on Joseph, then passed over him to linger on Bros.

"That one," he said, as though she hadn't already refused. "The dark one. We'll take him on when the cargo is brought to you."

"No," Joat said firmly.

"Yes," Belazir said, equally firmly. His eyes widened slightly and his lips lifted from his teeth in a snarl. "Captain *Simeon-Hap.*"

He knows, Joat thought and her heart sped again and her mouth went dry.

"You will do as you are told. Or you will not be leaving this place. Do you understand?"

"Yes." *Master and God,* her mind supplied treacherously.

She gripped the console, resolved to tell him that she understood, she just wasn't going to do it, when Bros's hand came down on her shoulder, making her jump.

She glared up at him and he surprised her by the regretful tenderness of his smile.

"I'd better go," he said softly.

"But . . . !"

He was out the hatch before she could continue.

"Most wise," Belazir murmured approvingly, "very wise indeed."

The screen went blank, and Joat was on her feet, rushing after Bros.

✧ CHAPTER SIXTEEN

"This isn't right," Joat insisted. She'd caught up with him at the cargo bay hatch; he stood looking back at her, hand on the dogging wheel. "I don't want you to go."

Bros smiled down at her.

"Would it surprise you to know that I agree with you? I don't want me to go either."

"Then don't!"

He cocked his head and looked at her affectionately, reaching out to brush her cheek with the back of his hand. Joat started and flinched away from his touch, then scowled at him.

"Is that a look to send a man out to battle with?"

"You're not going to battle," she snapped, "you're going to commit suicide. I can talk him out of this, Bros, you don't have to go."

"He'll kill us all, Joat. He knows who you are and he wants you dead." Bros leaned close, trying to catch her eyes. "Seg and Amos are too important to Central Worlds to risk. And I got you into this."

There was the sound of the caterpillar lock grappling on and filling with air. Bros snapped forward and kissed her lightly before she could protest. He straightened and glanced at the lock, then back down at Joat.

"And you're too important to me," he said as the lock opened with a hiss and a pair of black-clad mercenaries stepped out. "It's a far, far better thing I do . . ." he murmured as they led him away.

Joat watched him go; he never looked back as he was hustled along between his guards, and his step was firm and springy. She could still feel the soft warmth of his lips, and it was as though his kiss had sealed hers shut, for she couldn't speak. She could only watch with wide eyes as more mercenaries dragged an escape pod down the tunnel that linked their ships.

Joseph's touch made her gasp and she spun 'round in shocked surprise.

"Don't *do* that!" she snarled. "Why is everyone sneaking up on me today?"

Joseph suppressed a smile.

"Sometimes, Joat, you are more like my Rachel than you would care to admit."

"How shall we stow this, Captain?" Alvec asked.

Joat closed her eyes for a moment, grateful for Al's understanding. She led him into cargo hold C.

"Here," she said and indicated a rack which would accommodate the rescue pod's awkward shape.

They were busy for several minutes securing it to the mercenaries' satisfaction; the noncom in charge checked with finicky care.

"See them out, would you Joe?" she asked. "I want a few words with their Captain."

"Get me Belazir," Joat said to the dead-faced woman on the screen.

"Who?" the woman asked.

"*Belazir*, you bitch! Do it or I'll open fire on the mother ship."

Belazir's face appeared on the screen, his golden eyes laughing, though his face was stern.

"You wished to speak to me, Captain?"

"I'll be back for my crewman," Joat said tersely.

"Will you?" Belazir asked with a raised brow. "How very nice. You may be sure I shall look forward to seeing you again, Captain Simeon-Hap." He paused, considering. "So much do I wish for such a meeting that I will caution you most strongly, do not open the rescue pod. On pain of death," he said, his voice firm with sincere warning.

Then he was gone and by default the screen returned to the view of Belazir's fleet.

"Only a Kolnari could or would say *on pain of death*," Joseph said with disgust. "Even then, only Belazir could say it and not sound ridiculous. Come with me, Seg. Let us see what the Kolnar have entrusted to us."

"Wait," Joat said. "Let's get a little distance between us. They might have some kind of tell-tale attached to it."

Joseph sighed impatiently, but nodded and took his seat, while Joat checked out the flight plan the Kolnari had given them.

"It's what we expected," she said, her throat dry and tight. "Our course is set for Bethel."

"I am sorry, Joat," Joseph murmured. "I would rather he had chosen me."

"Don't be sorry and don't be stupid," she snapped. "This isn't finished."

But it was, she told herself. Finished before it was begun. A freighter with a single laser cannon and a few illegal side arms was no match for the Kolnari-mercenary fleet they were leaving behind. And while they ran like cowards Belazir was taking apart the first and only man she'd ever felt something for.

The fighter was designed to do one thing, fight, and it offered few amenities and little comfort. Karak was at the apex of a three-seat triangle, overseeing the other two. None of the seats were moveable; they were designed to put the occupants within touching range of everything essential, and Kolnari ship designers made even fewer concessions to comfort than the Central Worlds Fleet.

It had been part nightmare and part comedy getting everyone suited and out. He'd handily connected the unconscious Sung to the various catheters and waste tubes built into the space armor. But Soamosa had refused to let him help her, even though she obviously had no idea how to proceed.

Karak eyed her worriedly. From time to time she shifted in a way that spoke of discomfort. But she didn't complain and he felt a little glow of pride towards her for that.

"I have laid in a course for Bethel," he told her. "We can expect to arrive in four days."

Soamosa started.

"So close!" she said. And she asked herself what the Kolnari were going to do that required their fleet to lie so close to her home. *Fool!* she told herself. *The disease of course! They will want to come and gloat.* She wondered if they would be content with what they saw, or would they amuse themselves by bombing the helpless people of Bethel. The way they had before.

"At the end of four days, my love, it will not seem close, I promise you." His voice was tinged with amusement.

Captain Sung began to stir and in moments a thin, heart-broken wailing filled the small cabin they shared. Soamosa leaned towards him and began to murmur soothingly, reaching out for his shoulder.

The Captain batted ill-temperedly at her and increased the volume of his weeping.

Four days! Karak thought in despair. *It will be an eternity.*

❖   ❖   ❖

"Seg," Joat said, "put on an EVA suit, grab your bag of tricks and report to cargo hold C. We're going to lock you in and put the air in there on a sealed cycle."

!T'sel looked surprised. "How is it you can do that?"

"That hold's designed to ship live cargo. Why else d'you think it's got a double lock?"

"For sterilization procedures, of course," Seg murmured approvingly.

"And Seg, take everything you can think of. Once you're sealed in I don't want to keep opening that outer hatch any more than necessary."

!T'sel nodded solemnly.

"I understand and approve, Captain."

"I will accompany you," Joseph said.

Didn't ask my permission, this time. He'd always been careful of such courtesies before.

"You will also wear a suit, Joe."

He glanced at her in mild surprise and then nodded once. *Meaning, it's still my ship.*

"Yes, Captain," he said and followed Seg.

"Rand? Give me a multiple close-up on the pod."

"Yes, Joat."

Rand flashed four different views of the Kolnari escape pod. Then he brought each view to maximum magnification. The surface was some pebbled synthetic.

"Good," Joat said. "Polarized?"

"Most probably, from the composition—single-molecule silicon and carbon composite," Rand said.

"So far, we're in the clear," Alvec said, watching the Kolnari fleet on his screen. "No one's following, no weapons firing. Looks like we're safe." His voice had a flat, low-affect deadness to it.

"We're not leaving him there," Joat said. "We got Amos out, we'll get Sperin out."

He turned his chair around, his face like a lugubrious hound's.

"Boss, they wanted us to take Amos," he said gently.
"I know that." It was moments like this that you
realized Alvec was a very dangerous man.

Joat turned to watch the pod. Behind her, Alvec
smiled slowly as he studied the set of her face and the
way she held her shoulders. He could almost feel sorry
for the Kolnari fleet.

Bros was escorted down long, narrow corridors
smelling of dry, recycled air and the metallic-spicy
Kolnari body scent. The light was harsh enough to
make him squint and the gravity was tangibly heavier
than Earth standard. The temperature varied wildly,
from chilly to a more common dry baking heat. He
was uneasily aware that things he *couldn't* sense
might well be killing him slowly; heavy-metal salts,
strong UV, radiation . . . the Kolnari's ancestors had
adapted to them, on their hell-planet. But that had
taken gen-erations, and they were still a short-lived
race.

By the time they locked him into a spartan cell he
was panting slightly and a fine sheen of sweat slicked
his brow. He turned to take in his surroundings. Two
bunks that folded down from the wall, a sink, and a
toilet. The light was recessed into the ceiling, well out
of his reach, even if he tried for it from the upper
bunk. Clever. He assumed it would never go out.

Bros examined the bare walls, looking for the surveillance equipment. It was there, he knew, but it
certainly wasn't obvious.

"Clever," he murmured to himself, running his fingers
over the slick metal-fiber composite. *Not quite state-
of-the-art, but they're good engineers in their way.*
Probably spy-eyes and holo-projectors combined. He
went to the tap and drank deeply, ignoring the unpleasant chemical smell and taste of the water, and the high

salt content. The latter at least would be beneficial; he could feel the dry heat wicking moisture out of his skin.

Hands on his hips, he turned and looked at the closed hatch. Then, with a wry twist of his lips, he went over and tried it. Locked. *Ah, well, it was too much to hope for,* he thought. *The Kolnari are big, but they're not dumb.*

Not that he could easily escape anyway. They'd made him strip down to his underwear, even taking his socks. Weirdly enough, though, they'd let him keep his boots.

He went over and pulled down the lower bunk, sat and leaned his bare back against the cool white wall.

With a harsh *sssnnnaaapp!*, a jolt of electricity sent him leaping from the bunk.

As he reached for the burn on his back a woman's voice said calmly: "Sitting or lying on the bunk is forbidden until lights out."

"Yyyouu *bitch!*" Bros muttered, gently touching a rising blister.

There would be no lights out. Of that he was absolutely certain. Clearly Belazir had long-term plans for him.

He wondered if he dared to sit on the floor. Then he sighed. *No, I'll wait until I'm tired. No sense in getting a burnt butt before I have to.* He glanced at the commode. *Oh no, not unless I'm desperate.* There was no reason to start that phase of his torment before he absolutely had to.

Bros stood in the center of his cell, breathing deeply, his eyes closed, attempting to put himself into a trance state to make the time pass more quickly.

A little corner of himself wondered how long it would take for him to want to die.

❖   ❖   ❖

Seg leaned closer to the life pod and read the bio-display on the capsule's external screen. It showed that the being within was alive, conscious and in good health. Naturally the computer couldn't show if Amos, assuming it *was* Amos, was infected with an unknown disease. But, encouragingly, the brain scan showed no anomalies.

Joseph swore softly, unused to reading through the restricted view of an EVA helmet and not certain he fully understood what he was reading anyway.

"It looks good," Seg told him. "His brain scan appears normal."

"Let us open the capsule then," Joseph insisted. "I must know that it is the Benisur Amos."

"Joe," Joat's voice halted him, "check the capsule for booby traps first. They might have rigged it with explosives. Perhaps that's how they intended to spread the disease."

"And what harm to us could that be in this chamber, in these suits?"

"Amos might get hurt," she said reasonably.

He cooled down instantly. Joat was right. He must not let his emotions destroy his caution. He would proceed slowly, Amos's life was in the balance.

Joseph examined every inch of the outside of the capsule; Seg worked with him, using a sonic scan and circuit-tracer. A cable snaked out of the wall and put Rand in control of the internal circuits.

"Nonstandard design," the AI said. "But simple and straightforward. The controls are exactly what they seem to be."

Unless they contain a trap so subtle . . . Joseph thought, then forced his mind away from the infinite-reduction series.

Seg was having better luck with the bio-readouts than Joseph was with his devices. Life-pods were constructed to be impervious to virtually everything an unfriendly universe could throw at them, including probes, some of which could be deadly to living tissue.

By connecting his own diagnostic devices to those contained in the pod Seg was able to determine that Amos was in very good health. Whatever indignities he'd suffered at Belazir's hands, gross physical torture hadn't been among them.

"No damage to the myelin sheaths," Seg said. "His nervous system has not been overloaded."

"I have done all that I can," Joseph announced at last. "I can find no evidence of trickery here." He ran his hand over the top of his helmet in a nervous gesture, as though stroking his blond mane. "Surely it would make no sense for them to do something violent. If they had planned for the disease to spread by stealth they would want people to rush in to see Amos, to touch him . . . and each other." His lips thinned. "Let us open this and see what they have done."

"I agree," Joat said, smiling wryly as Joseph gave a little start at the sound of her voice. *Poor Joe,* she thought, *he's freaked. This is so hard for him.*

Seg nodded and stepped aside, allowing Joseph to open the pod.

The seals released with a hiss of air and the unit snapped open along its length.

Within, Amos lay still, eyes closed, breathing peacefully.

Amos heard the seals release and sensed the lid rising. Light pressed against his eyelids with an almost tangible weight, and he expected his eyes to open of their own accord in response to it. A sense of free space surrounded him; he could hear air pumps and the sound of a ship's engines. The need to open his eyes was an overwhelming frustration, like an unscratchable itch.

"Elevated heartbeat," an unfamiliar voice said—unfamiliar and inhuman, like words produced by some beautifully-made musical instrument.

Inside himself Amos cringed away from the hand that suddenly touched him. The brief sound of movement he'd heard, a strange crunching sound, hadn't prepared him for the cold, hard touch of the gloved hand.

"Amos," Joseph said, in a voice high and tight with tension. "Benisur?" he attempted when Amos lay still and unresponsive.

Joseph? Amos went alert, tensed within himself to the point of pain. *My brother!* he thought joyfully, then horror filled him. *I am death, my brother, do not touch me! Leave me, leave me!* He thought the words with all his might, with all his soul, as though he could force them into his friend's mind.

Joseph reached out and grabbed Seg, flinging him hard against the open life-pod.

"Do something!" he snarled.

Amos felt the life-pod rock as Seg's body struck its side. *Another?* he thought. *How many?* he wondered desperately, imagining a room filled with victims, and Kolnari laughter.

"I'm a bio-engineer, not a doctor, dammit!" Seg snapped.

"You said he was conscious," Joseph said, his eyes narrowing menacingly. "Does he look conscious to you?"

"The bio-readings on the pod said he was conscious," Seg objected. "Just back off so I can attach my diagnostic equipment to him directly and maybe we'll see what's going on."

"Could he be drugged?" Joat asked.

"Of course. There are dozens of drugs they could have used that would leave him conscious but immobile. Or they could have pithed him," Seg chattered on, unaware of the thunder in Joseph's eyes. "They wouldn't be needing him after this. And there are ways of doing it that are so subtle they wouldn't show up on these scans."

"Pithed him," Joseph repeated, shaken.

No, only drugs, Amos silently reassured him.

"There's a certain strategic value in essentially destroying your planet's religious leader," Seg pointed out. "Though catastrophe-wise it's lame for the Kolnari."

Who is this fool? Amos wondered indignantly. Reflecting that it was no surprise that Joseph threw him around like an ill-mannered cur. The creature actually *was* an ill-mannered cur.

"It's drugs," Joat said positively. "Look, Joe, there's no need to glare at Seg that way. If there's one thing I'm sure of when it comes to the Kolnari, it's that they don't do subtle quietly. Whenever one of them actually manages to be subtle they throw a party and boast about it."

"But why do *this*?" Joseph asked wildly.

"So that he couldn't warn anybody," Seg assured him grimly, tapping the screen on his diagnostic unit. "Because he's definitely a carrier. He's unaffected, so he must be immune, but he's positive. They paralyzed him so that he could only lie there knowing that simply by breathing he was destroying his people. Then when the drug wore off, he'd be one of the few able to help."

Seg was unusually solemn, as though he'd just discovered the real meaning of what he was involved in. He looked up into one of the cameras. "I'd say there's a great deal of subtlety in that," he said.

"Well," Joat agreed, "they know all about cruelty."

Joseph leaned close to Amos and quietly said, "Benisur . . ." He paused, his mouth tight, his eyes suspiciously bright and once again he grasped Amos's arm.

I am here my friend, Amos thought. *Be at peace, I am with you.*

Joseph took a deep breath and tried again.

"My brother, we know the Kolnari plan and we are prepared. We are immunized and cannot get the disease you carry. Even so we are in EVA suits. You need not fear for us."

Amos felt tears of joy roll down his cheeks. They were safe! His people were safe. *Ah, bless the God that gave me allies like Joseph, my thanks! My most heartfelt thanks.*

Belazir sighed contentedly as he watched Bros Sperin standing in his cell and drank deeply from the glass of cane spirit in his hand. Then he frowned and reached over to add a pinch of salts of mercury and a dash of copperas and lead oxide.

Ah, better.

The scumvermin spy had been standing for approximately eighteen hours now and still stood rock solid. But a sheen of perspiration glistened on his hard-muscled body and darkened the waistband of his shorts.

Belazir hoped that he'd be watching when the Central World's Security operative eventually fell over. He grinned. How he loved to watch them hop around when the electrical charges hit them. Perhaps if he lowered the temperature . . . shivering would wear him out faster. *No, it will be more informative to see just how long he can last. Besides even in one's pleasures one should exercise a modicum of discipline,* his eyes sparkled with amusement. *It builds character.*

"No Central Worlds Fleet," he said aloud. "Fool." He'd been prepared to run again, to scatter the painfully accumulated strength amid the dead stars. The High Clan did not need living planets, not since their exile from Kolnar.

But eighteen hours after he'd captured Sperin the mercenary escort he'd sent after Joat Simeon-Hap reported that the *Wyal* maintained its silence and its course for Bethel.

Belazir raised white-blond brows.

Perhaps her crew did not know his identity, he mused. Somehow he doubted that. *Ciety has a lot to answer for.* Belazir's brows snapped down. *First, the insult of Simeon's "daughter" thrown in my face, next a professional spy is among her crew.* He was pleased that he'd sent for Ciety. Never mind that his reasons had been less than rational at the time. *He and his wench are either traitorous or stupid. If the former, I shall kill them.* He smiled as imaginative images swept through his mind. *If the latter, I will punish them. That should give them an incentive to be more alert in future.* Even the most minor members of the crew had to maintain discipline. Without it, all was chaos.

"Rand, I want you to tight-beam this message to the nearest Central Worlds Naval facility," Joat began entering the *Wyal*'s coordinates and a Mayday. They were now far enough away from the Kolnar fleet that such a message should be safe to send.

"That's probably not a good idea, Joat. We're being followed. If we alert the Kolnari, they'll be gone by the time a task force can get here."

There was no way to track a ship on interstellar drive from more than half a light-year away. Once the pirate fleet had scattered, only sheer chance would let the Fleet intercept even the slowest. No doubt they had a rendezvous arranged for just that eventuality.

"Followed?" Her head snapped up. "Show me."

"Indicating."

Rand opened a screen onto the rear view of the *Wyal*. The view showed a corrected view of the sidereal universe as it would have appeared to an object with the ship's pseudospeed. Even at FTL, only the nearer

stars showed any apparent movement; space was *big*.
A point of light strobed, and a line of figures ran down
the screen beside it.

"Less than a hundred tonnes mass," the AI said. "But
high-powered. Fighter equivalent, nonstandard."

"How long has it been there?"

"I first noticed it four hours after we left the Kolnari
fleet," Rand said. "I didn't know just what it was at
first. I thought it might be just a probe. The pilot has
been careful, and for the most part was able to stay
just far enough away to be unidentifiable. But occasionally, like now, it's strayed just this side of the line
of scanning range and over time I've been able to
determine that it's a small fighter."

Rand showed her a composite picture of a fighter,
small and fast, and exceedingly well armed. "I'd suppose
it's probably crewed by a mercenary."

"Yeah," Joat murmured, nibbling on her thumb.
"They're not likely to risk one of their own on what
could turn out to be a suicide mission. From the size
of their fleet it doesn't look like they've got any Kolnari
to spare . . . that thing looks just barely large enough
to go interstellar."

She raised one brow and smirked with satisfaction.
Channa would tell her that she shouldn't feel so pleased
about it. But Channa was too soft-hearted for her own
good. When you came across a killer disease you
eradicated it. You didn't let it live out of pity.

"I'm going to guess," she said, "that his job it to make
sure we go where we've been sent."

"The pilot has been sending periodic communications
in the direction of the Kolnar fleet. But they were tight-
beamed and I couldn't catch anything."

"Don't sound so embarrassed Rand. We're not a spy
ship." *We're really not,* she thought with amusement,
even though we've been spying.

"Hmmm. He's there to insure that Amos is delivered to Bethel. Maybe Belazir is afraid we'll grab the life-pod and go running off to the nearest Central Worlds outpost screaming for help. But I think his real fear is that we'll open it and be wiped out by the disease before his revenge plan has a chance to happen." She tapped the screen. "And this poor fool is to board us and take over the piloting if we show signs of going out of our minds."

"That was my assessment too," Rand said.

"So let's get him over here," Joat said. "Let's ask Seg for a complete list of symptoms."

Skating along on the narrow edge of his scanners capacity Kraig Rendino du Pare followed the *Wyal's* trail.

He was bored. To the point of pain.

He reckoned that fighters were made to be uncomfortable so you couldn't go to sleep on duty. And you had to stay in your suit, which cut down on your options for personal fun. You couldn't even open the helmet in vacuum, so you couldn't get at yourself. For good or ill. *Merde!*

This particular assignment was *agony*. The ship ahead of him did nothing but proceed quietly on its way.

Damned Kolnari paranoia, he thought sullenly.

When he'd become a mercenary ten years ago he'd done it in hopes of excitement, adventure, loot. Usually, though, it was as dull as regular duty in the Navy had been. With the added drawback that the pay was irregular. Not to mention the bad maintenance, so you had to check everything yourself if you wanted to live.

It's still hurry up and wait, he thought. *Still do what you're told, no matter how stupid it is.* He was going to quit. The pay was okay, but it wasn't high enough to counter Kolnari arrogance. *Or missions to nowhere that last forever.* And they were weird, even if they spared you the lectures on mental hygiene. *Come to think of it, they seem to like it better if you're crazy.*

Yeah. The Kolnari'd hired more head-cases than he'd ever even seen before. Another good reason to quit.

Uh oh. They were broadcasting on an emergency band. He risked scooting closer to pick it up.

"Mayday, Mayday, Mayday, Mayday, Mayday," a clipped male voice recited calmly, over and over.

Alright with the Maydays, Kraig thought impatiently, *get to the message.*

"Mayday."

Oh, Jeeesh!

"Um . . . Mayday."

The speaker seemed to have run out of steam. Almost a minute went by in perfect silence, except for the crisp sound of an open com.

"Mayday?"

Kraig started to laugh. On the other hand, there were compensations. The Fleet would have expected him to charge in and rescue these idiots.

"Tell them we're in trouble," a woman's voice prompted.

"We are?"

Silence.

"I . . ." the woman's voice, sounding uncertain. "Yes, I'm sure we are."

"What's wrong? Are we in trouble?"

"Mayday," she said. "Keep saying . . . May-something."

Merde! Kraig thought in disgust.

This was what he'd been told to watch for. If the crew of the *Wyal* showed signs of disorientation he was to go over and check it out. If necessary he was to carry out their mission to drop a life-pod into Bethel's atmosphere.

Merde!

❖   ❖   ❖

"Attaboy," Joat said with a grin as the distant fighter began to close with them. She felt a tingling alertness, far more agreeable than the sour taste of fear. "Come to mama. How long before he gets here, Rand?"

"About ten minutes." Rand had long since discovered that humans didn't really want to know *exactly* how long until an event occurred. They were more interested in generalities. He'd often wondered how they'd accomplished all that they had, including his own invention, given their evident distaste for precision.

"Has he sent anything to Belazir yet?"

"No. Perhaps he's waiting until he has concrete information."

"*Verrrryy* good," she said, eyes bright with satisfaction. "Can you intercept any messages he sends once he's in range?"

"I assume you mean stop rather than intercept. If so, no, I can't."

"But," Alvec said. "Even a tight-beamed message can be interrupted so that it's garbage when it's received. I'll show ya how Rand."

"Thank you, Alvec," Rand said. "I'd appreciate that."

"You're a wonder, Al. I don't know what I'd do without you," Joat said, smiling at him over her shoulder. "The things you know . . ."

"I had an unfortunate adolescence," Alvec said piously.

Didn't we all. Joat keyed internal communications. "Seg, how are you doing with that antidote for whatever they gave Amos?"

"Not too badly, given the circumstances," he said, gesturing towards a looming Joseph with a none-too-subtle jerk of his head.

Joat pursed her lips.

"Will Amos come out of it on his own?" she asked.

"Eventually," !T'sel said slowly. "Why?"

"Because I'm going to have to ask you to stop what you're doing and come up here to administer some of those interrogation drugs you brought with you."

Joseph drew himself up indignantly, but Joat spoke before he could voice his outrage.

"Belazir put a tail on us," she said, "we're luring him in now. And somehow I don't think he's going to volunteer information."

Alvec barked a laugh in the background, making Joseph smile.

"Use your most effective drugs," he suggested to Seg, "so that you may return quickly. I loathe seeing the Benisur in this condition. And I assure you, neither the Kolnari, nor those they are likely to use as tools are deserving of mercy. If your drugs fail, call me. My knife will not."

"I'll . . . take that under advisement," Seg muttered.

He swallowed at Joseph's expression. Usually human faces were a little hard to read, immobile . . . but he suspected that a good number of sentient beings had seen *that* expression the very last time they saw anything at all.

Perhaps Bros wasn't completely wrong about adventure. Suddenly, his quiet, boring laboratory seemed much more attractive.

✧ CHAPTER SEVENTEEN

"Easy does it," Kraig said to himself. *"Pas de problème."* The High Clan certainly wasn't paying him enough to be a hero.

Nothing but nonsense on the com. He touched the sensitive pads under his gloved fingers, adjusting the fighter's trajectory. The ship itself continued on its way, apparently on autopilot, for neither speed nor course had changed.

He dreaded tight-beaming this information to the Kolnari. It made him feel as though *he* had failed. His mouth twisted wryly. It was definitely time to quit if he really gave a damn what the employer thought. *And they scare me.* He didn't like that sensation, either.

"Calling merchanter ship *Wyal*," he said, and waited for reply. He could hear sounds of consternation from her crew as his voice came through their speakers. *Merde, merde, merde!* he thought. *I don't wanna do this!* Every instinct that had kept him alive for the last fifteen years told him to stay off that ship. And the same instincts told him that if he left now the Kolnari would track him down and make him regret it.

"Kraig to command," he said; the machine intelligence of the fighter would relay and encrypt it automatically. "Crew incapacitated. Am approaching *Wyal*."

It was near enough for visual scan now, an elongated spindle, more streamlined than most freighters—built for landing on planetary surfaces. He was mildly surprised that the Kolnari had let it go; it would be perfect as a fleet auxiliary for surface raids.

This mission must be important, at least to whatever passed for brains inside those silver-blond heads.

Delicately, he established zero relative velocity and nudged his fighter towards the airlock, marked out by its square of strobing lights.

"So, Al, how're we going to handle this?" Joat asked, crossing her arms behind her head and stretching. The black Kolnar fighter approached delicately on the screen, like a cat advancing on a suspicious bit of string. She could think about this and *stop* thinking about Sperin.

Alvec's brow went up.

"I thought Joe was our resident warrior," he said.

"He is," Joat grinned. "But Joe's not likely to leave Amos's side now he's got him under his eye." She glanced over at her crew. "Besides, he knows we can handle this."

"He'll be wearin' space armor," Alvec said gruffly. He frowned and made a clicking sound with his tongue. "Can't charge a guy in space armor."

"Figure he's a merc," Joat mused, "so he won't be wearing Kolnari armor. That's a plus." She folded her hands on her middle and stared into space. "Ninety per cent of the space armor manufactured has lousy surge protection," she said at last. "Give 'em a sustained charge and," she snapped her fingers, "they're fried."

Alvec chuckled. "Set a trap?"

"Either side of the entry hatch," Joat agreed.

"Easily done," Rand said, and displayed schematics of the areas involved. "These segments—" bars of yellow flashed on the screen to indicate the spots he referred to "—are underlaid with support grids constructed of conductive materials. Actually I'm a little surprised at that," it added disapprovingly. "Anyway, they're . . ."

"I see it," Joat said quickly. "Just cut the power there to give us a chance to work. Then when our visitor steps onto those grids . . ."

"You can make him dance," Alvec finished, rising to follow a grinning Joat out the door.

"Actually," Rand said, mildly puzzled, "if this works properly he shouldn't be able to move."

Kraig's attempts to communicate with the *Wyal* had been met with half-hysterical nonsense and unending repetitions of "Mayday."

I'm going to kill that son-of-a-bitch who keeps sayin' that, Kraig thought. *Quick too, just to shut 'im up.* In the twenty minutes it had taken him to catch up with the merchant ship and align the locks he'd conceived a serious hatred for the prattling lunatic on the com. *Aw, Ghu, he's crying now. I'll be doing the jerk a favor.* Weight left him as he switched off his fighter's internal field.

He'd have done the woman a favor, too, if he could only get out of this damned suit. The mercenary shuddered. No chance of that, not with some bug loose on the ship. He disconnected his suit from the fighter's feeds and drifted out of his seat. Gripping hand-holds built into the minuscule cabin he pulled himself over to the hatch. Pausing there for a moment he ran a weapons and systems check on his suit.

All green, he thought, relieved. Even knowing he was unlikely to run into any opposition, Kraig was nervous. "Stage fright," one of his friends called it. *Yeah, stage fright. Well, curtain up.* He hit the control for opening the hatch.

Grapple fields held the two craft less than arm's length apart; the hard flat light of vacuum shone on every irregularity of hull and plating, and the undiffused glow of the airlock lights made the controls of the *Wyal's* entryway stand out.

e-n-t-r-y, he punched into the pad.

The *Wyal's* hatch opened after a second's pause to purge atmosphere. He crouched down and waited a full minute, alarm bells going off in his mind. It was always this way for him when things were too easy. He flipped across, catching the handbars by the merchanter's lock and orienting himself so that the internal gravity field would pull him down on his feet. Vibration shivered beneath him as he stood and swung the exterior door closed. Air hissed in automatically; the readouts below his chin showed it breathable.

He wished he had some of the fancy equipment the Kolnari had access to. Getting a nice, safe view of that corridor out there would suit him fine. As it was he'd have to rely on his eyes, and the few enhancements from his face-plate. Sonic and electromag monitor showed no weapons profiles from the access corridor. He readied the needler built into his cuff and stepped out into the ship.

Carefully, exposing as little of himself as he could, Kraig angled himself to look out the hatch in either direction. Nothing. That didn't mean they weren't there, it just meant they weren't *obviously* there. The suit's sensors would tell him more once he was actually in the corridor.

He pitched himself out of the lock and flattened himself against the wall opposite, his heart hammering. Nothing. The sensors confirmed it.

He took a deep breath and let it out in a soft whistle.

Then he grinned. *'Cause sometimes when it's easy, it's just . . . easy.* Kraig set off for the bridge with a jaunty walk.

"Now," Joat said.

The mottled armor froze in a spectacular shower of fat blue sparks. Ozone drifted through the *Wyal*'s corridors, and the life-support system whined in overload to carry it off. The suit toppled forward slowly in midstride, left leg frozen half-raised. The three hundred kilos of mass struck the decking with a clamor that echoed through the hull.

Help! Kraig thought as the power-armor toppled and he crashed helplessly to the floor, a prisoner inside it. Inertia flung him against the padded restraints inside, hard enough to bruise. His jaw struck the readout panel and blood filled his mouth with a taste of iron and salt. *I've fallen,* he thought in disbelief. *And I can't get up!*

A blond woman sauntered into sight, wearing a coverall with an amazing number of pockets for microtools Kraig didn't recognize. He *did* recognize the arc-pistol in the hand of the bruiser walking beside her. She squatted down beside the fallen mercenary and went to work with one of the tools. A minute later the faceplate came free; Kraig rolled his eyes at the whirring head of the tool. Her thumb stroked the control, setting the tiny Phillips' head up and down the scale from a low burr to a tooth-grating whine.

"*Tsk.* Now, that's the downside of cut-rate equipment," she said sweetly. "When it breaks down it's worse than useless. Doncha hate it when that happens? I'm Captain Joat Simeon-Hap, by the way. This is my engineer, Alvec Dia. He doesn't like pirates."

"I'm . . . I'm just a freelancer!" Kraig wheezed. He was lying face-down, his limbs clamped in midstride position as firmly as a tangler-field could have done.

The arc-pistol came closer; he turned his eyes until they ached in their sockets, enough to see the four pointed prongs of the guide-field projector at the end of the weapon. They were pitted with use.

"I don't like mercenaries who work for pirates, either," he said in a voice like a gravel crusher.

"Rand," Joat went on. "Lower the corridor gravity for a second, would you?"

The mercenary felt himself lighten; not that it made any difference, since he still couldn't move anything but the muscles of his face. The face-plate began to swing shut again.

"No!" he shouted. "My air's off!"

"I know," Joat said.

They shoved him onto a cargo sled and brought him to the bridge; a Sondee awaited them, with a medical kit resting beside him.

"I don't want to do this," Seg said.

"Neither do I," Joat said, digging in her toolbox for something to manually open the mercenary's space armor. "But we need information and we need it now."

"No we don't! Amos will be all right whether I come up with an antidote or not. It's just a matter of time."

"Oh yeah? This guy is supposed to signal Belazir that we've accomplished our mission. I need to know what that signal is. What's more, he knows things that'll get me into Belazir's ship," she said grimly. "You may have forgotten Bros, but I haven't."

"Jeeez boss, you can't go back there." Alvec came away from the bulkhead with a startled lurch. "You'll get yourself killed. Let Central Worlds handle it, they've got the manpower."

"Thank you, Al, that reminds me. Rand, send that tight-beam message to the nearest Central Worlds facility."

She turned to Alvec while she continued to manually trip the helmet's locking system. "I guarantee you, I'll bet this ship on it, that they can't get anybody here for two weeks or so."

"Well?" She looked Alvec in the eye. "You want to take that bet?" She turned to Seg. "You?"

They both shook their heads.

"The Kolnari can be beaten," she said positively. "I've seen it happen."

The helmet popped off in her hands.

"Well, hello there," Joat said sweetly to the gasping mercenary. "Welcome aboard."

Kraig looked frantically around him, surprisingly fine dark eyes filled with panic. He was about thirty, balding, with dark hair and a narrow face.

"I won't talk," he said.

"Really?" Alvec said, sounding pleased.

The mercenary laughed. "You're worse than the Kolnari? I don't think so. And if you aren't, I'm not going to risk getting on their bad side. You know what I mean?"

"You're already on their bad side," Joat purred from behind him. Leaning close she continued, "And they're in no position to hurt you right now." She grabbed his sparse hair and yanked his head back. "But we are," she said, smiling pleasantly.

He went white to the lips.

"My name's Kraig . . ."

"I don't care," she interrupted him cheerfully, shaking his head.

"There are laws, lady!"

"You're working for the Kolnari and you're talkin' about laws?" Alvec said with disgust.

"What's civilization coming to?" Joat coolly asked the room in general. "Seg," she said, glancing at the young Sondee. "Prepare Kraig here a shot of one of those wonder drugs you've been telling us about."

Seg's mouth was sphinctered tightly shut and his golden eyes were half-closed, his face gray with tension, the ear whorls nearly white. But he set down his bag and opened it, slowly.

"Joat," Rand said, "I'm receiving a distress call."

"You're joking," she said.

Instead of answering, Rand opened the com for all to hear.

"Mayday," an obviously distraught young woman was saying. "Mayday! Our pilot is ill, he's unconscious, if you can hear me please help us. We must get to Bethel, it's a matter of life or death! Mayday! Please, someone, answer me. Mayday." Her voice disintegrated into helpless sobbing.

Belazir steepled his hands beneath his chin and settled himself more comfortably on his thronelike chair, gazing placidly at Nomik Ciety.

I think this one has some trouble with his internal mapping of reality, the Kolnari warlord thought.

He lounged back, resting his chin on the fingers of one hand. Behind him a holographic night-scene showed a plutonium volcano on Kolnar. Down either wall stood Kolnari warriors, naked except for briefs and their weapons, armored in their leopard deadliness.

Nomik bristled. "How *dare* you kidnap me and my associate?" he shouted. He ignored the subtle stirrings of the warriors, their bronze eyes riveted on Belazir. "Do you have any idea the trouble you've just bought yourself? Do you realize that I'm under the protection of Yoered Family?"

The woman beside him had been glancing about. She looked at the collection of plants in their netted cages, and at the shape of the gnawed bones beneath them.

"Mik . . ." she whispered urgently. The man shook off her hand.

"Answer me, you mutant goon! What do you want?"

He paused, panting and glaring at Belazir's mildly interested face.

Fascinating, Belazir thought, bemused, *the creature seems to think I should be frightened of him. Apparently I am supposed to be intimidated.* If this was an example of intimidating behavior it was no wonder the scumvermin races were so easily conquered.

"*You* are dead meat!" Ciety snarled.

At Belazir's almost imperceptible gesture, two of the Kolnari picked Nomik up and flung him down on the floor hard enough to knock the wind out of him.

The moment they'd moved Silken had flung herself at Belazir's throat, one hand stiffened into a blade. He watched her approach with astonishment and flicked her aside like a butterfly. She crashed to the floor and rolled to a stop not far from Ciety and the two of them writhed, breathless at the Kolnari's feet.

"She is brave," Belazir said to Nomik. "I shall speak with her first as she is so eager to approach me." He smiled into Ciety's furious and frightened face. "But I shall try not to keep you waiting long."

Well, that was disappointing, Belazir thought as the guards dragged Silken's half conscious body from his quarters. He'd expected more fire from a woman who'd thrown herself at him unarmed. Ah well, some of them considered it properly stoic to affect total disinterest. Though he hadn't made that easy for her.

Who to speak to now? He sat down before his bank of screens, running a quick check on the day-to-day affairs of his people. Then he called up Bros Sperin and Nomik Ciety's cells.

Sperin was on his feet again, his body bearing yet more burns on his legs and sides. He swayed precariously, his jaw slack, eyes bruised-looking and swollen from lack of sleep.

Nomik was pacing energetically. He turned suddenly as the hatch opened. Two guards thrust Silken into the cell, where she collapsed in a boneless heap before Ciety could reach her.

Nomik knelt beside her and gathered her slender form into his arms, rocking her tenderly and whispering her name over and over as he stroked her matted black hair.

Bleh, Belazir thought. *That is enough of that; Karak was bad enough. It is time I interviewed Sperin, anyway.*

And the houseplants were hungry. It was time to cultivate a new crop, in any case. What the spores did to living flesh was *very* amusing.

Bros Sperin wavered. When he closed his eyes it felt as though his body was moving in a circle around the anchor of his feet. He tried not to close his eyes for too long; that meant he kept falling asleep and then over. The crisp white sheets of the bunk mocked him with taunting cruelty. Soft music was playing through the com system, soft soothing music—

He screamed as his knees struck the flooring and current arched through them. Still screaming he touched his hands to the floor to push himself up, then nearly staggered into the wall. Blisters burst on his kneecaps and palms, drooling liquid.

He was very thirsty. He'd promised himself that if he counted to a thousand one more time he could go to the sink and get some water. But he seemed to be stuck on eight hundred sixty-seven. For the life of him he couldn't remember what came next. Or before, for that matter. Eight hundred sixty-seven kept intruding itself into his efforts, offering itself every time he sought the next number.

The bottoms of his feet were numb, but his ankles ached and his calves burned. Inside as well as out.

The thought struck him as funny and he began to laugh. *Wonderful,* some distant, still sane part of him thought, *I'm getting hysterical. That should move things along nicely.*

That same part of him was waiting for Belazir to make an appearance. It unnerved him that the Kolnari hadn't come to gloat. It signaled unexpected new depths of self-discipline in the volatile pirate.

"Wake up, scumvermin," a gentle voice urged.

Painfully, Bros opened his eyes. Slowly, they focused on the face before him, and the wide yellow eyes blazing into his. He gasped and staggered back, almost losing his balance on his numbed and clumsy feet. Bros pinwheeled his arms and regained his balance barely in time to prevent himself from crashing into the wall.

Then he stood there panting, head down, heart beating rapidly, glaring at Belazir from under his brows.

Belazir chuckled delightedly and crossed his arms over his chest. He was pleased that he'd taken the time to dress for this interview in a long, open-necked robe of watered green silk accented by fretted silver jewelry glittering with fire-opals. It nicely emphasized the difference in their status. A refinement Sperin was definitely intelligent enough to recognize, on some level, semiconscious as he was.

"Are your accommodations to your liking?" he asked politely.

"I was more comfortable on the *Wyal.*" Bros straightened slowly and found himself equal to Belazir's imposing height. Which pleased him a great deal more than it did the Kolnari, he was sure. "You look older than I'd expected," he said conversationally.

A tiny seed of fury burst into existence in Belazir's heart. His mortality gazed back at him from his mirror with every new wrinkle and hair gone from silver-golden to white. Leaving him ever more aware of the hot breath of ambitious underlings on his neck; well-honed blades clutched in their sweaty young hands.

To be so casually insulted by a man he was torturing was intolerable. Lightning flickered at the edges of his vision. If they were truly in the same room he would teach the scumvermin how little his age mattered.

But wait! Profound surprise flickered across his mind. *Could Sperin be attempting to provoke me? To manipulate me?* He raised one white-blond brow. *Clever, foolish spy.* How interesting that he was so eager to die. It promised useful information as well as excellent entertainment.

"Do you think," he asked casually, "that it is wise to make me hate you, Bros Sperin?"

"I don't particularly care how you feel about me," Bros said.

Belazir smiled serenely.

"Ah, but you will," he said with utter confidence. "And in a very short time, too."

He decided to begin with the drug that caused pain. As yet he'd had no one to experiment on and Sperin should make a fine test case.

Three Kolnari entered the cell, one of them smaller and pudgier than the other two and tremblingly subservient; a half-caste castrato slave, the usual type assigned the low-status occupation of medicine. He bowed to Belazir's image over the small satchel he carried.

The two guards took hold of Bros, one on either arm and he slumped between them, making them stagger as he let them take his full weight. It felt almost good, not having to hold himself up anymore.

"The drug that causes pain," Belazir said to the cowering medical technician. He turned to Bros. "An invention from the Phelobites, some of Central World's most clever allies. It ignites the nervous system, I am told, causing exquisite suffering."

Bros looked up at him, tired, but contemptuous.

"You make it sound almost sexy, Belazir. Is this how you people have fun when you get old?"

Again the creature taunted him, and he didn't care to have the issue of his age mentioned before his crew. Rage snapped through him like a power whip and was quickly suppressed. He coiled it in, to be used later. Rage always had a use if turned to the right purpose.

"We are a disciplined people," Belazir observed with a calm smile. "We seldom allow ourselves to have "fun." However," the smile became wolfish, "I anticipate that you will provide us with some occasion for merriment in the near future." He gestured for the med-tech to administer the dose of pain-inducer and watched Sperin's eyes as it was done.

Bros looked back at him as calmly as though they sat across a table in The Anvil.

The dose went in with no more sensation than the touch of the injector to his skin. But inside, almost instantly, a vile sensation—like worms writhing beneath his skin—began to spread through his body.

Belazir watched eagerly as Sperin stood upright, taking his weight on his own feet and his face wrinkled into a mask of profound . . . distaste.

"Eeyaaahh, that's disgusting!" Bros said, shaking his hands and rotating his shoulders. All the while praising Seg !T'sel within his heart. *What would this have been like without the antidote?* he wondered.

Belazir showed no sign of his shock or disappointment beyond a tightening of his jaw. It wasn't working. Perhaps the drug was unstable and had begun to lose its power.

"Try the drug for fear," he ordered harshly.

The med-tech licked his lips and his dark flesh turned pale gray with terror.

"Great Lord," he said in a voice that shook, "there is a possibility that combining the two drugs could poison the prisoner."

"Do it," Belazir snapped. *Or I will have you gutted where you stand,* he thought viciously, but did not say. It would show too much of what he was feeling.

"Yes, Great Lord."

The second injection acted as quickly as the first, complicating the unpleasant sensation below Bros's skin with a sense of anxiety. His heart speeded up and sweat broke out on his brow. He found himself panting slightly and licked dry lips with a dry tongue. It was very unpleasant.

Almost as much of a strain as the effort not to laugh. The combined effect was about as bad as going three days without a bath or shave; and it was making him less sleepy, too.

Seg, you are a genius. Whatever they're paying you at Clenst it's not enough. If the little Sondee had been before him, Bros would have kissed him passionately.

Fortunately he was still too tired to smile.

Belazir's apparent calm hid a rage that almost frightened the Kolnari. He stood with his back stubbornly turned to his fury; a ravening beast that would overwhelm and devour him if he gave it one moment's attention.

"Leave him," he said coldly to his men, and watched them march impassively from the cell. Then he studied Bros for a moment longer, hating his victim's lack of reaction, hating his men for witnessing this humiliating incident.

"I see we shall have to think of some other means of helping you pass the time," he said to Sperin. "I shall return quite soon."

"Get some rest," Bros said, "at your age this kind of excitement isn't good for you."

"I am going to take you to pieces," Belazir promised him, "One millimeter at a time."

Belazir flung himself into his chair before the bank of screens. Breathing heavily . . . he forced himself to be still; his fury as hot as the core of a sun within him. He held up a hand before his face, and the fingers trembled. There was a time when they had been rock-steady, however hard the pulse of rage drummed in his ears.

He would personally kill that med-tech. *How dare the creature care for the drugs entrusted to him so poorly they have gone off!* He would tear the little eunuch apart! Belazir's mind filled with images of blood that soothed him somewhat.

He reached for the com, intending to have the creature sent to one of the rooms where discipline was administered, when his eye caught a movement in one of the screens before him.

Nomik sat beside his aide, Silken, on her bunk, holding her hand and talking. He'd reached up to brush her hair aside and that movement had earned him Belazir's attention.

Belazir watched him coax the shadow of a smile from Silken. *My other prisoners,* he mused.

Yes, his other prisoners.

Civilians.

Sperin was a trained spy, perhaps he'd been instructed in methods of resisting drugs, or he might have a natural immunity. Or there might be an antidote of some sort.

Belazir considered that. Those who had sold him the drugs had assured him that no counter-agents or immunizers for them existed. But he'd been dealing with thieves, and salesmen, who were also notorious liars. Anyone who trusted a Phelobite would ask a Kolnari for an insurance appraisal.

He slid down comfortably in his chair and steepled his hands before him, gently tapping the fingertips together. Yes, he would try the drugs on Ciety. Let Silken watch. The female had demonstrated her loyalty already. His lips twisted in a wry smile. *Let us see what her loyalty will bring me,* he thought, anticipating a pleasant interlude.

"Where is she, Rand?" Joat asked.

"Less than an hour away, and on our heading."

"Well we can't do anything tied to that fighter."

"I can pilot that," Al said. "Or did you just want t' let it go?"

"No, we're keeping it. Like I said, that ship, and this fellow's call signs are going to help us rescue Bros." She jerked her head downship, indicating that Al should go, cutting off his inevitable protest.

"You're crazy!" Kraig yelled. "You're fardling crazy!"

Joat ignored him. "Respond to that call, Rand. Tell her help's on the way." Then she stood with her fingers tapping her lips, staring off into space while Seg nervously watched her.

"Joat," he said quietly. "You're serious about rescuing Bros, aren't you?"

She looked at him from the corner of her eye and nodded once.

"It's suicide," Seg whispered in a pleading tone.

"You're fardling right it is!" Kraig snarled. "And not the easiest way to do it either. Do you have any idea what those people are like, lady?"

She nodded.

"I was on a space station they took over."

He went still. "The SSS-900-C?"

She nodded again, her lip curling slightly. "You may have heard of some of the tricks we played on them there." She leaned in close, filling his field of vision and whispered, "So you have some idea of what *I'm* like. Don't you?" He nodded and she nodded with him. Joat leaned still closer, resting her elbow on the shoulder of his frozen suit. "Think about this," she said confidentially. "If you help us out, we'll send you to Bethel a hero. You were sent to destroy us, but sickened by the Kolnari, you decided to help us instead. How does that sound? Hmmm?"

He stared at her uncertainly.

"You'd do that?"

"Um hmm." She nodded.

For a moment he almost smiled, then the frown was back.

"It sounds great, but it wouldn't sound so good when the Kolnari catch up with me."

Joat looked at Seg's disapproving face, then moved to block Kraig's view of him.

"Well, you know what, Kraig? You're not with the Kolnari, you're with us now. And now is all you should be thinking about." She smiled sweetly. "Given that I am one nnaaaaasty, dangerous woman.

"But if you're so *hot* to get back to the Kolnari, here's what we could do. After we torture the information I need out of you, I can fix your air pump, put that helmet back on and take you with me when I go." She smiled encouragingly into his horrified face. "Now, how would that suit you, hmmm?"

He went so pale that even his lips faded to white.

"Jeeeeezzz," he breathed. "You *are* crazy."

"You can't do that, Joat," Seg said raggedly.

"Oh, yes I caaaan," she said, playfully tweaking Kraig's nose.

"But they'll kill me," Kraig pleaded.

"I know. It's good to see that you understand your options." She straightened and stood before him with her hands on her hips. "You can either be a hero or a statistic. Your choice. I'll give you a few minutes to think about it."

Without another word, she turned her back on him and sat in the gimbaled pilot's couch.

"Rand, any word from Central Worlds?"

"No, but . . ."

". . . I wouldn't expect any, as yet," she finished with him.

Rand paused, as though nonplused by her knowing what he was going to say.

"Even if we hear from them in the next instant, Joat, that doesn't mean they will be here anytime soon."

"Tell me about it," she sneered. "Even *Simeon* couldn't get them to move their butts. It was two weeks before the station got help." She was silent a moment, remembering all too well the horror and anxiety of those slowly passing days.

There was a shudder through the ship as Alvec disconnected the fighter's caterpillar lock from theirs.

"So, any word from the Mayday Ms.?" she asked flippantly.

"I've had her stop her ship. She said that it is also a fighter. That she is a Bethelite and her companions are the former Captain of the *Sunwise* and a Kolnari."

"What?" Seg and Joat shouted together.

"Her name is Soamosa bint Sierra Nueva and the Captain's name is Sung."

"She captured a *Kolnari*?" Joat asked.

"She said he was one of her companions," Rand said carefully. "She made no boast of capturing one."

"Hmmmph! Interesting. The *Sunwise* was Amos's ship," Joat said. She keyed up cargo hold C. "Joe, Amos, does the name Soamosa bint Sierra Nueva mean anything to you?"

Joseph's head had lifted with a start at the sudden sound of her voice, Amos simply lay there, as unresponsive as ever.

"She is the Benisur's young cousin," Joseph said. "She was traveling with him when the Kolnari captured him." He straightened. "Why do you ask this?"

"Because we just picked up a Mayday call from her. She's in a ship ahead of us, en route for Bethel. Rand says we'll catch up with them in about forty minutes. Joat out."

She lives! Amos thought exultantly. *And she is sane. Oh, dearest God, my thanks. Your kindness is as sweet as honey, a balm to my heart and spirit. How astounding that Belazir told me the truth!*

He felt Joseph's hand take his and extended his will to respond.

Joseph felt the merest quiver in Amos's fingers, but he knew it was deliberate, that the Benisur *was* conscious and would, indeed, recover.

"My Lord," he said in a voice harsh with relief.

Soamosa had wakened to the sound of tears. A soft, strained, high-pitched whining, followed by a series of sobs. A sound of heart-breaking loss and confusion.

She blinked her eyes free of sleep and turned to Captain Sung, wondering if this time he would accept the comfort she offered him. *I think Karak may have been a little rough with that catheter,* she thought uncomfortably. Just the idea of a catheter made her squirm. She was certain she had installed her own incorrectly. Resolutely she turned her mind from that path.

There is nothing to be done about it now except to think of something else. It is not as though I lacked distraction, she thought wryly.

That was when she noticed that Captain Sung was quite still, his eyes closed, his face calm. He was snoring gently, she realized.

Then what is it that I hear?

Slowly, her eyes widened with horror and the hair on the back of her neck rose in a ripple that made her shudder. That awful weeping, the sound of a lost and wounded child, was coming from Karak.

Slowly she turned, her heart thudding like a horse's hooves and her mouth dry. *He is having a nightmare,* she thought desperately. *My poor love.* But instinctively she knew that the sound she was hearing never came from a sleeping man.

He was leaning over his console, the helmet almost resting on the boards before him. Then he flung himself back in his couch and flailed his head from side to side as if trying to fling off his helmet.

His face was gray and slicked with sweat. When his eyes opened it was like looking through two golden hued windows into the heart of a furnace. As she watched, tears spilled over and rolled heavily down his cheeks.

Karak touched gloved hands to his head, to be stopped by the face-plate. He groaned and threw his head forward again.

"Karak!" Soamosa freed herself from her couch and pulled herself rapidly over to him. "Speak to me, Karak. My love, can you hear me?" She placed her trembling hands on either side of his helmet and gently lifted his head. "Karak, you must answer me. Can you hear me?"

She was terrified. He could be dying and there was nothing she could do to help him. Locked into their suits like this she couldn't even touch him.

He opened his eyes and after a long moment, he seemed to recognize her. He smiled and moved a hand, as though to caress her, then stopped, as though the effort, even in zero-g, was too great.

"My sweet," Soamosa pleaded desperately, "if you can hear me you must give me some sign. Can you speak?"

He looked puzzled for a moment, then shook his head.

"Are you in pain?"

He nodded and his face crumpled like a child's, great fat tears falling unchecked down his sweat-slick face.

"Take a sip of water," she advised him.

He looked at her blankly through the plastic that separated them. Then he looked around, as though expecting a glass to materialize from nowhere. When it didn't, he looked accusingly at her and licked his lips; thirsty now that she had mentioned water.

"Sip on that," she said, pointing at a small flexible tube near his mouth.

He complied and his eyes widened with pleasure when the water came in response to his sucking.

Soamosa smiled reassuringly at him and then turned to the array of tell-tales built into the front of his suit.

Each suit of space-armor had a very basic auto-doc built in, to offer pain-killers and antibiotics, to apply pressure in order to control bleeding, and to administer up to two pints of plasma. Soamosa directed the suit to administer pain-killers. She noted that his fever was one hundred and four and reduced the interior temperature of his suit, hoping to combat the heat in his blood.

"Sweetheart," she pleaded, "why is this happening? Kolnari are never sick. Their bodies are too strong, they fight off everything. Why is this happening to you?"

He smiled bravely at her through his tears and mouthed the words: "I fight." Then his eyes crossed and rolled back in his head and he lay quiet beneath her.

She had panicked then, rushing back to her seat and activating the com, putting out a frantic Mayday call, hoping desperately that it would not be the Kolnari who answered it.

"Answering Mayday," a voice said in her ears. "This is free merchanter *Wyal*. Report your position and status."

Wyal, she thought. *That is . . . that is Joat's ship.* Every child on Bethel knew about the Jack Of All Trades and what she'd done against the Kolnari on SSS-900-C—girls especially knew. *She is the abomination's daughter.*

That thought brought her up short, like a mild slap to the face. She had thought, "abomination's daughter," without the slightest bit of rancor. It was merely an identifying tag, like the security director's wife . . . or the Benisur's Lady. She blushed to remember how she had yearned for that title.

Well, she thought wryly, *I suppose that if I have been impetuous enough to fall in love with a Kolnari, I have no business tossing epithets about. Nor aspiring to be the Benisur's wife, for that matter.*

"I am aboard a Kolnari three-crew fighter craft," she said, her voice a little hoarse. "With me are Captain Sung of the Benisur Amos's ship *Sunwise*. And . . . ah, and a Kolnari. Captain Sung and the Kolnari are ill, very ill—some sort of tailored disease which affects the memory functions. Help us, please!"

The waiting was almost harder than the fear had been. Captain Sung slept on, for which she was grateful. She considered authorizing the suit to give him a sleeping dose, but fought the urge. It would be selfish of her, and might harm him. Who knew how this awful disease had marred the functioning of his brain?

Releasing herself from her couch, she once again floated over to Karak. His eyes were closed and his temperature remained high, but at least had risen no higher.

"Oh, be well, my dear one," she whispered fervently.

"I could not bear it if you became like the Captain."
Her breath caught on a sob.

For that must be what afflicted him. And his body,
in typical Kolnar fashion, was just different enough to
cause this violent battle for supremacy over the disease
that had broken the Captain's mind. She prayed that
his body would be different enough to win.

An eternity later, the *Wyal* slid out of the night.

"Stand by for force-docking." A distant part of her was
surprised that a merchanter was equipped for that . . .
but this was *Joat's* ship, after all. The smaller vessel
shuddered violently as the freighter's lock clamped on
to it.

A small explosion of air, part sob, part laugh, entirely
relieved, escaped Soamosa's lips.

She heard someone thumping awkwardly through the
narrow tube connecting their ships when a thought
struck her.

"Wait!" she cried frantically, just as she heard
someone's gloves clack against the lock-face.

"What is it?" Rand asked.

The thumper had either heard or been warned to
stop, for suddenly there was no sound back there.

"I should have thought of this," Soamosa apologized
raggedly. "There is sickness aboard our craft. A very
dangerous illness, we dare not expose you to it." She
could feel the blood drain from her face as she spoke.

Ancient tales she had once enjoyed, describing noble
heroines buried alive for their principles, slipped into
her mind. *We're going to die out here,* she thought
numbly. *This ship will be my tomb.* Her heart picked up
its pace, as though her oxygen were already running out
and she gasped for air in sympathy with the thought.

There was a pause, then a woman's voice broke
the silence.

"This is Joat Simeon-Hap, Soamosa, captain of the *Wyal*. I assume the disease you're referring to is the one that destroys a part of the brain, leaving its victims like very young children?"

"Yes," the younger woman choked. Soamosa pressed her fist uselessly to her face-plate and then snatched it away with an annoyed sound.

"We're immunized and we have a controlled environment on the ship where we can lodge you."

"Oh!" Soamosa cried out in relief, and her heart filled to overflowing with gratitude.

She disconnected from her couch and flung herself at the nearest hand-hold. Scrambling towards the lock, all elbows and knees, Soamosa felt tears warming her cheeks. She reached the keypad, released the lock and flung herself into the suited arms of the woman who waited without. Their helmets knocked together with a resounding *clang*.

"Easy, girl!" Joat said, laughing. "These helmets cost a fortune." She held the girl awkwardly, feeling her trembling even through their suit's thickness. Joat gave Soamosa an occasional thump in the area of her shoulder blades in hopes the girl would soon feel comforted enough to release the death-grip she had on Joat's waist. "C'mon now," she said bracingly, "who've we got here." She gently but firmly pried Soamosa off and turned her towards the fighter's interior.

"It is Karak who is most in need of aid," Soamosa said urgently. "His fever is one hundred and four and he has been unconscious for over an hour." She began to tug Joat into the fighter.

"He the Kolnari?" Joat asked.

"Yes, he saved us."

"He *did*?"

Joat quickly saw that the Kolnari would have to be removed first, before the other figure in the lower seat could get out. Soamosa was lithe and slim and so could maneuver in that tight space with ease. But Captain Sung was both older and significantly thicker bodied. And one glance into his frightened, confused eyes told her that getting him out was going to be a project to remember.

"Okay," she said somewhat impatiently. "Karak goes first. Grab his other arm, Soamosa, then get at his feet and keep his rear end from catching on anything. Rand?"

"Yes Joat."

"Could you ask Seg to meet me at the air-lock with that cargo sled?"

"He's on his way."

Once in the *Wyal*'s gravity Karak seemed to weigh a ton. What with the thick, metal-heavy Kolnari bones and the great, muscled length of him, they nearly herniated themselves getting him onto the cargo sled.

Joat stood back and blew out an exhausted breath, put her hands on her hips. *I should have asked Rand to flux the gravity, like we did for the power suit.*

"Who did you say this osco was?" she asked aloud.

"He is Karak t'Marid," Soamosa answered in a tight, anxious voice, never taking her eyes off him.

"t'Marid?" Joat frowned.

Soamosa looked at her and licked her lips.

"He is Belazir's eldest son," she said, then she looked at him again.

"Can we use him as a hostage?" Seg whispered eagerly.

"No way," Joat told him with a dismissive gesture, "the Kolnari eat their young."

"Only very rarely," Soamosa protested. "For special ceremonies, Karak said, or under the most dire of circumstances." She looked up into their stunned silence and blushed. "In any case, you may be sure that if they did ransom him it would only be to destroy him. You must not return Karak to them," she cried passionately.

"He saved us, even the Captain, which was very awkward. Please help him! He is deserving of your aid, I promise you. He warned us of a plot to destroy Bethel and he was taking us there to thwart Belazir's plan when he was stricken." Her gaze turned defiant and she cradled Karak's massive paw in her own small hands. "And what is more, I love him."

Oh, wow! Joat thought. *That oughta jump-start Amos. He'll probably come out of that box like he was spring loaded.*

She held her hands out at chest level in a soothing motion and said, half-laughing, "Look, if giving him back would make them happy, that's the *last* thing I'm going to do. So just relax and we'll get him into cargo hold C so that Seg here can take a look at him." *I should have put a revolving door on that place*, she thought uneasily.

Joat tapped in the destination on the cargo sled's keypad and they followed it down the corridor. Soamosa carrying the big Kolnari's hand and cooing reassurance, Seg dragging info out of the auto-doc that no one else she knew could either get or understand.

In years to come, she thought with a grin, *I'm going to wish I had a holo-snap of Joseph's face when he realizes just what her hero is.*

✧ CHAPTER EIGHTEEN

Buster Rauchfuss read the memo from Dana Sherman regarding Bros Sperin's request for one hundred and twenty thousand credits.

Is Sperin crazy? he thought. *No documentation, no explanation, no report of any kind? Just a bald-faced demand for more money than I'll ever see in my lifetime.* He couldn't authorize this. *Even if I wanted to!*

Besides, Sperin was on leave from his department, so this request shouldn't even have come to him.

I'll just kick it up to Mancini, Buster thought with sour satisfaction. *Let him lose sleep over it.*

He hadn't liked the way Sperin had been removed from his supervision without explanation. "Security reasons," Mancini had said. *Like I'm some kind of neo who can't be trusted.* Sperin had been his man, dammit. And he'd felt a certain cachet just being the supervisor of such a distinguished field agent.

Then Buster glanced at the memo in his hand, suddenly relieved that Bros Sperin wasn't *his* any longer. He hummed as he composed the memo he'd be sending.

Dear Paul, he began. *I'm sure you know more about this than I do . . .*

When the lock opened, Joseph rushed forward anxiously, his hands outstretched.

"Lady Sierra Nueva," his eyes appraised her, "you are well?"

"Quite well, thank you, Ser ben Said," Soamosa responded with automatic graciousness. "Though my savior is in sore distress, as you can see."

Joseph glanced down at the figure on the cargo sled and choked, his eyes fairly bulging. A tide of intense red swept from his neck to his hair line, making the blue of his eyes still more startling.

"A Kolnari?" he said, with a quiet viciousness more deadly than a shout. "I will not allow this creature to share a single molecule of air with me!" He glared at Joat. "Space him," he commanded.

Joat raised one eyebrow and pursed her lips. After a moment of strained silence he muttered: "If you would, Captain."

"I've done it before, Joe, so don't go thinking I'm squeamish. But apparently this boy rescued the lady *and* Captain Sung for no other reason than he loves her."

Joseph barked a high-pitched sound of disbelief.

"What's more, he was piloting her to Bethel to warn them about Belazir's plot."

"You cannot believe that!" Joseph protested. "I can see an innocent, inexperienced young girl falling for such nonsense. But Joat, you have seen and known a great deal more than *she* has. You cannot be such a fool."

Joat shrugged.

"I can't see any benefit to Belazir in this." She pointed at the body on the sled. "This is his son— according to Soamosa—his oldest son. You tell me, why would he sacrifice him?"

Joseph turned away with a disgusted sound, then he swung back and said in a low fierce voice, "We have only his word that he is Belazir's son. I do not call that proof."

"It's not like you to be blinded by prejudice, Joe. *Look* at him. If there's one thing I'm not likely to forget, it's what Belazir t'Marid looks like. That boy is a copy of him. In any event, the first time in recorded history that a Kolnari does a good deed, I don't think the proper response is to stuff him out the air-lock. So, you're just going to have to be patient with me and put up with him."

Without another word Joseph turned and walked over to Amos, leaning close to speak with him.

Joat rolled her eyes and clicked her tongue in dismay. The quarantine hold wasn't that big. *Hah!, the ship isn't big enough to hold this kind of rancor. Wake up, Amos! We need you.*

She strolled over to the sled and tapped Soamosa on the shoulder.

"I need you to help me get the Captain in here."

"Oh," the girl looked distressed. "Must I go?" She indicated Seg with a fluid gesture. "Could not your assistant aid you?"

"My friend is helping your friend," Joat explained patiently. "Besides, the Captain will know you, where he doesn't know us."

"No," Soamosa murmured, shaking her head sadly, "he will not. Nor does he recognize anyone else, or anything." Her eyes filled with sorrow: "It is truly terrible, what they have done to him."

"Yeah," Joat agreed. "The Kolnari specialize in that sort of thing. And I'm not too happy about what they've done to Amos, either."

"Amos? The Benisur Amos?"

For the first time the girl looked around her. Immediately, her eyes fell on Amos, laying deathly still in the rescue pod, looking like nothing so much as a man in his coffin.

She shrieked and fell to her knees, babbling, "No, oh no, oh no . . ." over and over.

Joseph walked over to her again and knelt beside her, putting a gentle hand on her shoulder.

"He is well, Lady. Only drugged, but the Benisur is conscious, he knows you are here. Will you come and speak to him?"

Soamosa looked at him in horror.

"He is well, I assure you. Dr. !T'sel here was looking for an antidote to the drug the Kolnari gave him. But then he was distracted." Joseph glared at Seg as he said this.

"This is a very sick man," Seg told him firmly, "I'm afraid that takes precedence. The Benisur will recover from the drug very nicely all on his own. Karak here is going to need some doctoring."

Joat watched Soamosa's distress grow, the girl's head whipped from Karak, to Joseph, to Amos and back again.

She laid her hand on Soamosa's shoulder and said briskly, "You'll have plenty of time later to talk to Amos, and Karak is in good hands with Seg. Meanwhile I need help with Captain Sung and you're already in a suit." She gave Soamosa a reassuring smile. "We'll only be a few minutes."

Soamosa closed her eyes and took a deep breath, releasing it slowly, she stood.

"Very well," she said calmly, her voice shaking only a little.

Joat raised a brow, impressed. *Not quite the sheltered Bethelite maiden she seems. I think this oasis rose was carved from steelite.*

Soamosa turned to Joseph and spoke with the hauteur of twenty generations of aristocrats: "Ser ben Said, if you can not reconcile your feelings for the Kolnari, then I suggest that you keep away from my friend. For I will not suffer him to be hurt." She narrowed her eyes. "Neither will I tolerate any insult being offered to him. Do I make myself clear?"

"Quite clear, Lady," Joseph answered quietly.

Well said, young cousin, Amos thought. *I am sorry that you have had this terrible experience, and yet, you have grown. You sound like a woman now and not a silly girl.*

To find her changed so much for the better, in spite of the pain and humiliation she had endured at Belazir's hands was nothing short of a miracle. Inside his mind he smiled. *I do not think your mother will find you very easy to manipulate after this.* He imagined her mother's face as Soamosa presented Karak as her dear friend and hero.

Oh child, he thought in amused dismay, *she will never speak to either of us again.* For that matter, they'd probably be stoned to death anywhere on Bethel, unless he put guards around them every hour of the day—and he would have to pick the guards carefully. No Bethelite would accept any Kolnari on equal terms; never mind as a potential son-in-law. They had lost too many loved ones to the Kolnari's casual cruelty. Not a family on the planet had been untouched by the brief but violent occupation. And the pirates had planned to sear the world down to bedrock when they finished looting it.

This will not be easy, he thought. *It may not even be possible. Child, child . . .*

Joat sank exhausted into her chair on the bridge. She didn't know what was worse: Sung's blank-eyed terror and the small shrill sounds he made when they'd suddenly passed into the *Wyal*'s gravity, or the infantile gratitude with which he'd hugged Soamosa when she took off her helmet.

She shuddered. Then she popped the top on the container of coffee she'd grabbed from the galley and gratefully took a sip of the hot, fragrant brew.

Kraig's nostrils flared at the scent, but he remained quiet, watching her carefully from the prison of his frozen suit.

"Rand, patch me through to Al, will you?"

In a moment Alvec's voice came through the com.

"Yo, boss. You wanted to talk to me?"

"Just wanted to know how it's going out there, buddy."

"Quiet. Nothin' to report, really. *Wyal's* where the action is."

"You've got that right, Al. Would you believe Soamosa's in love with that Kolnari she brought in? Joe wants me to space him, Seg, I don't doubt, wants to study him, and Amos just lies there. Who knows what *he* wants."

She sighed wearily. "I think we should blow the fighter they came in. It's contaminated and we can't be bothered to salvage it, not with so much else to do. Can you manage that for us?"

"No problem, boss." By his voice Joat knew his eyes were gleaming. "You should see this weapons system ol' Kraig's got here."

"Yeah, when it comes to weapons there's no such thing as enough, for the Kolnari. Only things left regretfully behind."

Seg came quietly onto the bridge.

At Joat's questioning look he said, "I've got the young Kolnari stabilized. Fascinating reaction. I can't tell you how much I miss my lab!"

It was obvious from the passion in his voice. Joat smiled. Seg was a different being when he was in professional mode. As an espionage wannabe he might be a figure of fun, but as a scientist he was definitely a being to respect.

"I'm receiving a transmission from Central Worlds," Rand announced.

"Attention merchanter ship *Wyal*. Message received.

Repeat, message received. We will act on your information immediately. Message ends."

"That's it?" Joat sat forward in outrage. "That's all they have to say?"

"Well, they wouldn't tell us anything that might be intercepted," Alvec mumbled. Under his breath: "I never did like those straight-leg bast . . . children of irregular origin."

"You can't intercept a tight-beam message," she snapped. She flung herself back in her seat. "It could be days. It's already *been* days." Her lips narrowed to an angry line, and her fingers beat a rapid tattoo on the arms of her chair. "We've got to do something or he's dead."

Her eyes strayed to her prisoner and met Kraig's. She smiled, showing her teeth and his Adam's apple bobbed prodigiously. "That's right," she murmured, "be afraid—be very afraid."

Seg cleared his throat.

"You're determined to carry through with this idea of rescuing Bros?"

She nodded.

"Al can take the rest of you in the *Wyal*," she said. "I assume Clenst has some sort of facility for this sort of thing? Decontamination, debriefing?"

"Yes, the very finest," Seg assured her. He drew himself up to his full height. "Um. I have . . . certain discretionary," he waved a hand uncertainly, "powers, I suppose you could say. I can authorize the engagement of up to a battalion of Yoered Family mercenaries."

He stood looking at her eagerly, his large eyes round, like a schoolboy awaiting praise and fearing censure.

Joat's smile was brilliant as she rose from her chair and gave a sweeping bow: "The com is yours."

"Joat," Rand said, "perhaps you should discuss this

with Joseph. He will both need and want to know what decisions are being made here."

Joat blinked.

"Rand, that's downright sensitive! You're becoming more human every day."

"Thank you, Joat. I know you meant that as a compliment."

She blinked again and raised her brows. Then she went to Alvec's station.

"Rand, give me cargo hold C."

They'd brought in cots and a small store of self-heating food for their passengers' comfort, and they'd rigged up a curtained off area with a port-a-potty in it. Their passengers wouldn't be able to wash, but they'd survive that.

And even if I get my debt to Ciety cleaned up— amazing how unimportant that seemed now—*I still can't afford to have the whole ship decontaminated.* Viruses were nasty little things, even natural ones. Designed for durability, you might have to put the ship into a graving dock stationside and strip her to the hull to get them all.

Cargo hold C was designed for live cargo and was a self-contained, self-sterilizing facility. So even if they did impound the *Wyal* for a few months they'd be hard pressed to find an excuse for destroying her.

Of course it wouldn't matter then, because after a few months of not earning any income, *Wyal* wouldn't belong to her any more. *Come to think of it, legally, it already as good as belongs to dear, old Uncle Nom.* Even if they returned from this mission, which he clearly didn't expect, she couldn't see him quietly writing off a hundred twenty thousand credits. *And who do I have for witnesses that he'll give* Wyal *back to me in exchange for running this errand?* No one the Yoered Family would pay attention to.

Joat frowned at the unwelcome thought, then brushed it aside. She sat forward, her eyes fixed on Joseph where he sat at Amos's side, glaring at Karak.

"Joe."

His head came up. "Yes Captain."

Fardles! Still prickly. Aloud she said: "We've heard from Central Worlds. Basically all they did was acknowledge our message."

Joseph snorted. "What a great surprise that is. Did they at least imply that they were going to respond in any other way?"

She smiled bitterly. They'd both had experience with the ponderous bureaucracy of Central Worlds.

"In the broadest possible terms. Um. We're going to have Al destroy the fighter our friends came in. We can't bring it and we dare not leave it and risk the spread of this contagion."

"Wise," he said laconically. "Thank you for keeping me informed. Is there anything else?"

"Uh. Yes. Alvec will be taking all of you on to a quarantine facility where, hopefully, you'll be cleansed of any trace of this disease."

Seg nodded positively at her.

"At least Seg firmly believes so."

Joseph's eyes narrowed and the cant of his head became alert.

"And you, Joat? Where will you be while we are being purged?"

Back to Joat, she thought, *we're making progress.*

"I'm taking the other fighter and I'm going to get Bros Sperin."

His brows rose. "Just like that?"

"Suggestions are welcome," she said.

"I will go with you."

"Amos needs you," she said. "And so do Rachel and the children. This isn't like the SSS-900-C. You can't just act for yourself now; you're a father and a husband, Joe."

"I am also a man. And I have a great need to see this finished, Joat. If I can, I will kill Belazir. He has done too much to us. I cannot live with my hatred."

Joat sighed. She knew what he meant. If there was one thing she understood it was how unsated rage and hatred could poison your life.

"I wish Amos were awake to talk you out of this," she muttered.

I would not, Amos thought into the pause that followed. *I know my brother's heart too well. And he is right. He has a great need to take action. That is his destiny, Joat, do not fight him. You cannot forbid fate.*

"But he's not," Joat continued. "And I admit I'm selfish enough to be glad of your company, Joe. I've got some stuff to take care of first, then we'll suit up and meet at the air-lock." She cut off contact and sat back, her hand idly stroking her chin. Suddenly Al's voice startled her out of her reverie.

"Hey! You don't even ask me? I been watching your back for how long and you don't even ask me?"

"I'm asking you to take Amos and the rest to that Clenst facility. And who else would I let pilot the *Wyal?*"

"Rand," he said positively. "You know it can do it."

"You also know that I insist on at least two competent pilots aboard, including the AI. That's minimum safety rules, Al. I wouldn't leave this many lubbers with less. Especially since one of them is my adoptive mother's sweetheart. C'mon Al, don't give me a hard time over this. I need your support."

There was a long pause, redolent of ill temper and resentment. Then, "Okay," he mumbled, stabbing viciously at the firing stud.

His plasma gun fired an ultra-miniaturized, laser-triggered deuterium fusion pellet focused by magnetic fields. The abandoned fighter exploded in a brilliant burst of sun-hot violence, the whole mass of it reduced to gases in seconds.

Alvec's face-plate darkened to black automatically, protecting his eyes. He felt better, not perfect, but better. With a wry smile he maneuvered the fighter into position just over the air-lock and waited for Joat to grapple him.

"I don't want to do this," Seg mumbled mutinously.

Joat rolled her eyes with exasperation.

"Can you get Amos back on his feet?" she asked reasonably.

He shook his head. "No, not without more elaborate lab facilities. There are too many variables."

"Can you do anything else for Karak?"

Seg's mouth sphinctered shut in distress.

"No," he said at last. "The serum will either help him or it won't. Only time will tell."

"Well . . . you *can* help me. And you can help Bros Sperin by helping me. So do it," she said through gritted teeth.

"But it's wrong. Don't you understand?"

Joat's lips thinned to a straight line and she leaned forward in her chair, her eyes holding his.

"You wanted to be a part of Sperin's world. Well, now you are. Sometimes you're called on to hard things, Seg. It's not like I'm asking you to kill him, for crying out loud!"

Kraig's eyes bugged and he flicked his gaze frantically between them. But his lips were compressed into a firm white line. As though he'd resist speech by sheer will-power.

"And if we don't get the codes and call signs from

this man, an even more unethical bunch of people are going to rip Bros Sperin into little, screaming pieces!"

She sat glaring at Seg. "Meanwhile, I'm sitting here, captaining a blasted *hospital* ship, doing nothing! Oh, Central Worlds is sending help," she said quickly, cutting off Seg's protest.

"Just as soon as ever they can," she added sarcastically. "And you and Clenst are sending help, again, just as soon as they can. But I don't trust any of them, because they don't care! You know who cares?" She tapped her chest. "I do. They took him off *my* ship, and as far as I'm concerned that makes it my responsibility. So you choose one of those drugs and you inject him. Or I will."

In the end, Seg chose the drug that induced pleasure and an overwhelming desire to please. Kraig, awash with glorious sensations and having the time of his life, surrendered every secret he knew, up to and including the combination of his locker.

He even approved Joat's cobbled-together mercenary uniform.

"Oh yeah!" he enthused. "It's black an' it's tight. No one's going to look further than that."

Joat raised a brow. "Thanks," she drawled.

"No, problem, black and tight, way to go. Mmm-mmmmm."

Joat looked uncertainly at Seg.

"He'll quiet down as the drug wears off," Seg assured her.

"Jeeeez, I hope so," Alvec growled. "I don't like the way he's lookin' at me."

"At everybody," Joat agreed. Then she shrugged. "Seg, would you join me in the galley please?"

Puzzled, and wondering if he was going to receive another lecture the Sondee followed her into the galley/lounge.

There was a display film covering the tabletop, and beside it was a box about a meter long and half as wide and deep.

Joat inserted a datahedron into a slot at the edge of the display film and a schematic blossomed upon the screen. Seg automatically leaned towards it and began to read. After a moment he glanced up at Joat, read a bit more, flipped through several more schematics and then straightened. He looked at her in perplexity, a most unhappy look on a Sondee face.

"This is top secret," he said.

"This is synchronicity," Joat said with a grin. "Simeon and I were working on this idea for a signal jammer and I'd almost finished the prototype when Clenst announced their own version. Talk about disappointed." She pursed her lips and shrugged. "All for the best though. If we'd sold it then we wouldn't have it here to use. What I need is help in finishing up the dispersal unit."

Seg checked her data.

"You manufactured ten thousand transmitter/receivers by yourself?" he asked in wonder.

"It's not that hard to make 'em," Joat said. "And as you've noticed it's a long way between systems. So time isn't a problem."

"It's amazingly like ours," Seg murmured. "Except . . . I think the sine-wave control function may be a little better. For some purposes."

"Well, the concept is identical. Lots of miniature receiver/transmitters catching signals and sending them back out with various time lags. Result; hopelessly garbled messages. Think it'll work?"

"Actually . . . in some ways it's more efficient than our design. Clenst might be willing to negotiate for those improvements."

"Music to my ears," Joat said, smiling. "Let's get to work, shall we?"

"I see you're using a rocket propulsion system."

"Keep it simple," she agreed, "that's my motto."

"Have you got rocket fuel?"

"You purists," Joat scoffed. "All we need is a volatile liquid." She put a couple of bottles of cleaning fluid on the table. "We'd never have gotten farther than the moon if we'd waited for guys like you. If it'll make you feel better I've got a form you can fill out before we begin."

Seg laughed nervously.

"There's no control-board indicated on your design," he objected.

"That's because there are cheap, readily available ones already on the market. Why reinvent the wheel?" Joat slapped a tiny control-board on the table beside the cleaning fluid. "That's a spare from the food processing unit. So, it'll think it's dicing carrots when it fires up the rocket. I won't tell it if you don't."

All of Seg's eyes were shining as he smiled delightedly at her.

"This is *real* hands-on, seat-of-your-pants stuff, isn't it?" he said enthusiastically.

"Hands on the seat of your *pants*?" Joat asked, bemused. *Jeeez, these Sondee have weird sayings.* "Whatever you say, Seg."

Joseph was fully suited when she met him at the lock, her helmet balanced atop the box in her arms. With a glance at the box he placed the helmet over her head and locked it down. She smiled her thanks nervously.

"Our suits look awful," he complained. "They *look* like they have been painted."

"Nothin' we could do about it," Joat said with a shrug. "Kraig said they had to be black." She snorted in disgust. "Only the Kolnari would insist on black space suits. But then, I can't see them rescuing someone who managed to drift off. So why would they want to make them visible enough to pick up easily?"

Joseph grinned at her, his blue eyes alight with a fierce joy. "I am going to eat Belazir's beating heart," he said happily.

Absolute cold flashed over Joat's body and she stared at Joseph as if she'd never seen him before.

"Joe," she said quietly, like a patient mother addressing a particularly wanton five year old. "This is a rescue mission. We can't stop for lunch. Especially if we want to get away. So, we're not going on a Kolnari hunt, is that understood?"

His mouth twisted and his eyes flickered away as he nodded.

Joat kicked him in the shin.

"Don't you patronize me," she snapped. "Either it's understood that I am in command and that our mission, our *sole* mission, is the rescue of Bros Sperin, or you're not going. End of story."

"I need to finish this," he told her, his voice so rough it was almost a growl.

"But this isn't the time." Her eyes held his. After a moment she smiled. "If we can carry this off, Joe, Belazir will eat his heart out for us."

Twelve hours later they received a tight-beam message from the *Wyal*.

"Greetings, my brother," Amos's voice was husky from prolonged thirst, "and Joat, my friend."

"My Lord!" The joy in Joseph's voice seemed to brighten the inside of the cramped fighter.

"Good to hear from you, Amos," Joat said with a relieved grin.

"It is good to be able to speak, I assure you. I wanted to tell you that my prayers go with you."

"Every little bit helps," Joat assured him.

"Thank you, Benisur. Your blessing strengthens my purpose," Joseph said.

"So if you could clarify his purpose for him I'd appreciate it," Joat suggested. "He hasn't spoken to me since I told him he couldn't eat Belazir's heart this trip."

There was silence for a moment.

"Surely, my brother, you would not needlessly risk your life. There is Rachel to consider, and the children. And I would find it hard to bear if you were to die like a fool."

Wow! Joat thought, *I didn't think Amos knew how to be that blunt.* She had grown so used to his parables and subtle persuasions. Joat wasn't even the target of his remarks and she felt like she'd been hit with a rock.

Joseph gasped. Then: "I stand rebuked, Benisur. You are correct, of course. It is shameful to indulge myself at the cost of the greater good."

"I am pleased to hear it, my brother. This is an attitude that will serve you well in the coming years."

A contemplative silence followed. *And if that doesn't beg "C'mon, ask me what I mean," I'm a Shapelitic Nun,* Joat thought.

"What do you mean?" Joseph asked.

"My young cousin means to marry her Kolnari captive," Amos said. His voice seemed to smile.

"My Lord!" Joseph bellowed. "You cannot allow that!"

"Hey!" Joat snapped, her ears ringing.

"I am sorry, Joat. Benisur, you cannot be serious. The Lady's family will disown her. She shall be shunned. The shame will kill her mother."

Amos sighed. *I suspect my young cousin's mother is one of those who are immune to shame. Else she would be unable to use it so effectively as a weapon.*

Aloud: "Just before we were captured by the Kolnar I asked Soamosa how she would like it if the people looked on her as a prophetess. And, of course, being a modest maid, she said she was no such thing and surely no one could take her for such. But now, I find myself seeing her in just such a light. For she truly loves this Karak and it is just as plain that he loves her. It seems to me, my brother, that she has given his humanity back to him. Perhaps we should try to join her in this task."

"My Lord!" Joseph groaned and then drew his breath in a great gasp. "Just because *one* of that demon breed shows signs of being human does not mean the rest are salvageable."

"He has a point, Amos," Joat said.

Amos didn't laugh, but the smile was still there in his voice.

"God does not challenge us by presenting us with circumstances that we welcome. And if Soamosa's family disowns her, I shall not. She shall be my heir, and I shall support her with all of my heart."

"She is too young to make such a decision, Benisur."

"Joseph, you would not be making such an objection if I had decided to marry the girl myself. Now would you? In fact, when it was arranged for her to accompany me, it was you who smoothed out so many of the details. Wasn't it?"

Joseph was so silent that Joat glanced down at him, wondering if his suit mike had broken down.

Then he said, "You would love having children, my brother," in a quiet voice filled with pained dignity.

Joat felt a little spurt of outrage. *Channa's not that old!* she thought. She'd always suspected that Channa was just working out her contract before she ran off to Bethel with Amos. *All she needs is a little time.*

"Prophet is not a comfortable family business," Amos observed. "I am not sure that I ought to have children. I might enjoy having them, but I am not so sure that they would enjoy being my offspring. Channa and I have discussed this and we feel that perhaps we should adopt our children."

Joseph was silent again. The kind of silence that fills a room with powerful, undefined emotion.

"On behalf of adopted children everywhere, Amos, go for it," Joat said with a smile.

"I shall," he said. "As I have said, I will adopt Soamosa. And her children and Karak's shall be my grandchildren. As she is my cousin, they will share the same blood as I." He paused. "Interesting. That would mean that Belazir and I would share the same blood."

"NO!" Joseph roared.

"Ow! Joe! Watch the volume control!"

"You go too far, my Lord."

Amos sighed. "Yes, perhaps you are right, my brother. But perhaps also, there are other Kolnari like Karak who do not wish only to kill and to steal. This could be a sign of hope for them and the beginnings of peace for both our peoples."

"Is it all right this trip if we at least hurt the Kolnari's feelings?" Joat asked dryly. "I'll really miss that sense of closure I'd get otherwise."

Amos laughed. "I have not lost my mind, Joat. I merely present a new idea. This may not be practical; and in any case, you have my cheerful permission—both of you—to annihilate Belazir t'Marid and as many of his followers as seems convenient, while you pursue your mission."

"Good luck, Amos." She shook her head in wonder.

"We will discuss this upon my return, Benisur," Joseph growled.

"It pleases me to think that I have given you still another reason to be cautious with your life, my friend. I look forward to our conversation."

"Joat?"

"Hey Rand, what's up?"

"Your ETA is twelve hours, correct?"

"Well, thereabouts, anyway. Depends on what we run into. Why?"

"Yoered Family anticipates being at those coordinates in fourteen hours."

Joat raised her brows. Not that she'd doubted Yoered's professionalism; but this kind of timing indicated a high level of commitment for what was a fairly casual contract.

"Well, I'm impressed. Clenst must be paying a premium."

"They are," Seg assured her. "It might be wise to coordinate your efforts with them."

Joat rolled her eyes. "You mean subordinate my efforts to theirs. No way, !T'sel. Two hours could make a major difference in Sperin's life span. You tell your flunkies to watch out for us. Out." She cut contact with the *Wyal* before anyone could protest.

"Give them back their humanity?" Joseph murmured in stunned tones.

"Poor Amos," Joat said. "The trouble with giving people back their humanity is that a lot of the time they don't want it returned." *Crikey, the last thing a thief and murderer wants is an active conscience. Poor Amos.*

"But the Kolnari? Has my lord gone mad?"

"No Joseph. You're just looking at the down-side of loving a living saint. They *will* do uncomfortable things."

"But the Kolnari?"

"Yeah. Let's plan what we're actually going to do when we find them," Joat said, cutting off what she recognized as an endless conversational loop.

"Perhaps we should try giving them back their humanity."

She laughed. "Yeah, then we'll shoot 'em while they stand there frozen in shock."

Joseph chuckled.

"I should not laugh at the Benisur," he said. "But truly, this is beyond everything."

"One thing at a time, Joe. You can talk him out of it when we get back."

She ran through the data again. Their plans were actually as set as they could be, on what amounted to— *It is* not *a suicide mission.* Joat had gone through her copy of Janes's *All the Galaxy's Spaceships*, a gift from Simeon, and found Belazir's flagship. It was not quite a light cruiser; a destroyer-leader, built to command a flotilla of lighter craft, a Central Worlds Navy vessel, heavily refitted for Kolnari use. Probably it had once been a Navy surplus ship owned by a planet the Kolnar had stripped, then destroyed.

She'd called up the schematic and Kraig had guided them through it.

"Avoid the A and B corridors if ya can, that's Kolnar territory, an' they like to hassle anyone that doesn't belong there."

He indicated where the brig was located. A fairly large section of the ship deep in its center. And he enthusiastically described what he knew about their security system.

"It's fantastic, man! If they ever went straight they could make a fortune designing security for rich guys."

He'd recited the security codes and their answers so that Rand could record them. And Rand had made up a program that would answer the question asked, regardless of the order in which the codes were presented.

"Security's pretty light on the decks the mercs use," Kraig had told them. "I mean who's going to be stupid enough to sneak . . ." He'd blinked at them. "Hey, I din't mean anything." He'd apologized for several minutes before they could convince them they weren't offended.

✧　　✧　　✧

Joseph dubiously eyed the large ball of ice Joat held ready in front of the lock.

"*This* is your secret weapon?"

"Yup."

"A snowball?"

She chuckled. "The ice is imbedded with approximately ten thousand transmitter/receivers which will be dispersed at a controlled rate determined by the speed at which the *snowball* is traveling. We're going to push it right through Kolnari space and mess up their communications big time."

"They will blow it up, Joat."

"And if they do, some of the t/rs will be destroyed. The rest will be in a good position to do what they're designed for. It'll work, Joe. Trust me." She looked up at his scowling face. "Seg was really impressed."

He grunted and opened the lock.

Joat shoved her burden through the open hatch and Joseph closed it again. Then she picked up a control plaque and pressed the firing stud. The rocket ignited and her faux comet was off.

"You really like that alien, do you not?" Joseph asked as he strapped himself back into his seat.

"Yeah. He's a nice kid."

"He is a tactless, interfering busybody."

"But basically a sweetie."

"He is hideous to look upon and he is a fool."

"I knew you liked him."

Joseph growled. "It is hard not to. He is so much like a happy, bouncy little puppy."

They were silent a while, monitoring the discreet Kolnari signals. Kraig had warned them to linger just outside the Kolnar security perimeter and wait to be recognized.

Joat did and didn't mind.

The waiting was hard, largely because her excellent imagination kept conjuring possible disaster scenarios. Kraig might have left out something vital, or they might be given close escort to Belazir's ship. In which case they were sunk. The success of the whole plan depended on their being handled like a friendly.

Yet the longer they sat here, the more time her "snowball" had to do its work.

Suddenly there was a flurry of questions from the Kolnari. Rand's program answered as designed and they were given leave to proceed.

"Welcome back, Rendino du Pare," a woman's voice said.

"Thanks," Joseph muttered, "out."

"I hope that's not his girlfriend," Joat said.

"I would not worry," Joseph said quietly. "I am sure the Kolnar do not encourage chatter in their space."

They proceeded quietly on their way, watching the distant Kolnari fleet loom larger as they approached.

"Joat, may I ask you a question?"

"Sure."

"Your ship, the *Wyal*, what does its name mean? I have tried to find a reference to it everywhere that I can think of; without success. And knowing you, I am sure it has some significance."

"It's an acronym," she said with a grin. "Does that help?"

"Are you going to tell me or not?"

"It means While You Ain't Lookin'."

Joseph laughed silently. "Appropriate. It is pleasant to know that creeping respectability has not entirely obliterated the feral child I knew and loved."

They're not all watching me, Joat told herself. *This is normal. And this is the end of a normal mission.*

Lights on the floor and ceiling guided her to a berth.

She parked neatly and powered down. The hangar was cramped, nothing like the cavernous hold of an assault carrier. It was a little unusual for a ship of this displacement to carry fighters at all, but she supposed it was useful when you didn't have an elaborate military organization with specialized vessels. The tips of the fighter's weapons pods just barely cleared those of the other three; there was one empty berth—that would be the one Soamosa had taken—and a scurry of crew and robots, doing maintenance work.

No, they're arming up and fueling. Somebody's suspicious. Oh, joy.

"They're going to be expecting only one person to disembark," she said nervously.

"Kraig told you that security was light in the mercenaries' section, almost casual. My advice is to disembark with me, acting like you belong here. I doubt anyone will look twice, or bother to question us. As I said before, I am much more nervous about the paint on our suits."

"Don't worry," she said, "we'll shed them as fast as we can." *They do have a kinda orange undercast.*

Joat wondered if the suited figures servicing the fighters around them were mercenaries or Kolnar slaves. Either way, Joe was probably right. The ones who knew how many people should be returning from this mission sure as blazes weren't working on this deck. She grasped the strap on her black shoulder bag and followed Joseph across the floor to the locker area.

Joseph was keying in Kraig's locker combination when a message came through his suit's receiver.

"Rendino du Pare, you are to report to Captain Hobsbrowm for debriefing at fourteen hundred hours. Room C-780."

"Acknowledged, out."

Joseph finished the unlock code and pulled open the door. Then he took off his helmet and spoke to Joat.

"Now we know how much time we have. I am to meet with my debriefer at fourteen hundred."

Joat was already half out of her suit.

"It's twelve hundred now. They're not too eager to talk to you, are they?"

There were two uniforms in the locker, Joseph proceeded to put both on.

"It works to our advantage, of course. But I wonder what is going on."

Joat brushed her hair smooth and retied it in a ponytail.

"If we're lucky," she said, "Belazir's asleep and no one wants to wake him. If we're not . . . then he's with Bros."

"Or he is in conference with his captains, or working out, or just generally busy. Let us not worry about how Belazir is occupied until we must conclude otherwise."

"Joe," she said as she stuffed her suit into Kraig's locker beside his, "you're being reasonable. I really, really hate it when I'm being hysterically pessimistic and people insist on being reasonable."

"I shall try not to restrain myself," he promised with a smile.

"Well, all right," she said, "see that you don't." Joat looked him over, straightening his collar.

"Okay. Let's do it."

The Kolnari had sealed a number of the access panels into the repair tunnel that ran between corridors C and B, no doubt for security reasons. The remaining few were carefully locked.

Joat pulled Sperin's override gizmo out of her shoulder bag and set it against the lock mechanism. It hadn't taken her long to figure it out. The thing was designed to be simple to use and she had a natural affinity for mechanical objects.

Still, she was nervous and her hands were slick with sweat. Even with Joseph's beefy body partially shielding her from view she felt conspicuous.

The fact that they'd sealed so many panels made her believe those that weren't sealed were under observation. That "everybody's watching you and they don't like what they see" feeling was raising chills up and down her spine.

The lock clicked open and she slipped through, half expecting to be met by a snarling crowd of armed Kolnari. *What are you doing here? Hands up! Behind your head! On your knees! March!*

There was no one there. She breathed a soft sigh of relief.

"How I wish we could use one of your little scramblers, Joat," Joseph murmured nostalgically. "I would feel so much more secure."

"You and me both," she said, smiling. "But they're just as likely to set off alarms these days as to get you by them."

They backtracked until they found the access panel they wanted. One that was located quite close to the Kolnari Brig. Predictably it was welded shut.

Joat pulled a roll of what looked like putty from her bag and began to stick it around the seam of the panel. When she was through she stuck a suction cup with a handle attached onto the center of the panel and pulled on it to test its grasp.

Then she and Joseph drew their sidearms and after carefully regulating the laser's temperature they melted the coil of heat activated acid they'd drawn around the seam. Slowly at first, and then more quickly, it liquefied and began to eat its way through the welds. Joat exerted a gentle outward pressure on the suction cup. What

fumes there were stayed with them in the narrow
tunnel, unpleasant, but nontoxic. For the most part.
Kolnari would probably hardly notice them. A small
alarm she'd built into her coverall was complaining
about the *Dreadful Bride*'s toxic atmosphere in increasingly insistent tones anyway. She reached up and turned
it off. *I know already!*

As the panel came free, Joseph reached out to
support Joat's hand and they lifted it slightly, but held
it in place, not quite touching the frame it had once
joined.

They listened tensely for sounds of voices or people
walking by and were rewarded by silence.

Cautiously they lifted the panel outward and stepped
into the deserted corridor. Then they fitted it back into
place, reset their lasers and proceeded to the Brig.

✧ CHAPTER NINETEEN

The woman behind the Brig's reception desk was a heavy-worlder, no question. Her bones had been genetically altered for thickness and her height was somewhat below human norm. But her expression was curious, and relatively friendly.

"Yeah?" she asked. "Help you?"

"We're here to see a Mr. Bros Sperin," Joat purred.

Beside her Joseph stood impassively, eyes front, hands clutched behind his back in an automatic parade rest. Just so much muscle, ready to spring into action.

"Yeah? What for?"

Joat raised one brow.

"We have a specialty," she said smiling slightly.

"Oh?"

"Conversation. People can't seem to resist talking to us."

The woman chuckled evilly.

"Oh, yeah, I heard about that. I been expecting somebody like you. The Big Black Baddies tried with one of their creepy little medics and got nowhere. You'll have to leave your guns, though," she said.

Joat pursed her lips. "I don't mind leaving mine here, but I'd rather my companion kept his. Sperin is reputed to be an . . . educated man. I'd like to know he has a weapon pointed at him."

The woman was shaking her head and her expression was a lot less friendly.

"Or perhaps," Joat continued, "he could surrender it to the guard on Sperin's door." She arched a brow. "I assume there *is* a guard on his door?"

"Unh hunh. Let me see your ID."

A little hole appeared in the center of the woman's forehead and intelligence ran out of her eyes as though escaping through it in a narrow wisp of steam.

Joseph shook his hand, scorched by the backrush of burning gases where the laser had burned its way through the holster. A scorched smell insinuated itself through the sour chemical stink of Kolnar-normal atmosphere.

"I did not want to do that," he said ruefully.

Joat frowned. She didn't like killing, didn't like the waste. And like Joseph she hadn't wanted to see this almost-friendly hired killer die.

"It couldn't be helped," she said grimly. "We don't have ID."

When at last they'd taken the deliriously happy Kraig out of his suit, they'd checked his ID thoroughly. It was entirely too complex to duplicate with the equipment they had. And as time was a factor, they'd decided to go without.

They arranged the mercenary's body so that it was turned slightly away from the entryway, hiding the hole in its . . . her head. Even the single second gained by the small deception might count.

"Let me get to work."

Joat went down on one knee behind the control console. *Ah . . . dedicated system, just like Kraig said.* That was safer, in a warship subject to viral attack; a worm program could be stopped by a series of specialized interfaces, and it also made damage control in combat easier. The down side was that none of the subsystems was as capable as one big one, and data transfer was slower.

"This will take a second."

She eased one of her tools out from behind the belt of her mercenary uniform and set to work, whistling silently between her teeth. *Ah, not too unusual.* The Kolnar had been savages before the High Clan left their planet—although it was a peculiar type of savagery, you could mine raw metallic plutonium there with picks and shovels, they'd had nuclear-powered steamboats. The basic technology of the space-going Kolnari clans was copied from Central Worlds–derived models.

"Here." She snipped a fiber-optic line and spliced it into a converter, then plugged a datahedron into the optico-magnetic device. The screen before the dead woman cleared and began to show an uneventful corridor.

"There. That ought to keep the surveillance systems out of our hair, until someone notices the repeating pattern."

The main doors to the prison recognized them, routing though the intercept she'd placed on the computer. They proceeded through them as calmly as possible. The computer had indicated which of the cells was Sperin's and they moved confidently down the corridors.

There was a Kolnari standing guard outside the cell and Joat could feel Joseph going into high gear.

The guard showed no sign at all that he was aware of their approach. His posture had the relaxed alertness of a hunting beast.

Arrogant jerk! Joat thought. *Probably thinks there's no need to get excited about two scumvermin mercs. Oh baby, are you in for a surprise.*

"We are here to question the prisoner," she said, crisply, but with deference.

The Kolnari stared at the opposite wall, as though thinking deep thoughts that couldn't be disturbed.

After a full minute had elapsed Joseph said quietly, "We are here at the Great Lord's orders."

That got a reaction. The body remained rigidly in place, but a brass-yellow eye glanced in their direction. After a brief pause the guard spoke.

"I have received no orders that the prisoner is to be allowed visitors."

Then he returned to deep thought mode.

"Obviously the Great Lord has been detained," Joat observed, looking at Joseph.

"We will wait," he said grimly.

Joseph and the Kolnari stood like statues in contrasting colors, but after a few moments Joat began to pace.

She walked back and forth, spinning on her heel every four paces. Then she began to whistle through her teeth while clapping her hands before her and then behind her back.

Her fidgeting annoyed the guard. A very small wrinkle appeared between his brows. The equivalent of a full blown tantrum in any other people; he turned towards her, lips peeling back from his teeth.

Joseph's laser took him in the back of the skull, and the Kolnari collapsed, falling stiffly, like a giant tree.

Joe caught him before he hit the floor and Joat snatched the key from his utility belt. She aimed it at the door and it slid open obediently. Then she grabbed the Kolnari's feet and helped Joseph pull him into the cell.

Bros stood with his feet braced, swaying. He watched them enter with no reaction whatsoever, like a man viewing a holoshow.

Joat couldn't suppress an exclamation at her first good look at him. He was covered with burns. Some no more than reddened patches, but large areas were blistered and bleeding plasma. His face was slack with exhaustion, shadowed by his beard, his reddened eyes sunken in deep blue circles. He smelled awful; of infection and stale sweat and charred flesh.

Joseph's hand came over her shoulder, offering the shirt he'd just taken off and she jumped.

"Yeah," she said, as if Joseph had spoken. "Bros, you've got to put this on," she said clearly and calmly.

She took hold of one hand and slid the sleeve of the black shirt over it, ignoring the oozing wounds. He made a sudden sound of agony and began to struggle. Coaxing him to cooperate, she slid the other sleeve up and over his shoulder. Awareness flickered back into his eyes.

"Joat," Bros said, his voice hoarse, his breathing harsh. "I've been having this dream that you'd come for me since yesterday. But this is the first time you've worn something so sexy. Does it mean something?" he leered.

Good grief! Joat thought. *There's resilience for you.*

"I think it means your subconscious really, really wants you to get out of here. So why don't you just relax and go along with it?"

Fortunately the trousers were quite loose and slid over his boots with little trouble. Bros lost his balance at one point and started to fall, but Joe caught him. Blisters broke under Joseph's big hands and Bros gasped and cursed, but the pain seemed to make him more aware.

"Can you walk?" Joat asked anxiously.

"You're really here," he said and touched her face gently.

"Can you walk?" she repeated.

"Anything you can do I can do better," he quipped.

"If I'd known you were going to take that attitude I wouldn't have come," she grumbled.

He leaned forward.

"Give me a kiss, Joat, and I'll follow you anywhere."

Joat frowned and glanced at Joseph who nodded impatiently. She kissed Bros's lips gently, then smiled. *Like you'd have stayed with Belazir if I'd said no. Bros, you've got style even when you're nuts with pain and fatigue.*

"C'mon," she said.

They retraced their steps; Joat let the signal disrupting transmitter/receivers trickle from her pockets in their wake; Bros was stumbling forward in defiance of gravity, Joseph hovering nervously behind, ready to catch him if he fell.

When they reached the locker room Joat broke into the locker next to Kraig's with Sperin's lock pick and pulled out the suit it contained.

Then, she and Joseph stripped Bros of the mercenary uniform and shoved him into it without regard to his wounds.

Forgive me, Bros, Joat thought, *there's no time to go easy on you.*

She and Joseph hurried into their own suits, hearts pounding, waiting for an alarm klaxon to sound, waiting for discovery.

They sealed and checked each other's helmets and then marched out onto the flight deck, towards one of the green lighted fighters; fueled and ready for takeoff.

Joat boarded first and Joseph boosted Bros into her waiting arms. Between the two of them, they wrestled him into his seat, got him connected to life support and strapped down.

There were codes for taking a fighter out as well as in and Joat inserted the datahedron they'd made for it into its slot. Then she powered up and began rolling the big machine out of line. *Ghu, but I've got to pee.*

And she *hated* doing that with the catheters in. They hurt, and they always leaked a little. The universe was unfair to females.

Kraig's voice responded appropriately to every code and query until, at last, they were given permission to launch. And if there were any questions as to why someone who had just returned from a very long mission was going out again, they went unasked.

And that's the downside of disciplining the initiative right out of your troops, Joat thought with glee.

They launched and she keyed in a course that would lead them to Seg's Clenst facility. When she felt they'd traveled far enough, Joat brought out the control board for the signal jammer and turned it on. Communications chaos blossomed all around them.

"It works!" Joat shouted. "I can't believe this, we're out! No one's following, no one's shooting, this is incredible." She wanted to dance and hug Sperin and hear Simeon tell her how smart she was. "We're going to make it! Prepare to go hyper!"

A high-energy particle beam flashed across their bow, causing their face-plates to darken.

"What the . . ." Joat said. She killed velocity and backed frantically until she could at least see who was firing on her.

A sleek, bright-yellow fighter with red markings hove into view and lined up to fire on them again.

"That is the symbol of the Yoered Family," Joseph said in astonishment.

Joat brought their fighter to a halt and dove, just as the Family fighter fired again. She grabbed the control board for the signal disrupter and hit the off control. Nothing happened.

"Fardles!" she snarled. "I can't turn it off."

"What?" Joseph asked.

"The signal disrupter. It's not receiving my signal to turn off. Apparently it's disrupting that too."

"You are joking!" Joseph said in disbelief. "This is not funny, Joat. Turn the cursed thing off!"

"It's just a prototype, Joe. It's never been used before. There are bound to be problems."

"We're being fired on by our *allies* because of one of your famous gadgets, Joat? Is that what I'm hearing here?" Bros asked.

"Yeah," she growled.

Bros started to laugh.

"It's not funny, Sperin."

"Truly, it is not," agreed Joseph.

"Now I'm sure this is really happening," Bros said. "I don't have this kind of an imagination."

"We've got to go back," Joat said.

The ship rocked as the Family fighter hit one of their fins with its beam.

Joat spun the ship 'round and ran flat out for the *Dreadful Bride*.

"I don't believe this!" she said. "I don't believe that Belazir t'Marid is my only hope of survival."

"He will kill us," Joseph predicted grimly.

"But not right away," Bros assured them.

Joat didn't deign to answer either of them.

The Family fighter hit one of their altitude-adjustment coils and the little craft tumbled helplessly for an agonizing minute before the gyroscopic system righted their ship. *At that it probably saved our lives.*

The sensors were showing multimegatonne explosions in a rapidly expanding pattern.

Joat gasped. "Well, that kills one option. I was hoping to linger outside the *Bride* for as long as possible and maybe escape in the excitement. But the Family has put *paid-in-full* to that idea, now hasn't it?"

"Joat, wait!" Joseph snapped. "If they cannot hear you they will not have the hangar doors open."

"For cryin' out loud, Joe. They can't hear us, but they can *see*. If they don't open the doors we're going to smash into them. They're not going to let that happen. Trust me."

"Trust . . . you?"

It's probably hard for him to talk with his heart in his mouth like that, Joat thought, as she aimed the fighter at the stubbornly shut hangar doors. *I know that's where mine is.*

"Pull up, Joat," Bros suggested tensely.

"Pull *UP!*" Joseph seconded at top volume.

"I can't steer," she said. "I'm hoping they can see that."

Just when she'd begun to give up hope, the huge doors began to move. She throttled back, trying to give them time to widen and flitted through the narrow gap with just meters to spare.

Two tears of relief rolled down her cheeks and she made a strange sound, half-laugh half-sob. Her male companions cursed imaginatively, particularly Joseph.

"Daughter of a mangy, limbless goatherd and a ruptured swine!" he shouted. "You little spawn of Shaithen! Don't you *ever* frighten me like that again."

She laughed outright.

"Blame the Family, buddy. Or Bros here, or Amos for that matter. None of this is my doing. I'm just reacting here and doing the best I can." She unstrapped herself from her seat. "People are going to be running around crazy out there. My advice is to run around with them until we can find a safe place to lie low."

"And then?" Bros asked dubiously.

"Hope the Family wins. But doesn't total the *Bride* while we're on it. And if they don't, try plan A again." She shrugged. "Woulda worked this time if the timing had been just a little better."

"I don't want to spoil your plans, Joat," Bros spoke carefully to avoid slurring his words, "but I'm not up to much running around."

"I know," she said, releasing his restraints. She pursed her lips. "Maybe we could stuff you into Kraig's locker."

He glared at her.

"I'm not that far gone," he said between clenched teeth.

"Be reasonable. It's nearby and I'm positive no one will look for you there."

"I'll keep up," he snarled.

Joat glanced over at Joseph, who shrugged.

"Suit yourself," she said briskly. "It's your funeral."

They descended from the fighter to a welcoming committee of battle-armored Kolnari and black-suited mercenaries.

"Who is your commander?" one of the Kolnari barked.

"Captain Hobsbrowm, Sir!" Joat snapped out.

"Report! What is the meaning of this?"

"Sir!" Joat said. Facing the Kolnari, she sketched a salute. "Yoered Family fighters have infiltrated the perimeter. Communications are down. There are indications that the Family people are affected by the jamming also."

There was the briefest pause, as though the Kolnari within the huge battle armor was taken by surprise.

"Very well," she said. "Report to your squad leader. Get another ship and join us outside."

"Yes sir!" Joat and her companions saluted and trotted off. After a moment they cut right behind the body of a fighter and out of sight of the Kolnari and her friends.

They paused a moment to look around and Joat saw a cluster of black-suited figures emerging from an elevator.

"There," she said and pointed. The others followed her and they slid in just as the doors were closing.

Bros leaned against the wall, gasping for breath. His face was pale and slick with sweat. Joat thought he looked ready to pass out. He opened his eyes and met hers. Then he straightened up a bit.

"I'm all right," he panted.

"Where are we going?" Joseph demanded of her.

"B corridor."

"*Kolnari* territory?" he asked in disbelief. "Surely you are joking?"

"Jeez! You really think my sense of humor is getting the better of me today, don't you?"

Bros grinned. "The Brig," he said. "Last place they'll look for us."

"We couldn't all fit into Kraig's locker," she muttered. The elevator doors opened onto B corridor and a scene of organized chaos. "And we couldn't very well slip into that repair tunnel without being seen, now could we? I figure the Brig's our best shot." She glanced at Joseph. "Suggestions are welcome."

"Speak with authority and behave as though we belong," he said.

"Don't I always?" she asked and lead the way.

They rounded a corner and blundered into a squad of Kolnari.

"YOU!" bellowed their leader. "What are you scum-vermin doing here?"

"Sir!" Joat saluted. "We are to report to Captain Hobsbrawm. Sir!" All she could see in his black faceplate was her own reflection, looking determined. *Thank the powers-that-be for Captain Hobsbrowm,* her mind babbled. *I wonder if Hobsbrowm's a he or a she? How long can I keep referring to him/her without using a personal pronoun?*

"Hobsbrowm is not here," the Kolnari sneered. "You will fall in with us."

"With all due respect, Sir. I am under orders," Joat said.

"What is wrong with that man?" the Kolnari demanded unexpectedly, pointing at Bros.

"He's still getting used to the heavier gravity," Joat said. "He's a light-worlder."

"Phah! Weakling." He said it almost indifferently, as though thinking of something else.

He's wondering if he dares to interfere in the kind of "orders" that would allow me to defy him, Joat thought. *Make up your mind, creep!*

"Hobsbrowm does not need three of you. I will take this one." He pointed at Joseph. "Fall in!" he bellowed.

His face a blank, Joseph did so.

"What is your name, Sir?" Joat asked. "So that I can tell the Captain where this man is."

The Kolnari went very still. The way they did when they thought they might have made a mistake, but weren't certain yet what it might be.

"Skarik na Marid, petite-noble, commander of a section, is my name," he growled. "And I tremble at the thought of displeasing your captain. What is your name, scumvermin?"

"Rendino du Pare," Joat said crisply and rattled off Kraig's ID number. *It's not like he can check it out,* she thought nervously. *It just has to sound right.*

"On your way, scumvermin, before I change my mind."

Then the Kolnar barked an order and his squad marched off, Joseph bringing up the rear. Joat watched them out of sight. Joseph never looked back.

Silken jammed her fist into her mouth as though she would ram her scream back down her throat. She bit down until she broke the skin, and blood, hot and salty spurted onto her tongue. She flailed out with one hand, as though to clutch Belazir's green robe; only to have it whisk through thin air.

Nomik Ciety screamed. A hoarse bubbling scream like she'd never heard before. He was balanced on the crown of his head and his heels, his back arched in a great bow, arms held stiffly at his sides with his fingers clawing the air. Nomik's eyes were wild with disbelief and foam dribbled from his mouth.

Belazir watched with satisfaction, his heavy arms folded across his chest and his expression one of sensual enjoyment. Pleased that the drug was working as it should this time.

The med-tech stood by the hatch looking almost as aghast as Silken. The two Kolnari guards watched with academic interest.

"Please, Master and God," Silken begged, blood running down her chin, "make it stop, please! Whatever you want, we will do, I *swear*. Only make it stop!" She collapsed in incoherent sobs across the holo of Belazir's feet.

He looked down at her in mild interest.

"You are not as strong as I thought you would be," he remarked. "But I am generous to women, I will instruct you in the causes of my displeasure." He frowned slightly; it was difficult to make himself heard over Ciety's screaming.

"First," he said, raising his voice slightly. "You sent to me the daughter of our worst enemy to perform an important task for us. I cannot help but feel insulted by your lack of sensitivity." He sighed in exasperation as Nomik's screams reached new heights. "Kick him onto his face," he instructed the guards. "Perhaps it will stifle some of his noise."

He turned back to the wide-eyed Silken, who had

her hands pressed against her mouth, as though that would somehow help to silence Nomik's cries.

"Where was I? Ah, yes. Second, as part of this woman's crew, what do I find? I find Bros Sperin! One of Central Worlds' most notable covert operatives." He spread his hands, raising his brows.

"What am I to make of this? One thing was bad enough—sending me the girl when I could not torture her to death without wrecking my greater scheme—but the other . . . ? It is intolerable. So . . . you are fools or you are enemies. Either way you must be punished. Surely you understand this? Incompetence and insults must always be addressed."

Nomik's body collapsed and he lay panting, whining slightly.

"Ah. It is over." He turned to Silken and said reassuringly, "There are supposed to be no permanent effects."

"You bastard," Nomik gasped, "you bastard."

Belazir compressed his lips.

"Of course," he drawled, "sometimes, with some individuals, a lesson must be repeated a number of times before its meaning is comprehended." He raised his hand to signal the med-tech.

Suddenly another Kolnari appeared beside Belazir.

"Great Lord!" he said excitedly.

Belazir backhanded him, knocking the man to his knees. His yellow eyes blazed.

"How *dare* you enter here? What is the meaning of this intrusion?"

"I abase myself before you Great Lord," a one word expression in Kolnari. The soldier bowed his head and placed both fists on the floor where he knelt. "Communications are down," he said urgently. "The fleet is under attack by Yoered Family fighters."

"What?"

"They've come because of us, you fool," Nomik lay on his side, glaring at Belazir. "You can't kidnap someone from Rohan and not answer to the Family for it. They're going to kick your butt, asshole."

Everyone went still, Belazir drew a deep angry breath, his nostrils grew pale and pinched.

"Give her the antidote," he snarled at the med-tech, "give him the disease. Then report to your stations." Then he disappeared form the cell.

One of the guards grasped Silken's arm and raised it. The med-tech touched it with an injector. He moved over to Ciety and applied another to one of his arms. Then the three of them fled the cell and Silken crawled over to hold Nomik in her arms.

Belazir threw off his silk robe and strapped on a utility belt, checking the charge in his plasma gun.

"Report," he barked.

"There is little more, Great Lord. Ships have been launched to meet the foe, the battleworthy ships have closed around the mother ship in protective formation. With communications out we can do little but wait."

"Fool!" Belazir snarled and marched out of his quarters moving towards the bridge.

Outside the door Skarik na Marid's small squad formed up around Belazir in a protective square.

Joseph strode along behind Belazir, eyes blazing, his heart full of hate. Amos's words rang in his head, "It would grieve me, my brother, to have you die like a fool."

Benisur, what am I to do? God has placed our enemy in my hands. Can I turn away in fear for myself and still call myself a man?

He could almost hear Amos's answer. "Wait for your best moment before you strike. And do not condemn yourself as a coward if no such moment arrives."

Before them an elevator opened and disgorged another crowd of Kolnari warriors running to their battle stations.

Joseph's whole body pounded with his heartbeat, it was all that he could feel, the blood raging through his veins. *Never have I felt such desire, not even in the arms of my beloved.*

He grabbed Belazir by the neck and flung him into the empty elevator with a mighty shove, drew his laser and threw himself in afterwards just as the door closed. He hit a floor at random, then spun and kicked Belazir's legs out from under him, bringing the butt of his pistol down on the back of the Kolnari's neck with a vicious crack.

Joseph fired on the elevator's control mechanism and they lurched to a halt. Then he turned back to his prey, his blue eyes alight with joy.

"*You!*" Belazir screamed, staggering to his feet. The blow would have killed any normal human. "*You!*"

The Bethelite cast his weapon aside and drew the long curved knife. He could hear Amos's voice again— this time condemning him for a fool. *And I do not care. Some things are beyond even loyalty, my prophet and friend.*

The lift cage was large, built to transport a section or more of troops in power armor. Belazir sidled crabwise, tearing off the remnants of his robe. His body was matte-black except where the dusty gray of scars seamed it, a gaunt thing of massive bones and muscles shrunken and knotted and still powerful enough to crack teak beams. There was no mind behind the golden eyes now, and a string of saliva dangled from one loose-curled lip.

"*You!*" he screamed, and leaped with his hands outstretched to tear.

❖   ❖   ❖

Joat was relieved to see that the corpse she and Joseph had left behind was still on duty behind the reception desk. Bros labored along beside her and at last she felt safe enough to put his arm around her shoulder and give him some support.

"No," he said, resisting her. "Not until we're behind a locked door. There's no telling who we might run into."

She blushed and compressed her lips. He was right, and she was embarrassed. It wasn't like her to get soft like this.

They moved into the Brig and she started trying doors, looking for one that wasn't locked.

Around the corner came two Kolnari and a med-tech, moving so fast they almost collided.

"What are you doing here?" one of the guards demanded.

"We've been sent to relieve Kolnari guards for duty elsewhere," Joat said.

"No," the other guard said, looking hard at Bros. "No, she lies. He is a prisoner."

"Ridiculous," Joat snapped. "We are heading *into* the Brig, not out of it."

"This is Bros Sperin," the guard insisted. "I know him."

The other guard and the med-tech began to grin.

Oh shit! Joat thought and went for her laser.

The first guard slapped her hand aside and kicked her legs out from under her. Joat lay for a single instant, stunned; she'd forgotten over the years, the inhuman speed of the Kolnari.

Bros is unarmed! she thought as she crashed to the floor and she saw both guards moving in on him. Before she could get her stunned body back in action the med-tech had her in a hold that immobilized her. He stripped off one of her gloves and pressed an injector against the inside of her wrist.

The last thing she saw as her vision darkened was Bros going down in a flurry of kicks from the two Kolnari guards. She heard something snap, and then there was nothing.

She woke to the sensation of something heavy resting on her lap, holding her against a wall. Her eyes flickered open and she snapped them shut, the light in the room was so bright it drew tears. Cautiously, she slitted her eyes open and looked down to see what was so heavy.

Bros lay in her lap. He was perfectly still; blood trailed from his mouth. She snapped the locks on his helmet and tossed it aside, touched her bare hand to his pulse.

Chief Family Enforcer Vand looked down at her impassively.

"He is alive?" Vand asked.

Joat nodded wearily, then glanced up at him. Vand was much taller than she'd expected and twice as intimidating as he was on a screen.

"It would seem they questioned him very thoroughly," he observed. He looked away, his eyes never resting long on any place or thing.

Just as well, Joat thought. *When he looks at me I feel like I'm about to be dissected.*

"The Family would very much like to interrogate Mr. Sperin," Vand said, considering the notion.

Joat made a small flinging gesture and a knife slipped into her hand, she pressed it up under Bros's jaw.

"But you won't," she said with fierce determination.

"No," he said, his face still impassive, but a look of something like respect touched his cold eyes. "Of course not. In addition to restoring the Family's honor, the object of this mission was to rescue Mr. Sperin. It would hardly do to compromise Yoered's honor immediately after saving it. Now would it?" He smiled, and she wished he hadn't. "Our honor is an extremely valuable commercial property."

Joat had the impression she was being laughed at, though nothing visible backed it up.

"You must excuse me. We're in the process of teaching the Kolnari a rather sharp lesson on maintaining a certain standard of professional etiquette when in a Family port. Remain here," Vand commanded. "I have some med-techs on the way."

Then he was gone, moving lightly despite the bulky battle-armor.

As if I was about to scamper off and get into trouble, Joat thought sourly. She leaned her head wearily against the wall and closed her eyes. When she opened them she found herself looking into Silken's.

Silken sat on the floor across from her, with Nomik's head leaning against her breast, in a pose that mirrored her own.

Tears ran down Silken's cheeks and her expression was tired beyond all bearing. Her hair was wild and there was blood around her mouth, bruises on the porcelain skin.

Joat knew a moment's sympathy for her, realizing that Silken must be broken indeed if she was too weary to make threats.

Eventually the promised med-techs came and suited them up in quarantine outfits like the ones they were wearing. They lifted Nomik and Bros onto pallets. Each of the women walked beside one, looking down.

Joat wavered, wondering if she should try to find and destroy Belazir's store of stolen virus.

Then Bros opened his eyes and looked up at her and she found herself taking his hand and walking beside the pallet.

Ah well, she thought, *if I did find it Vand would only take it away from me. Whereas if they don't know about it then they're very unlikely to find it.* Joat was uncomfortably aware of how unlike her it was to hope for a miracle.

Then again, sometimes they happen, she thought dazedly. There were other pallets waiting at the lock, with med-techs working around them. One in particular seized her gaze. A thick-bodied blond man lay on it; the uniform had been cut away from most of his body, and devices hummed over it. She could see broken bone on one flank where the ribs had been hammered as if with a maul, and the tech's fingers were straightening the left arm above and below the elbow, so that the positioning sleeves could be fastened. Inflatable casts already covered the whole lower half of his body, and it was only just possible to tell the color of his hair, because something had ripped half the scalp off his head as if it were a wig.

She walked to the side of the pallet. Incredibly, the blue eyes were open.

"Joe," she whispered.

He tried to smile. She bent closer.

"No . . . pain," he whispered. "Drugs . . ."

Joat closed her eyes. "Thank God you're alive."

"Thank . . . the God indeed."

"Who did this to you?"

"Belazir . . . t'Marid."

Joat's hands clenched. *That debt keeps building up and up!*

Joseph saw her expression, and tried to smile again. Blood ran down his chin and his eyes rolled sideways. Joat looked down on the floor.

The head was quite recognizable, despite the cuts. She could never forget those eyes, and they were open and staring.

✧ CHAPTER TWENTY

Buster Rauchfuss chewed his lip and considered this second request for clarification and/or credits from their contact on New Destinies.

Mancini had never bothered to get back to him. Obviously he hadn't dealt with the situation either.

Typical, Buster sniffed. *Kick somebody up a notch and they think they're too good to answer their mail.*

Well, Paul would answer this one.

Dear Mr. Mancini, Buster wrote. *This matter is growing more urgent. Perhaps you should look into it yourself. Surely I shouldn't even know about this. After all, when Mr. Sperin was removed from my department you'll recall that I was told nothing for security reasons. I must say that it worries me, therefore, that I keep getting these messages.*

Let me know if I can be of any help on this.

That oughta shake Mancini up.

Buster received a reply that same afternoon, lightning speed for interoffice communications at CenSec.

Buster, it began.

All I know about your man Sperin is that he was taken off a Kolnari battle-cruiser in the company of Nomik Ciety and that he's in security quarantine.

You can tell your contact on New Destinies that we

*have no intention of giving that many credits to a
station notorious for graft and bribery. Certainly not
on the say-so of a man under that kind of a cloud.
Word it however you like, but the answer is no.*

I would hate to see you pursue this. Buster noticed
the "your man Sperin" and the lack of signature and
he felt a little frisson of alarm tickle the back of his
neck.

*I can't believe that Bros would have anything to do
with the Kolnari,* he thought dubiously. *The guy hated
them.* But the bare facts were damning. He frowned.
It sure looks bad. And it was rumored that Ciety could
convert a saint to the devil's cause. He shook his head.
Enough credits can get to anybody.

Certainly with this to go on he couldn't be expected
to stick his neck out. Buster chewed his lip, then sighed
and began composing a note for Dana to send to Sal
on New Destinies.

*Clal va Riguez was not authorized to make this kind
of payment.*

Short, sweet and to the point. *That oughta take care
of that,* Buster thought with satisfaction. It had the
virtue of being the absolute truth, too.

Joat left the *Wyal* glumly; she ignored the cluster
of newshounds and floating pickups—even on Rohan,
you couldn't avoid the media. Lies and distortions would
be flying all over the human part of the galaxy, many
times faster than light. At least on Rohan, they didn't
try to grab her arm to force an interview.

She smiled bleakly. Not with Enforcer Vand backing
up *The Rules;* the bloody lesson taught the Kolnari had
shown just how seriously the Family took them. She
forced her legs onward.

Not a word since we got back to Rohan. She wondered uneasily whether Silken intended to honor Ciety's

stated intention of canceling the *Wyal's* debt; maybe she'd just been waiting to recover fully before putting in the knife.

Joat had been relieved that Silken hadn't required her to do anything blatantly illegal. Several times, she'd been ordered to ferry some rather creepy passengers to equally creepy destinations. And who knew what contraband they had in their personal luggage? But no outright smuggling.

Joat sighed. She'd been so sure that Bros—her mind shied away from the fierce disappointment she felt in him—or someone representing him at least, would have released her from the debt that bound her to her uncle and his concubine. *So much for being a hero. Not even a message.* Beyond the pain was a sadness that frightened her.

They'd been separated by the med-techs as soon as they were brought aboard the Family ship. Despite her protests she'd been taken into a cubicle to have her own wounds treated. Then a sedative had been pressed on her and she'd been escorted, dizzy and sleepy, to a berth and sealed in. She'd slept through most of the journey.

When they reached the quarantine facility she woke up in a Spartan room wearing nothing but a pair of plastic slippers and a disposable shift. They kept her locked up for three weeks, until her wounds were well healed and they were certain she carried no trace of contagion. She was able to communicate with Al and Seg, Amos and Soamosa right away. Then Joe, when he'd recovered sufficiently. But never Bros.

Joat sighed. Maybe he thought it was fair turnabout. She'd abandoned him on Belazir's ship, after all. *No! I went back!*

She'd attempted to relay messages, both directly to CenSec and through her old contact at The Anvil on

New Destinies. To be blandly told that they had or
would be forwarded to Sperin.

Not that she'd expected them to be eager to con-
tribute that many credits to Nomik Ciety and Rohan's
burgeoning economy. In fact, it would seem to go
against their charter.

But *damn* this was like being a slave! Joat hung on,
hoping that Silken was at least crediting the work she
was doing against the debt. *At least that. If she won't
return the* Wyal *to me outright, at least let me work
it off.* Though so far, Joat was paying her own expenses.

She'd seriously considered enlisting Simeon's aid in
getting through to Bros, but had been too ashamed to
send her father anything from her Rohan address. Or
from any of the other ports she'd been in lately.

I will not whine.

When she entered the bland waiting room at N.
Ciety, Research and Development, there were two
rather nondescript individuals seated in the lounge area,
but no one was behind the reception desk.

She huffed impatiently and put her hands on her
hips, frowning.

"Excuse me," one of the men in the lounge said,
rising and coming over to her. "Are you Captain Joat
Simeon-Hap?"

A sort of icy foreboding swept over her in a numbing
tide.

"Who wants to know?"

They looked like accountants, mild and innocuous,
with smooth, chubby faces. They smiled little, amused
smiles at her response. Joat was willing to bet they were
carrying weapons and that they weren't amused at all.

"Why don't we just cut the crap and get right to the
point," the taller man said. "We represent New Destinies and we've come to repossess your ship in lieu
of the debt you owe for a fine levied against the *Wyal.*"

Her mouth went dry and it felt as though all her blood had run down into her extremities.

After what seemed a long time she croaked, "What?"

"We're foreclosing on your debt," the smaller one said slowly.

"But . . . Nomik Ciety bought the debt from New Destinies. I was working it off for him."

"I'm sorry," the tall man said. "We have no record of any such purchase." He actually did look marginally sympathetic. "You can file a complaint, and if there's been an error, you're certainly entitled to recompense." He paused. "Now, we'll require you to vacate the *Wyal* immediately. Obviously you'll only be allowed to take personal possessions. Any items which might be considered integral parts of the ship will naturally have to remain."

Rand! she thought for the first time. *What's going to happen to Rand?* This wasn't supposed to be happening. She'd never believed that CenSec would let her down like this, not once.

"Let me talk to Silken," she said, trying to keep her voice from shaking. "She's running things here, perhaps she can explain this." *And it had better be good or I'm going to rip her pretty, little face off.*

She sat behind the receptionist's desk and after a moment got the comp to release Silken's private number. A few moments later Silken's face, looking thinner, sharper and deeply annoyed filled the screen.

"You!" she said in astonishment.

"Me," Joat confirmed. "There are two men here claiming that there's no record of Ciety's purchase of my debt from New Destinies. Do you know what's going on?"

"Ah, yes," Silken murmured, leaning back with a half-smile. "I've been so busy that I'd forgotten. When Mik told you that he'd bought your debt he had every intention of doing so. But," she made a little moue, "your extremely negative reaction changed his mind." She shrugged and said indifferently, "Too bad. But it's not like it makes any difference. You never could have paid it off in any case."

"I notice you didn't forget to use me to ferry your friends around," Joat snapped.

"I told you, I forgot." Silken's eyes were disdainful, as yielding as stone. "Even you have to admit I have a great deal on my mind."

"Yeah, like how to keep my Uncle from drooling on the carpet."

Silken went white.

"You heartless, spiteful, cruel, vicious bitch," she said, each word a separate insult, sincerely meant.

"You're right," Joat said, ashamed. Suddenly, she understood Silken's malice so completely that she was utterly disarmed. Enough so that she couldn't forgive her own. "That was uncalled for, I'm sorry."

"There's nothing that could happen to you that would make you sorry enough to appease me," Silken told tightly. "That damn ship is the only thing you care about and I'm *glad* you're going to lose it. It's not enough, it's not nearly enough, but it will do for a start.

"I'll be watching you," she continued, fire beginning to kindle in her cold green eyes. "And whenever it goes sour for you, whenever you lose or miss out or get passed over," she tapped her chest with one slender finger, "— that's me. My work. I promise you. You don't know what sorry is, you slime-hag. But you will."

The screen went blank and Joat just sat there, staring at it.

One of the repo-men cleared his throat awkwardly and she looked up.

"We . . . might as well get this over with," he said.

She nodded, feeling freeze-dried inside, hard and

brittle and shredded. Joat rose carefully, weirdly numbed, and began to ask pertinent questions as the three of them left the office, headed for the *Wyal*.

They gave her permission to download her logs and personal correspondence and to tell her crew herself.

Joat sat in her pilot's couch for the last time, listening to Alvec curse.

"I never would've believed it," he said for the twelfth time at least. "Jeez, he seemed like an all-right guy. Y'know? This isn't right!"

"Excuse me," the taller repo-man said. "We'd like to get our own crew on as soon as possible. Could you speed this up a little, please?"

Joat started to speak and merely squawked, she cleared her throat. "I'd, ah, like to leave the *Wyal* as ship-shape as possible. You know, tidy her up."

He smiled knowingly.

"Yes, we get a lot of that kind of thoughtfulness. One of our debtors was so 'tidy' that his ship didn't blow up for three weeks. Killed a family of five. So I'm afraid you'll just have to pack and go, leaving things just as they are."

She nodded coolly.

"Just a few more minutes," she said.

"Five," he said, holding up his spread hand for emphasis.

Alvec rose and walked directly towards him, as though he didn't exist, leaving the hapless debt collector to leap aside or get walked over.

"I'll meet you on the dock, Boss," Alvec called over his shoulder.

Joat turned her chair and looked at Rand's blinking "face."

"What about you, Rand?"

After a moments silence, it said, "Obviously I can't leave, can I?"

"No," Joat said, her voice soft with shame. Even if they would allow her to download Rand's personality she had no access to a computer powerful enough to receive it. Through all of their troubles and misadventures, she'd somehow managed to overlook *this*. She'd failed to protect a friend, one who had done far more than his share to help her.

Yes, his *share*. Rand was most certainly not an "it" any longer. *What a fardling stupid time to realize that!*

"I'm so sorry," she whispered, ashamed of her powerlessness and fighting to keep her tears from falling.

"Like you, Joat, I find I don't like the idea of a life of servitude."

"Oh," her voice creaked. "Might not be that bad. They'll probably declare you an AI ship and send you out on your own. You'd be making your own decisions and not getting yourself in the kind of trouble I've lead you into."

"AI assignments tend to be the most tedious kind," Rand said. "No crew, no stimulation, not even an allowance for virtual reality in port—computers don't get paid. And I would scarcely be making my own decisions Joat, other than: "Should I allow myself to be hit by this rock or should I avoid it?" I'd scarcely call that autonomy," Rand said with scorn.

One side of her mouth crooked.

"You sound like me," she said.

"And why wouldn't I? You've put a great deal of yourself into me."

And children often resemble their parents, she thought morbidly.

"Excuse me," the tall one said, "are you through yet?"

"Just a minute!" she snapped. The repo-man glared, but withdrew. Joat thought she heard him say, ". . . think they've got an AI on board." Turning back to Rand, she said: "It's not over yet, buddy. Maybe there's still something we can do. At least now I'm free to move around."

"Correct me if I'm wrong. You have no credits."

"You're wrong. Little Silky owes us a considerable amount, and she *will* pay us."

"Why should she," Rand asked reasonably enough. "You can't make her."

"I may not love him, but I'm Nomik Ciety's niece. A quick genetic scan will prove our relationship, and the Family is very fond of backing family rights. Probably, all I have to do is make the claim and I could put his whole empire, such as it is, on hold."

"You can't hope to win such a claim," Rand's voice was almost surprised.

"Of course not. But it would cost more to hire an assassin than it would to pay me what she owes, and it would cost twice that to retain an attorney."

"She could challenge you to a duel."

"I can take her."

"If I were human, I would laugh. Silken hates you, Joat. To the point of obsession. I'm sure that nothing would give her greater pleasure than killing you herself. Probably she hasn't challenged you simply because it hasn't occurred to her."

Joat grinned savagely.

"Oh, it's occurred to her all right. But she won't risk leaving Ciety alone and at the mercy of the Family. If he were dead we'd have crossed swords long since."

"So you'll be able to leave."

"Yes. And I'll be able to call in favors, perhaps get a loan," she was silent a moment, "maybe even get through to Bros. So don't give up on me. Okay? I won't make that an order."

Philosophers might debate whether it was *possible* for a computer to commit suicide, since it wasn't certain that they could be self-aware in the first place. Rand's "impassive" face blinked multicolored lights for a few moments.

"Very well, I will abide. But, if I am sold to someone else, Joat, I won't serve them. If worst comes to worst I've saved a copy of Seg's worm program. Should some other bidder obtain the *Wyal* I shall trigger it. If I don't fight it, it will be very quick."

"You can't be serious," Joat whispered. She couldn't believe her ears. "Aren't you even willing to give a new owner a chance to prove their worth before taking such a drastic step?"

She wondered if she'd programmed him for self-preservation. *Of course I did! I couldn't possibly have left it out, it's too important.* Not that it was unknown for Rand to erase bits of programming he didn't want anymore. She'd never locked down any part of him, preferring to leave that . . . freedom, for himself.

"I am an individual," Rand insisted, "there is no more individual choice than this."

Joat sat still, too horrified to speak.

"All right, that's enough," the shorter repo-man struck the back of her chair, making it spin towards him. "Stop yakking to the computer, go pack up your belongings and get lost."

Her mind was wholly on Rand, or she would have kicked his tubby form through the bulkhead. Instead she gave him a disgusted look and headed off the bridge.

"Hey! Don't forget these," he said and handed her the collection of datahedrons she'd made.

"Personal files, erased," said Rand mechanically.

Joat sat in the auction room with her heart in her mouth.

It was an enormous hall, too brightly lit, with a strange sharp smell to it. The hall was furnished with ugly, uncomfortable chairs each having one arm that terminated in a small computer with a display screen. Currently it displayed the ship being bid on. There were a few controls that would call up information on the ship, schematics, history, and beside them a slot into which a successful bidder's credit chip would go. Almost every seat was filled with junk dealers, purchase agents, and bargain hunters.

She had with her every credit she could beg, borrow or earn and it was still forty thousand credits short of the fine.

Wyal was going on the block.

It was third on the list and the closer it got to the top the faster her heart beat. Her palms were sweating and she rubbed them surreptitiously on the fabric of her dark blue business suit. The strange, formal garment she wore in hope of looking more respectable only succeeded in making her feel obvious and awkward. *I should have robbed that bank. I should.* Robbing banks on Rohan . . .

The hammer went down and the *Wyal* moved one place closer to the block. Her breathing grew nervous and ragged.

She knew, she *knew* that she wouldn't get her ship back. Silken was certain to have agents among the bidders who would know to the credit how much she had. Agents who were, no doubt, instructed to bid just one credit more.

Alvec, who was working short, freelance hops, had offered his life savings.

"I can't take this," she'd told him, horrified and deeply touched, as well as terribly tempted.

"So make me a partner," he'd said.

And she'd smiled, hope blazing.

But it hadn't been enough. It had never been enough and Bros Sperin remained beyond her reach. So here she was, facing certain defeat, feeling humiliated before she even began.

How could I have been so stupid? she railed at herself. When had she grown so soft that she would put her freedom on the line, for someone else, mind you, with no expectation of cost or reward? *My own fault. Playing at spy,* she mocked, *I'm no better than Seg !T'sel.*

Alvec was furious with her for not asking Amos for help.

"I asked my father," she'd said. Though of course she hadn't told Simeon *why* she needed credits. "That's as much as my pride can take."

That was partially true, it had hurt to ask Simeon for help. Even though he gave it willingly and offered to take out a loan for more, no questions asked, it hurt. She'd felt like a complete failure. First Brawn school, and now this.

Nor did she dare to ask Amos for help. Bethel was a poor planet, most of her credits already committed for years to come. And though he was very rich, Amos was in the habit of pouring most of his wealth back into his world's struggling economy. She couldn't very well ask him to choose her needs over the good of his people. And she didn't think he would really understand about Rand.

Joat wondered if Joseph and Amos hovered in the same state of anxiety that tortured her, wanting to give, not daring to offer. Or if they even knew.

Either way she simply couldn't afford the time or the money it would cost to ask, only to be told no.

A deeper truth was that she felt Amos should have offered. Or Joseph should have. *He* knew all about the debt. Yet the total silence from all the powerful people she'd counted as friends—or more than friends—never varied. In the end she was just a forgotten detail, an unimportant loose end.

Joat frowned. *Oh, stop it,* she thought disgustedly, *there's no poison deadlier than self-pity. The mistake was yours and so's the punishment.*

Although that last wasn't completely true. Rand had made it very plain that he didn't count himself as part of the ship.

Rand's threat had certainly inspired her to new heights, and depths, in her fund-raising efforts. Sometimes, late at night when she couldn't get to sleep for thinking about it, Joat told herself that was why he'd made it. To get her over her shyness about asking friends for help.

Probably he doesn't mean to erase himself at all, she comforted herself. *Hah! A computer that plays with you. Somehow I don't think this idea will sell.*

Joat knew that if she lost the ship, and Rand erased himself, for the rest of her life, she was going to feel like a failure and a murderer.

There might still be time to get through to Amos on Bethel, she thought.

The next ship up was a tasty offering that seemed to have excited a lot of interest. Of course sometimes those were the ones that came on and off the block so fast you couldn't get a decent look at them.

Then there was the cost to consider.

A tight-beam interstellar com-link could cost me four percent of what I've got. On the other hand . . . On the other hand Silken's bidders wouldn't let her have the *Wyal* anyway unless she could exceed Nomik Ciety's entire fortune. And she couldn't even pay the fine.

She closed her eyes and took a deep breath. When she opened them she saw that she'd been right. The bidding was over and the ship had sold.

"I have an announcement," the auctioneer said. "The *Wyal*, which is the next ship on the list, has been withdrawn from bid. We're sorry for any inconvenience this may have caused. I'll repeat that. The *Wyal*, a merchant freighter ship, has been withdrawn from bid."

Joat's felt the bottom of her stomach lurch into zero-g. *My ship! What have they done with my ship?*

Absently she noted two bidders that turned to stare at her. Silken's people, no doubt. Well, they seemed satisfied by the look of white-faced horror that she knew she must be wearing. They'd be happy to report this disaster to their employer.

"They can't *do* that!" Joat said desperately.

The Sondee next to her looked up when she spoke.

"How can they do that?" she asked.

The Sondee shrugged. "Sometimes they get a private bid that more than meets the minimum price. In this case it wouldn't take much. The *Wyal* is a crummy little ship."

Joat raised an eyebrow and glared.

Instead of defending the honor or her ship she spoke: "What if you had questions about something like this? Where would you go to ask them?"

"Why, at the same office where you were assigned your seat. Through that door, down the hall, first door on the right," the Sondee said helpfully, then pointedly turned back to the auction.

Joat found the office empty, which infuriated her. She swore and muttered, pacing back and forth before the tall counter more and more rapidly.

At last frustrated beyond bearing she shouted, "Hello? Is *anyone* working here?"

No one answered.

She marched out into the hall, determined to open the first door she detected a being behind and demand service.

At the end of the corridor she turned left, at the end of that one, she found the president's office and went briskly in.

"I'd like to speak to someone in authority," she said to the surprised secretary.

"Do you have an appointment?" he asked politely.

"No, but I do have questions."

"Perhaps I can help you."

"I *said* someone in authority. That wouldn't be you." She marched over to the door of the inner sanctum and before the secretary could disengage himself from his desk, she was through it.

A well-dressed human in his mid-sixties sat behind the wide, wooden desk, a pleasant smile frozen on his face by her entrance. The younger man seated before him turned to see who had entered so precipitously.

It was Bros.

"You!" she said, her voice a near shriek.

He rose smiling and extended his arms as though to embrace her.

She backed up a pace and stood glaring at him, breathing hard, wanting to hit him and knowing that if she landed a blow it was because he let her.

No thank you, she thought, *I think I've been humiliated enough lately.* She turned and walked away thinking over and over, *I'm going to kill him, I'm going to kill him . . .*

"Excuse me," Bros said over his shoulder and followed her.

She was moving pretty fast when he caught her by the arm and pulled her through the first door they came to. It was an empty office. He shut the door behind him and leaned against it.

She paced back and forth, too furious to speak, glaring at him.

"I don't blame you for being angry," he said at last.

"But there was nothing I could do until now. I didn't even know that this hadn't been acted on. I *told* them about it in my report, I insisted that we had an obligation to see that your debt was canceled, reduced or paid. But I didn't know it hadn't been done." He held out a datahedron.

"This is yours, *Wyal's* papers."

She took it carefully and swallowed hard.

"And where were you that you couldn't answer any of my messages? That you never attempted to get in contact with any of us?" She stood with her arms folded, looking him square in the face and asking with her eyes. *And how could you leave me believing that stuff about caring about me? How dare you make me believe in you like that?*

"You have to understand, Joat, I was interrogated by the enemy. It's customary to hold an agent incommunicado for at least two months afterwards. There are very solid reasons for it. If the Kolnari were a more sophisticated people, I wouldn't be free now." He frowned at her unchanging stare. "Look, I came as soon as I knew, okay?"

She nodded reluctantly.

"So, what happens now? Can I just leave? I've really got my ship back?"

He nodded and gravely watched Joat smile.

She couldn't help herself, the tension disappeared and joy broke over her face like a sunrise.

"How . . . how did you find out? You must have just been released. Was it the first question you asked?" She blushed "I mean, did you say: 'What's going on with the *Wyal*?' or what?"

"Simeon told me. He's the one who speeded up my release in fact. Officially, I should still be in quarantine for three days."

"My father?" she squeaked. "How could he possibly have known?"

"Rand sent a message blip to a passing brainship, who relayed it to a city manager and so on and so on."

"Oh fardles!" she clutched her hair. "They're the biggest gossips in Central Worlds. This means that literally everybody knows about this." Her voice had grown hollow and she leaned weakly against the desk. "I'll never be able to show my face in port again. And as for visiting the SSS-900-C . . . " She hid her face in her hands and groaned.

Bros grinned at her and shook his head.

"Talk about looking a gift horse in the mouth. It was a private letter and was treated as such. The problem your father had was wondering why you didn't ask him for help. You were certainly entitled to it."

"I did ask him for help. I asked him for a loan, a huge loan and he gave it to me, no questions asked."

"Oh, I wouldn't say that," Bros said, laughing. "He had a million of 'em for me."

Joat looked at him earnestly. "It simply never occurred to me to ask him for official help. You were the only one I thought could help me, because *you* guaranteed our expenses. I tried every avenue I could think of within CenSec." She shrugged helplessly. "But Simeon never occurred to me."

"And what about the Benisur?"

"I couldn't afford to go personally. Travel time was time I wasn't earning credits. I kept wanting to contact him, but time was short and I didn't dare risk the credits a tight-beam would cost. What if he couldn't afford to help me? What if he had to say no? Then I'd be out all those credits for nothing."

"Good thing Rand was thinking more clearly than you were."

She laughed. "Yes, it was. He's very bright, don't you think?"

Bros nodded, smiling.

"I brought this for you," he said and held out another datahedron.

"What is it?" she looked from the hedron to Bros. He straightened.

"Well, after *this* and ten years, I've gone about as far as I'm going to with CenSec and still be allowed to do anything," he explained as he casually closed the distance between them. "But I've got a strong suspicion that Joat Simeon-Hap Enterprises is going to go far. And you'll definitely need a good security man."

Suddenly Joat found herself wrapped in a warm embrace. She stiffened and opened her mouth to object.

He kissed her lightly and smiled warmly down at her. Then gently pressed her head against his chest, resting his chin on her smooth blond hair.

"It's okay to lean on your friends, Joat. There's no harm in it."

"Oh, all right," she grumbled. "You're hired."

"Good." He kissed the top of her head.

She looked up. She could just see an earlobe beyond the curve of his lean jaw.

"Are you sure you want to do this? Silken could be a problem."

"I'm sure she will be."

"And some of the Kolnari got away. You know what they're like."

"Yes," he said comfortably and stroked her back. "I do."

Joat wriggled unhappily, enjoying the sensation but not trusting it. She couldn't help wondering what he really wanted.

Bros smiled. *I'd love to tell you that I bought* Wyal *back for you with my retirement fund, but I don't dare. You'd never let me get away with that.*

He'd also resigned from CenSec over their refusal

to help Joat. Though to be honest, he'd been disappointed and surprised when they'd accepted it so quickly.

Still, it was the least I could do for you, he thought. *Considering what Belazir would have done to you if . . .* He let the thought slide, his embrace tightening unconsciously.

"And we can still work for Central Security sometimes. Right?" he asked. *After all, I'd hate to feel completely cast off.*

"Don't push your luck," she said and pulled away to grin up at him.

That's better, she thought, feeling more in control. All she'd needed was a handle, a reason behind his behavior. *Clearly CenSec thinks they can use me, so they've sent Bros along to be their agent-in-residence. Hah! Still . . . might be fun.* In fact, she was already looking forward to it. She'd enjoyed bargaining with Sperin. *Especially since, in the end, I got the better of him.*

Bros smiled down into her amused blue eyes, aware that she thought she had his number, and sighed in his mind. *This thing is going to take a lot of time,* he thought. *Good thing I've got plenty to spend.* There was a slight pang at the thought of his lost career.

"So," she said stepping out of his arms, "let's get going."

"Yes, Boss."

Joat snapped him a look.

"You realize that you're not going to be making big credits right away."

"Yes, Boss."

"I'll bet you expect me to make you a partner one day, don't you?"

"Yes, Boss."

"Don't count your chickens before they're hatched, Sperin. You'll have to earn it."

"Anything worthwhile has to be earned, one way or another," he said.

Joat let out a long breath, feeling the stiffness flow from muscles she hadn't known were tense. She smiled, and turned her head away.

"Yeah."